# When Wolves Gather

## CW Browning

Copyright © 2022 by Clare Wroblewski

All rights reserved.

Cover design by Dissect Designs / www.dissectdesigns.com
Book design by Clare Wroblewski

No part of this publication may be reproduced, stored in or introduced into a retrieval system, or transmitted, in any form or by any means (electronic, mechanical, photocopying, recording or otherwise), without the prior written permission of the copyright owner, except by a reviewer who may quote brief passages in a review.

This is a work of fiction. All of the characters, organizations, and events portrayed in this novel are either products of the author's imagination or are used fictitiously. Any resemblance to actual persons, living or dead, or events is entirely coincidental.

CW Browning
Visit my website at www.cwbrowning.com


First Printing: 2022

ISBN- 9798356819605

## Author's Note:

On June 14, 1940, Nazi soldiers entered Paris unopposed. The Battle for France had been lost. While pockets of fighting continued in the south of France, the government knew that it was over. On June 22, 1940, in the Compiègne Forest, in the same railway carriage that was used to sign the 1918 Armistice ending World War I, the French surrendered to the Third Reich. Germany allowed the French government to retain an unoccupied zone, but took for themselves the entire western seaboard and north of France. With complete control of all the French ports along the Channel and the Atlantic Ocean, Hitler was in position to attack his last remaining foe.

In his famous speech given on June 18, "Their Finest Hour," Churchill said, "It seems quite clear that no invasion on a scale beyond the capacity of our land forces to crush speedily is likely to take place from the air until our Air Force has been definitely overpowered."

The Luftwaffe was coming for Great Britain, and only one thing could stop them. The fate of every Briton, spread across the globe, rested squarely on the shoulders of the Royal Air Force pilots. At a severe disadvantage in both airplanes and men, the world watched, and waited, for the inevitable destruction and invasion of the British Isles.

# When Wolves Gather

"But the traitor moves amongst those within the gate freely, his sly whispers rustling through all the alleys, heard in the very halls of government itself."
~ *Marcus Tullius Cicero, 106-43 BC*

# Prologue

**London, England**
**June 5, 1940**

A well-dressed man made his way through the crush of people exiting the platform and headed towards the steps up to the street. He'd arrived on a train from Plymouth not half an hour before, and taken the underground to St. James. The journey from France to Plymouth should have been uneventful, but given the state of affairs in both France and the Channel, it had been anything but. While the operation for the evacuation of Dunkirk had officially ended the day before, the Luftwaffe were still taking pot shots at any ships they happened to fly over. While his particular conveyance had arrived in Plymouth unmolested, they'd heard on the radio that another one had not been as fortunate. It had departed from Le Havre not four hours before them, and had been torpedoed by a U-boat. When Henry asked if the U-boats were common in the Channel, the Captain had laughed and asked where he'd been. He was lucky to have left from Bordeaux rather than further north, he was told matter-of-factly. The bloody Germans were trying to stop as many of those poor boys from getting home to England as they could. They weren't paying any mind yet to the rest of the sea. That would soon change now that they'd got most of their boys home. It was lucky he'd come back when he did.

Pushing past a heavyset woman with a screaming infant on her hip, Henry started up the steps. The newspaper that he'd picked up in Plymouth was filled with news of Winston Churchill's latest speech to the House of Commons, made the day before. The new prime minister had been very eloquent, as was his wont, and had sworn that England and her people would continue to fight. They would fight on the beaches, he said, and the landing grounds. They would fight in the fields and the streets, and in the hills. Good old Winston, always the optimist. Did he honestly believe that the country could be defended by the commoners in the streets? Was he really trying to rouse the country to fight against the invaders as if they could win?

Henry's lips twisted as he stepped out onto the busy city street. Afternoon sun touched his face, and he took a deep breath, pausing for a moment outside the entrance to the underground. The unavoidable fact was that the German Army would be in London by the end of the summer, and no amount of old men with pitchforks would be able to stop them. It was inevitable, and Winston, of all people, should know that. He'd seen how quickly Europe had fallen, and how quickly France was succumbing. He knew once France fell completely, England would be alone, and there was no possible way they could hold off Hitler and his armies. It was only a matter of time, and then no amount of high endorsements to fight in the streets would make an ounce of difference. The whole speech was ridiculous.

Someone brushed past him and Henry felt something hard press against his gloved palm. Turning, he began to walk up the street in the opposite direction, glancing down. A small plastic tube was in his hand, and he slid it into his pocket before continuing to the next block, where he stepped into an alcove. Concealed from the street, he pulled out the tube and extracted the slip of paper.

*Instructions received. Meet with contact, codename Mata. Dorchester Hotel. 9pm. Evaluate for possible collaboration.*

Henry scowled and shoved the message and tube back into his pocket before stepping back onto the sidewalk. He didn't like working with others. He didn't trust them not to be caught. He had worked too hard to stay above suspicion for over two years now, and he had no desire to see it all go to Hell because of one slip from someone who hadn't the faintest idea how to conduct themselves. Yet it appeared that he was going to have to take his chances. He'd been given his instructions, and now had no choice but to follow them. Striding up the road, the scowl deepened. He would have to collaborate with others or risk losing any standing he still had with Berlin.

After failing once again to recover the package that Robert Ainsworth had hidden before his death, Henry couldn't afford any more negative marks against him. The lead that he'd thought he had in Bordeaux hadn't been any lead at all, and by the time he returned to Paris, the trail had been cold. He knew someone had been to the house in Switzerland, but he had no idea who, or what they'd taken away— if anything. He was back to square one, and he knew Berlin was keeping score. He'd have to find that package; that was clear. But in the meantime, his handler was giving him a new assignment.

He would have to go to The Dorchester at 9pm. If Berlin wanted him to collaborate with others, he had no choice. He would have to meet with this Mata, and he would have to play the game. He was no longer the only spy in London, and he was expected to work with these new recruits.

## When Wolves Gather

Henry's lips tightened and his eyes narrowed. He would do as he was told, but he'd be damned if he'd go down with them if they were caught.

## Chapter One

Sir William Buckley looked up at the knock on his office door. He glanced at his watch and called the command to enter, laying down his pen and sitting back with a sigh. It was getting late. Marguerite would be expecting him for dinner, but there was still so much to be done.

"I'm sorry to disturb, sir." His assistant Wesley entered the office carrying a leather portfolio and stack of signals from the radio room in his hands. "I have the latest reports from France, and another batch of communications from our agents there."

"What's left of them," Bill muttered, holding out a hand for the stack. "Thank you. Anything from the French network?"

"No, sir." Wesley cleared his throat. "And nothing from Norway, either."

Bill glanced up with a wry smile. "Am I that predictable?"

"Not at all, sir. I just know that you're anxious for word from the resistance there."

"Well, thank you for these, at least."

The telephone on the desk rang, forestalling any response Wesley would have made, and Bill reached for it, waving his assistant away.

"Yes? Buckley speaking."

"Still there, Bill?" a voice demanded. "It's almost seven!"

"Yes, sir." Bill cradled the receiver between his shoulder and ear as he flipped through the messages from France. "There's quite a bit going on at the moment."

"Well, since you *are* still here, why don't you come up to my office? Or, better yet, I'll come down to you. I could use a walk to stretch my legs."

Bill snapped his fingers to get Wesley's attention just as he was reaching for the door handle. When he turned his head questioningly, Bill held up a finger, asking him to wait.

"Very well. I'll be here. Shall I have tea sent up?"

"Have you still got that scotch in your cabinet?"

Bill grinned. "Yes."

# When Wolves Gather

"I'll have that, if you don't mind. I'm on my way."

Bill hung up and looked across his office at Wesley.

"Montclair is on his way down. I don't know how long he'll be in here, but there's no need for you to wait about until he's finished. I'll just scan through these messages now and if there are any that need a response, you can have them sent, and then head home."

"I don't mind staying, sir," Wesley said. "I know there's quite a bit happening just now."

"My dear Wesley, it won't improve as the war continues. You must learn to pace yourself. No sense in wasting all your ammunition before the main battle."

"And does that apply to you as well, sir?"

Bill let out a bark of laughter. "It does, indeed, but I'm not very good at following my own words of wisdom, I'm afraid."

Wesley grinned and stood quietly while his superior went through the stack of messages before him, scanning each one thoroughly.

"Is it as bad as they say?" he finally ventured.

"Just about," Bill murmured, glancing up. "Your brother…Percy, is it?"

"Yes, sir."

"He's made it back all right from Dunkirk?"

"Yes, thank you. He arrived back last week. He was brought back by a private yacht, captained by an ex-Navy Lieutenant from the last war. He said there were a few hairy moments, but his captain was cool as a cucumber and got them back. Amazing what some of those ordinary citizens did in the effort." Wesley cleared his throat. "Percy has a nasty wound in his shoulder, and his leg took a fair beating from shrapnel, but the doc says he'll be back with his regiment in no time."

Bill nodded. "Good. That's what I like to hear. I'm glad he made it home."

"Sir?" Wesley broke the silence again a moment later.

"Yes?"

"It's about your agent. The one who made it out of Bordeaux."

Bill glanced up. "Yes?"

"Well, I was just wondering if she's made it back all right?" Wesley cleared his throat and a faint flush stained his cheeks. "It's just that we've been hearing about ships being sunk by U-boats in the Channel, and I haven't heard anything more about her since she left Bordeaux."

"Ah. Quite right. She made it to Plymouth right enough. She'll be here tomorrow."

"That's good news, sir," Wesley said, a look of relief on his face.

"Yes."

There was a single, brisk knock on the door and Wesley moved to open it, admitting a man who was on the shorter side with a stocky, square frame. Seen in a crowd, one wouldn't look twice at the man. However, what Jasper Montclair lacked in stature, he more than made up for in personality.

"You're still here too, Fitch?" he demanded in a booming voice. "Is everyone working late?"

"There *is* a war on, you know," Bill said, getting out of his chair and coming around the side of his desk. "But I've just told Wesley he can go."

"I don't mind staying, sir."

"Yes, I know, but none of those messages require a response this evening. Go on and get yourself some dinner."

"Very well, sir, if you're sure."

"I am. Thank you. I'll see you in the morning."

"Good night, sir."

Wesley nodded to Jasper and went out of the office, closing the door quietly.

"He's a good man, young Fitch," Jasper said, crossing the room to seat himself in one of the arm chairs before Bill's desk. "Not surprising, given his family. His father is a legend in the Houses. You're lucky to have him."

"Yes, I know. He's a tremendous help." Bill went over to a tall wooden cabinet and pulled a key from his pocket. "His brother's just returned from Dunkirk."

"Has he? Good show." Jasper crossed his legs and watched as Bill unlocked the cabinet. "That's one battle, at least, that's over. We rescued more men off those beaches than Churchill ever thought possible when he dreamt up the scheme. Not only did we get all our troops off, but that last night they took off twenty-six thousand French troops. A resounding success, it was, thanks in no small part to the armada of private boats that answered the call. They're calling it the Miracle at Dunkirk."

"Yes." Bill poured two glasses of scotch and turned to carry one over to Jasper. "His brother came back on a private yacht captained by an ex-Naval man."

Jasper sipped the scotch appreciatively and watched as Bill took the other arm chair.

## When Wolves Gather

"You've heard the news from France about Daladier?" he asked after a moment.

Bill nodded, rubbing his forehead tiredly. "He's been removed from his position, and de Gaulle is now the Under-Secretary for Defense."

"Know anything about him?"

"De Gaulle? Not really. Only that he's an officer in the French army. Tanks, wasn't it?"

"Quite right. He was made a Brigadier-General a few weeks ago. He led one of the few successful counterattacks against the invasion, for all the good it did." Jasper exhaled and shook his head. "The French won't hold out for much longer. Our forces are being pushed south, and the losses are heavy. I don't see that there is much hope left for France."

"No."

"England will be alone."

"Yes."

Jasper sighed heavily and pinched the bridge of his nose. "Sometimes I wonder if perhaps we will be better off."

Bill raised an eyebrow. "Why would you think that?"

"Well, we won't be committing the defense of England to France, for one thing." Jasper dropped his hand and sipped his drink. "And Churchill won't have to fight with Paris on every little thing that he wants to do."

"There is that." Bill was quiet for a moment, then he shook his head. "But how on earth we're going to keep the Jerries on the other side of the Channel is beyond me."

Jasper nodded glumly. "Winston is putting great faith in the radar. Chain Home is the one thing that might save us."

"The radar towers *are* key," Bill admitted. "They'll give our pilots advanced warning to intercept the bombers…and fighters."

"Let's hope it's enough."

Both men were silent for a moment, then Jasper cleared his throat.

"Has Jian returned from France?"

"Yes, and she brought Oscar with her. He is already in London and is debriefing. She will be here tomorrow."

Jasper raised an eyebrow. "Why the delay?"

"She had to return to Northolt before coming to London. It was only a few days delay, and Oscar has given his account, so I saw no harm in it."

"And the package?"

15

"She gave it to me before continuing on to Northolt. It contained some rather interesting plans for the underground munitions factories that the Germans are building beneath the plants in Stuttgart. I've forwarded the information on."

"Good!" Jasper nodded in satisfaction. "Very good. And Oscar?"

"The amount of intelligence he's managed to gather, as well as the sheer amount of information that he already knew, is staggering. It's slow going. There is so much!"

"Will he be willing to go back?"

Bill let out a bark of laughter. "That's all he wants to do. He says he won't rest until the Nazis are out of Prague."

Jasper grunted. "I suppose he would feel that way. Is his information good?"

"The best I've seen in quite a while." Bill leaned forward. "He has intimate knowledge of how the SS work and conduct their business. More than that, he knows exactly what is required for identity papers for the Reich."

Jasper looked startled. "Heh?"

"That's what he did before leaving Prague and making his way to Holland. He issued papers and credentials for the Reich."

"Well, that *is* helpful! Where in blazes do you find these people, Bill?"

"Oscar found me. Or at least, he found one of my agents in Amsterdam. They alerted me and, well, now here he is."

"Thank God for that. And no one knows who he is?"

"Jian does, but no one else."

"Not the French network?"

"No."

"Good. Then he will be the ace up our sleeve." Jasper cleared his throat. "Once Jian has debriefed, what are your plans?"

"I don't have any. I was going to give her some time off. I think she's earned it."

"Don't do that just yet."

Bill raised his eyebrows in question and Jasper took another sip of scotch before setting the glass down on the desk.

"There's a new training course that's being put together," he said slowly, deliberately. "You know the stock Churchill puts in intelligence, yes? Well, he's convinced that once France falls, the only way to go is to have people on the ground who will…well, there's no good way of putting it. He wants to send people to engage in guerilla warfare against the Germans."

## When Wolves Gather

Bill grinned. "That sounds just like Winston. What does he have in mind?"

"He wants to train them here, and then parachute them in. They'll make contact with any French resistance and, well, do their thing."

"You don't sound like you approve."

"It *is* rather underhanded."

"Jasper, we deal in intelligence. Our very business is underhanded."

"Yes, but that's different," Jasper muttered, waving a hand dismissively. "What Churchill is proposing is…well, it's ungentlemanly."

"I can assure you that the Nazis are not being gentlemen themselves," Bill muttered, recalling some of the accounts from the villages in France. "By all accounts, they're shooting innocents and bludgeoning their way through France. I'm with Churchill on this one. What will he call it?"

"Oh, he's had a few ideas, but I think the current favorite is the Special Operations Executive."

Bill waited for a moment and, when nothing more was forthcoming, he frowned.

"What does this have to do with Jian?" he finally asked.

"Others in the cabinet aren't convinced of the need for such a group. The main objection seems to be the amount and intensity of training that the men, and women, would have to undergo. To address that particular obstacle, an experimental training program is being set up in Scotland."

"And you want Jian to take it?" Bill asked incredulously. "She's not a saboteur. She's a spy!"

"Yes, and I'm not suggesting that she be moved to this new group, if it ever gets off the ground," Jasper said hastily. "It's simply that I saw the training plans, and I think she would benefit greatly from the course."

Bill's brows came together. "Why? What will she be learning that she hasn't already learned from us?"

Jasper cleared his throat uncomfortably. "I know her father was a close friend of yours, and I suspect that you think of her almost a daughter."

"Yes, I suppose in some ways I do. However, I treat her the same as I treat all my agents."

"Yes, yes, I have no doubt of that." Jasper finally raised his eyes to Bill's. "She would learn, among many other things, how to kill enemy sentries quickly and, above all, silently. Now, my own personal feelings regarding the role of women in a theatre of war aside, if she is to be sent back into France once it has fallen, then this is a skill that I think will only help her. Don't you agree?"

Bill was silent for a long moment, thinking of her proficiency in a martial art which no one knew anything about. Jasper believed Jian needed to learn to kill, but Bill knew she'd already learned that years ago in Hong Kong. Mistaking his silence for reluctance, Jasper exhaled and leaned forward.

"She would also undergo very strenuous physical training and testing. The men who drew up the training plan have been training the BEF. Have you heard of the Commandos?"

"No, I don't believe so."

"It's another one of Winston's ideas. They're to be a special branch of the army, made up of soldiers who volunteer for special training to carry out raids against the enemy. Small groups of men who will be able to go where a whole battalion cannot. Or, at least, that's the general idea as far as I can tell. The men who will be training those chaps are the same ones who are undertaking this training, and they have some rather maverick ideas. They are adamant that very specific skills be taught, as well as extreme physical endurance. They don't expect even half of the trainees to complete the course. Their conservative estimate is twenty percent to complete it and pass. If you don't think she can do it, then it's best not to—"

"I have no doubt that she can do it," Bill interrupted, swallowing a mouthful of scotch. "You've seen all her training reports."

"Yes. They're exemplary, which is precisely why I thought of her this morning when I saw the training outline."

Bill considered him shrewdly for a moment. "There's another reason you want her there," he said bluntly. "Spit it out, Jasper. What is it?"

Jasper had the grace to look sheepish.

"I was asked to submit an agent from MI6 to the training. There is some discussion as to the type of person who can excel in such an environment, and I thought perhaps someone like Jian would open a few minds to possibilities that they might not have considered otherwise."

"You want someone you think will surprise them."

"Something like that, yes."

Bill shook his head and finished his drink. "Well, she would certainly do that. Are there any other women going?"

## When Wolves Gather

"Not yet, and to be perfectly frank, I don't think any others will go on this run. As I said, it's all rather more of an experiment. If it goes well, then it will be the basis for the training platform for this new project of Winston's. If not, well, then a few people will come away with very specialized Commando training." He looked at Bill quizzically. "Will that be a problem for her?"

"Not having any fellow females about? No, I don't think so," Bill said thoughtfully. "I'll certainly mention it, but I'd be surprised if she balked at that. She's not one to balk at any challenge."

Jasper visibly relaxed. "You'll arrange it then? Good. I'll submit her name first thing."

"And if she doesn't complete the training?"

"Then I'll lose a rather large wager with the Commando instructor heading up the project," Jasper said cheerfully, standing.

Bill laughed, getting to his feet. "Ha! I should have known."

"Well, when they implied that our agents weren't capable of the kind of physical and mental conditioning that they have in mind, what was I supposed to do?"

"Quite right, Montclair. Quite right. Let's hope that Jian is up to the task."

## Chapter Two

**St. James Underground**
**June 10**

Evelyn Ainsworth looked at her watch and sighed. She'd just missed the train to Paddington. Bill had wanted to talk to her about Oscar, or Finn as she knew him, delaying her departure from the building on Broadway that was headquarters to MI6. He had some questions about their flight south ahead of the German army, and her impression of the Czech-turned-Nazi-turned-Allied-spy. While Finn was still being held for debriefing, there was some concern that perhaps he was a double agent for the Germans. Or at least, that was what she surmised from Bill during his very careful questioning. It was an understandable suspicion, she supposed, but she would be very surprised to find that it was the case. She didn't believe a man could fake the hatred she'd glimpsed in Finn's eyes for the SS soldiers. And so she'd told Bill, but not, apparently, before he'd made her too late to catch her train.

Turning, she made her way across the platform to a bench. She would have to wait for the next one, and it would mean getting back to RAF Northolt much later than she'd planned. This delay would mean waiting for over an hour at Paddington Station for the train to Northolt, and then she still had to walk to the RAF station where she was ostensibly posted in her position as an Assistant Section Officer in the WAAFs.

It really was infuriating, she thought as she sank onto the bench and settled her handbag on her lap. She'd been in London for two days, debriefing from her latest romp across Belgium, France, Switzerland, and then France again. At the end of it, she'd returned to Northolt, only to be called back again not twenty-four hours later. This time she'd had to spend two days with the radio group, learning how to operate the newest model of portable radio. She shook her head now and rubbed her forehead tiredly. It really was ridiculous. They kept teaching her how to use the radios, but they never sent one with her when she went abroad. It seemed to her that it was all rather a waste of time.

## When Wolves Gather

"Evelyn!"

A voice called across the platform and she looked up in surprise to see Bill's assistant, Wesley, running towards her, his tie askew and his jacket flapping open.

"Mr. Fitch!" she exclaimed, standing quickly. "What is it? Is everything all right?"

"No. Well, yes." He stopped before her, breathing heavily. "What I mean is, no."

Evelyn stared at him in some consternation, a laugh on her lips.

"It's not a difficult question, Mr. Fitch," she said humorously. "Either everything is fine, or it isn't."

"It isn't." He took a deep breath. "Sir William just received a call from Northolt. You must get back immediately!"

"I am trying, but I've missed the train to Paddington, in no small part because of Sir William himself."

"Yes, I know. I'm to drive you, but we must hurry!"

Wesley put his hand under her elbow and began to guide her quickly towards the steps leading up to the street.

"Drive me to Paddington?" she demanded. "Don't be ridiculous! The train will have me arrive long before you can make it through the traffic."

"Not Paddington. Northolt," he clarified. "Sir William says the train will never get you back in time."

"In time for what?" Evelyn pulled away from him in exasperation. "Really, Mr. Fitch, what on earth can be so urgent?"

Wesley stopped on the bottom step to the street and looked at her.

"Flight Leader Miles Lacey."

Alarm shot through her and Evelyn felt her chest tighten painfully as breath caught in the back of her throat.

"Miles? Is he hurt?" she asked quickly, her heart pounding. "Has something happened?"

"No, no, nothing like that. But he's standing in your office right this minute while a young corporal is supposedly out on the station looking for you!"

Evelyn gasped. "What?! But I'm not there!"

"Clearly," Wesley said dryly, starting up the steps. Evelyn needed no urging to hurry now, and she ran up the steps lightly beside him. "Your assistant didn't know what to tell him, so she said that you must have stepped out and sent a corporal to locate you. Then she called Sir William to find out when you would be back!"

"Oh good Lord, what a ninny!" Evelyn muttered under her breath. "Why would she do such a thing?"

"I gather she was rather flustered at him showing up unannounced, seemingly convinced that you were on the station. Why would he think that? Does he know that you're back?"

"No. I haven't spoken to him, or even written to him yet. I haven't had time. I've been running back and forth to London!"

They emerged onto the street and half ran down the pavement towards Broadway.

"That's not all, I'm afraid. There's also another pilot there, an Officer Fred Durton?"

"Oh dear! I suppose he's looking for me as well?"

"Quite." They stopped on the curb, waiting for a traffic light to change so they could cross the road. "So you see, Sir William is rather anxious to allay any suspicion on their part."

"Yes, I suppose he is. What a muddle!" Evelyn looked at him, a reluctant laugh pulling on her lips. "Things are never easy, are they?"

He grinned. "Not in this business, or so I'm learning. I've had my car pulled around. I can get you back in half an hour. The rest, I'm afraid, is up to you."

"What did Bill tell her to say to them? Where am I supposed to have been?"

"He didn't. He thought it best for you come up with something that would be likely to be believed by both of them."

The light changed and they jogged across the intersection to where a black Vauxhall was pulled up alongside the curb. The driver got out as Wesley approached.

"Thanks so much, Tommy," he said with a nod. "I appreciate it."

"No problem at all." The driver nodded and turned to walk back towards the tall, unremarkable building that was the headquarters on Broadway.

"Wasn't that Sir William's driver?" Evelyn asked as Wesley opened the passenger door for her.

"Yes. He sent him round for my car while I tried to catch up with you."

Evelyn got into the car and waited while he ran around the front to climb in behind the wheel.

"I do appreciate you taking the time to run me back," she said. "Thank you."

## When Wolves Gather

"There's no need to thank me," he said with a smile, pulling into the flow of traffic. "Let's just get you back so that we can avoid any unnecessary complications, shall we?"

### RAF Northolt

Flying Officer Fred Durton whistled cheerfully as he strode down the corridor on his way to Assistant Section Officer Ainsworth's office. He turned the corner and continued on, wondering as he always did why on earth her office was so far removed from the rest of the WAAF officers. It was almost as if she'd been shoved in the back corner where she was out of sight, and out of mind. The out-of-the-way position of her office probably wasn't helping her displeasure with the state of the WAAF accommodations on the station, and he couldn't say he blamed her for that.

He chuckled to himself. She complained often enough about the lack of proper officer quarters, particularly in relation to the WAAF officers' mess. On one occasion, that conversation had led to her dressing up as a man in an RAF officer's uniform and accompanying him to *their* officers' mess. The chuckle turned to a laugh at the memory. He'd had to help her out a back window in the end.

It had been some weeks since he'd seen Evelyn, and he was looking forward to seeing her now. She was away more than she was present on the station, but this time it was his fault. He'd just returned from a glorious seven days of leave, and he couldn't wait to tell her all about it. He still wasn't quite sure how he'd managed to finagle the time off, but he'd had a wonderful time. Of course, now he couldn't wait to get back up in his Hurricane, but first, he had every intentions of dragging the lovely ASO out to dinner. It had been entirely too long since he'd teased her. He needed his semi-regular dose of Evelyn humor to help him carry on, after all. Flying was a dangerous business, and after Dunkirk, they were really in it now.

He ran a hand carelessly through his hair as he came to her office door and reached out to turn the handle and enter quickly. The cheerful greeting died on his lips when, instead of the fair Evelyn, he found a tall man standing at the window looking out. He turned as he entered and Fred recognized him instantly. He was his friend Barney's mate, the Spitfire pilot he'd met a few months ago.

Evelyn's pilot.

"Oh!" Fred exclaimed, drawing up short. "I say, aren't you Miles Lacey?"

The man nodded with a smile.

"Flying Officer Durton, isn't it?" Miles asked, moving forward with his hand outstretched. "Nice to see you again."

"Thank you, but where's Evelyn?" he asked, looking around the office.

"That seems to be the question of the day," Miles answered wryly. "I arrived nearly an hour ago. A redheaded sergeant showed me in here, then said she would have someone go and see if they could discover her whereabouts. That was the last I saw of her."

"Good Lord, really?" Fred pulled off his hat and tossed it carelessly onto the edge of Evelyn's desk. "The station isn't that big. Where on earth has she got to?"

"I've no idea." Miles pulled out a cigarette case and offered him one. "She isn't on one of her training sprees. At least, I don't think she is."

"Well, Sergeant Cunningham would have told you if she was," Fred said logically, selecting a cigarette. "Ta. Anyway, there's her mac. She takes it with her when she goes away."

He nodded to an RAF-issued raincoat hanging on the coat stand in the corner and Miles glanced at it.

"Then she's definitely here," he said, shoving a cigarette between his lips and pulling out his lighter. "I wouldn't have thought it would take so long to find her."

"Neither would I." Fred rounded the desk and dropped into her chair, crossing his legs. "Strange thing, that. You don't suppose she's ill, do you?"

"She didn't say anything like that in her last letter. I just received it yesterday."

Fred looked up at him through a haze of cigarette smoke.

"I say, what do you think about all these trips she's always taking?" he asked suddenly. "It's damned odd, really. I know she's training her chicks, but they really do keep her moving about, don't they?"

"Her chicks?" Miles grinned, going back to the window and glancing out. "Is that what you call them?"

"She *is* rather like a mother hen at times." Fred grinned. "That night we saw you at the pub, she was keeping a close eye on the two enlisted WAAFs with us, more's the pity."

Miles was quiet for a moment, then he turned away from the window to consider the other man thoughtfully.

# When Wolves Gather

"To be honest, I can't imagine why she should possibly travel around as much as she does," he admitted. "I don't like it, and I know it bothers her brother. He's never able to reach her when he needs to discuss family affairs."

"She keeps mum on what it is that she trains the girls to do. I thought for a bit that it must have something to do with the plotters, but then I realized that wouldn't necessitate nearly as much travel. I mean, she was in Scotland not long ago! We don't have plotters in Scotland, at least not that I'm aware of."

"Well, there's no use asking her. She won't give anything away." Miles exhaled and looked at his watch. "I think that silly sergeant has gone and got herself lost as well."

No sooner were the words out of his mouth than the office door opened unceremoniously. Both men looked towards it expectantly, sighing audibly when a young WAAF pushed in a trolley with tea.

"Sergeant Cunningham asked me to bring you tea, sir," she said, glancing up as she came in. She smiled cheerfully at both of them. "She saw you come in, Officer Durton, so I brought an extra cup."

"Thank you."

"Is there any word yet on the Assistant Section Officer's whereabouts?" Miles asked.

"Not yet, sir. The sergeant is still looking. She'll be along shortly, I'm sure."

The young girl saluted smartly, turning to leave, and the two pilots watched the door close behind her with a firm click.

"Well, I'd think we'd warrant at least another visit from the venerable sergeant," Miles muttered, walking over to inspect the tea tray.

"Perhaps she did get herself lost." Fred put out his cigarette in the ashtray on the desk and stood up with a yawn. "I was going to ask Evelyn to join me for dinner, but I'm famished. I'm off to the pub. I suppose you'll wait for her?"

"Yes. I've waited this long, I'm loathe to pack it in now."

Fred nodded and picked up his hat. "Well, tell her I said I'll see her tomorrow. And tell her it's no use trying to hide from me. It won't take *me* half the day to hunt her down!"

Miles grinned and shook the offered hand. "I'll tell her."

Fred went to the door, then paused, his fingers on the handle.

"How did your squadron make out over Dunkirk?" he asked suddenly, turning.

"We lost three pilots and four Spits," Miles said grimly. "You?"

"Four pilots, and four planes." He shook his head. "One was a flight leader."

"I lost my flight leader as well. I ditched in Belgium and had to make my way back."

Fred turned to stare at him. "Really? How did you get back?"

"Through Dunkirk."

"Good Lord, you were there?!" Fred came back into the office and took off his hat again. "What was it like? Tell me everything!"

Miles stubbed out his cigarette. "I thought you were going to the pub?"

"Well, I was, but I want to hear about what it was like down there."

Miles sighed and went over to the coat stand where he'd hung his hat.

"In that case, why don't we both go to the pub. I'll have a pint while you eat."

"And Evelyn?"

"I'll leave her a note." Miles went over to the desk and picked up a pen, pulling a piece of paper off the pad. "I'll come back. I don't really fancy another hour spent in this dreary office. I don't know how she stands it."

"Well, she's not in it very much, is she?" Fred pointed out.

Miles let out a short laugh.

"No, I suppose not."

He scrawled a note to Evelyn and left it in the center of the blotter where she couldn't miss it. Then, with a final glance around the office, he joined Fred and they went out the door.

# When Wolves Gather

# Chapter Three

Miles climbed out of Fred's car with a sigh of relief. When the other pilot had presented him with the disaster on wheels, he'd stared at it in dismay, wondering if he really had to get in. The passenger's door was actually tied on with string. It was airplane rigging, admittedly, but string just the same. Seeing the look on his face, Fred had made it a point to mention that Evelyn rode in it frequently, and with pleasure. After muttering something about Fred trying to kill her, he had nonetheless climbed into the jalopy. To his surprise, it had carried them to and from the pub without incident, the only caveat being that he had to climb over the driver's seat to get in and out.

He watched as Fred hopped back behind the wheel before grinning up at Miles through the open window.

"Give Evelyn my regards," he said cheerfully. "Tell her I'll drop by tomorrow."

"Yes, I will."

Fred waved and put the car in gear, pulling away. Miles watched him go in bemusement. How on earth could anyone voluntarily drive a car held together with string? He'd seen some things in his time, but that had to be the strangest one yet.

He turned towards the office building behind him and looked at his watch as he walked up the shallow steps to the door. Anticipation surged through him at the thought of seeing Evelyn again. It had been well over a month, closer to two, since he'd seen her last. While they corresponded regularly, it was no substitute for seeing her gleaming gold hair and sparkling blue eyes. As he opened the door and went into the building, he was conscious of a sense of frustration that even now, when he'd managed to steal a few hours to come and surprise her, it was still an ordeal to pin her down.

After giving his name to the sergeant at the desk, he waited while the same visitors' badge as before was handed to him. He clipped it onto his breast pocket and waved away the offer to show him the way.

"It's quite all right. I was here earlier," he said, turning towards the corridor that would lead him back to the corner where Evelyn's office was tucked away. "Thank you!"

He looked at his watch as he strode down the corridor. That sergeant had better have located her, or he would have to leave and miss this one stolen chance to see her. A moment later, he stopped outside her office door and hesitated for a moment before knocking. A combination of relief and pleasure rolled through him when he heard her unmistakable voice call the command to enter. Opening the door, he strode in as if he owned the building.

Evelyn sat behind her desk writing. She looked up when he entered and her face lit with a smile, her eyes sparkling.

"Miles!"

She laid down her pen and jumped up. Miles grinned and closed the door behind him as she came towards him quickly, her hands outstretched.

"Sergeant Cunningham told me you were here. I was so disappointed to have missed you!"

Miles drank in the sight of her and ignored the outstretched hands, catching her around the waist instead. He swung her in a half circle as she burst out laughing.

"God it's good to see you!" he said, his voice sounding hoarse even to his own ears.

And it was, he suddenly realized, staring up into her beautiful face. This was what he'd been missing, and what he had so desperately needed after Dunkirk. He set her on her feet and lowered his lips to hers, anxious to feel them warm beneath his and know that she was really there before him. Her arms went around his neck, and he felt her fingers slide into the hair at the back of his head. His heart thumped and his arms tightened around her as if he would never let her go. After a dizzying moment when he seemed to lose track of time, she pulled away breathlessly and spun out of his arms.

"Now, none of that, if you please!" she said, looking over her shoulder with a teasing smile. "I'm a respectable Assistant Section Officer in the Women's Auxiliary Air Force."

Miles grinned, his eyes glittering.

"Yes?" he asked politely, advancing towards her purposefully.

Evelyn laughed and backed up to put the desk between them. "How would it look if my Section Officer came in? Or worse yet, the Squadron Officer?"

"Don't they knock here?" he asked, glancing at the door. "They do at my station."

"Well, everyone does except Fred," she admitted with a sheepish smile. As he came around the side of the desk, she added

## When Wolves Gather

quickly, "But that doesn't change the fact that this is terribly inappropriate behavior for two RAF officers!"

"Speaking of Fred," he said conversationally, backing her up against a filing cabinet.

"Were we?"

Evelyn sounded breathless and Miles looked down into her face, smiling faintly.

"Yes. I've just been to the pub with him."

She didn't look surprised at all to hear that, and he filed that bit of trivia away while he stepped closer to her.

"Did you?"

She was definitely breathless, and that made him very happy. At least he knew that he wasn't the only one affected by that completely spontaneous kiss just now.

"Yes. He drove."

Evelyn burst out laughing. "Oh dear! How did you fare in the Vehicle of Waiting Reprisals?"

Miles straightened up at that, momentarily diverted.

"Is that what you call it?" he asked with a grin. "I was told that you ride in it frequently, and with great pleasure."

A flash of something close to irritation went across her face, but it was gone so quickly that he wasn't sure if he imagined it.

"Fred likes to think that every woman rides in it with great pleasure," she said dryly.

"And do you?"

"Only when I'm very late coming to meet you at a pub."

Miles smiled slowly and placed his hands against the filing cabinet on either side of her head.

"That's perfectly acceptable then," he murmured, lowering his lips to hers once more.

He half expected her to try to pull away again, but instead she seemed to sigh into him and her arms went around his waist, pulling him closer. In that single instant, Miles felt as if he could conquer the entire Luftwaffe single-handedly. The nagging feeling of anxiety that had plagued him ever since Dunkirk, and which had become more pronounced while he was relating the experience to Fred, receded, and Miles felt as if he'd finally, truly come home. Unwilling to let the feeling go, he deepened the kiss, dropping his hands to her hips to pull her up against him.

Miles had no idea how much time had passed, though he was sure it was only a moment or so, when the strident ring of the telephone jolted him back to reality with a shock. He lifted his head and looked towards the desk. He let his arms fall away as Evelyn let out an unmistakable exclamation of frustration and moved towards the desk, a scowl on her face. Taking a deep breath, he chuckled and followed her, perching on the corner of the desk as she reached for the telephone.

"Yes?" she answered, her irritation clear in her voice.

Miles considered the prim bun at the back of her head and reached out to pluck at one of the hair pins holding the golden locks. Evelyn shot him a laughing look of reproach and slapped his hand away.

"Robbie! How are you?....Yes, he's here now. Did you want to speak with him?....Oh…What?"

Miles grinned as he snagged another pin from her hair, causing her to bite back a giggle as she scooted away from him.

"…What? I'm sorry. I wasn't listening….oh! Yes…Yes, they've arrived. They're with Mummy and Aunt Agatha now…yes…Are you?!...Oh, I wish I could, but I don't think I'll be able to get away…not this weekend, at any rate…"

Miles leaned forward to pull another pin from the ridiculous bun, chuckling when she slapped his hand away with more force.

"…oh, I don't know. I'm off somewhere, I'm sure, but they haven't told me yet…yes…yes, I will…Tell Mummy I love her and miss her…yes, and Aunt Agatha as well…I'll try to arrange a time to see you…I promise…Take care of yourself, Robbie. Goodbye!"

Miles watched as Evelyn hung up the receiver and let out a long sigh.

"What's wrong?" he asked in concern, seeing the laughter disappear from her face.

She dropped into her chair, shaking her head.

"That was Robbie. My Aunt and Uncle have come from France and are at the house in Lancashire. He's managed to get a day off to go home," she said, absently removing the rest of the pins from her lopsided bun.

Miles watched her drop the pins onto the desk and thread her fingers through the golden waves falling about her shoulders. He wanted to run his own fingers through them, but he forced his eyes back to her face.

"He said he was going to try to go home for a day or two. Is that a problem?"

"What? Oh, no. He was ringing to see if there was any chance of my getting home as well." Evelyn dropped her hands and sat back in the chair tiredly. "I'd love nothing more than to see Robbie and Mummy, and Tante Adele and Uncle Claude."

## When Wolves Gather

"I imagine they have some stories. It must have been difficult, not to mention terrifying, to leave France in the midst of the invasion."

A strange look passed fleetingly over her face. "Yes."

"You've just come back from a training stint, haven't you? Can't you request a day?"

"No. I have to prepare for another one. They haven't told me where yet, but I'll be leaving again in the next few days." She rubbed her forehead tiredly. "Sometimes I think this war really is the pits."

Miles slid off the desk and reached down to take her hands, pulling her to her feet.

"Have you eaten?"

"Not yet."

"Come on, then. Let's go and have dinner and forget all about the bloody WAAF for a few hours."

"But haven't you eaten already?" she asked, swiping up the pins from the desk and going over to a small mirror hanging on the wall.

"No. I thought I'd wait for you." He went over to her and took the pins from her hand. "Don't put it back up. I like it down."

"Miles, I have to do something with it," she protested. "I look a fright!"

"Well, for God's sake, don't put it back in that awful bun. It reminds me of an old maid."

She met his gaze in the mirror and laughed.

"But I *am* an old maid, darling! At least, I am by some people's standards. My mother says I should have been married off long ago!"

"Good Lord, no! Then I wouldn't have had a look in!"

Evelyn turned to face him and rested her hands on his chest.

"Oh Miles, I do wish we'd met sooner. This is a rotten time to…well, it's just rotten timing."

Miles put his arms around her and pulled her close, smiling faintly as she rested her cheek on his chest.

"Yes, it is," he agreed quietly. "But we have right now, this evening. We can pretend that there is no war."

The woman in his arms made a sound that was a cross between a sob and a laugh and lifted her face to his.

"You're right."

He winked at her.

"I know I am. Now fix your hair and let me take you out for a meal. I'm positively starving."

## Chapter Four

Evelyn sat across from Miles at a table in the corner of the pub, basking in the comfortable familiarity of the heavy, scarred wood tables and low-beamed ceilings that were so typically English. After over a month of traveling across Europe, she was looking forward to her first taste of good, hearty English food since returning.

She smiled faintly as she thought of how much her life had changed. Just two years ago, she'd only ever stepped inside a pub once when Robbie had dared her to accompany him. They simply weren't places young ladies of her stature frequented. But the war had certainly changed all that. The war was changing a lot of things.

"What are you smiling about?" Miles asked, pulling out his cigarette case.

"I was just thinking about the first time I ever stepped foot inside a pub," she said. "It wasn't that long ago. It was the summer of '38."

"Do tell."

"I was about to leave for Paris. I spent the summer there with my Tante and Uncle, and my cousins Gisele and Nicolas, of course. Before I left, Robbie challenged me to go to a pub with him. He didn't think that I would."

"You'd really never been inside one before?" Miles asked, raising his eyebrows. "Not at all?"

"Never. It wasn't something Mother would have allowed, and it never occurred to me to go behind her back." She laughed, shaking her head. "I'm not sure what I was expecting. Something much more debauched than I encountered, I'm sure. I remember saying to Robbie that it was delightful. I think that shocked him."

"Really?"

"Yes. I don't think he expected me to feel comfortable at all."

"And now you're a seasoned pub-goer. Whatever will we do with you?" He winked. "What did your mother say when she found out?"

"I don't think she ever did, to be honest. I left the next day for France." Evelyn opened her handbag and pulled out a cigarette case.

## When Wolves Gather

"When I returned, all anyone could talk about was the possibility of war. Once I joined the WAAFs, it was all over as far as she was concerned. I'm quite a hopeless case, now."

Miles grinned and pulled out his lighter, holding it out for her to light her cigarette.

"Don't despair, m'dear. Provided we can curtail these unbecoming pub tendencies of yours, you may still have a chance to snag yourself one of the Yorkshire Lacey's."

Evelyn choked and laughed. "Might I? I must be sure to mention that in my next letter. It will give her and Aunt Agatha something to discuss for hours."

Miles tucked his lighter away and watched as she sipped her drink.

"Tell me, why did it take your sergeant so long to find you today?" he asked suddenly.

Evelyn shrugged, setting her drink down with a silent sigh. She'd known he would get around to asking eventually. She was surprised he'd waited this long.

"It took her so long because I wasn't there."

He looked surprised. "What? Where were you?"

"When you arrived I must have been on a train. I was in Weymouth, you see, for a last minute training meeting."

"Well, why didn't she say? Both Fred and I were told you were on the station!"

"She didn't know." Evelyn swallowed, uncomfortably aware of a pair of green eyes studying her from across the table. The look in them was shrewd, though his face was unreadable. "It's really very simple. She was away on a two-day pass to London when I left. She just returned today and I suppose no one told her that I'd gone."

Miles pulled out his cigarette case, never taking his eyes from her face. "When did you go?"

"I left on Friday evening. I caught the last train."

She blew smoke towards the ceiling. She was doing her best to put on a carefree front, but her heart was suddenly thumping in her chest. He didn't believe her.

The realization shot into her mind in an instant, and she knew she was right. Not even by the flicker of an eyelid did he betray as much, but she knew that he didn't believe her story at all. But why? It was seventy-five percent true! She *had* left by the last train on Friday night, after being back in Northolt for a scant sixteen hours or so. The only difference was that she hadn't gone to Weymouth, but to London.

And it hadn't been for a training meeting, but for a crash course in radio transmitting.

"Weymouth! For the weekend? How lovely! You don't seem to have caught any sun. Didn't you go to the beach?"

Evelyn laughed lightly and tapped her cigarette ash into the tray on the table.

"Hardly. It was a training meeting, Miles. I spent two days in a sooty old bunker with a lot of terribly important relics from the last war."

The faintest smile crossed his face. "Poor you! Never mind. I'm sure you'll have many other opportunities to visit the seaside."

He bent his head to light his cigarette and Evelyn allowed herself a silent sigh of relief. It appeared that he was going to let the matter drop.

"The letter I received from you yesterday was postmarked from Scotland. I could swear you said that once you returned to Northolt that you didn't have any trips planned."

So much for him letting the matter rest. Evelyn resisted the urge to squirm in her chair and reached for her drink instead. Why was he so persistent about this? Why couldn't he simply accept her perfectly reasonable explanation like a good boy and leave it alone?

"And so I didn't. This wasn't really a trip. It was more of a jaunt."

Green eyes lit with laughter as they met hers. "A jaunt? To Weymouth?"

"All right, perhaps more of a long weekend. I knew nothing of it until I returned back to the station earlier this week."

"They really do have you moving around a lot, don't they?"

"Yes."

"And you absolutely cannot tell me what it is that you do?"

"Miles! You know I can't!"

He grinned. "I know, but you have me intrigued. Fred made a valid point about plotters today, and now I'm beginning to question that particular theory. But never fear! I'll figure it out, y'know. Don't think I won't!"

She swallowed and forced herself to laugh lightly.

"I'd be absolutely shocked if you did," she said truthfully. "But enough about me. Let's talk about you. I haven't seen you in an age."

"There isn't much to say. The flying is becoming more intense. We're running into the bloody Jerries regularly now." He took a sip of his drink. "I know that I've been saying I wanted to get into the fight, but now that it's here, it's all rather anti-climactic."

## When Wolves Gather

"I very much doubt that." Evelyn put out her cigarette. "Being shot down is far from anti-climactic."

"Yes, well, perhaps not that."

"And neither is being promoted to Flight Leader, Lieutenant."

"Yes, but at what cost? I never wanted to earn a promotion by losing a pilot."

Evelyn exhaled and reached out to take his hand across the table.

"Was it very terrible?"

He looked at her and a flash of sorrow went across his face before being effectively hidden behind the reckless mask that he wore.

"I wasn't there. I'd already ditched on a beach in Belgium."

"Belgium!" she exclaimed, her eyes widening. "Where?"

"Just south of Ostend. I shouldn't be telling you any of this, you know."

Evelyn thought of the top secret intelligence that she was tasked to gather and suppressed a laugh.

"Don't worry. I promise not to tell the Germans where you landed," she said with conspiratorial wink.

"Well," he said, lowering his voice, "I put her down on the beach and must have hit my head because the next thing I knew, I was waking up to the smell of burning oil. I just made it out before…well, I wouldn't be sitting here now."

Evelyn swallowed and reached for her drink with her free hand. It was trembling only slightly, but Miles saw it and tightened his fingers around hers.

"I'm sorry. I shouldn't tell you."

"No!" Evelyn took a fortifying sip of her drink and set it down, looking at him resolutely. "I *want* to hear. I want to know what you experience up there. I need to know."

He considered her for a moment, then nodded, releasing her hand and lifting his cigarette to his lips.

"Very well. I ran into two Belgian soldiers and one of them patched me up on the side of the road. Nothing serious. I dislocated my shoulder in the crash, and bumped my head. Then they sent me on my way. I was going to try to make for Ostend, but they told me it had already been overrun by the Germans, so I went south. To Dunkirk."

She stared at him, her heart pounding. "You were there? At Dunkirk?"

"Yes."

She thought of the newspaper articles she'd devoured on her mad flight south, and remembered the waves upon waves of Luftwaffe bombers flying overhead, heading to the coast. A shudder went through her. While she had been witnessing the massacre of civilians by Stukas on the road south, Miles had been facing the same nightmare, trapped on a beach while their Royal Navy desperately tried to rescue them.

"What was it like?"

He was quiet for a moment, then he shook his head.

"I've never seen so many men in one place. They were all lined up in orderly rows on the sand, waiting for the next ship. I've never seen anything like it, and I hope to God that I never do again."

"You got on a ship, then?"

"Yes. A destroyer. It brought me back to England, and I was with my squadron again the following day. That's when I heard about Mother—or Lieutenant Hampton."

Evelyn was quiet for a moment, her mind still trying to grasp the realization that they had both been in France at the same time, both escaping the advancing German forces. Together, yet worlds apart.

A barmaid came to the table then, bearing their dinner, and she sat back as the woman set a steaming fish pie before her, the mashed potatoes golden atop the creamy fish sauce. She watched as a plate of beef stew was set before Miles and was suddenly overcome with the most bizarre feeling of homecoming. It was the only way she could think to describe it, this rush of warmth and belonging that was overtaking her. Looking across the table and meeting Miles' smile, Evelyn realized that this was what she had been longing for over the past weeks. Throughout the frantic flight from Brussels, and then again from Marle, and then yet again from Paris itself, she had clung to the memory of England.

But in an instant, she realized that the memory of England wasn't just of England at all. It was of Miles, and the life that she longed to have with him. A life that seemed to grow more and more impossible with each passing day, and each lie that she told him.

"Thank you."

His deep voice thanking the bar-maid pulled her from her reverie and Evelyn looked at the food before her. It was the solid, wholesome, English fare that she'd so been looking forward to, and she was suddenly ravenous.

"Can you tell me what happened?" she asked, picking up her knife and fork. A watermark on her knife caught her attention and she unconsciously rubbed it with the sleeve of her WAAF uniform jacket. "When you were shot down?"

## When Wolves Gather

"There's not much to tell. One of the bastards got me in my radiator and near my fuel tank. I think he must have nicked a fuel line because oil was burning by the time I set her down. I thought I could make it back, and Rob was to escort me to keep the Jerries off of me, but I realized my coolant was leaking and, well, I had the choice of putting it down in the Channel or trying for land. I chose the latter."

"And Robbie?"

"The last I saw of him, he was engaging two 109s to keep them away from me. I was a sitting duck. If they'd got to me, there wouldn't have been much I could do. I could barely keep my kite straight, let alone fight."

Evelyn felt a surge of pride in her brother, mixed with horror at the thought that she could have lost both of them in the same day; the two men she cared for most in the world.

A comfortable, companionable silence fell over the table as they ate, and Evelyn wondered suddenly if they would all make it through this war. Would all of them survive? Or just one? Or none?

"Did you see the news on the train?" Miles asked, breaking the silence after a few moments.

"I picked up a newspaper in the station in London," she said.

"Then you know the French government has fled Paris?"

"Yes." She set her cutlery down and wiped her mouth with a napkin before reaching for her drink. "They say that the Germans will be in Paris by the end of the week. It's too horrifying to think about. Can you imagine the Nazis goose-stepping down the Champs Elysee?"

"Appalling thought, isn't it?" Miles shook his head. "Can you believe it's only been one month today since Hitler launched his offensive against Belgium and Holland? One month, and they're already to Paris. It doesn't seem fathomable!"

Evelyn remembered the speed of the German tanks tearing across the French countryside and suppressed another shudder.

"Blitzkrieg," she said in a low voice. "Mögen sie für alle Ewigkeit in der Hölle verrotten."

Miles looked up sharply, his eyes narrowing. "What?"

She cleared her throat. "Nothing."

He looked at her for a moment. "Rob said that you spoke several languages. I suppose I should have realized that German would be one of them."

"It's not one that I use very often, especially now," she said quietly. "I much prefer French."

"What other languages do you speak?"

"Fluently? Or for recreation?"

"Is there a difference?" he asked, laughter lighting his eyes.

"Oh yes. Some I'm quite fluent in, and others I only know enough to make myself understood."

He grinned and wiped his mouth with his napkin before reaching for his drink. "Fluently, then."

Evelyn shrugged self-consciously. Suddenly she was rather embarrassed by the number of languages she'd learned. She certainly didn't want Miles thinking that she was a bluestocking. As she hesitated, his smile widened.

"Oh, come now. Confess! How many, and what are they?"

"I speak eight languages fluently. It was seven, but I've learned another in the past year."

"In all your spare time?" he asked wryly. "No. Don't answer that. I'm sorry I said it. What are they?"

"Is this really necessary? Why do you want to know?"

"I want to know everything there is to know about you, Miss Evelyn Ainsworth. I find you fascinating. So tell me, what countries are we destined to travel to when this blasted war is over?"

She swallowed. "I speak French, German, Italian, Cantonese, Spanish, Portuguese, Russian, and Norwegian," she said in a low voice, avoiding his gaze. "And I'm becoming fairly proficient in Japanese, although I haven't been able to concentrate on it as much as I'd like."

He stared at her, his dinner forgotten, with a stunned look on his face.

"All of them?" he finally got out. "You're fluent in all of them? Russian as well?"

"Yes."

"Good Lord, Robbie wasn't exaggerating! He said you were the linguist in the family, but I assumed it was French and Italian, and possibly Spanish."

He fell silent as the bar-maid returned with fresh drinks, another pint for him and another glass of wine for her. Once she'd left again, he shook his head.

"Cantonese? Why did you learn that?"

"Surely Robbie told you that I lived in Hong Kong for a time with my parents?"

Miles frowned. "No, actually, he didn't. You lived in Hong Kong?"

"Yes. My father was sent there for a few years for his work. Mummy and I accompanied him. I was there for, oh, six years or so."

"How extraordinary!"

## When Wolves Gather

"Not really," she said with a shrug, setting her wine glass down and picking up her knife and fork again. "It was in the early thirties and Daddy was attached to the embassy."

"When did you leave?"

"In '36. As it turned out, it was fortunate that we did. The Japanese moved into China shortly after we left."

Miles was silent as they ate and Evelyn wondered what he was thinking. Her mother had told her often enough that men didn't like smart women, but she'd never really cared much what men thought of her.

Until now.

The comfortable silence between them was broken a moment later when a farmer burst into the pub, his hair disheveled, waving a newspaper in his hand.

"They've gone and done it!" he cried. "Italy has declared war on England and France!"

Evelyn's head snapped up and her knife and fork paused over her plate as she and Miles stared at the man.

"Bloody hell!" someone cried. "What next?!"

"You've got that wrong, Bill. You must have!" The landlord spoke from behind the bar, his voice carrying over the suddenly hushed pub.

"No I haven't! It's right here, in the evening edition. Mussolini Declares A State of War. See?"

He flourished the newspaper and took it over to the bar. The landlord snatched it up and scanned the headline blazoned across the front page. After a stunned moment, he lifted his head.

"It's true," he announced. "At midnight, we'll be at war with Italy."

"Bloody Italians!" A voice was heard from a table nearby to Evelyn and Miles. "Fascist pigs, that's what they are!"

Evelyn tamped down a wave of anger and looked across the table at Miles. He looked grim.

"We knew it was coming," he said in a low voice. "It was only a matter of time. Mussolini has been in Hitler's pocket for the past year or more."

"Yes, but it's still rather shocking to have it happen," Evelyn replied, laying down her cutlery. Her appetite was suddenly gone and she pushed the plate away, reaching for her wine instead. "Now we have another front to fight, and we still have troops in the south of France."

"And our allies are losing on all sides." Miles also pushed his dinner away and pulled out his cigarette case. "Norway surrendered today. King Haakon has escaped to London with his cabinet. He will form a government in exile."

"Thank heavens that he escaped!"

"It was inevitable that Norway would fall, of course. The Germans have had control of most the country for months now."

"They were still fighting in the north," Evelyn said, accepting an offered cigarette from him. "I'll say that for the Norwegians. At least they fought to the bitter end."

He crooked an eyebrow. "Unlike the Belgians and French?"

"I didn't say that!" She bent her head to his offered lighter. "It's different. The terrain, the people, the culture; it's all different in Norway."

He watched her with an unreadable expression on his face. "Is it? I don't know very much about the Norwegians, I'm afraid."

Evelyn waved her hand vaguely, wishing desperately that she could take the words back.

"Neither do I, but you've only to look at a map to see that the whole country is made up of mountains. It's a completely different theatre of war."

Miles lit his cigarette, his eyes never leaving her face.

"Do you know, I think you're the most interesting woman of my acquaintance?" he decided, snapping his lighter shut. "You know the most extraordinary things!"

She forced a laugh.

"My father was a very well-versed and popular diplomat. I know something about almost all the countries in the Western Hemisphere, and most in the Eastern. It was inevitable. Does it bother you?"

"Not a'tall! It makes for the most unexpected and fascinating conversations." He winked.

Evelyn relaxed. "Oh good. My mother and Robbie are constantly telling me to mind what I say because no gentleman likes a bluestocking."

"Well, this gentleman thinks it's enchanting," Miles assured her with a warm smile. "And you are as far removed from a bluestocking as I can imagine."

"Oh? And what do you imagine a bluestocking to be?"

"A prim and plain person who belongs in a library hidden in stacks of books," he said promptly. "Musty, old-fashioned, and dull as ditch water."

# When Wolves Gather

"And that's not me?"

"Good Lord, no! You belong on a dance floor, surrounded by glittering lights and music. You're beautiful, and you know it."

She laughed, grateful to be back on familiar footing with him. Societal flirting she could handle; the unreadable look in his eyes that convinced her that he saw more than she wanted him to, she could not.

"Thank you for noticing."

"Rob did warn me, you know," he said conversationally. "He told me I hadn't a chance in hell."

"Well that wasn't very nice of him."

"On the contrary, it was the best thing he could have said." Miles put out his cigarette. "After hearing about all the broken men you've left scattered about London *and* Paris, I was only more determined."

"Good grief, you make me sound like some kind of femme fatale! I'm not nearly as elusive as my brother would have you think. I simply know what I want, and I'm not willing to settle for anything less."

"And what is it that you want, Assistant Section Officer Ainsworth?"

"That, Lieutenant Lacey, is something you will have to discover for yourself."

## Chapter Five

"When are you due back to your station?" Evelyn asked as Miles opened the door for her to step outside into the night.

"Tonight. I had to go to London to meet with my father and the solicitor, but I only had the day." Miles took a deep breath and looked around the small, gravel parking area in front of the pub. "I'm not ready to take you back yet. Would you care for a walk?"

Evelyn tucked her hand through his arm. "I'd love one."

Miles covered her hand with his and they walked out of the pub yard and onto the narrow street that wound its way through the village.

"I still can't seem to get used to the blackout," she said as they strolled down the dark lane. "It's so strange not to have any light at all. You'd think I'd be used to it by now, but it's just so bizarre not to see lights in the windows, or anywhere."

"Necessary, though. There's no point in helping Jerry out by showing him where to drop his load."

She looked up at his profile. "I suppose you fly at night?"

"Yes, of course."

"What's it like? Up there in the pitch blackness?"

He looked down at her for a moment, then he smiled. "You ask the strangest questions, Evelyn."

"Do I?" She was surprised. "Hasn't anyone else asked about your flying?"

"Who is there to ask? Everyone I spend time with is a pilot themselves." He chuckled. "I'm sorry. I didn't mean to tease you. When I first began night flying, it was very disconcerting. You have to rely completely on your instruments, you see. There's no sense of space or distance when you look outside. It's a black void."

"Can you see the ground when you land?"

"Not until you're right on top of it."

"However do you manage?"

"The instruments. I let them guide me. They tell me exactly where I am. At first, it wasn't easy, but I'm used to it now." Miles shrugged. "Tell me, do you ask Durton these kinds of questions?"

## When Wolves Gather

"Fred?" Evelyn laughed. "No. I can never get a word in with him. He did tell me once that he almost collided with another airplane during night training, but nothing more. Does it bother you? My asking you questions about the flying, I mean."

"Not a'tall." He looked down at her. "I wish I could ask questions about what it is that you do."

"Oh, it's not nearly as exciting as what you and Robbie are doing," she assured him with a light laugh. "I know it all sounds mysterious, but it's really very dull, I promise you."

Evelyn resisted the urge to cross her fingers behind her back. Oh yes. Standing on a ridge above a road filled with Wehrmacht troops and confronting a German Major was very dull work indeed! An icy chill went through her and she swallowed. That entire encounter could have gone very differently, and if it had, she wouldn't be here now, walking next to Miles with his strong hand covering hers in the crook of his elbow.

"Now why don't I believe you?" he murmured, drawing a sharp glance from under her lashes. Before she could reply, he changed the subject. "Rob tells me that your cousins didn't come to England with your Aunt and Uncle. Did they really stay behind in France?"

"I believe so." Evelyn exhaled silently in relief at his apparent willingness to drop the topic of her war work for the time being. "That was the last that I heard, at any rate."

"They must know that…"

His voice trailed off and Evelyn looked up at him. "That they will be trapped when France falls?" she asked bluntly. "Yes. I'm sure that they realize that."

"Then why on earth would they stay when given an opportunity to go to safety?"

"I would imagine that they feel they can do more to fight for their country from within France than from England."

"Your brother seems to think that they're looking for adventure."

"Very likely." Evelyn shrugged. "Nicolas and Gisele are quite headstrong, and they never were ones to shy away from trouble. In fact, sometimes I think they thrive on it!"

Miles stopped walking in front of an alcove to a shuttered shop. Turning to face her, he looked down into her face curiously.

"You don't sound very concerned," he said slowly. "Aren't you worried that they'll become involved in a resistance?"

"Worried? No. I pray that they do! I'm afraid I'd be rather disgusted with both of them if they remained behind only to turn a blind eye to what the Nazis will do to their country."

Evelyn spoke before she could stop herself, her voice low. Aware of his green eyes watching her closely, she forced a shrug and a smile.

"I know that if the Germans succeed in invading England, as everyone seems to think they'll try to do, I would do everything in my power to resist the occupation. Who am I to say that Gisele and Nicolas should not?"

"And if they are killed?"

Evelyn remembered a blond man sitting in a snowy ravine, blood pouring from his leg, and swallowed with difficulty. Peder had been doing what he could to help her escape from Norway while his country was being overrun. When he was shot, he chose to sacrifice himself to help them escape. The whole scene flashed across her mind's eye in an instant, and another shudder went through her.

"Then I hope they take a few of the bastards with them."

Her voice was hard and Miles frowned, staring at her in thoughtful silence for a moment. Before he could speak, however, they heard voices, muffled at first, but growing louder in waves. They both turned towards the strange sound, peering down the narrow, dark street. A glow was becoming visible around the bend at the end of the street, and Evelyn squinted, trying to make it out.

"What's happening?" she asked.

Miles shook his head, grasping her elbow and pulling her into the alcove behind them.

"I don't know, but I don't like the sound of it."

While they couldn't make out what the voices were saying, they could hear the anger and force behind them. The glow at the bend grew brighter, and then, suddenly, the source of the light became visible.

Evelyn sucked in her breath as a large group of people came around the corner, brandishing flaming torches above their heads.

"Good Lord," Miles exclaimed, drawing her deeper into the alcove and moving so that his own body shielded her. "It's a mob!"

"What?!"

Evelyn strained to see over his shoulder, but it was no use. She couldn't see a thing. Moving to the side to peer around him, she watched as a crowd of at least a hundred people poured down the narrow lane, carrying torches and chanting something that was, at first, unintelligible. As the swarm drew closer, however, the words became clear.

## When Wolves Gather

"Down with Duce! Down with traitors!"

"Duce?" Evelyn stiffened. "This is about Mussolini?"

"And the Italians," Miles said grimly, glancing at the dark storefront behind them. "What is this store?"

"It's a bakery."

"Is it Italian?"

"No. At least, I don't think so."

She started at the sound of breaking glass and pushed forward to stand next to Miles, ignoring his attempt to press her back behind him again.

"Stop trying to protect me," she exclaimed in exasperation. "I hardly think..."

Her voice trailed off as she got a good look at the mob swarming the street and coming towards them. Two young men near the front brandished clubs and as she watched, a brick was thrown through the front window of a shop a few doors down from them.

"Italian traitors!"

"Burn it down!"

Another rock was thrown and more glass shattered. The mob had stopped before the shop, shouting and tossing whatever they had at hand towards the storefront.

"Burn it!"

"Down with Duce!"

As she watched torches lighting strips of cloth hanging out of bottles, anger surged through Evelyn. She remembered the stories of Kristallnacht, the night that Jewish business were looted and burned throughout Germany and Austria in the fall of '38. She had been just beginning her training with Bill and MI6 when they'd heard the news of businesses being attacked in coordinated riots throughout Nazi Germany. She remembered her horror that any human being could do such a thing to others.

"Traitors!"

"Burn it!"

She started forward, her whole body shaking with rage, only to have Miles grab her arm and haul her back.

"Evie, no!" he exclaimed, a sharp note of alarm in his voice.

"I can't let them do it!" she hissed, trying to pull away. "Let me go!"

"Evie, listen to me!" Miles clamped a hand on either arm and held tight, staring down into her face. "There are too many of them. You'll only get hurt!"

"But they're going to—"

"Yes, I know, but we can't stop them."

She glared at him. "So we do nothing?!"

"I don't like it any more than you do," he said grimly, pulling her deeper into the alcove and into the shadows. "But what would you have us do? If we go out there, we're outnumbered by at least a hundred to our two. And it won't stop them!"

As if to reinforce what he was saying, another round of volleys was thrown into the shop and more glass shattered. An eerie, unnatural silence filled the street for a moment, then the crowd cheered as the unmistakable smell of smoke filled the air.

Someone yelled from the end of the street, and a new wave of cries went through the mob.

"Police!"

Whistles could be heard over the crowd and Evelyn watched as they dispersed, running up the street and past them without a glance into the darkened alcove. Frustration mixed with her rage and she found her whole body shaking as she watched faceless people with torches, clubs, and iron pipes scatter ahead of the arrival of the policemen. The smell of smoke was getting stronger and there was another sound of breaking glass as flames broke through the windows of the shop a few doors down.

"Oh my God," she breathed as lights came on in the buildings up and down the street.

Miles wrapped his arms around her and pulled her close, watching over her head as the mob disappeared just as quickly as it had come.

"It's over," he said after a moment.

"No, it's not." Evelyn pulled away and shook her head, her jaw clamped together. "It will keep happening, over and over again. Different nationalities. Different cities. Different thugs. It won't be over until the war is over, and all this hate is laid to rest."

*15th June, 1940*

*Dear Miles,*

*It was lovely to see you last week, even if the evening did end on rather a sour note. Did you see what happened in Edinburgh? They're saying the entire city was in flames. I suppose we were lucky that it was only that one incident here. Fred says that it is inevitable, and that he's surprised it hasn't*

## When Wolves Gather

*happened more often, with both the Italians and the Germans. Of course, most of the Germans are interned now. While I understand the reasoning behind it, it makes me ill to think that we're treating our neighbors and former friends as badly as the Nazis treat their enemies. I know we have to be careful of spies, but to put them all in internment camps? There must be a better way. This isn't us. This isn't England.*

*I've just finished reading the newspapers. Paris has fallen. We knew that it would, but seeing the images of the Nazi flags along the Champs Elysée is horrific. It seems like only yesterday that I was shopping and having lunch there with Gisele. Will it ever be the same again? Will I ever see my beloved Paris again? And what of Tante Adele and Uncle Claude's house? Will it become the province of German officers? Heaven forbid!*

*I do worry about Gisele and Nicolas. I know that when you asked, I said things that you didn't understand. I don't really understand how I feel myself. At that moment, I wasn't worried for them. I only wanted as many French men and women as possible to have the courage to resist the Nazis. Now, seeing the photographs of Paris as they marched in, I see that perhaps it would have been better for my cousins to accompany their parents to England. My mother says that they are at the chateau in the south, and so they are safe for now. My uncle is still trying to convince them to come to England, but he was unable to get through to them the last time he tried. I fear the communications have already been cut off by the German forces.*

*Verdun has surrendered, and they have advanced to Le Havre. It can only be a matter of days now before Reynaud gives in and France capitulates. What will happen to us then? The Nazis will be across the Channel, and they will turn their attention to their last remaining foe: England. How will we withstand the full force of the German Luftwaffe and Kriegsmarine? Certainly many have tried to cross the Channel in the past and failed. Yet I feel that this time is different. This time, the threat is very real.*

*I'm hoping to have a few days leave in July. I'm off to another training post in a few days, but when I return I'm due for some time off. I'd like to get back to Ainsworth Manor to see my Mother and my Aunts and Uncle. If I do manage it, I'll try to get to London for a few days as well. Wouldn't it be lovely if you could arrange another visit to your solicitor at the same time? We could dine at the Savoy and pretend that the most powerful army that the world has ever seen isn't just over the Channel, waiting to attack us.*

*Take care of yourself and your Spit. No more grand tours through Europe, if you wouldn't mind.*

*Always yours,*
*Evelyn*

## June 16

Evelyn closed the small leather-bound notebook and tucked it into her purse, turning her attention out of the window. The train swayed soothingly as it sped towards London and she leaned her head back on the seat, watching the fields roll by.

Bill wanted to see her again. He wouldn't say why over the telephone, but there was nothing strange in that. It wasn't his custom to divulge any information over the telephone. After five days at Northolt, she wasn't at all surprised to be on the train to London. She had a suitcase with her, knowing from experience that she may be on the verge of being sent off to some training exercise. MI6 seemed to be taking every advantage of her forced stay in England to update her training as much as they could.

And it didn't look as though she would be able to leave England again in the immediate future.

Paul Reynaud had resigned, and Philippe Petain had become prime minister in his place. As the German armies overran France, it was expected that Petain would surrender forthwith. It would be some time before she would be able to go back to France, and Evelyn swallowed, wondering how Josephine was doing amidst the invasion. She'd left her just outside Bordeaux, intent on starting a new life in the south until she could resume her fight against the Germans.

And Jean-Pierre? Had he fled Paris with the government? Was he, even now, staying with the crumbling government as France fell around him? He'd said that he would, until he could no longer be of any use to the resistance in his current position.

Evelyn lifted her head and exhaled. How strange it was to think of the remnants of the network Bill had built up through France,

## When Wolves Gather

and those that were left of the Deuxième Bureau, as the resistance. That they should become a resistance movement under Nazi occupation was something that was unthinkable just six months ago. Now, it was a terrifying reality for all of them.

Her heart ached for the citizens of France, her throat growing tight at the thought of what they were experiencing right this very minute. Their government had grossly misled them, assuring them that the invasion tearing through their country could never happen. They had created a false sense of security with the Maginot Line, and then compounded it by ensuring that the press supported their claims of military strength. All the people believed that Germany didn't have the soldiers, tanks, or weapons to match the French and English armies. When it became clear that they did, they felt betrayed by their government, and rightly so. People across France were losing everything as the Germans advanced, destroying crops and bombing villages and cities with total abandon. Men and women like Josephine, Jens, and Jean-Pierre were prepared, and willing to fight, but the majority of the population was not. Her flight south had shown her just how confused and frightened the people of France were, and Evelyn swallowed painfully. She and Finn had been able to leave, but they could not. They were stuck there to face the Gestapo and the SS.

Miles had been startled by the vehemence in her tone when they discussed her cousins remaining behind to fight the Germans. She had been unable to conceal her anger from him, and she knew that it was a dangerous slope she'd slid down that night. Miles wasn't stupid. He saw far more than his bored, aristocratic demeanor betrayed, and that was what made her slip so dangerous. He was already unduly curious about her work, and suspicious. She knew that. She had had one too many slips with him, and he was beginning to realize that she wasn't where she said she was all the time. She was sure of it. And now he knew exactly how she felt about resistance movements and fighting the Nazis with all available force. These were not sentiments consistent with an heiress and WAAF officer. He was bound to begin putting two and two together. And that was no good for either of them.

Evelyn exhaled and pinched the bridge of her nose. She had to find a way to guard her tongue around him, or she would end up in a very awkward position indeed. He could never know that she worked for MI6. No one could. She was bound by the Official Secrets Act, punishable by imprisonment and charges of treason should she ever break it.

Miles Lacey could never realize that the woman he believed to be a WAAF was, in fact, a spy.

For that matter, neither could anyone. Her family, thankfully, seemed to have no inkling that things weren't exactly as she said they were. Her mother had no idea how things worked in the RAF and so had no notion that it was unusual for her daughter to be traveling about the country so often. Robbie, who *did* know how things worked, hadn't raised any questions, which was a bit surprising. She wasn't about to look that particular gift horse in the mouth, however. If Miles was the only one asking questions, she could handle him. She simply had to be more diligent about her stories from now on.

She frowned. She really had no idea what gave her away this last time. It was a perfectly plausible story, and so close to the actual truth that it really was annoying that he had clearly not believed a word. And he hadn't. She was absolutely sure of it.

The conductor came down the aisle, calling out the time, and Evelyn looked at her watch. She would be in London in ten minutes, and then there would be no time for worrying about Flight Lieutenant Miles Lacey. Bill would expect her full attention, and she had every intention of giving it. The question of Miles would work itself out in time, and as long as she got better at lying to him, all would be well.

And that very thought made her stomach clench. How could they ever have a relationship if everything he knew about her was a lie?

But how could she ever walk away now?

# When Wolves Gather

# Chapter Six

Evelyn showed her identification to the guard at the top of the stairs and smiled cheerfully.

"Good morning."

"Good morning, miss." His face relaxed as he examined the card before stepping back to allow her to pass. "Lovely weather we're having today."

"Yes, isn't it?" She tucked her identification back into her purse. "It almost makes you forget there's a war on!"

She went down the long corridor towards Bill's office, sighing inwardly. The sun was shining brightly over England, and it promised to be a warm day. It was the perfect day for a picnic, and no doubt if the world hadn't spun out of control, she would have been dressing to go on such an outing instead of walking down a drab and dreary hallway, dressed in an equally drab and uninspiring WAAF uniform.

A moment later, she knocked on a door, hearing Bill's familiar voice call for her to enter.

"My dear Sir William, you really shouldn't be cooped up here on such a fine day," she announced, sailing in. "We should go to the park. You could use the fresh air."

Sir William Buckley looked up from the papers strewn across his desk, his face creasing into a smile.

"Could I indeed? What makes you say that?"

"I've got to know you quite well this past year," Evelyn said, crossing the office as he stood and came around the side of his desk. "I'll wager you've been here since before dawn."

"Guilty as charged." He took her outstretched hand. "How was the train down?"

"Perfectly uneventful." She began to remove her gloves as she sank into a chair before the heavy wooden desk. "Have you seen the headlines this morning? Reynaud has resigned. Petain is prime minister of France now."

"Yes, for as long as France remains." Bill offered her a cigarette from the box on his desk and she shook her head. "He will sue for peace with Hitler. England will stand alone by the end of the week."

She stared up at him. "Do you think so?"

"Yes." He seated himself in the other chair before the desk, crossing his legs comfortably. "He is a military man. He knows there is no hope for France now. Our prime minister is preparing for it."

"Poor Churchill. He's only been in office for a month. It doesn't seem possible, does it? That all of this has happened in such a short amount of time?"

"No. No, it doesn't."

"What's being done about our agents in France?" She smoothed her gloves and laid them in her lap, looking at him expectantly.

"I'm doing what I can to get the ones out who want to leave, but it's very difficult. As you experienced yourself, finding a port to flee from is becoming more and more of a challenge."

"Can I help in any way?"

He smiled and shook his head.

"No, my dear Evie. Your job is done for now. At least, as far as France is concerned." He held up a hand when she would have spoken. "The time will come soon enough for you to return, but it isn't now."

"And Finn? Is he going back?"

"Not yet. I'm not taking any chances with my best agents. You and Finn, and a handful of others, are staying right here in England where it's safe for the time being."

"Safe for how long?" Evelyn made a face. "Hitler will turn his attention to us now that France is all but won."

"Yes." Bill was quiet for a moment. "How is your pilot faring?"

"Miles? He seems to be handling everything all right. He was shot down over Dunkirk, but he went right back up again. He says the experience gave him a rather large chip on his shoulder."

"I'd imagine it would. And your brother?"

"The same. You know Robbie. He's just happy to be flying."

Bill chuckled, then sobered almost immediately.

"If what they're saying is true, the RAF is about to face the full force of the Luftwaffe. Hitler will require full control of the skies before committing his troops to cross the Channel."

"Yes. I know."

He met her steady gaze.

"Right. Of course you do." He cleared his throat. "Well, while we're preparing for what now seems to be an inevitable battle for our

## When Wolves Gather

small island, you'll be on your way to Scotland. There's a training course that I want you to attend."

"In Scotland?" She raised her eyebrow. "I thought I'd completed all the courses MI6 had."

"You have. This isn't one of ours."

She stared at him, surprised. "Then whose is it?"

"I'm not really sure, to be honest. It's a new scheme of Winston's."

"Churchill's?!" she exclaimed. "Whatever for?"

"You know he's always been very supportive of the need for intelligence agencies and agents," Bill said slowly. "Well, if nothing else, the absolute debacle in France has convinced him that more drastic measures need to be taken on the continent. He's hatched an idea for a new department, but he's meeting stiff resistance."

"What kind of a department?"

"I can't say. Suffice it to say that many in Whitehall and Parliament think it would be disgraceful."

"Many have said the same about MI6," Evelyn pointed humorously.

"Quite."

She studied him for a moment, then raised her eyebrows questioningly.

"And what of this training course?"

"It's highly confidential. They've put together something of an experiment, really. It's expected to last three to four weeks, and is being run by a couple of Commando instructors."

"Commando!"

"Yes, I thought that would get your attention." Something like a grin crossed Bill's face and he got up to get a cigarette from the box on his desk. This time she nodded when he offered her one. "It's rather difficult to explain without telling you anything you're not authorized to hear, but I'll do my best."

He pulled out his lighter and lit her cigarette before lowering his head to light his own.

"You see, the vision that Churchill has isn't of a department of soldiers and military personnel, but rather one made up of civilians. Ordinary people, from all walks of life, who have certain skills and can be trained to go into occupied territory. Of course, they'll have to be trained by the army." He seated himself and crossed his legs again. "That's all I can really say."

"Civilians? Yet the army is in charge of the training?"

"Yes." He cleared his throat. "I can tell you this: many of the objections stem from the belief that civilians are not capable of withstanding military training."

"I beg your pardon?" Disdain dripped from every word as Evelyn's spine stiffened. "What are soldiers if not civilians before they join the army?"

"Quite. I didn't say I agreed with the opinion, only that it is a driving force behind the wave of resistance that Churchill is meeting. While everyone agrees there's a need, in theory, of what he's proposing, there are varying views on how to accomplish it."

"And what *is* he proposing?"

"I'm not at liberty to say."

She sighed impatiently and lifted her cigarette to her lips. "If I'm to go through the training, I'll find out myself, won't I?"

"Not unless someone sticks their foot in it."

She blew smoke up to the ceiling, her eyes on his face. "Very well. Why do I feel that you have much more to say?"

He chuckled. "I do, I'm afraid. There are a few requirements for prospective participants, and they vary depending on the person in question. What makes you a candidate, for example, is different from what will make someone else a potential candidate."

"That sounds suspiciously like they don't know what they're looking for."

"On the contrary," he said, shaking his head, "they know exactly what they're looking for, and very few will make it through the training."

She frowned and studied him for a minute. "Bill, I really wish you could hear yourself," she finally said, leaning forward to tap ash into the ashtray on the edge of the desk. "You want me to attend a training, but can't tell me what it's for. Now you say that most won't complete it. Why on earth should I go if I don't even know what it's for and probably won't complete it? It sounds like a complete waste of time. What is my incentive?"

"Jasper Montclair has requested you personally."

"That is not much of an incentive, I'm sorry to say." She sat back in her chair and looked at him. "You would have done better to say that *you* wish me to go."

They were quiet for a moment, then she exhaled loudly.

"Very well. I'll bite. Why does Montclair want me to go?"

"He was invited to put forth one agent for consideration," Bill told her. "The Security Service was also asked for one agent."

## When Wolves Gather

"MI5?" She was surprised. "Really? But they focus on internal threats here in England. They don't go onto the continent."

"Yes, but remember, this is a test of sorts: of civilians." Bill shrugged. "Beyond our two agencies, I have no idea where they're getting the other candidates. They could be canvassing the local pubs for all I know."

"Why was my name put forward? I would have thought that Montclair would be eager to send one of the men. Finn would be an ideal choice," she said thoughtfully, pausing to give it some consideration.

"No doubt he would, but I'm afraid he wouldn't fit in with the spirit of the thing." Bill cleared his throat. "You see, there are some rather large wagers being placed on what type of individual will be able make it through the course."

"Good Lord, of course there are." Evelyn stood up to put out her cigarette. "I think I've just realized why I'm such an attractive candidate."

"As far as I'm aware, you're the only woman who's been accepted."

"I've been accepted then? They have my file?"

"Oh yes. You leave tomorrow on the first train, unless you have any objections?"

"Would it make any difference if I did?"

"No, I suppose not." He got up to stub out his cigarette. "Evelyn, I wouldn't have agreed to send you if I didn't think that what you'll learn will be useful. From what little I've been told, I think it should be required for all our agents, but especially for you. You already have very dangerous enemies on the continent, not least of which is Eisenjager. I can't impress upon you enough just *how* dangerous he is. Even the small amount that we've been able to glean from various sources regarding who he is, and where he came from, is enough to make my blood run cold. If you are to have any chance of survival when we send you back to France, you *must* be on a par with him, or at the very least, as close as we can get you."

She looked up at that. "And this course will get me closer? Have you seen the training, then?"

"I've seen part of the outline that was sent to Churchill." He turned to lean on the desk, folding his arms over his chest as he looked down at her. "It's tremendously difficult and that wasn't even half of it. It will, however, teach you invaluable skills that can not only save your life, but the lives of those working with you. And, of course, skills that will help you to go toe-to-toe with Eisenjager."

"Well, when you put it that way…"

"When you finish, and I have no doubt that you *will* finish the training, you'll have two weeks leave to do with as you like. It's already been arranged. The people at Northolt don't expect to see you back for at least eight weeks, perhaps longer."

"Two weeks leave!" She stared at him. "Why so long?"

"Trust me, my dear, you'll need it. You're not in for an easy time of it, and this will only be the beginning. If I have my way, you'll be undergoing more training before the summer is out." He tilted his head to the side. "I didn't expect you to balk at two weeks holiday."

"I'm not balking, I'm simply surprised. I was hoping to talk you into a few days," she said with a laugh.

"Well, you have fourteen waiting for you once you've finished in Scotland." He turned to go around the desk. "Wesley has all the paperwork that you'll need, and he'll give you all the details. See him on your way out."

"I will." Evelyn stood up, pulling on her gloves. "How many people will be training with me?"

"Not more than twenty, I shouldn't think." He seated himself and looked up at her. "Oh! Before I forget, I thought you'd like to know about the packet you brought back from France."

"Yes?"

"It contained some tremendously useful information regarding the bunkers the Germans are building beneath their munitions factories. I thought you'd like to know how important it will be to the war effort."

Evelyn nodded. "Thank you. That's something, at least."

He frowned. "I don't like the sound of that," he said, sitting back. "What do you mean by it?"

She shrugged. "I don't know. I suppose I feel that I haven't really done very much at all. I spent an entire month running all around Europe with not very much to show for it in the end."

"Is this because that address in Switzerland turned out to be nothing? I've told you that's the way of it sometimes. I'm sure there will be something else, another clue. Your father left something behind, and you will find it in time."

"No, it's not that." Evelyn finished pulling her gloves and hooked her handbag over her arm. "I suppose it's just that I've left Josephine and Jean-Pierre behind to face the Nazis alone while I ran home to England. Jean-Pierre told me that it was for the best, and that it was more important for me to get that package back here than to stay and fight, but I suppose I feel like I let them down in a way."

## When Wolves Gather

Bill shook his head. "Your job, Evelyn, is to gather information and bring it to us. Your destiny is different from theirs. They have to fight now, and that is their responsibility. Yours is to help them by getting information to us that will help us defeat Hitler."

Evelyn stared at him for a moment, then nodded.

"You're right," she said slowly. "It's just difficult to leave when they're fighting against such unfair odds. They need help."

"Yes, but that's what this training experiment is all about. If it's a success, they will get help, I can promise you that."

"But not from me?"

"No. You are far more valuable to us in your present role. Never doubt that."

◉

**London**
**June 20**

Henry climbed out of the back of the car and nodded to the man holding the door for him. His driver closed the door without a word and went back behind the wheel while Henry looked up at the impressive facade of the town home before him. Located in Mayfair, it stood in exclusive company among some of the oldest and most distinguished houses in London. His own town residence wasn't far from here, and he had instructed his driver not to remain. He would walk home when he was finished.

He went up shallow steps to the glossy black door with a shining brass knocker and pushed the bell with the knob of his cane. He had come straight from dinner at the Claridge Hotel, and this was the last place he wanted to be on a Thursday evening, but here he was just the same. He didn't have any choice, really. His instructions from Berlin were very clear.

The door opened and a man in a dinner jacket holding a whiskey in his hand looked out at him.

"Ah! You must be Henry," he said jovially, waving him inside. "Pleasure to meet you at last. The name's Martin."

Henry stepped into the marbled foyer as the man closed the door behind him.

"Hope you don't mind the lack of servants," the man continued. "Mata felt it was better to give 'em the night off. Less chance of being overheard, y'see."

"I understand." Henry removed his hat and looked around. A long narrow console table along the wall held an assortment of gentlemen's hats. "I suppose I'll just set this here?"

"What? Oh yes! Rather a muddle, that. I've told Mata that in future we really must keep at least a footman around." The man watched as Henry removed his gloves and set them with his hat. "I feel certain I've met you before. Have I?"

"We belong to the same club," Henry said, turning with a smile.

"I thought I must know you. Then you're aware of my real name, and I suppose with more time, I'll remember yours." The man sipped his drink and led Henry across the hallway to a room with the door ajar. "That's another one of Mata's fancies. We all must be known by our codenames, which seems rather silly when I think most of us know each other. Still, it's best to keep the women happy, wot?"

"Certainly."

Henry followed him into a fairly crowded drawing room and looked around. Lights blazed behind the blackout curtains, filling the room with dazzling light as the gathered company spoke in quiet tones. Most had drinks in their hands, and all were dressed in evening wear. This was not their first stop this evening, just as it wasn't his.

"Henry!" A woman came towards him, her face wreathed in smiles and her hands outstretched. "I'm so glad you could make it."

Henry inclined his head, accepting one of her hands. "Lady—ah, but Martin has informed me that it is to be codenames only this evening. Mata, it's very good to see you again."

"Yes, I thought it best to stick to anonymous names for gatherings such as these." Mata tucked her hand through his elbow and turned to survey the room. "As our ranks increase, there will be more and more faces that are not necessarily familiar. While it may seem silly now, I think over time it will be for the best. Don't you agree?"

Henry made a neutral sound of agreement in his throat as he slowly took in the faces present. He knew a surprisingly large number of them. They moved in his circles, and many of them knew his real name. In fact, looking about the room, there were only a few that he was unfamiliar with.

"You see that we have a number of influential members," Mata said, watching his face. "They are all committed to the cause as passionately as you and I. I hope this sets your mind at ease."

He looked at her in surprise and she let out a tinkling laugh.

"My dear man, it was quite obvious that you were reluctant to join forces with us. I'm well aware that you were ordered to by our

## When Wolves Gather

handlers in Berlin. As you can see, however, we are not such a disreputable group of amateurs. I'm sure you recognize Rodney, there in the corner."

"Yes, of course." Henry nodded, inclining his head as the duke caught his gaze across the room. He received a royal nod in return. "And he is known as Rodney?"

"Yes. I'll introduce you, or reintroduce you, as it were, to everyone in time. But before we do, Rodney is going to lead a short discussion on the state of affairs and where we stand now." Mata led him towards a cart that was laden with bottles and glasses. "Please, help yourself to a drink. You are the last to arrive, so I'll just go tell Rodney that we can begin."

She turned to move down the long, narrow drawing room towards the duke. Henry watched her go before picking up a decanter of brandy. What was he doing here? This was the absolute height of folly. The more people operating in London, the more likely they were to be caught. The Security Service had rounded up all the spies Berlin had sent into the country at the beginning of the war, and now they were in the process of doing the same with the fifth columnists. No matter how many times he warned his handler that they were not to be underestimated, it seemed that the Germans were intent on disregarding his warnings.

And now they had made it clear that he was to work with Mata and her network of bored aristocrats who fancied themselves as spies and saboteurs.

He sipped his brandy, turning to observe the collection of people that she had managed to gather. She wanted him to believe that she was the one who had founded the group, but he knew better. His eyes shifted to the duke thoughtfully. That was the man responsible. Rodney, was it? Well, Rodney was the one who was in charge. Mata was simply the right hand. It was the duke who had all the power, and the financing to back it.

While he admitted to feeling some surprise at the gathered company, it didn't make him feel any happier about being part of it. He counted four titles present, not including the duke, and several MPs. Mata herself was wife to a lord of no small distinction, the conspicuous absence of whom he found interesting. And yet, for all their privilege and breeding, they were all tarred with the same brush: they were all amateurs.

And Henry didn't know if there was anything quite as dangerous as an amateur playing at being spies in the heart of London.

"Ah, I see you've discovered the brandy!" Martin was back, his glass empty. "Quite palatable, or so I'm told."

Henry smiled politely as he refilled his glass. "It's quite tolerable."

"I prefer scotch myself," Martin said, lifting his glass in a silent toast. "Have you heard the latest news from France?"

"Which news?" Henry asked, sipping his brandy. "There's quite a bit these days."

"The Germans captured Lyon today."

"Oh yes. I did see something about that."

"I suppose it's all rather anti-climactic now," Martin continued thoughtfully. "Petain will sign the armistice with Hitler in two days, and then it's all over."

Henry shot him a sharp look. "Two days? Where did you hear that?"

"We all have our ways, Henry." Martin grinned. "Does it make a difference? What matters is that France has surrendered, and soon we will be welcoming the Germans into England. Mata is quite looking forward to our role in that. Has she told you about the plans they're setting in motion in Dorset?"

"No, I don't think so."

"Well, suffice it to say, when the invasion comes, they'll find it easy-going at Weymouth and Bournemouth."

Henry looked across the room at Mata and the duke consideringly.

"Is that so?"

"You really must ask her to tell you about it," Martin said cheerfully. "It looks as though old Rodney is ready to start." He lowered his voice. "Take my advice, Henry. Go over and snag that comfortable chair while you can. You'll thank me for it."

Henry chuckled. "Long-winded, is he?"

"Rather! But don't despair. Mata will reign him in eventually." He glanced at Henry's glass. "You might want to fill that up again, though."

Henry nodded and watched as Martin moved away with his drink, heading for a spot on a sofa. He splashed some more brandy into his glass and turned towards the armchair reluctantly. It appeared that he was in for a long night.

**When Wolves Gather**

# Chapter Seven

**London**
**June 23**

Bill thanked the maitre d' who showed him to the table and smiled as Jasper rose from his seat, holding out his hand.

"Good evening, Buckley," he greeted him cheerfully. "I'm so glad you could join me. While I detest being bothered at lunch, I do hate to eat dinner alone."

"Thank you for the invitation," Bill replied, shaking his hand and seating himself at the white-clad table set with china and crystal. "Marguerite has gone to our house in the country, and I was contemplating a solitary meal myself."

"How is your wife?"

"Growing restless. This business with the Armistice has upset her dreadfully, to be honest."

"Yes, of course it has. She's a Frenchwoman, after all." Jasper lifted a finger and a waiter came towards the table. "What will you drink?"

"Scotch and water, I think," Bill said after a moment.

"You've been spending time with the prime minister."

He chuckled. "We had lunch the other day," he admitted.

"I know. He told me." Jasper ordered their drinks and waited until the man had retreated before continuing. "He was quite impressed with you."

"Was he? I can't imagine why. I was rather blunt with him."

"Were you? Good! That's what he prefers." Jasper sat back in his chair and looked across the table with a faint smile. "You certainly made an impression, and that is a good thing, believe me. Your intelligence will get a closer look from him."

"Well, that's all that counts, isn't it?"

"How long will Marguerite be away from London?"

"I'm really not sure. She's considering traveling up to Lancashire to visit Madeleine Ainsworth. Her sister and her husband have arrived from France. They're staying with her for a few weeks until they make other arrangements."

"Ainsworth? I didn't realize that Marguerite was friendly with Mrs. Ainsworth."

"Oh yes. They are great friends."

"Oh, well, I suppose it stands to reason, doesn't it? They're both French."

Bill looked amused. "Yes."

"Perhaps it's best for her to leave the city for a bit," Jasper said after a moment. "If Hitler does try to invade, London will be a target for his bombers."

"That's what they said when war first broke out, and I haven't seen one bomb fall on us yet."

"Yes, well, we've been very lucky, haven't we?"

They fell silent as the server returned with their drinks, setting them down before taking their dinner order. Once he'd gone, Jasper cleared his throat and reached for his glass.

"I'm afraid our luck won't hold out much longer now that the French have signed the Armistice," he said. "Hitler's taken the entire western seaboard and north of France. The Wehrmacht and Luftwaffe are just over the Channel, only thirty-one miles away. They can launch an invasion from any point on the coast of France, and Churchill is convinced that they will."

"Oh, Hitler will try," Bill agreed. "There's no doubt about that. We're the only ones standing in his way now."

"And yet he claims that Britain is not Germany's natural enemy. He has all along."

Bill made a rude noise in the back of his throat. "Herr Hitler has claimed many things over the past few years, and not one of them has turned out to be true."

Jasper grunted. "That's a fair point. Did you see that he's visiting Paris? The man's on holiday, seeing the sights!"

"Wouldn't you? Look at what his generals have been able to accomplish in just over a month! I'd take a holiday as well!" Bill shook his head and reached for his drink. "Don't let's discuss the little corporal. It only gives me indigestion. What do you think of General de Gaulle?"

"He's certainly determined to rally the French to himself," Jasper said. "He's only been in London a short time, but he's already attempting to mobilize the French soldiers in England and the French territories in Northern Africa. He's been broadcasting through the BBC. Not a bad idea, really."

"When he arrived last week, no one knew who he was," Bill said with a grin. "Now, people are learning quickly. It's amazing when

## When Wolves Gather

you think that he's really only a junior officer, relatively speaking, in the French army."

"At the rate the French are going, he'll be the last ranking member left standing."

"It certainly took some courage to oppose his new prime minister and leave France. He must know that he will be considered a traitor by Petain and his new government."

"To hear him tell it, Petain is the traitor." Jasper sighed. "What a world we are living in! London has become the refuge of kings and queens from across Europe, governments-in-exile, and now a little known general who hopes to lead his country in a fight against its occupiers. Just one short year ago, would you have ever dreamt it possible that it would have come to this?"

"One year ago? Absolutely."

Jasper chuckled. "Ah, yes. You did try to warn all of us, didn't you?"

"I did. No one wanted to listen."

Jasper looked at him shrewdly. "Yet you managed to find the few who did listen, didn't you?"

"Didn't do much good in the end. We're right where we all swore we didn't want to be: standing alone against Germany, the Soviet Union, and now Italy."

"I think we can blame that more on the French and their pigheaded ideas on how to conduct a defense rather than our intelligence. Our agents have been productive. It's the ground war that broke down."

They fell silent once more as the server returned with their dinner, setting the plates before them. After he left, Bill picked up his knife and fork.

"I do feel that we were getting actionable intelligence," he said thoughtfully. "Now that France has been overrun, who knows how long it will be before it starts coming in again. It's a complete shambles over there. Radios are being destroyed before they can fall into German hands, and the agents themselves have gone to ground. I have no way of knowing which are still alive, or if any have been captured. It's a right mess."

"How many have you been able to get out?"

"About half. The rest either couldn't be located, or chose to remain."

"And the two new ones?"

Bill looked up from his dinner. "You mean Jian's cousins? They're safe for now. They're at the family chateau in the south. As it transpires, they're on the right side of the line."

"In the unoccupied zone?"

"Yes."

"Well, that's something, at least." Jasper ate in silence for a moment, then cleared his throat. "The Security Service has rounded up some more Italians for internment. All of them have some kind of ties to the fascist regime or the fifth column."

"So I've heard."

"They're trying to vet everyone coming into the country, but with the number of refugees pouring in, it's almost impossible."

"I don't envy them their task," Bill said, looking up. "Ours is hard enough. I can't imagine trying to locate traitors and threats right here in England."

"Do you really think there are threats here?" Jasper asked, his knife and fork pausing over his plate. "I mean, really?"

Bill thought for a moment, then nodded slowly.

"Yes, I suppose I do. As much as I hate to think of it, it's only to be expected. I've got informers and agents in other countries. It's only common sense that Hitler would have the same here. Well, we know that he does. Just look at Henry, and all the trouble he's caused us."

Jasper grunted and returned to his meal. "I suppose you're right. Damn disconcerting, though. Henry is one man, and we know where to look for him. We can contain the damage until we find him. But when you think of the entire nation, and people we don't have any idea of yet…"

"And that is why I do not envy the Security Service. Who knows who the sympathizers are, or where they are, or even what they're organizing!"

"Do you think they're organizing at all?" Jasper asked, glancing up sharply.

"I'd be very surprised if they weren't." Bill set down his utensils and wiped his mouth with a linen napkin before reaching for his drink. "It won't be long before Hitler launches an attack against Great Britain. When he does, I'm very much afraid that we'll find quite a few people who would welcome the Nazis in, and do everything they can to help them."

"Sabotage?"

"I think so. Don't you?"

## When Wolves Gather

"The local police forces, especially in the coastal regions, certainly do. They're taking every precaution they can."

"And that will go a long way. It's the everyday people who will win this war for us, Jasper. Not old buggers like you and I."

Jasper was silent for a long time, finishing his dinner. When he finally did look up, he looked very tired.

"How do you think it will all play out in the end?" he asked. "Do you think we'll be able to hold out?"

"God-willing, yes. And if not, then I'll tell you this: we'll go down fighting. I wouldn't want to be in the boots of a Nazi soldier if they have to fight their way through the East End."

"The everyday people?"

"Precisely."

*30th June, 1940*
*My Dear Evelyn,*
*It's been a quiet couple of days here. After a busy time over the Channel and North Sea, we've fallen back into a rather dull routine of flying patrols. I'm sure it won't last, but I think we're all enjoying the slight respite while we have it. Have you heard any more about the possibility of taking a few days away when you return? Perhaps I'll be able to get away to meet you in London.*

*Jersey and Guernsey have both been taken by the Germans. They walked in unopposed after bombing them on Friday. It seems unbelievable to think that they're on the Channel Islands. What's next? Actually, I don't think I'll ask that just now. Perhaps ignorance is bliss in this instance. I do feel sorry for the people there, though. They didn't have any chance at all.*

*The Yank was reading the newspaper this evening and came across a little tidbit that I thought was interesting. Do you remember Oswald Mosley? He was arrested last month for his party, the British Union of Fascists, which has now been banned. Well, they've just arrested his wife, Diana Mitford. She was expecting their son when he was arrested, and so they waited until after she gave birth to arrest her. But what I found interesting, and think you will as well, is that they were married in 1936 in Berlin. Do you know where? In the house of one Josef Goebbels! And Adolf Hitler was their guest of honor!*

*Chris, the Yank that he is, was rather shocked by the whole thing. There was no point in trying to explain to him that many of our fellow countrymen saw nothing wrong with Hitler in 1936. In fact, I rather fancy that several of my father's acquaintances attended various state functions in Berlin as guests of honor of Herr Hitler. Still, it's rather jarring to see that two such public figures as the Mosely's were on such chummy terms with him. It makes one wonder who else was? And are they still? Rather disconcerting, that.*

*I must put out the light now. We're up early tomorrow, flying patrols. My batman will be calling for me at half-past four, so I really must get some sleep.*

*I pray you are well and can't wait to see you again.*

*Always yours,
Flight Lieutenant Miles Lacey*

## RAF Coltishall
## July 4

Miles slid some coins across the bar to the landlord and reached for the two full pints that had been set in front of him.

"Quite a good voice the lad has," the landlord said, nodding to the back corner where Chris was pounding away on a piano, singing a jazz tune from America. "I've never heard 'alf of wot he's played, though."

Miles grinned. "Sadly, we're becoming well acquainted with American jazz," he said, picking up the pints. "Even more sadly, some of it is quite good!"

The landlord laughed. "Well, if he'll insist on entertaining us, who am I to quibble? Just so long as you lads are enjoying yourselves."

Miles turned and made his way to the back of the pub where Rob was tossing darts at the board in a solitaire game.

"I quite liked that one," Rob said when Chris came to the end of the tune. "Who was it?"

"Louis Armstrong," Chris replied, taking the pint Miles handed him. "Thanks!"

## When Wolves Gather

"Never heard of him."

"He's a pretty big deal back home." Chris sipped his beer and set the glass on top of the piano, pulling out a cigarette. "He did When the Saints Come Marching In."

"Never heard of that either, I'm afraid."

"Uncultured," Chris announced, lighting his cigarette. "That's what you are. Uncultured swine."

"Good Lord, Miles, I think the Yank's learned a new word!"

"Which one? Swine?"

"Uncultured. Do you think he got it from us?"

"Quite possibly." Miles sat in a chair and crossed his legs carelessly. "We do throw it about a lot."

"There're just so many opportunities!" Rob walked over to the dart board and pulled out his darts. "But I do think he's a bit off on this one. We may be many things, you and I, but uncultured is hardly one of them."

"It is when it comes to music," Chris said cheerfully, spinning around on his stool. "Anyone who's never heard of Louis Armstrong...well, I mean, he's...he's Louis Armstrong!"

"So I gather," Miles said dryly. "We're very lucky to have you here to educate us, Yank. Whatever would we do without you?"

"I have no idea. Here. I've got one for you!" Chris spun around again to face the keys. "Boogie Woogie!"

"Another of Armstrong's?"

"No. Tommy Dorsey," Chris said over his shoulder, beginning to play.

"I don't suppose you'd play something from a Brit, would you?"

"Not a chance! I should be at home eating hot dogs and watching fireworks, celebrating my country's Independence Day from you lot. Instead, I'm here, drinking warm beer, and helping defend the Mother Country."

"And having a jolly time doing it," Miles pointed out.

"True. But for one night, you can humor me." Chris looked over with a grin. "At least I'm not playing the national anthem."

"Thank the Lord for that!"

Miles shared an amused look with Rob and drank some of his beer. Dropping into the seat across from him, Rob pulled out his cigarette case.

"I had a letter from my mother today," he said. "Tante Adele and Aunt Agatha are getting along much better than anyone expected. At least, they were. I'm not sure how long that will last."

"Why do you say that?"

"Well, we've gone and blown up half the French fleet, haven't we?" Rob lit his cigarette. "I can only imagine what Uncle Claude and Tante Adele will have to say about that, and it will only lead to arguments with Auntie Agatha."

"Wait, we did what?" Chris stopped playing and turned to face them. "Say that again?"

"Don't you read the newspapers?" Rob asked, raising an eyebrow.

"I didn't today."

"The Royal Navy attacked the French fleet at Mers-el Kébir last night," Miles told him.

"Mers-el-where?"

"Kébir. It's at Oran, in Algeria, dear boy. Really, your geography is appalling. Don't they teach you anything in the States?"

"Oh sure! I know where all the states are, and Mexico and Canada. And I can tell you all the state capitals, and what their primary economic output is." Chris grinned. "I stopped paying attention when it went to this side of the pond. If it's not in Europe proper, I'm hazy on it."

"No wonder the Americans all want to keep to themselves," Rob muttered. "Why choose to help a country fight a war when you don't even know where it is?"

"Hey, that's not fair," Chris said with a frown. "We fought in the last one. We'll end up fighting in this one, too. Mark my words. There are a lot more who think like I do."

"Quite right you are," Miles said soothingly. "Don't pay any attention to Ainsworth."

"So what happened at this Algerian port?" Chris asked after a moment.

"A portion of the French fleet was there. Part of the Armistice terms was that the fleet would remain under French command." Rob put out his cigarette in the ash tray on the table and reached for his half empty pint glass. "We attacked them yesterday."

Chris looked from one to the other, a frown of confusion on his face.

"Why?"

"Because, my dear boy, one of the worst things that could happen right now is for Petain to hand over the French fleet to Hitler," Miles said. "The last thing the little corporal needs is more toys."

"Was that likely to happen?"

## When Wolves Gather

"Very doubtful, but who can say?" Rob shrugged. "The French are in an uproar, of course. Over a thousand Frenchmen were killed in the attack, and they see it as a direct betrayal."

"Well wasn't it?" Chris asked, reaching for his beer. "I mean, you were their ally."

"Yes, until they broke that alliance by suing for peace with Germany," Miles said sharply. "No separate peace, that was the agreement. And Petain broke it."

Chris shook his head. "Even so, it's a dick move."

Rob raised his eyebrows and glanced at Miles. "Just when I think we're making some progress with our colonial friend, he comes out with little gems like that," he complained. "Really, I'm ready to give up on him all together."

"He does have some interesting turns of phrasing," Miles murmured. "I'm still waiting for the definition of…fudder, was it?"

Chris choked on his beer.

"FUBAR, and I said I would tell you when it was appropriate," he gasped.

"Well?"

"It's not appropriate yet."

"Do you think the Germans would have taken the fleet?" Rob asked Miles, returning to the primary discussion.

"I think it more likely that the Italians would," he replied with a shrug.

"So now what?" Chris asked. "What happens now that you've gone and bombed the French fleet?"

"Nothing. Oh, they'll probably retaliate, I suppose," Rob said.

"They already have." Miles pulled out his cigarette. "I heard it on the wireless before coming here. They've attacked Gibraltar."

"Good Lord. Well, there you have it, Yank. We're taking aim at each other in Africa and Spain." Rob finished his beer. "Rather like shooting rubber bands at each other on the playing field at school."

"Only with larger rubber bands." Chris pressed his lips together. "I just don't get it. Why bother?"

"Because our continued existence on this earth depends on England being able to defend herself," Miles said grimly. "Right now, we are outnumbered in men, tanks, and airplanes. If we're to have any chance at all, we can't allow ourselves to be outnumbered in ships as well."

"Do you really think it's as bad as all that?" Chris asked.

"Yes. I do." Miles pulled out his cigarette case. "And what's more, so does our prime minister, which is why he authorized the attack on the French fleet."

"I guess when you put it that way," Chris sighed. "What a mess."

"Yes, it is."

"I'm for another pint," Rob said, standing up. "For heaven's sake, play something upbeat, will you? I'm feeling rather gloomy all of a sudden."

Chris nodded. "So am I."

"Play that Jeepers Creepers song," Rob said, turning towards the bar. "That'll do it."

Chris turned obediently to the keys and began playing an up-tempo version of the popular song as Miles lit a cigarette. He tucked his lighter into his breast pocket and watched Chris play absently, a pensive frown on his face.

He wasn't sure that bombing the fleet at harbor in French Algiers was the correct call, but he also wasn't sure what else could have been done. If the fleet fell into German hands, the already-beleaguered Royal Navy would be done for. While Chris was right in saying that it was a "dick move," the French had made their fair share of them as well. The Yank was right. It was a complete mess.

The only thing that seemed certain was that they were about to be faced with the full force of the Luftwaffe as Hitler turned his attention to England. An invasion was imminent. Everyone knew it. And if that happened, then it wouldn't make an ounce of difference whether they'd bombed those ships or not. The war would be over, and Hitler would have won.

And the RAF was the only thing standing in his way.

# When Wolves Gather

# Chapter Eight

*6th July, 1940*
*Dear Evelyn,*
*I hope this finds you well and having as grand a time as we are here. Our reprieve was brief, and now we're back to running into Jerries almost every day. How are the Hurries holding up on your station? I expect they're as busy as we are, probably more so. We've heard that 11 Group is right in the thick of it. We're up multiple times a day now. Yesterday we had a terrific scrap over the Channel. Jerry is going for the convoys, the bastards, and it's all we can do to try to keep them off of them. We've had several engagements with the bandits, but we're holding our own. At least we haven't lost anyone this week.*

*What do you think about Vichy severing all ties with us over the Mers-el Kébir incident? I say good riddance. At least we're not saddled with a craven ally now, our own relatives notwithstanding. I'm not sure why the newspapers are making such a mountain of it, though. Cutting off diplomatic relations with London really doesn't affect anything one way or the other. They've already lost to Hitler and are becoming a puppet government for the Nazis, so I really don't know why people are so upset. Of course, I'd never dream of saying such a thing to Mother or Tante Adele and Uncle Claude, but I know you'll understand.*

*I really do think we're better off without them, even if it does mean that we're the only ones left standing against Hitler, Stalin, and Mussolini. The Yank seems to think that the Americans will come around and join in, but I have my doubts. I don't think they'll get involved unless they're hit directly, and that will never happen. I will say this for the Yank though: he's a bloody good flier. He shows no hesitation in charging into a mess of fighters. If many more of his countrymen are like him, then God help anyone who picks a fight with the United States.*

# CW Browning

*I'm sure you've heard, but what about Jerry bombing Plymouth today? That's the third city bombed so far this month. I suppose we can look forward to more of the same as things go on. I wonder when they'll try for London? For they will, you know. Only a matter of time.*

*I hope all is well on your end. Mother wrote that you might get some leave soon. If you do manage it, be sure and keep me informed of the state of affairs at the pile. I have a small wager riding on how long it will be before Tante Adele and Aunt Agatha come to blows.*

*Before I sign off, do me a favor, will you? Answer Miles' letter. The man is becoming downright irritable to be around. Damn pathetic, actually.*

*Your most loving brother,*
*FO Rob Ainsworth*

---

### July 10

Miles slid his canopy hood closed, cutting off the stream of air pouring into the cockpit, and looked to his right. Chris was there, off his wing, sliding his own hood closed. On his left, one of the new pilots was struggling to retract his undercarriage. He shook his head. Thomas was his name, and he had absolutely no hours on a Spitfire before he arrived to join 66 Squadron three days ago. Miles had thought the CO would burst a blood vessel when he realized they'd received a pilot that hadn't even sat in a Spitfire before, let alone flown one. But the lad had handled his first flight well enough, even if he *had* waited a little too long before taking off. Rob and Chris had wagered that the glycol tank would boil before he got her airborne, but thankfully that hadn't happened. In fact, the young pilot showed considerable stamina in getting up to speed in the fast, notoriously touchy fighter.

"Close up, Blue Three," Miles said now. "Stick to me like glue."

"Roger, Blue Leader."

The rest of the squadron was already airborne, and Miles flew through a cloud bank to emerge behind A flight. Ashmore was leading, with Rob as his number two. Yellow section was being led by Charles Halloway, a veteran pilot who had come to the squadron shortly after

## When Wolves Gather

Miles returned from Dunkirk. Miles liked him, even if he did enjoy discussing his hemorrhoids rather too much.

Turning his head, he looked further back to Green section. Another experienced pilot who had recently transferred from Duxford, Billy Lloyd, was at the helm there. He'd arrived two weeks ago, and Miles hadn't said more than a few words to him. He kept to himself, and Miles was loathe to intrude on his self-imposed isolation. He did feel bad for the bloke, though. While he had one unfledged pilot in his section, Billy had two, both of whom had just arrived in the past week. Miles supposed he would happily take Chris' skill along with a new pilot's inexperience over having two wingmen who hadn't a clue.

And this was how they were expected to defend England?

"Bandits approaching from the south," Ashmore's calm voice broke the silence on the radio. "Eleven o'clock high and below. Blue Leader, take Green section and go high. We'll tackle the gaggle below."

Miles looked up and saw what his CO had seen just seconds before: a mass of shadows above them. There were ten light bombers above with their fighter escort. Looking below them, he saw more of the same.

"Roger that, Red Leader," he acknowledged, angling upwards. "Watch for the escort, lads."

He led his flight towards the Dornier 17s, his head constantly moving as he searched for more enemy fighters. The escort was well above the bombers, but Miles knew from experience that there could very well be more lurking about.

"Keep an eye out, Green Three," Billy said over the radio. "And for God's sake, get in closer!"

Miles focused on one of the bombers and raced in behind it, pressing the firing button on his column as the outline of the enemy plane centered in his crosshairs mounted on the dash.

"Here they come!" Chris called out just as Miles' Spitfire shuddered from the Browning guns firing from his wings.

Miles broke away from his attack, arching up and through the bomber formation as the Me 109 fighters fell on them from above. The DO 17 that he'd just hit fell out of formation, black smoke pouring from the starboard wing. Miles just had time to feel a spark of satisfaction at the sight before a 109 shot into his peripheral vision and dove in behind him.

"Bugger!" he swore, twisting his kite away from the firing 109.

He flew out of the bomber formation, avoiding the return fire from the rear gunners skillfully. The gunners on the bombers didn't concern him as much as the twenty fighters swarming around them. Twenty enemy fighters to their six. Hardly seemed fair, that.

But the Spitfire was fast, maneuverable, and responded to the slightest touch. Within seconds Miles had maneuvered himself behind his opponent. He focused on the sinister black swastika on the wing and pressed the button on his column, sending a short burst towards the fighter before peeling away as another two got on his tail. Leading them in a tight spiral, he shot upwards before diving down again to return to the bombers. While the fighters were swarming all over them, it was the bombers they had to stop.

"On your six, Blue Leader!" Chris cried suddenly.

Miles instinctively pulled to the right, whipping his head around in time to see a line of tracers stream past his left wing.

"Damn, that was close," he muttered, pulling up into the clouds to come back around. He got behind the bandit, but before he could fire, the pilot darted out of range just as another two shot in behind him. "God, they're like ants at a picnic!" he swore.

He pulled back on the stick and climbed, relying on his plane's speed to outrun the persistent fighters. Entering a cloud cover, he changed direction swiftly, turning to dive back down. He dove towards the writhing mess of fighters below him, blinking against the glare of bright sunlight. There was no hope of getting to the bombers now. To do so, he had to get through a thicket of enemy 109s.

An Me 109 with distinctive markings shot into range, trying to get an angle on Chris.

"Four o'clock, Blue Two!" he called.

Chris dove just as the fighter fired, just missing the stream of bullets. Miles didn't have time to do more than exhale in some relief before the deadly little fighter turned towards him.

"Come on, you bastard," he muttered as the Messerschmitt came directly towards him.

Clenching his jaw, Miles opened up the throttle and stayed on course, speeding towards the German head-on. The enemy didn't flinch, holding his course as solidly as Miles and, for a blindingly terrifying second, it seemed as if they would collide. Miles pressed the button on his column, feeling his machine shudder as the guns unloaded a burst of ammunition towards the fighter. At the last possible second, he broke away, sending another burst as he did so. While he didn't see any indication that his shots had hit the other fighter, it suddenly twisted into a dive, dropping out of the dogfight. There was no smoke, nothing to show that it had been hit, but the

## When Wolves Gather

small plane was suddenly disappearing over the sea back towards France.

"I'll be damned," Miles breathed. "The bugger's out of ammunition!"

He felt like laughing, but his heart was pounding and he didn't dare. Instead, he turned his attention back to the rest of the fighters. The bombers had disappeared, and so had half the fighters, but the new pilot was in trouble with two on his tail. Miles dove down to get in behind them, pressing his gun button to send a stream of bullets towards the one closest to Thomas.

"Break left, Blue Three," he barked into the radio.

Thomas did as he was ordered, breaking to the left. As he did so, Miles fired again, sending a burst of rounds into the side of the enemy fighter. Smoke began pouring from the wing, and the 109 dropped out of the fight, a thick, black line showing his progress. He evened out after a few hundred feet, turning to make his way back across the water.

"Red Leader to Blue Leader," the radio came alive with Ashmore's voice. "Where the hell are you lot?"

"We got tangled with some 109s, Red Leader," Miles responded. "It looks like they're heading home now. Most likely low on fuel."

"Well, get out of there and bear angles two four zero. It's the bombers we want!"

Miles glanced at his instruments and turned his plane accordingly. "Roger that, Red Leader. You heard him, Blue section. Leave the stragglers."

Chris and Thomas turned towards him, joining him on his flanks as they sped away from the remaining enemy fighters. Miles glanced to his left and saw that Thomas was right next to him. His lips twisted wryly. No need to tell him to close up this time. He wasn't taking any chances. Good. He was learning fast. He just might last the week.

They broke out of a cloud cover a moment later to find a formation of Dornier's below them, with A flight battling the return fire as well as another escort of fighters.

"Joining you on your right, Blue Leader," Billy said over the radio.

Miles glanced back at the three extra Spitfires. "Glad to see you, Green Leader."

And he was. That Green section had come out of that mess with both inexperienced pilots still intact was a miracle in itself. *God must be with us today,* he thought, turning his attention to the fight raging below them.

"I don't suppose you lot would care to join in?" Yellow Leader Halloway demanded.

Miles couldn't help the grin that flashed across his face.

"For once we're above the bastards, lads," he said cheerfully. "Let's give them a taste of their own medicine."

He led B flight in a dive and they dropped down on the enemy fighters out of the sun. With the bright sunlight behind him, Miles had no trouble picking out an iron-crossed target below. He dove down, focusing on the black cross emblazoned on the wing, and fired before the other pilot even knew they were there. His shot was true and satisfaction coursed through him as smoke exploded from the 109. The wing came apart from the airplane, sending it into a steep dive towards the choppy water far below, and Chris let out a whooping noise over the radio.

"Bulls-eye!" he caroled.

Miles grinned again, heading for the bombers. He weaved between two fighters, breaking through them with speed and surprise. When one of them pursued him, he led him up into a tight spiral, away from the bombers.

"Scratch two!" Chris called a second later as he fired at the fighter behind Miles.

"Thanks, old man," Miles gasped, turning to dive back to the bombers.

He was just coming up behind the formation when he saw the silhouette of a Spitfire flash through the formation, a 109 on his tail. As it passed behind one of the Dornier's, return fire from the bomber caught the tail, sending the Spit into a spin.

"Bloody hell, I've been hit," Rob drawled, somehow managing to sound both bored and breathless at the same time.

Miles felt his chest tighten and he broke away from his attack on his bomber to follow Rob down. The airplane spun for a few more rotations before Rob got the machine under control and leveled out below the bomber formation.

"All gauges are functioning," he announced.

Miles came up beside him, casting his eyes over the wounded Spitfire.

"You've been hit along the back and on your arse near the wheel," he said over the radio. "And they caught your tail. It's pretty shredded up."

"Best get on home, Red two," Ashmore said.

## When Wolves Gather

"Roger that, Red Leader." Rob turned inland. "See you at tea."

Miles watched to be sure no enemy fighters went after him, then turned to head back to the bombers and fighters that were now some distance above him.

"Will someone get this bastard off me?" Thomas cried a moment later.

Miles swallowed, seeing a 109 in perfect firing position behind the inexperienced pilot. The pair were too far for him to do anything but watch and his gut clenched, waiting for the inevitable shots that would send another one of their squadron out of the fray. Before it happened, Chris shot in behind the enemy fighter, firing of a burst of ammunition. In seconds, the 109 was dropping out, thick black smoke and flames licking around one wing.

Relief went through him and he rejoined the fight above, trying once more to reach the bombers. With that hit, Chris had just pulled ahead of him in the unofficial pool the squadron had going.

"I think that puts me ahead, Blue Leader," Chris said cheerfully.

"Days not over yet, Yank," Miles retorted.

"Quit the chatter!" Ashmore barked.

Miles grimaced. He was right. They were tying up the radio with unimportant chatter, and they both knew better. But Miles knew that Chris was feeling the same rush of adrenaline mixed with relief that Rob was off home safely after being hit by the return fire, and this was their way of dealing with it. Still, there would be time enough later to discuss the score.

Blinking against the blazing early morning sun, Miles squinted and focused on the bulbous front of a Dornier 17. He flew up under it at an angle, his eyes on the markings on the wing, and let off a stream of bullets towards the airplane. Then, breaking away, he hooked around, coming back for another run.

Out of the corner of his eye, he saw an enemy fighter coming towards him from above. With a low curse, he released another short burst of bullets, gritting his teeth as he arched up and away from the pursuing fighter. Twisting his machine around into a tight spiral, Miles caught the 109 mid turn and pressed his gun button, catching the 109 right in the fuel tank. He broke away just as flames exploded around the small fighter. It dove downwards and, a second later, came apart in an explosion that seemed to rock the sky. Miles stared at the flames, stunned. The pilot never had time to even think about bailing out.

He was aware of a horrible sense of fascination, staring at the streaks of flaming debris falling to the sea below. Yet, strangely, he felt no horror at what he'd done. He thought he should probably feel something, but at the moment, all he really felt was the need to return to the bombers and try again. This was his job, and if he didn't do it, those 109 fighters would be landing on RAF bases all over England.

Swallowing, Miles dove around to come up on the bombers again. All at once, he saw in his mind's eye men stretched out on a beach, helpless and exposed, as German dive bombers descended, firing on the columns of soldiers waiting for a ship.

Miles' jaw tightened and the feeling of numbness shifted swiftly to one of determination. He focused on the black Iron Cross before him, pressing the button on his column. He had a job to do.

And he'd be damned if he gave them any more mercy than they showed the boys at Dunkirk.

When Wolves Gather

# Chapter Nine

*14 July, 1940*

*My dear Evelyn,*

*I have quite a bit to tell you, and not much time to do so. I'm writing this between sorties in the dispersal hut while my kite's being refueled and rearmed. At least I came in just as the tea cart was brought round, so I have a fresh pot beside me.*

*We're engaging the enemy every day now. They're going for our convoys, and just this past week alone we've flown over twenty sorties. Rob was hit the other day, but both he and his machine are fine, the lucky blighter. We were attacking a formation of Dorniers and he was caught by return fire. It rather shook us all up, to be honest. I don't think we ever really considered that some of the German rear-gunners might be good shots. They are though. One of the new pilots was shot yesterday. He wasn't as lucky. The last anyone saw he was heading down into the drink.*

*Did you listen to Churchill's speech? It was all a bit over-the-top in morale boosting, but I suppose I can see the need for it. It's up to him to keep Great Britain calm in the face of the onslaught that we all know is coming. Well, as far as we're concerned, it's already here. Jerry is sending more and more planes over and, even though they're mainly focusing on the convoys, it's clear that won't last for long. We did get a mention in Churchill's speech, though, which gave us all a bit of a chuckle. Apparently Fighter Command has accounted for a loss of five to one in aircraft. That's what he said, anyway. I'll admit to questioning those figures. From where we're sitting, it doesn't look anywhere near that optimistic. But who am I to argue with His Majesty's government? I have one job: to go up and shoot as many of the blighters down as I can. I'll leave the bean-counting to the suits in Whitehall.*

*I think they've about finished with our kites, and the tea's gone cold, so it's time to be off again. It's been some time since you've written. I'm sure you're just as busy as we are, but I do hope and pray that you're well. As Hitler turns his sights on us, I don't suppose either of us will have very much time to write, but I hope to at least manage a few lines here and there. Do write when you have the time. It will give me something to read other than the depressing newspapers.*

*Always yours,
Flight Lieutenant Miles Lacey*

**London
July 19**

Evelyn lifted a hand to knock on the door, inwardly grimacing at her lack of gloves. If her mother saw her out and about in London without gloves, she would have a coronary. Yet here she was, perfectly gloveless. It wasn't for lack of trying. She'd worn gloves onto the train, but the train was where they remained, having been left behind in a hurry when she almost missed getting off at her station. She'd been fast asleep when the train rolled up to the platform. It was only the kind but insistent prodding of the older woman sitting across from her that had awoken her and got her moving just in time. Alas, her serviceable navy gloves had been left behind.

Hearing the command to enter, she opened the door and stepped into Bill's office, smiling when he exclaimed in surprise.

"Evelyn!" He rose swiftly to his feet and came around the side of the desk. "Good Lord, you look half dead."

"That's about how I feel as well," she admitted, shaking his hand with a laugh. "I'm afraid I slept most of the way down on the train."

"Have you eaten? Shall I ring for tea?"

"That would be lovely." Evelyn sank into one of the chairs. "I haven't had anything since early this morning."

Bill nodded and picked up the telephone, ordering tea and sandwiches to be sent up. When he replaced the receiver, he studied her shrewdly for a moment.

"Tell me how it went in Scotland."

"You haven't received the report?" she asked, surprised.

## When Wolves Gather

"I have, but it doesn't tell me how it went. It only tells me what they thought of you."

Something like a self-deprecating smile twisted her lips.

"I can't imagine that it was very complimentary. I had rather a run-in with one of the instructors, and I don't think they appreciated it very much."

"There's no mention of anything like that," Bill assured her. "What was it about, this run-in?"

"Oh, nothing very important. I took exception to how he was treating another one of the students. I'm afraid it was none of my business, but I managed to stick my nose in it anyway."

"I suppose I should have a stern word to say about that, but I'm really not very surprised. You've always been one to fight for others. How was the training otherwise?"

"Well, it wasn't the most difficult thing I've ever been through. My trek through the mountains of Norway still holds that dubious honor. It was bloody difficult, though, if you'll excuse my language. There were twenty-six of us that began, and only six of us to finish."

"Yes, so I was told." Bill sat back in his chair and studied her. "Did you learn anything useful?"

Evelyn let out a short, mirthless laugh. "Oh yes, and most of it shocking. Shall I tell you the highlights? Or would you rather read about them?"

His lips twitched. "By all means, tell me."

Evelyn grinned despite her exhaustion.

"It was really quite ridiculous. I don't think I've ever climbed up so many obstacles in my life. They seemed to have a particular fondness for making us scramble up structures of varying heights and difficulty, and then making our way down again. We lost points according to the amount of noise we made, or if we slipped at any point. I had to wear the most appalling coveralls, though they were very practical. And all the others had to wear them as well, so it's not as if I was singled out because I was the only woman." She opened her purse and pulled out a cigarette case. "May I?"

"Of course."

She extracted a cigarette from the case as Bill came around the desk with a lighter in his hand.

"Well, aside from climbing up and down, learning how to make a rope ladder, and crossing over a very narrow bridge built into the trees that was easily ten stories above ground, we spent quite a bit of time in the classroom." She leaned forward to light her cigarette. "Thanks."

"In the classroom?"

"Yes. Did you know that there's an entire methodology devoted strictly to sabotage and learning to recognize which targets are crucial, and which are secondary?"

"No, I didn't."

"Nor did I. It's all really very interesting, and I think it may come in useful at some point."

"Why do I feel like there's more?"

Evelyn chuckled.

"Because you know me very well, Sir William. There *is* more, and it's rather disturbing." She paused, smoking her cigarette for a moment, then looked up at him. "We were taught to kill a man silently, ensuring that he makes no sound to raise an alarm."

Bill stared down at her, shocked. "What?"

"Oh, there's no need to look like that. It's not as if I haven't learned to kill before. Wing Chun taught me much more than simply how to defend myself. But I must admit that there is a very large difference between knowing how to kill your opponent in hand-to-hand combat, and learning how to sneak up on an unsuspecting sentry and slit his throat without his making any sound."

"Yes, I should jolly well think so!" Bill glowered and strode back to his chair. "They should have made that part of the training quite clear. I would never have sent you!"

"Good heavens, why not?" Evelyn stared at him. "You sent me for sniper training and small arms training."

"That's different. That's necessary."

"Well, so might this be. I won't always be able to use a gun, and I'm sure there could very well be a time when it may be necessary to...well, to dispose of a guard."

"My dear Evelyn, your father must be spinning in his grave, and I shudder to think what your mother will say if she ever catches wind of any of this!"

Evelyn felt a laugh bubbling up inside her.

"I was thinking just now when I knocked that Mummy would have a coronary if she saw me abroad in London without gloves. If she had any idea of what I've been up to for the past two years, I don't think she would ever recover."

"My point exactly, and now we've gone and added to it by sending you away to learn how to kill a man."

"To be fair, I already knew how to do that long before I ever came to work with MI6," she said practically. "It's just that now I can do it rather efficiently with a knife. Oh, which they gave us to keep

# When Wolves Gather

when we finished the course. Would you like to see it? I have it right here."

"No!" Bill roared, missing the devilish laugh in her eyes. "I would not!"

Evelyn burst out laughing.

"Oh Bill, you *are* funny! It's really not worth getting all in a bother over. It was rather disconcerting at first, of course it was, but once I'd got used to the idea, I saw that it really is rather practical. Everything we learned was, and it will come in very handy, I'm sure. It may even save my life, or someone else's, just as you said. And I certainly feel much better prepared to face Eisenjager or Herr Voss now."

"I'm beginning to understand why only six of you made it through," Bill muttered, rubbing his face. "Let me ask you this. Do you think this is training that other women are capable of doing? And should we allow them to?"

"I don't think allowing them to is really an option," Evelyn said, getting up to put out her cigarette in the crystal ash tray on the desk. "Women will have to be sent into occupied France. Aside from the obvious fact that all the able-bodied men are busy fighting in the army, navy, or RAF, we can go places where men wouldn't be able to, and do things that men cannot do. It's a simple fact of life that a woman has the ability to manipulate men, and if we're to win this war, then German soldiers will need to be manipulated."

Seating herself again, Evelyn crossed her legs, inwardly wincing at the still-tender bruising on her right hip. She'd taken a rather nasty fall off one of the obstacles, and it had left her limping for the better part of two days. Her minor injury hadn't given her any passes, though, and she had continued as if it had never happened, probably aggravating it in the process. Now she was left with a gorgeous deep purple and green mass that covered her hip and went partway down her thigh.

"As for whether or not other women can complete the course, of course they can," she added briskly. "It's very difficult, and I haven't come away without any marks or bruises, but I *have* come away."

Bill sighed, but before he could say anything, a loud rap sounded on the door. He called to enter and the door opened to admit a young woman pushing a tea trolley.

"Oh, lovely!" Evelyn exclaimed, catching sight of a large pot of tea, cups and saucers, and, perhaps most pressing to her needs, a plate of sandwiches.

"Thank you. We'll serve ourselves," Bill said, standing.

"Yes, sir."

The woman nodded respectfully and turned to leave the office. When she'd gone, Evelyn got up to get a cup of tea, but Bill waved her back into her seat.

"Hitler addressed the Reichstag today," he said, going to the trolley and picking up the pot of tea. "Milk?"

"Yes, thank you."

He poured a bit of milk into one of the cups, then poured in the hot tea.

"He issued a rather stern warning to Churchill. Quite a cheek, actually. The little corporal really does have an ego on him."

"He can afford to now, can't he?" Evelyn asked, accepting the cup and saucer from Bill. "What did he say?"

"Among other things, he said that there was no reason for Germany to wipe such a great Empire from the map." He placed a selection of sandwiches on a plate and passed it to her. "He said that it is inevitable that one of us shall lose this war, and that while Churchill may believe it will be Germany, Hitler knows it will be England."

"One can't really fault him for believing it," Evelyn murmured. "After all, everyone else has fallen to his armies."

"Yes." Bill carried his tea around to set it on his desk before sitting again. "He reiterated that he sees no reason for this war to continue."

Evelyn made a noise in the back of her throat.

"No, of course not," she agreed sarcastically. "No need at all, just as long as we kowtow to his regime and bow down to his directives."

Bill was amused. "Quite."

Evelyn ate a sandwich hungrily, then sipped her tea. After a moment, she shook her head.

"We can't give in now. We just can't. We've come too far, and the people of Great Britain deserve more than that."

"Oh, Churchill has no intention of giving in, don't worry. Did you listen to his speech the other day?"

"Yes. They had it on in the recreation room and called us all in to hear it." Evelyn reached for another sandwich. "It was rather uplifting, wasn't it? Even though we're basically fighting a losing battle, it did make one want to fight to the last man, or woman, as it were."

"Do you think we are?" Bill looked up sharply. "Fighting a losing battle?"

She sighed and shook her head, swallowing.

## When Wolves Gather

"No, I suppose not. We've barely begun to fight, so it's not fair to say the battle's lost, is it? But it doesn't look very good, does it? I mean, they're training people like me to kill larger and stronger men with knives. There are old retainers marching outside the pubs with pitchforks and shovels in drills to defend the home front. Some of them look as if a strong wind will blow them over, but they're out there, training to fight with farm tools should we be invaded. I suppose this is all in case our pilots fail to keep the Luftwaffe from taking control of the skies, but it's not very hopeful, is it? When our last resort is women, children, and old men?"

"Isn't that always a castle's last resort?" Bill raised an eyebrow. "Don't tell me that you've forgotten your history." He sighed and set down his cup. "What would you have us do?"

"Oh, I understand the need for it." Evelyn shrugged. "Don't misunderstand me. I also recognize the effect it has on morale. But even you must admit that it's looking rather dark."

"Yes. I suppose it is."

"I'll tell you this, though," she said after a moment of thought, "if Jerry does make it to our shores, he'll have a very rude awakening. It won't be like France. For one thing, there is nowhere to run to, and so even the women and children will have to stand and fight. And I really wouldn't want to take on the Cornish on a good day, let alone when trying to invade their country."

Bill let out a bark of laughter. "That's the truth. And the East End here in London will put up a nasty fight as well."

"And the Scots?" Evelyn made a face. "Good Heavens, if the Germans know what's good for them, they'll stay out of Scotland!"

"Perhaps it's not such a losing battle after all, eh?"

She smiled ruefully. "No. Perhaps not. Don't listen to me today, Bill. I'm exhausted and when I get tired, I tend to become a much larger pessimist than I have any right to be."

"I do have something that will cheer you up," he said, watching as she consumed another sandwich. "Good Lord, didn't they feed you?"

She laughed ruefully, wiping a crumb off of the corner of her mouth with her pinky finger.

"They did, but you have no idea the amount of exercise we were subjected to! I could have eaten a horse every day for breakfast and still been hungry by lunch." She got up to pour herself more tea. "What is it that will cheer me up?"

"We've finally had a message from Norway," he told her. "From Erik Salvesen."

Evelyn spun around, the teapot in one hand and her cup in the other.

"Erik!" she exclaimed, her face lighting up. "He's alive?"

"So it would appear," Bill said dryly. "However, I want to be sure that it *is* him, and not Germans who captured him and the radio."

She frowned and finished pouring her tea.

"I can understand that. Although, I think he would have destroyed the radio before it could be captured if he thought there was a danger. He's an army lieutenant, after all."

"Yes, but we must be sure. Is there anything that you can think of that we can use to confirm that it's him? Something that only the real Erik Salvesen would know?"

Evelyn went back to her seat with her tea, her brow creased in thought. She was silent for a long while, thinking as she sipped the tea. Finally, she looked up.

"Yes! There is something!" she exclaimed. "Ask him how many tries it took the Englishwoman to hit the fence with his rifle, and whereabouts on the fence she aimed. We were the only two present. No one else could possibly know, and an interrogator wouldn't think to dig it out of him."

"And the answer?"

"Two shots, and it was the second post from the end."

Bill looked up from where he was scribbling on a notepad. "And you think he will recall this incident?"

"I think so. It was the first time I earned his respect. Before then, he really had no use for me." She shrugged. "Erik doesn't have a very high opinion of the English, I'm afraid. He made that very clear."

"I hope you're right and the incident holds as primary a spot in his memory as it does in yours." Bill capped his pen and laid it down. "If it really is him, this will be the first contact we've had with any of the resistance in Norway. It will be a huge step towards establishing a network that can support them."

"I hope and pray that we can help them," Evelyn said, her voice low. "If he confirms that it is, indeed, him, will you ask after Anna? I want to know that she is safe."

Bill nodded. "Yes, of course."

"Thank you."

"Do you have a message for them?"

Evelyn smiled slowly. "Yes. Tell them that I'm still fighting, and I expect nothing less from them."

Bill gave her an inscrutable look. "That's seems like a very strong message."

## When Wolves Gather

"Trust me, they are very strong people. And they will understand what it means."

"And what does it mean?"

"That I am committed to continuing to fight in this war until the end, whether that end be my own or the war's. It was a message that they were very adamant about getting into my head when I was doubting everything during that trek through the mountains. Just in case they're now feeling like I did then, I'd like to remind them of how important it is to keep fighting."

"Well, you can continue yourself after you've had a few weeks rest."

Evelyn finished her tea and set the cup and saucer down.

"Yes, well, before I can do that, I really must go back to Northolt," she said.

He frowned. "I wouldn't advise it. They don't expect you back yet."

"I understand, and I'll come up with something to say, but I really must go back. There are some items I need to collect to take back to Ainsworth Manor with me." She looked at him with a faint smile. "You'll recall that I had no notion that I wasn't immediately returning when I came to London a month ago."

He continued to frown, but finally nodded reluctantly.

"Very well. How long will you be there?"

"Just long enough to collect my things, and perhaps meet with Sergeant Cunningham and arrange matters for my absence."

"Ah yes, Cunningham. How is she working out for you?"

"Very well. Flying Officer Durton is terrified of her, so that's always a good sign." Evelyn laughed. "And when I've been away, she's been an absolute godsend at keeping all the questions at bay. Wherever did you find her?"

"On a station in Devon. Her father is in the House, and sits on the Home Defense committee. He's assured me of her discretion."

"Well, she's really quite competent. She takes care of everything that I'm supposed to be doing, and does it all much better than I ever could."

"As she should. That's her job. She's an Assistant Section Officer."

Evelyn looked at him, startled. "But...then why is she posing as a sergeant?"

"Because that's what we asked her to do. She thought it was a marvelous idea. She said that it would help her to see where improvements could be made for the NCOs, and give her a feel for what they had to contend with."

"How remarkable!"

"Yes, well, if you knew her father, you wouldn't think it so remarkable." Bill stood up as she rose from her seat with her purse in her hand. "Are you off then?"

"Yes, I'd like to get back to Northolt this evening in time for supper." She held out her hand to him. "You'll let me know what the verdict is on the training course, won't you? And tell Montclair that he can collect on his wager with my complements."

"Oh, I'm looking forward to that," he said with a laugh. "I don't think he really believed you'd do it."

"That will teach him to doubt the resolve of an Ainsworth." Evelyn turned towards the door. "I will admit to looking forward to a few days of rest and pampering, for all that."

"Give my regards to your mother, and to your aunts and uncle as well."

"I will, provided my Aunt Agatha hasn't started another war with all of them."

"Why on earth would she do that?"

Evelyn paused at the door and looked over her shoulder with a laugh.

"You don't know my Auntie Agatha. She is a very stoic Englishwoman who, if I'm not very much mistaken, would have approved mightily of attacking the French fleet after the Armistice."

Bill made a comical face. "Ah. Say no more."

"I shan't. I shall simply pray that there is still an Ainsworth Manor to return home to!"

# When Wolves Gather

# Chapter Ten

**RAF Northolt**
**July 20**

Evelyn waited for a truck loaded with ground crew to rumble by, then jogged across the road once it had passed. They were undoubtedly heading out to the landing strips where the Hurricanes were waiting to be fueled for the day's second round of patrols. She had been rather surprised to hear the squadrons taking off before the sun was up, but she supposed she shouldn't have been. Both Miles and Rob were up in the air at all hours now, and it was obviously the same for the pilots of Northolt.

Striding along the pavement towards the short, squat building where her office was located, Evelyn looked up as another flight flew overhead, coming back. It was always a welcoming sight to see the airplanes above, but today it made her feel unaccountably melancholy. While the pilots were doing their job, and what they loved, it couldn't be ignored that they were hopelessly outnumbered on the other side of the Channel. Now that France was lost, the full force of the Luftwaffe would be turned towards them, and all these young men who were already getting tired would have to try to stem the onslaught. And she knew they were getting tired from the tone of Miles' last letter. He had sounded just about fed up, and he wasn't even in the very thick of it yet.

Northolt was, though. As part of 11 Group, they were expected to see the brunt of the coming battle. If the constant drone of engines and clank of tools repairing aircraft were any indication, they already were.

"ASO Ainsworth!"

A very familiar voice called out, drawing Evelyn's attention from her gloomy thoughts, and she turned to see Fred waving from the other side of the road. He was dressed in his flying gear, his flight jacket over his shoulders despite the warm morning.

"Aren't you a sight for weary eyes!" he called, crossing the road towards her. "When did you arrive back?"

"Last night." She smiled up at him as he joined her on the pavement. "Goodness, aren't you hot? Why are you wearing your jacket?"

"It's better than carrying it. Damned heavy things, y'know." He shrugged. "I haven't had the chance to remove it, to be honest."

Evelyn frowned and looked at him more closely. He looked exhausted, and there was a grimness about his mouth that made her frown deepen. The usual twinkle and laughter were missing from his eyes and, all at once, she realized that he didn't look like the Fred that she had become such good friends with over the past months.

"Are you all right?" she asked. "What's happened? You don't look like yourself."

He let out a short, dry laugh.

"I don't feel like myself, my darling Evie. Are you going to your office? Any chance of a spot of tea?"

"Yes, of course."

They walked up the steps of the building before them and, a few moments later, Fred was shedding his leather flying jacket in her office with a sigh of relief.

"That's much better!" he breathed.

"I honestly don't know why you're wearing it!" she exclaimed, setting her hat on the desk and reaching for the telephone to ring for some tea. "It's already unbearably warm out there."

"It wasn't yesterday morning when I went up," he replied, dropping into a chair and pulling out a cigarette case.

"Yes, but it isn't yesterday." Evelyn turned her attention to the person on the other end of the line, requesting a tea cart, and then set the receiver back into the cradle. "I can't imagine that you would need it up there today."

"Probably not, but I'm still wearing my clothes from yesterday." Fred lit a cigarette and leaned his head back, letting out a wide yawn. "Lord, I'm tired. I was shot down, you see. Just got back an hour ago."

"What?!"

"Bloody inconvenient, too. I was just about to get my third kill when it happened, robbing me of my victory."

"What happened?" Evelyn demanded, sinking down into her chair and staring at him.

"I was hit by return fire from a Heinkel 111. Jerry got me right in the fuel tank. I was damned lucky it didn't go up right there and then." Fred looked across the desk at her and his lips twisted. "Would you still go about with me if I was terribly burned?"

## When Wolves Gather

"Of course I would," she said briskly. "Don't be ridiculous."

"It happens, you know. The tank right in front of the pilot isn't self-contained. If that goes up, well, it's all over. Even if you manage to bail out, chances are you're in flames when you do."

Evelyn stared at him for a moment, then nodded slowly.

"Yes, I've heard. But that obviously isn't what happened to you, is it?"

"No. I was hit in the left tank, which *is* self-contained, thank God." Fred got up restlessly and walked over to the window to look outside. "You wouldn't think the Jerries could shoot that well."

"I've heard that as well. My brother was shot by return fire from a Dornier, I believe it was."

He glanced over at her. "Was he? Is he all right?"

"Apparently so. Miles told me in a letter. Both Spit and Robbie are operational."

"Well, that's jolly good to hear." He turned his attention back out of the window. "My kite's toasted."

"Did you have to bail out?"

"No. I probably should have, in retrospect, but I thought I could land her. So I toddled off home. Unfortunately, a 110 followed me in. Turns out, I was also out of ammunition."

"What?!"

"Yes. That was a bit of a shock, I'll tell you." He turned from the window and paced back across the office. "I can't properly explain the feeling of horror when you press the button to fire only to have absolutely nothing happen."

"What did you do?"

"The only thing I *could* do. I opened it up and tried to outrun the bastard while I was leaking fuel and burning glycol. It's a bloody miracle I didn't explode all together while I was high-tailing it out of there. He got me on the left side when the cliffs were in view. That's what sent the tank over the edge, I expect, because the fire spread in a blink after that. I flew over Brighton in flames and put her down in a field. Would you believe Jerry followed me in?" He shook his head and sucked on his cigarette. "Bastard probably went back and claimed a kill. Don't suppose I blame him. I don't know how I managed to climb out before she exploded."

"And the flames?"

"I was going out one side of the cockpit as they were going in the other."

"Good heavens!"

"That's what I mean about being bloody lucky." Fred paused and shook his head. "I really don't know how I landed and got out when I did."

"Well, obviously the good Lord was looking out for you."

He shot her an unreadable look. "Was He?" he asked softly. Then, "Yes, I suppose you're right. Can't really explain it any other way."

He went over to put his cigarette out in the ashtray on her desk.

"Anyway, that was my day yesterday. How was yours?"

"Not nearly as exciting. I spent most of it on trains." Evelyn shrugged ruefully. "I'm afraid that I may have been napping while you were wrestling with a burning Hurricane."

"That sergeant of yours, Cunningham, seemed to think you wouldn't be back until next month at the earliest."

"Yes, I know. I shouldn't have been, but I finished early at one post and so I came back. I'm off again this evening. I'm just finishing up a few things before I go."

"Where is it this time?" he asked, dropping back into his chair. "Oh, I know. You can't tell me."

"Actually, I can. I'm going home for a couple of weeks," she said brightly with a smile. "I'm actually getting a spot of leave."

"Good Lord! It's about time! Where is home?"

"Lancashire."

"Well, I'm very happy for you. I mean it. You work all the time, and I've never known someone to travel so much. You've earned a break."

"It sounds as if you could use it more than me."

"Not a'tall. I just had a weeks leave not long ago." He grinned at her. "And after a few hours sleep, I'll be right as rain again. They've grounded me for today while they get another Hurrie ready for me. That's all the rest I need."

She shook her head, standing as a knock fell on the door.

"Well, I won't deny that I'm looking forward to some time to myself," she said, crossing the office to open it and admit a young WAAF pushing a tea trolley. "Thank you, corporal. Just leave it over there, will you?"

"Yes, ma'am."

"And how is Miles faring?" Fred asked once the young girl had left the room, closing the door softly behind her.

"He seems to be all right. It sounds as if they're spending more time in the air than on the ground, much the same as you are." Evelyn poured out a cup of tea and handed it to him. "Is it really very bad up there?"

He took the saucer with a smile of thanks. "Not yet, but I expect that will change in the coming weeks." He took a sip of tea gratefully. "Right now Jerry's focusing on the convoys."

"So I understand." Evelyn carried her cup of tea to her desk and set it down, seating herself. "Are you getting very tired?"

Fred looked surprised. "Tired?"

"Yes, tired. It can't be easy being in the cockpit more hours than you're out of it."

"I hadn't really thought about it." He sipped his tea. "They say to meet bandits at a certain longitude and latitude, and off I go. Simple as that."

Evelyn was quiet for moment. She hadn't missed the trace of impatience in his voice. She supposed she was being rather silly. It was their job to fly in defense of England. Questioning if they were getting tired already was perhaps a bit insulting.

"Did you really climb out of your Hurricane and walk away without a scratch?" she asked suddenly, tilting her head. "Not even a grazed elbow?"

A flash of ruefulness went across his face.

"Well, not precisely," he admitted. "I did bump my head a bit. The good doctor said it's nothing, but he advised remaining on the ground for twenty-four hours."

"Ah, so it isn't because they're getting another airplane ready for you. I thought that sounded fishy."

"Well, not entirely. They *are* getting another airplane ready for me, but I could have taken up a different kite until then." He swallowed the rest of his tea. "Not to worry, though. I'll be back at it in the morning."

"And I'll be riding my horse at Ainsworth Manor." Evelyn smiled at him. "I'll think of you up there while I'm galloping across the countryside."

"Please do." For once, there was no answering laugh on his face. "And perhaps send up a prayer to the Almighty for me. I have no pressing desire to repeat yesterday's experience."

"Well, that goes without saying."

He tilted his head and studied her for a minute. "Would you really go to the pub with me if I was burned and disfigured?"

Evelyn swallowed. "Of course I would. It would take some getting used to, but I enjoy your company for who you *are*, not what you look like." She forced a bright smile. "And anyway, I could hardly say no without being horribly rude, could I?"

He did laugh at that.

"And I can't imagine a world where you would ever be rude, Assistant Section Officer Ainsworth."

"Precisely." She finished her tea and sobered. "Do try to take care of yourself while I'm away, though. I can't think of anything worse than this station without you to make me laugh."

"I'll certainly do my best."

### Ainsworth Manor
### July 24

"All alone, Mummy?" Evelyn asked cheerfully, sweeping onto the terrace, her father's trio of hunting dogs at her heels. "Don't tell me everyone has deserted you!"

"They have, and I couldn't be happier," Madeleine Ainsworth said, shielding her eyes from the sun and peering up at her daughter. "I adore having them here, but there are times that a few moments of quiet are welcome."

"Then you won't want me here with Tom, Dick and Harry. Shall I go away again?"

"Please don't. Have a seat and tell me about your morning. Did you go for a ride?"

"Yes, I did, and it was lovely." Evelyn sat down at the small iron table across from her mother as the dogs sniffed the tiles before flopping down in the sunlight. "Did you know the south pasture is being dug up? Well, of course you must. But what's happening?"

"Robbie is transitioning it into farming land, on the advice of the steward, Damien. He seems to think that it's likely to be requisitioned if he doesn't do something with it."

"I suppose it's a fair assumption," Evelyn said thoughtfully. "I saw that they're building some kind of military installation on the old Patterson estate."

"Yes. Well, I suppose it's a good thing to put the pasture to good use, at any event. We'll be growing crops that Damien says will be sold to the food ministry for the home front." Madeleine waved a hand vaguely. "I'm not very clear on all the details. I feel as if our lands are not our own, but of course that's nonsense."

# When Wolves Gather

"Things are changing, and you're reacting to it, that's all." Evelyn smiled encouragingly and reached out to squeeze her mother's hand. "Growing food on the south pasture is a good thing! You'll see. It's a tremendous thing to do for the war effort."

"I suppose you're right." Mrs. Ainsworth smiled and pulled her hand away. "It's not as if the pasture has been used for much since the last war. And we didn't have to take in any of the children from London, after all. This is the least we can do for the war."

"Now, tell me about the row between Auntie Agatha and Tante Adele," Evelyn said with a twinkle. "I've been simply dying to know what happened since I arrived, but one of them is always around!"

Her mother made a face.

"It really was thoughtless of Agatha," she muttered. "They hadn't been here but a few days!"

"Did she really say that the French deserved what they had coming?"

"Unfortunately, yes. Or, at least, words to that effect. She was referring to the ships, of course, but Tante Adele took it to mean the people of France themselves."

"Good Lord. What did Uncle Claude say?"

"He tried to diffuse the situation, but it really was hopeless. Agatha had well and truly put her foot in it." Madeleine shook her head. "It was a few days before Adele calmed down enough to listen to reason. Even Claude couldn't talk sense into her."

"They appear to have got past it now, at any rate."

"I'm not sure how much of that is because they don't have a choice," her mother said humorously.

At that moment, Thomas exited the house and came towards them with a silver tray in his hand.

"The post has arrived, ma'am," he said, bowing slightly and holding out the tray.

"Thank you."

She reached out to take the stack of letters off the tray and Thomas turned back to the house.

"Oh Thomas? Could you ask Wallace to bring the car around in half an hour?" Evelyn called suddenly. "I want to drive into the village."

"Of course, miss."

"Here's one for you, Evelyn," Madeleine said, holding out an envelope.

Evelyn took the letter and glanced at the return address.

"It's from Maryanne Gilhurst!" she exclaimed, turning it over and breaking the seal. "How wonderful! I haven't seen her in ages. I wonder how she is?"

She turned her attention to the letter before her and fell silent as she read about the dwindling social scene in London. Her brother, Lord Anthony Gilhurst, was becoming increasingly frustrated and withdrawn as the war progressed. It wasn't like Maryanne to worry about her brother, but Evelyn received the distinct impression from her letter that she was very concerned for him.

"Oh dear," she murmured.

Her mother looked up from the letter she was reading. "Is everything all right?"

"What? Oh, yes. It seems that Lord Gilhurst isn't behaving as he normally does. Something about being frustrated with the course of the war."

"Aren't we all?" Mrs. Ainsworth went back to her letter. "And now they've gone and added another tax on luxury items. Heaven knows what they'll consider luxury items."

Evelyn looked up from the letter, her attention caught. "What? Another tax?"

"Yes. You know I don't read the newspapers, but Claude does. He told me this morning over breakfast. They've proposed another war budget and it was presented yesterday, I believe. It includes a twenty-four percent tax on luxury items."

"Did it say what those items were?"

"I have absolutely no idea." Mrs. Ainsworth lowered her letter, her brow creasing in a frown. "It's already getting terribly expensive to live, and the rations are an absolute nightmare. Millie went to do the shopping on Monday and came back with hardly anything. She said the shops were empty. What's the point in giving us rations if, when we go to use them, there's nothing in the shops?"

"It's because the Germans are attacking the shipping routes, and the goods can't get through. I'm afraid it will only get worse."

"Well something has to be done. Where's the navy? They should be protecting the ships!"

Evelyn thought of the U-boats and the Luftwaffe, and then of Rob, Miles, and Fred trying desperately to protect the convoys from attack.

"They are trying, Mother."

Madeleine was silent for a moment, then let out a sigh.

"I know. It's all so very frustrating. I wish your father were here. He'd know what was to be done."

## When Wolves Gather

"Even Father wouldn't be able to protect the ships from German U-boats," Evelyn said wryly.

"No, I suppose not."

Evelyn saw the sorrow that crossed her mother's face and immediately felt guilty for speaking without thinking.

"I'm sorry, Mummy. That was thoughtless of me." She set her letter aside and got up to lean down and wrap her arms around her mother's shoulders. "I miss Daddy, too. Even if he couldn't make it better, he would have been here with us."

Mrs. Ainsworth patted the back of Evelyn's head and smiled up at her as she pulled away.

"He would be very proud of you," she told her. "He always said you'd find your place in the world, and he would have been very proud that it was with the WAAFs."

Evelyn swallowed, ignoring the flash of guilt that went through her, and sat back in her seat, reaching for her letter.

"Maryanne writes that the Ramsay's are having a party on Friday. Quite a few of our old crowd will be there," she said, changing the subject as she refolded the letter to put it back in its envelope. "Perhaps I'll go to London and surprise them all. I'd love to see them again."

Her mother looked up in surprise.

"Go to London?" she repeated. "But you've only been home a few days!"

"It won't be for long, Mummy," Evelyn said with a laugh. "Only the weekend. I'll take the train down tomorrow and use the extra day to do some shopping. I can be back on Monday. I'll stay in the house on Brook Street."

"I don't think I like the idea of you being in London for any amount of time," Madeleine said with a frown. "What if there's a raid? They evacuated all the children for a reason, after all."

"Yes, and since they did, not one bomb has fallen on London." Evelyn stood up, her letter in one hand. "Don't worry! I'll be just fine. And it will do me a world of good to get out and about and see some of the old faces again."

"I just don't like the thought of you all alone in London."

Evelyn laughed and leaned down to kiss her mother on her cheek.

"Then don't think about it!" she advised. "I promise you that I will be careful."

She turned away to go towards the doors leading to the drawing room, a smile twisting her lips. Her mother was worried about her spending a few days alone in London. What on earth would she say if she knew that she had spent weeks fleeing across Europe during the German invasions? Or that she'd gone to Switzerland completely unaccompanied and traversed that country alone before getting into a small, private airplane with a single pilot to fly back to Paris?

The smile faded as she went through the doors and into the house. That all seemed very far away now, even though it was only a month ago that she'd arrived back from Bordeaux with a Czech spy in tow. It was amazing how quickly the time had gone. The training course in Scotland had certainly helped in that regard, and now she was enjoying her time home with her family. Yet, even though she was having a thoroughly nice rest, Evie was conscious of a nagging sense of restlessness. The rides across the country, the shooting with the groom, and the comfortable family dinners with her mother and aunts and uncle were lovely, but they had grown very dull in just a few short days. What once had occupied her time quite nicely was now pale in comparison to the danger she knew was waiting for her in this war.

And, God help her, she was looking forward to it!

# Chapter Eleven

**Dover**

Henry got out of his car and stretched, looking across the flat expanse of land as a brisk wind whipped around him, pulling at his jacket collar. He took a deep breath of salty air and closed the door, turning to walk towards the cliff edge in the distance. The sun was shining through patchy clouds above, and the breeze off the Channel was stiff, but warm. It was a fine, summer day in the South of England, but there were few out enjoying it. He had this little corner of Dover almost entirely to himself. The only other human that he'd seen was a few miles away when he'd passed a lorry with a bale of hay in the back. It was just as well. He wasn't in the mood to be sociable to anyone, least of all the local populace of Dover.

When Lady Rothman suggested that he drive down to the southern coast, he'd thought she was joking. It soon became apparent that she wasn't, however. He'd listened in growing astonishment as she detailed what she expected of him while he was on this absurd jaunt to the cliffs. She actually wanted him to scout out ways to sabotage the local defenses and aid an incoming invasion force.

His lips tightened as he made his way over the coarse grass towards the cliff edge. It really went beyond insult. A man in his position, being ordered about by a woman, an amateur, who was playing at being a spymaster! It was really the outside of enough. He'd been working hand in hand with the Germans long before she ever dreamt of becoming involved in anything more than her famously terrible tea parties. Ignoring his experience, she'd decided to send him on useless scouting missions in the South of England rather than utilize him in his full, and quite capable, capacity in London.

Yet here he was, for all of that. Berlin had been quite clear. He was to cooperate with Lady Rothman and her team, and assist in any way possible. And then he was to report back to them regularly and keep them updated on her movements, plans, and progress. If it weren't for those instructions, which he intended to follow to the letter, Henry would have cut ties and moved on without a backward glance.

## CW Browning

He paused and looked around as another gust of wind plucked at his collar. He hadn't put on his hat when he got out of the car. There was no point. He would only be struggling to prevent it from being ripped off his head and carried away on the wind. Lifting his hand to shield his eyes from the bright sunlight, Henry turned to look back behind him at the tall towers that loomed over the countryside. Lady Rothman wanted him to evaluate the telephone wires and electric poles for sabotage. That was child's play, parlor games for the unimaginative. He had absolutely no intention of wasting his time on something his ten-year-old nephew could do in less time than it took to blink. No. Those! Those towers were what he was interested in. Those were what could truly cripple England.

Henry looked back at the cliff edge, mentally calculating the distance to the road. Lady Rothman didn't know about the towers. Or, if she did, she completely failed to comprehend how crucial they were to the defense of England. He pursed his lips and turned to stare at the structures in the distance. Chain Home, that's what it was called. Those towers were part of a system that stretched along the entire southern coast of England. They were radar towers which could, by all accounts and tests, detect and relay the position of enemy aircraft coming across the Channel. The incoming threat was picked up by the radar towers, and then transmitted to Fighter Command Headquarters, where they could scramble the appropriate fighter response to intercept them. Those towers were the single most important weapon in England's arsenal at the moment.

And Lady Rothman wanted him to see about snipping telephone wires and blowing up bridges.

Henry's lips tightened and he turned to walk parallel with the cliff edge, staring thoughtfully out over the distant expanse of water. The Channel was the only thing stopping Hitler from continuing his Blitzkrieg right into England. Historically, it was the body of water that had protected England from others who wanted to invade her, most notably another corporal who had had similar ambitions to Hitler. But times had changed. While the English Channel still posed difficulties, it wasn't the barrier that it once was.

He looked up to blue sky with its patches of white cloud and watched as a flock of seagulls swooped towards the water. Now, they had airplanes. Hitler had the Luftwaffe. They were capable of bypassing the Channel altogether and flying over. Once they took control of the skies, the Channel was just another body of water that could, and would, be crossed with relative ease.

The only thing standing in the way was those towers.

# When Wolves Gather

Henry turned and began walking back towards his car. He wasn't about to share their existence with Lady Rothman if she wasn't aware of them. They were, after all, top secret. No one knew of their existence. The chain of towers along the coast were hardly inconspicuous, but the locals had no idea of their purpose. Lord only knew what they'd been told, if anything. He was only aware of their existence because of his position in Parliament, and all he knew was that the radar system was one of their government's best kept secrets. He certainly wasn't going to be the one who blabbed it to Lady Rothman and her Amateur Hour.

He would, however, share it with his handler in Berlin. That was his true purpose in following the ridiculous instructions to come down to Dover. He would start here, and then systematically go along the coast, noting the locations and approximate distance from the cliffs. He would then hand the information over to Berlin for them to do with what they would. Henry had come too far now to take a backseat to Lady Rothman. By the time he was finished, she would look like the amateur that she was.

And he would have made up for any lost ground over that damned Ainsworth business.

## London

Evelyn sipped her tea, watching as Maryanne Gilhurst finished tucking her hair back into place and snapped her compact closed.

"I really do like that hat," she said, setting her cup down in the saucer. "Where did you say you got it?"

"Oh, it's from last season. I picked it up in Paris when Anthony and I went over for a visit." Maryanne poured tea into her cup from the china pot on the table. "I don't suppose I'll get back to Paris now for a very long time, if ever. Do you think it will ever be same?"

"I don't know." Evelyn sighed. "I very much fear that it won't."

"No. I don't see how it can be. Did you see the photographs in the newspapers of the Nazi banners hanging from the Arc de Triumph?" Maryanne gave a shudder. "Ghastly!"

"Yes."

She sipped her tea as Evelyn reached for a bun from the three-tiered holder in the center of the table.

"Do you think we have any chance at all of winning this war?" she asked suddenly, her green eyes boring into Evelyn's. "Really?"

"I hope so, otherwise we'll be seeing the banners and goose-stepping here in London." Evelyn bit into her cream bun and chewed for a moment. "I can't think of anything worse," she added after a long moment.

"No." Maryanne shook her head and set her cup down with a clink. "I've got some news."

"Oh?"

"I've joined the ATS."

Evelyn stared across the table at her friend, her bun forgotten as her mouth dropped open.

"What?!"

Maryanne let out a delighted laugh at the look on her face.

"Oh, the look on your face is priceless, my dear. Absolutely priceless!" she chortled. "I wish you could see yourself."

"I'm just so surprised!" Evelyn said, setting down her bun and wiping her fingers on a linen napkin.

"I don't know why you should be. After all, you're the inspiration behind it." Maryanne considered the tiered holder for a moment before finally selecting a piece of fruit cake. "You joined the WAAFs before any of us knew what was happening. The war had barely begun!"

"Yes, but that's different. Robbie was already in the RAF, and I wanted to do my bit."

"Well, so do I." Maryanne set the cake on a plate and looked at her. "At first, I thought the whole thing would blow over. Everyone said that it would. It would all be over by Christmas. That's what they said."

"Yes. I remember."

"Well, here we are in summer and the Nazis are on the other side of the Channel." She broke off a piece of the fruit cake and popped it into her mouth, chewing thoughtfully. "I never dreamt France would fall so quickly. Did you?"

"I rather hoped it wouldn't fall at all, but no. It never occurred to me that it would happen so quickly."

"No. Shocking, really." Maryanne cleared her throat. "At any rate, that's why I've joined the ATS. This war is clearly not going away, and like you, I want to do what I can."

"But the army?" Evelyn raised her eyebrows. "What on earth made you pick the ATS?"

## When Wolves Gather

"I can drive," the other woman said simply with a shrug. "I might as well do it for the ATS. They need drivers, you know."

"But...how do you know that you'll be a driver?"

"Oh, Anthony's already had it all arranged," Maryanne said airily with a light laugh. "It's handy when your brother is a lord, really."

Evelyn choked back a laugh and reached for her tea cup. "I suppose it is. When do you leave?"

"I have to report here in town next week and go to training, then they'll assign me. I'm not really sure when I'll actually be posted, or where, to be honest. They weren't very clear about that." She made a face. "The uniforms are perfectly dreadful, aren't they?"

Evelyn laughed. "Yes, they are, and terribly uncomfortable. But you'll get used to it."

"I don't suppose I'll have a chance to wear that gorgeous dress I bought today," Maryanne said sadly. "Why on earth did you let me buy it?"

"Well I didn't know you'd joined the ATS, did I?" Evelyn grinned. "Besides, it looks wonderful on you. I wouldn't have stopped you even if I had known."

"It does look rather fantastic on," the other woman agreed. "Oh well. There won't always be a war on, will there? And there are still parties before I go. Speaking of which, are you going to stay for the Ramsay's do? I have no idea who will be there, but several of the old crowd are in town. And the Ramsay's always did have tremendous parties."

"Yes, I think I'll go. It's so nice to be back in town again, and it's been lovely seeing you. I'd love to see some of the others."

"Oh good! We can go together. Won't that be nice!"

"Is Anthony going?"

Maryanne wrinkled her nose and the smile on her face faded.

"No. At least, I'd be very surprised. He doesn't do much of anything anymore. He doesn't seem very interested in our friends, or in going out and about."

Evelyn looked up from her bun. "You said in your letter that you think he's depressed?"

"Yes. Well, who isn't nowadays? I mean, this war is hardly a barrel of laughs, is it?" Maryanne toyed with her tea cup for a moment, then shook her head. "I think perhaps he's feeling at a loss. He's been more active in politics, and our father is very pleased with the attention and respect he's garnering in the House, but I'm not sure it's what Anthony is really looking for. He told me that he's envious of me joining the ATS."

Evelyn raised her eyebrows. "What?"

The other woman nodded. "He did. I was rather taken aback, to be honest. I mean, I never once thought he wanted a military career. But then, I never once thought that we would be at war with Germany, Italy, and the Soviet Union."

"Perhaps he's just worried," Evelyn suggested after a moment. "These are very uncertain times, and your brother has always been a bit of a protector where you are concerned."

"I suppose. I do worry about leaving him when he's like this, though."

"I'm sure he'll be just fine." Evelyn reached across the table and squeezed her friend's hand reassuringly. "I can't image the level of pressure and stress the Houses are feeling at the moment. Goodness, Churchill has only been prime minister for three months, and Hitler is knocking on our front door. It must be unbearable."

Maryanne looked up, her lips pursed thoughtfully. "I never considered that," she admitted. "He could simply be feeling the pressure. I don't want you to think he's turned into some kind of moping Marley, for that's not the case at all. He's just not the same person he was a few months ago."

Evelyn thought back to herself a few months before and suppressed a sigh. She certainly wasn't the same woman she had been in the spring.

"War has a way of changing us," she murmured. "I haven't decided if it's a good thing or not, but we're all changing. It's inevitable, really."

"I suppose so."

They were quiet for a moment, then Maryanne looked up with a grin.

"Did Rob tell you that we ran into him a few weeks ago?" she asked.

"No! Did you?"

"Yes. We were having dinner at The Dorchester and he was there with another pilot. Miles Lacey." The grin on her face turned devilish. "I do believe you've been keeping secrets from me, Evelyn Ainsworth."

Evelyn was annoyed when she felt a flush steal up her cheeks.

"Don't be ridiculous. I haven't seen you to keep secrets from you."

Maryanne let out a laugh at the pink staining her cheeks. "Why Evie! You're blushing! Is it as serious as all that?"

"No, it isn't. Miles is a friend. That's all."

# When Wolves Gather

Maryanne tilted her head and studied her for a moment. "Well, you could certainly do much worse than one of the Yorkshire Lacey's," she said thoughtfully. "And he's terribly good-looking. His father is a Baron, and he's in line for the title, so that's certainly something. Tony says the fortune is stable, and the lineage is certainly impeccable. What's the trouble?"

"There is no trouble. We're just friends."

"My dear Evelyn, since when are you just friends with any man?" Maryanne demanded with a laugh. She held up her hands placatingly when Evelyn appeared affronted. "All right, all right. I'll rephrase. When is any man just friends with you?"

"How am I supposed to respond to that?" Evelyn demanded with a laugh. "There's no good way to answer that."

"Fair enough. But really, why aren't you jumping at the chance to land Miles Lacey? Don't you like him?"

"Yes, of course I do." Evelyn sighed and pushed her half-eaten bun away. "To be perfectly honest, I don't think I've ever felt this way about anyone before."

Maryanne stared at her. "Then what's the matter with you? Snag him while you can!"

Evelyn laughed and shook her head.

"I don't know if you've noticed, but there seems to be a war on at the moment," she pointed out dryly. "A war that we're both rather heavily involved in. Perhaps once the war is over…"

"Once the war is over? Are you out of your mind?" Maryanne sat back in her chair and stared at Evelyn. "What has the war got to do with anything?"

"Well, we can't very well go making plans, can we? Not when neither of us knows if the other will be…" She stopped abruptly and swallowed with difficulty. "It's just not practical, is it?"

"For heaven's sake, Evelyn, it's not unpractical. Everyone and their sister is rushing to get married precisely *because* of the war!"

"And if he's killed?"

"Then at least you would have been married."

"Maryanne!"

The other woman laughed and waved the protest away.

"I'm only having some fun. You know that. But honestly, you can't let the war stop you from pursuing a relationship with Miles Lacey if that's what you want. Why, this could drag on for years! Are you willing to wait that long?"

Evelyn thought of all the lies she told every day, and of how horrified Miles would be if he even knew part of what she did for the war effort. Her chest tightened and she swallowed again painfully. If she really was a WAAF, she supposed she'd be thinking just as Maryanne was. But she wasn't, and her war work left no room for anything like a husband, or even dreams of a husband.

"I really do find this conversation quite ridiculous," she said with a flash of a smile. "You speak as though it were all up to me. He hasn't even mentioned the future, and neither have I. Don't you think this is all a bit premature?"

Maryanne came as close to a snort as a woman of her standing could.

"You may not have mentioned it, but I'm not blind. As soon as your name is mentioned, Miles Lacey lights up like a torch. That man is head over heels for you, Evelyn. All you have to do is bat those long eyelashes of yours and he'll be on one knee so fast you wouldn't see him move."

"Maryanne, really!"

Her friend grinned, unrepentant. "Well, it's true. All the man needs is a little encouragement, and I'm completely at a loss as to why you won't give it to him."

"Maybe I don't want to get married just yet."

"If any other woman in London uttered those words, I wouldn't believe her." Maryanne tilted her head again and smiled at Evelyn. "But you've always been so different, Evie. That's why I adore you. Very well. I'll leave it alone."

"Thank you."

"He *is* very good-looking, though. If you don't snatch him up, someone else will."

"Oh for heaven's sake!" Evelyn exclaimed, laughing despite herself.

Maryanne winked. "Now I'm finished."

"I very much doubt that," Evelyn murmured with a reluctant grin. "I can't wait until you find one of your own. I'll be ruthless."

"I wouldn't have it any other way, darling."

When Wolves Gather

# Chapter Twelve

**RAF Coltishall**
**July 26**

Miles closed his newspaper and folded it, taking a deep breath and looking up into the cloudless blue sky. Rob stood a few yards away, chatting with Ashmore and a few of the other pilots while the squadron was down and refueling after being up most of the morning.

"Gorgeous weather," Chris commented beside him, lighting a cigarette. "Couldn't ask for a prettier sky."

"Mmm." Miles made a noncommittal sound and watched as the new pilot, Thomas, left Rob's group and came towards them. "What do you think of young Thomas, there?" he asked suddenly.

Chris raised an eyebrow. "Uncle Tom? I dunno. What should I think of him?"

"Well, he landed in the drink yesterday after bailing out, but this morning he was out here before the rest of us," Miles said. "That doesn't strike you as unusual?"

Chris shrugged. "So he has an axe to grind with the Krauts. Nothing unusual about that. I seem to recall you being the same way after your adventure over Dunkirk."

Miles looked at him. "Why do you Americans call the Jerries Krauts?"

"Because they eat sauerkraut," came the prompt reply. "Why do you Brits call them Jerries?"

"Because their helmets look like a Jerry."

"And what, for the love of God, does a Jerry look like?"

"An old chamber pot."

"I say, do you know what Ashmore just told us?" Thomas asked excitedly, joining them.

"I haven't the foggiest, old bean," Miles said, reaching into his jacket pocket for his cigarette case.

"That our squadron may be in line for a few days of leave!"

"Jolly good. But you had a day off yesterday, didn't you?" Miles asked, peering up him. "Don't see why you should get another."

"Oh, I say, that's not fair!" Thomas protested, his curly hair standing up as a breeze whipped around his head. "It's not as if I had much of a choice!"

"Don't listen to him, Uncle Tom," Chris said cheerfully. "He's pulling your chain."

"Pulling my what?"

"He's joking!"

"Oh!" Thomas looked flustered and shot Miles a look. "Really, sir?"

Miles couldn't stop his grin, although he did try.

"I'm sorry, young Thomas. You really do make it so easy!"

The young pilot visibly relaxed and laughed uncertainly. "Oh, well, that's all right."

"Where will you go?" Chris asked him as Miles lit his cigarette. "Where are your people?"

"Oh, they're down in Dorset. I'll go to London, I expect." Thomas looked around when someone called his name, waving him over. "I just thought you'd like to know that we might be getting a bit of a break soon."

He went back to the group of pilots and Miles glanced at Chris.

"How long has young Tom been with us now? A week?"

"Closer to two, I think. Or perhaps three?" Chris thought hard for a moment, then shook his head. "I have no idea. I can't keep all the newbies straight anymore. They come. They go. Who can say how long he's been here?"

"Well, however long it's been, it certainly isn't long enough for him to need a break as of yet. Good Lord!"

"Well, he did take a dive into the Channel yesterday," Chris pointed out placidly. "Maybe its rattled his nerves. It would have rattled mine."

They were silent for a moment, then Chris looked at Miles.

"Are we really due for some leave?"

"It's been mentioned. Ashmore is trying to get us some time off. I think he's worried about the strain." Miles ashed his cigarette and shrugged. "I certainly won't argue with him."

"You won't hear any complaints from me either." Chris tossed his cigarette away. "Have you heard from your girl?"

"I had a letter from her yesterday. She's enjoying a spot of leave herself. She's gone home for a bit."

## When Wolves Gather

"If we do get a day off, why don't we go to London and see if she can meet us there?" Chris asked. "I'm dying to meet her. I keep picturing Rob with long hair."

Miles glanced at him in amusement. "She's hardly that, I assure you."

"Well, let me see for myself." Chris grinned. "It'll be fun!"

Before Miles could reply, the window of the dispersal hut opened and the sergeant stuck his head out.

"Excuse me, sir," he called excitedly, "but you've been scrambled!"

Miles turned in his chair to stare at him. "Don't be daft, man! We're still refueling!"

"I know, but that's what they said!"

"Well, bloody well call them back and confirm!"

The sergeant nodded and ducked back into the hut.

"Did you even hear the telephone ring?" Chris asked.

"No, but I don't think we would out here." Miles put out his cigarette. "It must be a mistake. They know we're refueling!"

"We've never been scrambled before," Chris said. "It can't be for real. Can it?"

"With the way this war is going?" Miles shrugged. "Who knows!"

The window behind them opened again and the sergeant was back, his face flushed.

"There's no mistake, sir!" he called. "Scramble!!!!"

His bellow reached Ashmore and the rest of the pilots, and they all turned to stare. Miles got up.

"I don't know what the hell they expect us to do when our kites are still…"

His voice trailed off as Jones, his ground crew sergeant, came running from the directions of the airplanes.

"You're fueled and ready, sir!" he gasped.

Miles grabbed his Mae West from where he'd dropped it next to the chair.

"We're good to go!" Chris yelled to the others, joining Miles as he began running for his Spitfire. "Get a move on!"

The others broke into a run, heading for the squadron of gleaming machines in the distance. Miles reached his and leapt onto the wing, reaching into the cockpit for his parachute. Jones joined him and helped him clip it on before clambering off the wing as Miles climbed back into his cockpit. He felt as if he was spending more time in his Spit than out of it these days. Jones pulled the chocks away and Miles motioned to him that he was starting the engine. A moment later, he was taxiing down the landing strip with Chris close behind. As he turned the nose into the wind, he saw Ashmore and Rob both starting their engines.

He shook his head and opened the throttle, keeping one eye on the glycol tank as he hurtled along the grass, gaining speed. A scramble? Was it really happening, then? Were the Jerries coming after England at last?

His wings caught air and as his wheels left the ground, Miles reached down to retract the undercarriage. Chris was right. They hadn't been scrambled yet, outside of the drills. The RAF seemed to think they should be able to be airborne in two minutes. As far as he knew, no squadron had passed the two-minute drill yet. Was that what this was all about? Was this simply another drill?

Miles banked up into the sky and reached up to slide the canopy shut.

Or had the invasion begun?

### Reims, France

Obersturmbannführer Hans Voss stepped through the front room of the old farmhouse and looked around. His men had secured the house and the grounds, and the old man who lived there was in the front parlor.

"Search upstairs," he said shortly. "If you find anything, bring it to me."

"Yes, Herr Obersturmbannführer."

His subordinate motioned for two others to follow and they started up the stairs as Hans turned towards the parlor. He stripped off his gloves as he entered, his pale blue eyes falling on the man standing defiantly in the middle of the room between two SS soldiers.

"Yves Michaud?" he asked, examining the man dressed in work clothes.

"Oui."

"I'll make this very simple. I have information that you're supplying false papers and identities to members of the former French forces." Hans slapped his gloves against his thigh, his pale eyes never leaving the man's face. "Tell me who they are, and where they are

## When Wolves Gather

hiding, and this will go much easier for you. I may even allow you to remain here, in your home."

The man stared at him impassively, remaining silent, and Hans let out a loud sigh. He nodded to one of the soldiers. The soldier turned and punched him in his kidney, extracting a grunt of pain as the man fell forward to his knees. The soldier hauled him back up and hit him again, this time in his stomach. Hans watched dispassionately as the man doubled over from the blow, and raised his hand to halt the blows.

"My men are in the process of tearing your house apart," he said calmly. "They will find your equipment, and anything else that you might be hiding. If you cooperate now, the damage to your property and to yourself will be minimized. Do you understand?"

The man spit out blood and Hans nodded to the soldier. He pulled him upright and Hans stepped closer, watching as blood trickled out of the side of his mouth. His skin was weathered from the sun, and his hands were calloused, speaking plainly of his work in the fields adjacent to the house.

"If you choose not to cooperate, I will burn your vineyard, and this house, with you in it. Do I make myself quite clear?"

"If you kill me, you'll never find what you seek," the man rasped out.

The smile that crossed Hans' face was icy.

"I will learn all that I need to know. Of that, you can have no doubt. The only question is whether you suffer to keep secrets that will not be secret for very much longer."

Old brown eyes met his and Hans watched as the man considered his words. Before he could press his advantage, however, a young soldier ran into the room.

"Herr Obersturmbannführer! We have searched the barn. There is nothing there but vegetables and hay."

"Look harder!" he barked over his shoulder. "And don't come back until you've found something!"

The soldier gulped, saluted, and left hurriedly. As soon as he'd gone, Hans exhaled.

"Is it in the barn? Or is it in the house?" he asked. "Where is the room where you make these papers?"

"I don't know what you're talking about," the man said, flinching when there was a crash upstairs. "I am a farmer. I grow grapes that I sell to the winemakers on the other side of the town. I don't know anything about papers."

"You lie." Hans made the statement calmly. "To do so is foolish. I know that you provide new identities for people, and that those people actively oppose the Führer, and our occupation. I know that the papers are made here, along with the photographs. I know this because we've been informed of your work by one of your clients."

The man looked up at that and Hans smiled coldly.

"So you see, your loyalty is misplaced. They are not nearly as protective of you as you are of them." He motioned for the two soldiers to step back and, once they had, he stood very close to the man and lowered his voice. "I know that two women and a man came to see you in May. I know that you provided identity cards for one of the women. If you cooperate, and tell me what I want to know, I will personally guarantee that you will come to no harm. If you do not…"

He shrugged and stepped back, watching as the man remained stubbornly silent. After a long moment, he sighed and motioned to the soldiers.

"Take him outside and tie him to a tree overlooking his precious vines. Perhaps watching them burn will jog his memory."

The soldiers each grabbed an arm and began to force the man towards the door.

Yves Michaud spoke as they reached the door.

"Wait."

Hans motioned with his hand and the soldiers released him. He turned to face Hans, his lined face looking weary.

"Yes?"

"Do not burn the vineyard. If you kill me, someone else can tend the vines. If you burn them, you will burn four generations of grapes that make some of the best champagne in the region."

"Would you rather I burn you instead?"

"Oui." He spoke without hesitation, bringing a reluctant laugh to Hans's lips.

"The wine is that good?"

"Oui."

Hans threw his head back and laughed out at that.

"Who am I to debate wine with a Frenchman?" he asked. "Very well, old man. I will spare the vines." The laugh disappeared as quickly as it had come. "But I will not spare you. Take him to the car. I'll question him later, at the station."

He watched as they took the man away, then turned and looked around the parlor slowly. The old man was more stubborn than he'd anticipated, but he had his weaknesses. The vineyard was one, but where there was one, there were others. His eyes fell on a framed

## When Wolves Gather

photograph of a woman standing with a young girl. He just had to find them.

Crossing the room to the photograph, he picked it up, studying it. It had taken two months to get to this point in his search. As much as he despised the assassin known as Eisenjager, it had been that man who had provided the information leading to the old man. He had followed a trio through France as they fled ahead of their armies. It was he that discovered the extracurricular activities of the old man. The trio the assassin had been stalking were presumed to be members of the French intelligence network, the former Deuxième Bureau. Once Voss had their names, he could begin to hunt them down, and they would, in turn, lead him to the others.

But first he had to gain Yves Michaud's cooperation.

## Chapter Thirteen

**London**

The front parlor in the Ramsay's London house was packed to capacity, as was the back parlor where card tables had been set up for those disinclined to partake in the dancing underway in the ballroom. It seemed to Evelyn that half of London society was present for the Ramsay's party. Despite the war, they had managed to throw as close to a bash as those she remembered so well from pre-1939. Rationing had curtailed the usual spread of light fare that would have been found in the dining room, but the Ramsay's had managed to put together an acceptable offering for their guests that, while not as extravagant as it once would have been, was nonetheless respectable. A few servants circulated through the rooms, carrying trays of wine and champagne, and the overall mood was light and noisy. The city's elite were enjoying themselves, taking a welcome break from the realities of a war that had suddenly taken a turn for the worse.

"Why, look! It's Miss Ainsworth!" a voice exclaimed over the low drone of voices and laughter. "Evelyn!"

Evelyn turned to see a tall redhead dressed in a stunningly simple emerald gown waving to her. She smiled and made her way past a group of older women towards her.

"Why Maggie!" she exclaimed, joining the redhead. "It's been years! How are you?"

"I'm still here, causing trouble every chance that I get," Maggie replied, kissing the air beside Evelyn's cheek. "I thought you'd joined the WAAF. At least, that's what the rumors were."

"I did. I was given some time off, so I came to London."

"Fantastic! We must have lunch while you're here. You remember Lord Billingsley? And his sister, Gillian?"

"Yes, of course. How are you both?"

"Very well, thank you," Lord Billingsley said, shaking her hand. "How is Robert? Is he still flying Spitfires?"

"Oh yes. You couldn't tear him away," Evelyn said with a laugh. "How is your mother?"

## When Wolves Gather

"She's comfortably ensconced at the seat in Devon. She wanted to get away from London. She's been there since Christmas." He sipped his drink. "And yours?"

"She's well, thank you. She's doing much the same thing in Lancashire."

"We were very sorry to hear about your father," Gillian said. "We were in Spain when it happened."

"Thank you."

"I'm still trying to believe that you're here!" Maggie said once it was clear the civilities were over. "I haven't seen you since...well, since your father passed away, I suppose."

"I know. The WAAF has been keeping me busy. I don't get to town as often as I used to." Evelyn shrugged and laughed. "Maryanne Gilhurst is the reason I'm here now. We had lunch yesterday."

"I thought I'd seen her earlier, but then she disappeared!" Gillian exclaimed. "Is her brother here as well?"

"I believe she said he might look in later."

"There! You see, Charles? I told you it wouldn't all be old stuffed shirts!"

Charles looked uncomfortable. "All I said was that it might be dull, and I was clearly mistaken."

Maggie cleared her throat and looked at Evelyn. "What do you do in the WAAF?"

"I'm a training officer."

"An officer!" Charles nodded in approval. "Good show! What and who do you train?"

"I train enlisted ACWs, that's Aircraft Women. However, I'm afraid I can't tell you anything else." Evelyn smiled apologetically. "I'm sorry."

"Do you know, it doesn't surprise me in the least to hear that you're a training officer?" Maggie asked. "You were always so calm and collected. Nothing ever did ruffle you."

"Where do they have you stationed?" Charles asked.

"I'm at Northolt at the moment, but I travel quite a bit."

"Oh, that's not far from here, is it?" Gillian asked. "Yet we haven't seen you in ages!"

"She just said that she travels, Gil," Charles muttered. "Do keep up."

Evelyn swallowed a laugh.

"No, she's right. I'm not far away. I don't get to town as often as I'd like. Unfortunately, I don't get very much time off."

"I was thinking of joining the WRENs, but Charles doesn't think it would suit me," Gillian told her.

"It wouldn't," her brother said decidedly, "and besides, you need to be available for Mother. Lord knows I can't keep running to Devon every few days. I'm far too busy."

Maggie waved a passing servant over and took two glasses of champagne, handing one to Evelyn.

"Here. We must toast to your re-appearance, my dear," she said, holding up her glass. "To old friends and their mysterious pursuits! Cheers!"

Evelyn touched her glass to the others and sipped the sparkling wine.

"Thank you, but I assure you, they aren't very mysterious at all," she murmured.

"Well, they are if you can't tell us about them," Maggie retorted. "Do you like being in the service? Aren't the uniforms ghastly?"

"Yes, they are."

"Well, I don't suppose she had anything else to do," Gillian said. "After all, she's not married."

Evelyn raised an eyebrow.

"Oh, I'm so sorry. Have you been married since I've been away? I didn't know!"

Charles let out a bark of laughter as Gillian flushed a dull red.

"No, she hasn't," Maggie said cheerfully. "And neither have I. The war is taking all the men away from London, except those that are already married, or who are married to their work."

"I didn't mean…" Gillian began, then faltered.

"Yes you did," Evelyn said briskly, "and you're quite far off the mark, I assure you. I joined the WAAFs because I wanted to do something for the war effort. My mother was opposed to the idea, but I didn't see why Robbie should have all the fun."

"Is it fun?" Maggie asked, her brown eyes widening. "Do you mean that you really enjoy it?"

"Aside from the ghastly uniforms and terrible accommodations, absolutely." Evelyn smiled. "I never was one to sit around in a drawing room and pour tea."

"No. No, you weren't, were you?" Maggie grinned suddenly. "Oh Evelyn, I think we could use you around here. You really must try to get back to London more often."

"That is, if my sister hasn't offended you and put you off," Charles said.

## When Wolves Gather

"Not at all," Evelyn said with a laugh, glancing at that embarrassed young lady. "I'm not offended. I just thought I should set the record straight."

"Well, I for one, wouldn't blame you for not coming to town more often," Charles decided. "The restrictions are getting worse every day, and the rationing is ridiculous. If it gets much worse, I don't know what any of us will do. I've had to stop putting sugar in my tea in the afternoon! It's really the outside of enough."

The conversation turned to the hardships of trying to live comfortably amidst the rationing, and Evelyn's eyes wandered over the crowds, looking for Maryanne. It was a common theme this evening, as she'd realized after being in three different conversations already. They always came back to the personal discomfort of being in a war. At first, she had empathized. After all, the complaints were much the same as what she and her mother had said many times. But something was different here. Here, the complaints weren't made and then the conversation turned to something different. Here, the complaints led to several comments that made Evelyn distinctly uncomfortable. And she had no doubt that it would be the same again in a minute. Where *had* Maryanne disappeared to?

"Really, I do feel like the world has gone mad," Maggie was saying as Evelyn brought her eyes back to the other three. "I was at the Savoy, for lunch, you know, and I was shocked at who they're letting in these days! The table next to me had three women in uniform, and they were quite clearly not like you, Evelyn dear. It was evident that they were…well, they just didn't belong there. It really was quite shocking."

"It shouldn't be allowed," Charles agreed. "It's one thing to allow officers into the better restaurants, but quite another for all these girls in uniforms running about. Most of them come from Lord knows where, and their behavior is absolutely shocking."

"Of course, we don't mean you, Evelyn," Gillian assured her with a smile. "I'm sure you wouldn't dream of wearing your uniform to the Savoy."

"No, I don't, actually," Evelyn agreed, tamping down her irritation. "Although that has more to do with the fact that I keep clothes at the house in Brook Street, and less to do with the uniform itself."

"The uniform really hasn't anything to do with it. Not really. As Charles says, it's not the officers that are the problem." Maggie finished her champagne and set the empty glass down on a nearby table. "It's more the lowering of the standards that's got out of control. The uniforms are really only a symptom of the illness."

"I couldn't agree more," Charles said, nodding. "After all, once they start lowering the bar to get into our favorite restaurants and clubs, where will it end? The next thing you know, we'll have all sorts of undesirables running around as equals, and that's when the British society will crumble."

"It wasn't like it in the last war. My father says that this is all the result of the Fifth Columnists," Maggie said thoughtfully. "They're intent on destroying the class systems, you know. They don't believe anyone should have any more than anyone else."

"What do you think the problem is Evelyn?" Gillian asked, turning to her. "Do you think it's the Fifth Columnists?"

Evelyn swallowed and shrugged.

"To be perfectly frank, I haven't seen that there is very much of a problem," she told them, her voice steady. "But, of course, I'm not in town very often anymore, and when I am, I'm afraid I'm too busy enjoying myself to take very much note of who's dining at the table next to me. So I really couldn't put forth an opinion on the matter."

She swallowed the rest of her champagne in a gulp and set the glass on the tray of a passing server.

"I'm afraid I'm feeling rather flushed. I'm off to powder my nose and perhaps step outside for some air. It was lovely to see you all again! We really must have lunch, Maggie."

"Yes, we must!" That lady said promptly. "Are you staying in Brook Street?"

"Yes."

After saying her goodbyes and smiling all around, Evelyn made a hasty escape and slipped out of the overcrowded drawing room and into the hallway. As soon as she was out of sight, she exhaled and the smile disappeared from her face.

*Good Lord, have they always been that arrogant?* she wondered, making her way down the hallway to the ballroom. She would have thought, had she given it any consideration before now, that the war would have shown everyone the need to work together, regardless of social standing. However, it seemed to have had the opposite effect on many of her peers. The conversation she'd just suffered through was not the first of its kind this evening, and Evelyn knew that if she stayed for much longer, it wouldn't be the last. She had to find Maryanne and make her excuses and leave before she lost her mind and did something altogether shocking.

Stepping into the ballroom, she scanned the dancing couples, looking for her friend. Not finding her among the laughing and chatting occupants of the large room, Evelyn turned towards the

## When Wolves Gather

French doors at the back of the room that opened out onto the back lawn. She moved through the crowds at the edge of the room easily, smiling and nodding in greeting to old acquaintances as she went. Something about the set of her jaw and the determined stride prevented any of them from trying to stop her, and she was grateful. She needed a few moments of fresh air and quiet and time to herself. Her nerves were rubbed raw, and Evelyn was rather shocked at how angry she had become at the elitist views she'd been hearing all evening.

It was very disconcerting. After all, she was one of the elite. These people were once her only acquaintances, and these parties her only source of activity and amusement. Why, then, was she so angry? They were simply voicing their opinions, and discussing the world as they saw it. Why did it bother her so much? Her own outlook had obviously been changed by her experiences so far in this war, but they had had no such experiences. She could hardly expect them to be different people just because she herself was.

Evelyn slipped through the doors onto a stone patio and took a deep breath. A couple standing just outside the doors turned to look at her, smiling in greeting.

"Oh hello! It's been ages since I've seen you, Miss Ainsworth," the gentleman said. "How are you? How is Rob?"

"We're both doing well, thank you, Sir James. And you? How is your wife?"

"Very well, thank you. She's home with a headache tonight, more's the pity."

"What a shame. Do give her my regards!"

Evelyn smiled and, murmuring that she was going for some air, moved away into the darker shadows of the garden. The further she moved from the house, the deeper the shadows became, and she exhaled in relief. The night was warm and the air was filled with the scent of the roses that the Ramsay's were famous for. Their rose garden, positioned to the back of property if Evelyn remembered correctly, was renowned throughout England. Taking a deep breath, she moved into the shrubbery, stepping off the path and disappearing into the darkness. This was what she needed. Just a few moments alone, in the garden, to gather her thoughts and calm her anger.

Emerging into a small seating nook, Evelyn looked around before sinking onto an ornate iron bench. The area was cloaked in shadows and she couldn't see very much at all, but she didn't mind. She just wanted to sit quietly, and she didn't need to see in order to do that. Breathing deeply, Evelyn felt herself begin to relax as she looked up at the night sky. Through the smog, she could just make out a few stars above. She thought of Miles and wondered if he was flying. Or was he finished for the day? What would he have said to those people inside? Would he have agreed with them?

Somehow, Evelyn didn't believe that he would have. Miles, while being every inch the aristocratic Lacey that he was, had never once come across to her as being a snob. But then, she admitted to herself, she never would have thought of herself as a snob. Yet, if she were brutally honest with herself, before the war, she probably would have held the same opinions as Maggie, Charles, and Gillian. As far as they were concerned, everyone had a place in society that was determined, not by what they did, but who they were born to. Women had their roles, and men had theirs. It was the way things always had been, and furthermore, it was the way they were supposed to be. It was how their class was bred, and how they were taught to think. But she had never cared much for that particular belief, and she knew Miles didn't either. No. She couldn't believe that Miles would have agreed with most of what was said this evening.

Evelyn frowned and pressed her lips together thoughtfully. Before the war, before being caught in France during the German offensive, would she have been offended at the perceived encroachment of lower classes into the Savoy? Or into the better cafés in Paris? In all honesty, Evelyn had no idea. She almost couldn't remember what the world had been like before the Nazis began turning Europe into a killing zone. When she was on that road in France, helping to bandage the wounded after the Stukas attacked and killed so many, she hadn't given any thought to what social class any of them were. It didn't seem to matter. Those driving the expensive automobiles were killed right next to those in the carts drawn by donkeys.

She thought of the old man who had buried his wife, and her chest tightened as sorrow crashed over her. His grief was no less because he was a poor man, just as hers was no more when she heard the gunshots that ended Peder's life. When such evil was killing without compunction, what did it matter who your parents were? Or in what section of the city your house was located? Or where you went to school?

And why the bloody hell did it matter if a few women in uniform ate lunch next to you in the Savoy?

Evelyn shook her head in disgust. Clearly, she no longer had anything in common with those of her own societal circle. Of course, to be fair, she never really had. She'd always had her own ideas, and her own way of living. Robbie said she marched to the beat of her own

## When Wolves Gather

drum, and he was right. She had never cared for the limitations and restrictions placed on her by society and their expectations. Thankfully, she was blessed with parents who understood that, even if her mother *did* bemoan it every chance she got. Her father had recognized that the world was changing, and he had encouraged his children to change with it—within reason. As a result, she and Robbie were adjusting to this war and all the challenges it brought easily. She would take that over the close-minded, self-absorbed patronizing of people like Charles and Gillian any day.

Evelyn was just preparing to stand and go back to the house when she heard voices on the other side of the hedge behind her. She paused, reluctant to emerge and be faced with more of the same before she'd even got back to the party. After hesitating, she settled back on her bench. She would wait until the guests had passed before leaving the protection of her little haven.

"I suppose I don't understand why I have to go at all."

A female spoke as footsteps grew closer. Evelyn recognized the voice immediately. It was Bethany Milner, a woman about her age, whom she'd never much cared for. She had a very distinctive, almost whining, lilt to her voice that grated on Evelyn's nerves every time she heard it. She sat still on her bench and reflected how glad she was to have chosen to remain hidden. Of all the people to run into in her current mood, Miss Milner was one of the worst.

"Everyone has to go. It's a meeting."

The voice that answered was also familiar to her, and Evelyn listened intently, trying to place the man with Bethany. It wasn't Lord Gilhurst. And it wasn't Jerry Stanford. For some reason, the voice reminded her of both men. She frowned. Who was it?

"But why? Isn't it too dangerous?"

"Mata doesn't think so. She believes the benefits of getting everyone together outweigh any…well, any threats."

Sir Ronald! Evelyn exhaled silently, her shoulders relaxing. It was Sir Ronald Clark. He was in Parliament with Lord Anthony and Mr. Stafford. That was why she thought of them at the sound of his voice. Now that the mystery was solved, Evelyn gazed into the darkness, waiting for them pass.

"Yes, but what if we're caught?"

"By whom?" Sir Ronald sounded amused. "Really, Bethany, you do worry over the littlest things."

"It's not little!" Bethany snapped. "I'm not sure that it's a wise thing to get everyone together at once. And I'm not sure that I should go. You know what my father would say if he knew!"

"You're quite old enough to be your own woman, my dear. What your father would or would not say really shouldn't enter into it."

The pair stopped almost directly on the other side of the hedge and Evelyn sat very still, barely daring to breathe. She had no idea what they were talking about, but if they discovered her eavesdropping, it would be unbelievably awkward.

"Besides, as I've told you numerous times before, your father is, unfortunately, going to end up on the losing side when this is all over. You don't want to be there with him, do you?"

"No, of course not." There was a short silence, then Evelyn heard an exhale. "Very well. If you say I must."

"I do. You really must stop worrying so. Once you see everyone who's in attendance, you'll feel much better. You'll be amazed at the people Mata has recruited into the cause. Really, you must stop thinking that it's just us. This is much larger than you can imagine. Well, you'll see for yourself."

"But what if we're caught?"

One of them had begun to move away again, but stopped with her question.

"Why does that concern you so much?" Sir Ronald asked.

"Why doesn't it concern you?" Bethany retorted. "If we're caught, we'll be arrested and interned…or worse. That doesn't bother you?"

"Not in the slightest. The Germans will be here by September at the latest. Once they arrive, we'll be released and hailed as heroes by the Nazis." Sir Ronald spoke in a low voice. "You must realize that the old ways are over. The old England is over. We'll be the first to begin building something new! These are exciting times, Bethany. Stop worrying about what it will take to get there, and understand that we are a part of history! What we do in the next few weeks will help determine the course of victory for the Führer!"

There was silence after that, then the pair began walking again.

"Who is Mata?" Bethany asked as they moved away.

"That, my dear, you will learn for yourself at the meeting. I think you'll find that the Round Club has many surprises in store for you."

The voices faded again into the distance but Evelyn remained rooted to her bench. Her heart was pounding as she struggled to wrap her mind around what she'd just overheard. She almost couldn't believe it, and yet, at the same time, she could! There was an organized group of traitors in London! And, if what Sir Ronald had just said was true, several of her peers were part of it!

# When Wolves Gather

Evelyn rose to find her legs shaking along with the rest of her. Good Lord, there were Nazi sympathizers right here at the Ramsay's! She may have spoken and laughed with one of them! They believed Hitler's forces would be in London by September, and they would welcome them!

Anger such as she'd never known coursed through her, stopping the trembling and causing her face to flush hot. They would welcome the downfall of England, and everything she stood for, and watch as their former friends and family were subjugated by the Nazis. They would aid and assist the SS and Gestapo. Did they have any idea at all what, exactly, would happen to all of their family and friends who didn't go along? Did they know what the Gestapo would do to them?

And all of this would come after Miles, and Robbie, and Fred had all died trying to defend this island and those very people who were plotting against everything they were fighting for!

Evelyn stood very still, her body rigid now with fury. They were traitors, and Bethany was right about one thing. If they were caught, they would be imprisoned and charged with treason against the crown.

But first they had to be caught.

And Evelyn was going to make sure that they were.

## Chapter Fourteen

Evelyn watched as the breeze rippled the water in the lake, lost in thought. The day was partly cloudy, with the sun emerging for a few moments at a time only to disappear again behind thick clouds. It was one of those days when Mother Nature didn't seem able to make up her mind what to do, and Evelyn felt much the same way.

Turning, she looked around and began walking slowly along the path around the lake. She was in St. James Park and, as she walked, she couldn't help but reflect that it wasn't helping to lift her gloomy mood. Now home to an air raid shelter, the royal park had been absorbed into the war effort along with all the civilians. Military installations had sprung up in most of the parks in London, and railings had been removed to be melted down for ammunition. All the parks housed air raid shelters now, and even Greenwich had anti-aircraft guns set up in the Flower Garden. The inevitable result was that the once lovely parks which served as peaceful refuge from the hustle and bustle of city life had taken on distinctly utilitarian mantles, reminding her forcibly that she was committed to fighting in a war much larger than all of them. Even their beloved parks could not escape it.

She sighed and continued to walk, her eyes wandering over the lake again. Despite the grimness of some of the new additions, the lake was still lovely and many Londoners had come out on this warm Saturday morning to relax in their little patch of nature. If there were stark reminders of the war around them, they didn't seem inclined to notice, choosing instead to walk the winding paths, or picnic on the grass near the water's edge. The sight of a couple in uniform seated on a blanket together made her smile, and she wondered if she and Miles would ever have the opportunity to picnic next to a lake.

"Evelyn!"

She turned as her name was called behind her and smiled, stopping to wait for Bill to join her.

"Good morning!" she greeted him as he drew closer. "Lovely day, isn't it?"

"Is it?" He glanced upwards and shook his head. "I don't think it can decide."

## When Wolves Gather

"That's what I thought, but it could be worse. It could be raining."

Bill held up the umbrella that he carried with him everywhere. "And that is why I carry this."

She laughed and turned to continue, Bill falling into step beside her. He looked down at her.

"Well? What was so important that you insisted we meet?" he asked. "You're on holiday, you know."

"Yes, I know." Evelyn shrugged. "But this seemed like something too important to leave until I return."

He frowned. "That doesn't sound good. What's on your mind?"

"Have you ever heard of something called the Round Club?"

He thought for a moment, then shook his head. "No, I don't believe that I have."

"No. I hadn't either until last night. I went to a party at the Ramsay's with Maryanne Gilhurst."

"Did you? I'm glad. You should be enjoying yourself. You deserve it. How are the Gilhursts?"

"Doing well. It was lovely to see everyone again. It's been a long time since I was able to socialize in Town."

"You're being careful, of course?" he asked, shooting her a sharp look.

Evelyn laughed and waved her hand.

"Yes, of course. They believe I'm an officer in the WAAF. There's no reason for them to think otherwise."

He visibly relaxed.

"Good. Did you enjoy the Ramsay's party? I've heard that they still pack the rooms, despite the rations making a dent in their usual refreshments."

"I think I would have enjoyed it very much if…" She sighed and shook her head. "I don't know. They've all changed so much. Or perhaps it's me that changed."

Bill nodded slowly. "That was bound to happen, Evelyn. You've seen things that, well, change a person. You're not the same person you were before the war."

"No. No, I suppose not. I certainly don't have the patience to listen to much of the drivel that was being poured about last night. I went outside to get some air, and that's when I heard about the Round Club. I thought I should tell you about what I heard because, well, it involves national security."

He frowned. "Go on."

She stopped and turned to face him.

"There's no delicate way of putting it, so I'll just say it. I believe it's a group of Nazi sympathizers and traitors right here in London."

He stared at her.

"What?"

"The two people speaking didn't see me. I was sitting on a bench behind a hedge, so they spoke quite freely, believing they were alone." Evelyn began walking again. "They were discussing a meeting of the Round Club, and one of them was nervous that they would be caught and put in prison. The other said quite clearly that the Nazis would be in London by September and, if they were arrested, they would be released then and hailed as heroes. It was quite obvious to me that they fully expect England to fall, and are working to ensure that the Germans have a welcoming committee when they arrive!"

Bill was quiet for a moment, then he let out a sigh.

"I supposed it's inevitable," he finally said. "There are Fifth Columnists and other fringe parties that would welcome a regime change here in England. The Security Service is well aware of them, and is working to apprehend those that they can."

"But this isn't a fringe political party," Evelyn told him. "This is a group of our peers. These are high-ranking members of London society. They can't simply be dismissed as disgruntled workers or national socialist idealists."

He looked at her sharply. "How do you know?"

"I recognized the two speaking. You would have as well. They're quite well-known, respected members of society. And anyway, they were attending a party at the Ramsay's. They could hardly have been two individuals off the street, could they?"

Bill was silent for a moment, then he let out a sound suspiciously like a groan.

"You might as well tell me who they were," he said. "If it's as you say, I'll need to know anyway."

"I know." Evelyn stopped and looked at him, her gaze troubled. "I hate to do it, though. I feel like a school yard snitch."

"Yes, it's distasteful, but it must be done. Who was it?"

"Miss Bethany Milner and Sir Ronald Clark."

Bill was startled, but he managed to hide it swiftly. Nodding once, he began walking again, his umbrella tapping on the pavement.

"And you're sure about what you heard?"

"Yes."

"You'd best tell me everything."

## When Wolves Gather

Evelyn nodded and repeated the conversation that she overheard, leaving nothing out. When she was finished, he grunted in acknowledgment and they walked in silence for a bit, his umbrella keeping up its steady tattoo. Evelyn walked beside him, wondering what he was thinking. Was he as angry as she was?

While she lay awake most of the night fuming over the audacity of the pair, she had hatched a plan to at least discover who might be part of the so-called club. She knew it wasn't any of her business, really, but she couldn't sit idly by while her own peers were planning to help the Nazis in any way that they could. She also knew that Bill would balk at allowing her to do anything to help apprehend or uncover the traitors. Her job was with MI6, not the Security Service. But she was determined to do *something*. She just had to decide how to broach it with him.

"While I acknowledge that it's very upsetting, this isn't our business." Bill finally broke the silence, echoing her own thoughts. "This is the province of the Security Service. I'm sure they're aware of this Round Club and have it under surveillance. This isn't something you need concern yourself with."

"I know that it isn't in our regular purview, but I'm in a perfect position to obtain information about them," Evelyn said. "It seems rather silly for me to do nothing when I can be of some assistance."

"I'm sure MI5 has someone on it already." He stopped and looked down at her. "This isn't our concern. You're on holiday, for God's sake. You're supposed to be resting!"

"And I *was* resting! But really, there're only so many lunches and so much shopping I can do," she replied with a quick smile. "You can't honestly expect me to simply sit back and cool my heels when there are people—traitors—right here in London, planning God knows what. You've trained me too well, Bill, and I'm afraid you've created a bit of a monster. I can't just stand by and ignore intelligence when it falls into my lap, even if it *does* involve British subjects on English soil. Lord knows I wasn't looking for it, but now that I have it, I feel that I must act on it."

He shot her a look of amusement mixed with resignation.

"I've heard that tone before," he muttered. "And you're right. I trained you to do this very thing, but on foreign soil. Not here."

"What does it matter where the intelligence comes from if it will help us get a leg up in this war?"

He grunted.

"I can't very well argue with that, but you knew that before you said it. Well? What plan have you come up with? I know you have something up your sleeve, so what is it?"

Evelyn stopped walking and watched as two women on bicycles cycled past. Then she turned to face him.

"Sir Clark was very confident that the Nazis would be in London by September. He's getting his information from somewhere, and my guess is that they have contact with someone in Germany. Perhaps agents in the Abwehr, or perhaps even the SD. You know as well as I do that many of our peers, ourselves included, spent time in Germany before the war. They made friends there, and moved in the elite society of the Nazis. Why, even Sir Mulligan was on friendly terms with Hermann Göring."

"Yes. Go on."

"If this Round Club is predominantly made up of members of society, and I think that it must be or Sir Clark wouldn't be quite so enthusiastic, then it isn't a stretch to believe that they must be providing information to the Germans by way of agents or contacts on the continent."

"Agreed."

"Well, an organization like that will always need more contacts to move information," she said with a shrug. "They would want someone who they believe shares their sympathies, and who has a vested interest in seeing the Germans win the war. They would also want someone who has contacts in Berlin. A German."

"And you want to be that German?" he demanded in a low voice incredulously.

"I can speak German with a Berlin accent well enough to fool an Untersturmführer in the Sicherheitsdienst. If I can fool Herr Voss, I can certainly convince an Englishman that I'm German-born. All we have to do is present me as a contact who can get information out of England and to Berlin, and then we can control the flow of information. We can choose what is released and what is not. We can control the damage."

"And if they already have a contact?"

"I'll remove them from the equation."

Bill let out an exclamation and began walking again, his face a thundercloud.

"You can't run around England eliminating British subjects at will, Jian," he hissed. "That's not how it's done. We're English, for God's sake, not savages!"

## When Wolves Gather

"I didn't say eliminate," she protested with a laugh. "Heavens, I'm not that blood-thirsty! I said *remove*. I'm sure we can arrange to have them arrested for something."

"And then you step in as a replacement?"

"Exactly."

Bill was silent for a long time, then he shook his head.

"MI5 will never go for it. They're in the middle of a regime change. Kell was removed in June and the new director has his hands full trying to get everything reorganized. From all accounts, Kell left the place in a devil of a mess. That's partly the reason that they're having such trouble keeping track of the refugees coming into the country, as well as the threats that are already here. It's also the reason we're working to find Henry ourselves instead of turning it over to the Security Service."

"Oh, that's all right. I know someone over there. He's quite high up in the command chain, I believe."

Bill looked at her in surprise.

"What?"

"He was a friend of my father's, rather like you were," she said, flashing him a grin. "You know him as well."

"Who?"

"Anthony Marrow."

Bill raised his eyebrows. "I didn't know he was friendly with Robert." He paused, then a smile twisted his lips. "Although, I can't say that I'm surprised. Your father was a charming devil. He cultivated friendships and contacts wherever he went, home and abroad. You get that from him, you know. Watching you is very much an experience in déjà vu."

Evelyn swallowed the sudden lump in her throat at the mention of her father. Bill rarely, if ever, spoke of him. Hearing his casual observation on their similarities gave her a jolt of melancholy.

And guilt.

"Well, I believe Marrow is in a position of some authority in MI5," she said, clearing her throat.

"Yes. Yes, he is."

"I'll take this to him, then."

Bill looked at her. "Why haven't you gone to him already?"

"I would never do something like that without telling you first," she exclaimed, her eyes flaring. "I'm not trying to hide anything from you. I just want these bastards caught."

Bill let out a laugh at that.

"Well, I can't fault you for that." He sobered. "Very well. If you're determined to spend your holiday chasing down Nazis, I shan't forbid it. But Marrow can never know you work for us. You understand? No one can ever know. He can't have even the slightest inkling that you're not who he thinks you are."

"Yes, of course. Don't worry. As far as he will know, I'm simply an Assistant Section Officer in the WAAF who overheard something and brought it to him because I didn't know where else to go." Evelyn twinkled up at him. "Trust me. He'll never dream I could possibly be anything else."

# When Wolves Gather

# Chapter Fifteen

*28th July, 1940*
*My Dear Evelyn,*
*It was wonderful to hear from you. I'm so glad you're getting some time off at last. Are you enjoying yourself? How are Tante Adele and Auntie Agatha getting along? I think Rob is waiting for word that a second war has broken out in Ainsworth Manor.*

*We've been flying constantly. We were actually scrambled the other day, if you can believe that. Jerry is doing everything he can to stop our convoys, and another of our destroyers, Codrington, was sunk yesterday in Dover. The poor blighters are getting hit hard, despite our best efforts. I feel like we're very much in the fight now. I just pray that we can hold them off. The convoys are only the start. It's only a matter of time before they turn to England itself. It's already started with their sporadic bombings of coastal towns.*

*Ashmore, our CO, has managed to obtain permission for some twenty-four leaves for us. I'm not sure when, exactly, but we're told it will be in the next week. The Yank is keen to meet you, and I wouldn't be opposed to seeing you again myself. Rob will be there as well. Would you be willing and able to meet in London for a night out? I'd love to have dinner and a dance.*

*I'm off to dispersal now for another long day. What awaits us up in the blue yonder? The sun is shining and the forecast is fair, so I expect it will be quite a busy day.*

*I hope you're having a lovely holiday. Say a prayer for us when you have a moment. We can use all the help that we can get.*

*Always yours,*
*Flight Lieutenant Miles Lacey*

Evelyn looked up from her tea when the front door bell rang. She was seated in the kitchen, flipping through the newspaper while she finished her breakfast. Standing, she wiped her mouth with a napkin, then turned to go out of the kitchen and down the hallway to the front of the house. When she opened the door, a slim young boy whom she recognized as one of Broadway's couriers stood on the stoop.

"Morning, miss," he said, touching his cap. "A message for you."

He held out a sealed envelope and Evelyn reached out to take it.

"Thank you. Are you to wait for a reply?"

"Not as they said, miss. Just dropping off."

He grinned and waved and turned to leap off the step. Evelyn watched as he ducked around a couple strolling along the pavement and hurried away down the street, his errand completed. She smiled and closed the door. The boy had no idea who he worked for, nor did he probably care. He was paid to deliver messages, and that was an end to it. Sometimes she envied that innocence.

Walking into the front drawing room, Evelyn ripped open the envelope and pulled out the single sheet of paper. The message was coded and she went over to the desk to sit down. Opening the desk drawer, she pulled out the small, nondescript book that contained the standard codes. This was different from the codebooks she took onto the continent. This was a much simpler code, used only to maintain standard security here in England. She reached for a pencil and bent over the message, decoding it. When she was finished, she sat back in the chair thoughtfully.

RADIO MOSCOW BROADCAST THIS MORNING. THERE WILL BE CLEAR SKIES OVER THE RED SQUARE.

Nothing else was in the message. Nothing else needed to be said. The people who monitored international broadcasts had been told to listen for that specific phrase in the broadcasts coming from Moscow. If they heard it, they were to send a message to her immediately, wherever she may be. That was it. That was the extent of their, and MI6's, involvement.

Shustov.

The Soviet NKVD agent had something for her. They had set up the arrangement during a hasty meeting in Brussels before Hitler unleashed his Blitzkrieg across Europe. Evelyn had then put in place a

## When Wolves Gather

system where she could contact him in reverse if she had need of him. The system was outside of MI6 control, and that was something she knew both Bill and Jasper were not happy with. She hadn't actually thought that it would ever come into use, if the truth were known. Yet here was the code from Moscow.

Getting up, Evelyn picked up the message and the codebook and turned to leave the drawing room. She couldn't waste time. The breakfast things would have to wait. She had to change, and then she had to go out and send a telegram to the Bellevue Palace Hotel.

There was no holiday from Vladimir Lyakhov.

### Paris, France

Hans nodded briskly to the soldier standing guard outside of the cell. He saluted and turned to unlock the iron door, standing aside so that Hans could go into the small, stone-walled room. A minuscule window high up near the ceiling allowed a sliver of light to filter into the gloom below, slicing through the stale air that stank of urine and blood. He stopped just inside the door and studied the man sitting on the floor in the corner.

Yves Michaud was leaning heavily against the stones, his head hanging down over his chest. When Hans entered, he rolled his head back to lean it on the wall, lifting his face towards the door. One eye was completely swollen shut while the other was almost closed, only a slit allowing him to peer up at Voss. His jaw had been broken, causing his face to swell until he was barely recognizable. Blood was caked around his mouth and nose, and his shirt front was covered with more of the same. At first Hans didn't think the man could see him at all, but then his lips moved.

"The...vines?" he rasped out.

Voss let out a short laugh.

"You and your grapes!" he exclaimed. "Yes. They are intact, as is your house. You would be better served to be as worried about yourself."

Yves stared at him through the slit of his one eye. It was doubtful that he would have answered even if he had the energy and his jaw was not broken. After a second, Hans turned to call out the door.

"Come! Get him to his feet. I'm moving him," he ordered in German.

The guard called to another soldier and a moment later the two of them entered the cell.

"Be careful," Voss told them. "I don't want his face to undergo any more trauma. Much more and he will never speak again."

They nodded and moved forward. They each took an arm and hauled the old man to his feet.

"Not that you're capable, but don't do anything stupid," Hans said, switching back to French as they began to drag the man forward. "I'm moving you somewhere more comfortable. If you cooperate, I may even call in a surgeon to look at that jaw bone."

The soldiers passed through the cell door, hauling Yves along between them. He couldn't walk. He couldn't even support his own head. Following, Hans reflected that it was as if the men were dragging a rag doll. The human body could only withstand so much before the brain instructed the muscles to cease function. The brain was really a fantastic thing. Self-preservation was its priority. In order to keep Yves alive, and therefore itself, the brain knew that they could not waste energy on simple tasks such as walking or supporting themselves. They had to conserve energy if they were to have any chance at all. Amazing, really. The body could be broken, but the brain would keep it going until it could go no further.

"Take him upstairs. Put him in the back room and have someone clean him up. Ensure that they take care with his face. I don't want any more damage inflicted," he instructed, turning to go down a narrow corridor. "Stay with him until I come. If any additional harm comes to his face, I will hold you both personally responsible. Am I clear?"

"Yes, Herr Obersturmbannführer Voss."

Hans strode down the narrow corridor until he came to a stairwell. Jogging up the steps, he wondered if Yves would be willing to talk now. Two separate interrogators had been at it for two days, but he hadn't said a word. Until this morning. Then he'd simply said one: Voss.

If Hans wasn't so convinced that Yves had been making new papers and identities for the missing members of France's intelligence network, he never would have bothered with the old man. But Eisenjager, as everyone in the SS knew, did not make mistakes.

Hans had one job in Paris: to locate and apprehend all former intelligence agents. Once that had been accomplished, he was to monitor and arrest any new resistance members that emerged. He had been given a large unit of SS soldiers and Gestapo to help him achieve this lofty goal, and he had every intention of exceeding

## When Wolves Gather

Standartenführer Dreschler's expectations. His superior had entrusted Paris, the most coveted assignment, to Voss despite his failure to apprehend the courier who had carried stolen plans through Europe a month before. He would prove to him that the trust was not unfounded.

And he would begin with Yves Michaud.

Reaching the top of the stairs, Hans threw open the door and emerged into a large and brightly lit hallway. They had taken over a police station in the heart of Paris, as well as the large hotel across the street. The police accommodations were more than acceptable, and the hotel was a luxury that Hans was very happy to have. The theatre was not far, and the restaurants were also very close by. They had been closed for the first week they were here, but now they were slowly reopening. The Parisians were beginning to come out from their hiding, and soon they would adjust to the new regime.

He went down the wide hallway towards an office at the end. It would take some time for them to get Yves upstairs, into the more comfortable holding cell, and cleaned up and comfortable. He would review some notes before joining him. If the old man had any sense, he would agree to Voss's terms. If he didn't, well, then that would be the end of Yves Michaud.

**London**

The bell rang above the door as Evelyn entered the small, neighborhood shop. A woman stood speaking with the man behind the counter while her little boy, dressed in short trousers and a worn jumper, waited beside her. Evelyn looked around and moved over to a stand where the newspapers were stacked neatly in rows. She wasn't familiar with this particular neighborhood, which was close to the East End of London, but any feeling of discomfort that she might have felt a few years ago was nonexistent now. Her travels had quickly cured her of any feelings of being an outsider.

"Right. Well, careful as you go, Mrs. May," the man said as the woman gathered her purchases and placed them in her shopping bag. "Give my regards to Gerald."

"I will. Thank you."

The woman took her son's hand and turned towards the door, casting a curious look at Evelyn. She nodded politely and the woman smiled back before the bell rang again and she and the boy went out.

"Can I help, miss?"

The man was regarding her with a look of polite inquiry and Evelyn turned from the rack, a newspaper in one hand.

"Thank you. Just the newspaper," she said, walking over to the counter.

"I haven't seen you in here before, have I?" he asked, ringing up the newspaper. "Are you new to the neighborhood?"

"No. I was just passing."

He nodded and took her money, making change.

"Lovely day today, isn't it?" he asked.

"Yes. Quite lovely."

"Makes it hard to think there's a war on," he said, handing her the change.

Evelyn murmured in agreement and took her newspaper, turning towards the door. A moment later she was back on the pavement and she turned to walk up the street to the tea room she'd spied on her way here.

She had contacted the Bellevue Palace Hotel yesterday, and had received a telegram back last night. It had instructed her to come here, to this particular shop, to purchase a particular newspaper, at precisely eleven o'clock. She wasn't to take the top paper, but the third one down in the stack. That was where the instructions ended. The tea room was her own idea.

It was rather disconcerting, really. She'd been contacted by Shustov and had expected to be given a message in response to her contacting the Hotel in Bern. Instead, she'd been sent to pick up the message, right here in London. Was Shustov here? No. She dismissed that idea as quickly as it came into her head. It wasn't possible for the Soviet agent to come to London. It was unusual that he was allowed to traverse Europe at all, which spoke volumes of his rank in the NKVD more than anything else. But even that respect would stop short of Moscow allowing him to enter England unofficially and unaccompanied.

But someone must be here in London. Someone had inserted the message into the newspaper.

Coming on the heels of the discovery of the Round Club's existence, Evelyn admitted to herself, as she sat at a table near a sunny window in the tea room, that she was feeling rather dazed by everything. Each time she came home to England, she felt as if she

## When Wolves Gather

were returning to safety. Now it appeared that home wasn't entirely safe either, not for people like herself. Between traitors in London, and now a Soviet agent, Evelyn was beginning to feel as though she were back on the continent, and perhaps in enemy territory.

The feeling was a disheartening one. After all, if she couldn't relax and let her guard down in England, then what on earth were they fighting for?

"Good morning, miss!" A cheerful, matronly woman came over to the table with a wide smile. "Lovely day today, isn't it?"

"Yes, indeed," Evelyn agreed with an answering smile.

"And what can I get for you?"

"A pot of tea, please." Evelyn glanced at her watch. "Do you have any sandwiches?"

"Yes. I have cucumber, cheese and onion, or cheese and tomato. Which would you like, dear?"

"I'll have the cucumber, please."

The woman nodded and left her, and Evelyn turned her attention out of the window. Cars and lorries jostled for space on the busy street while women in house dresses and men in suits shared the pavement with workers and military personnel alike. London was bustling as usual, and she found a strange comfort in the busy chaos. While she was taken aback to realize that there were some in London who didn't share the same feeling of patriotism that others did, she had to believe that they were in a minority. And the men and women hurrying about their daily lives outside the window reminded her that, while some were trying to undermine everything England stood for, others were fighting to preserve it.

"Here you are, miss."

The kindly woman was back with a plate of cucumber sandwiches and a pot of tea with cup and saucer. Evelyn started in surprise. She had been staring blindly out of the window for much longer than she'd realized.

"Thank you."

The woman left again and Evelyn poured tea into her cup before reaching for the newspaper. It was time to get her head out of the clouds and see why Shustov had contacted her.

As she opened the paper to the classified section, a frown crossed her face. Who did Lyakhov have in London? Was there more than one? Her mind went back to the man in Stockholm, Risto Niva. He had been an NKVD agent, and he had been very confident in the fact that the Soviet Union had spies ensconced in London. In fact, he seemed both surprised and amused when it became obvious that she had no idea of their existence. At the time, it had seemed fantastic. Soviet spies in London? And yet, someone had inserted a message into the newspaper and placed it where she would retrieve it in a small, unassuming corner shop.

Folding the paper back, Evelyn scanned the page of ads and personal requests. She had no idea what she was looking for. The telegram had said simply to turn to the classified ads. Something caught her attention as she was scanning the ads and Evelyn looked closer. Someone had underlined a few words in pencil. Then, as she examined the page more closely, she found that several groups of words and some single letters were underlined. She sucked in her breath and opened her handbag to pull out the little notebook and pencil that she always carried with her. She opened it and began writing down the underlined words in order from the top of the page downwards. When she was finished, she sat back and let out a soft gasp.

ONE OF ROUND CLUB IN CONTACT WITH HANS VOSS. SEEKING INFORMATION ON YOUR WHEREABOUTS. PROCEED WITH CAUTION.

**When Wolves Gather**

# Chapter Sixteen

Hans walked into the holding cell and closed the door behind him before turning to look at Yves. He had been cleaned up, as instructed. The dried blood was gone from his face, revealing split and cracked skin. His shirt had been exchanged for a worn, standard prisoner's tunic, and a cloth strip had been tied around his head and under his jaw to hold it in place. He was sitting on a narrow cot built into the wall, his back against the wall and one leg drawn up on the thin mattress. His head had been leaning back against the wall, but as Hans entered, it lifted so that he could watch him through the slit of his one eye.

"You are comfortable?" Hans asked.

The old man looked at him but didn't answer. Hans sighed and pulled a wooden chair from the corner, seating himself facing him.

"It doesn't bring me any joy or satisfaction to see a man of your age in this condition," he said, crossing his legs comfortably. "There is no need for it. All I want is information. If you tell me what I want to know, there is no reason you cannot return to your home and your precious vines."

Yves said nothing, but he continued to look at Hans, clearly willing to listen. Hans considered him for a moment, then sighed again.

"Are you able to speak?"

"With…pain…" the older man rasped out in a whisper.

Hans nodded and got up. He opened the door and called to a guard.

"Bring me a pad of paper," he commanded, "and something to write with."

"Yes, Herr Obersturmbannführer."

Hans went back to his seat and sat once more.

"I have sent for some paper. You may write down anything you would say," he said magnanimously. "There is no reason for you to struggle to speak and increase your pain. If you cooperate, I will send for a doctor."

A moment later, the soldier came in with a pad of paper and a pencil. He glanced at the man on the cot as he handed the items to Hans.

"Is it wise to give the prisoner a pencil, Obersturmbannführer Voss?" he asked in a low voice. "What if he attacks you?"

"The man barely has the energy to lift his head, and probably will not be able to write without difficulty," Hans replied. "I do not think he will be much of a threat. If you are concerned, however, you may stay. Stand over there, if you must."

"Thank you, Herr Obersturmbannführer."

The soldier went over to stand in the corner, his eyes fixed on Yves. Hans returned his attention to the older man.

"Sturmmann Schmidt is concerned that you will attack me with this pencil if I allow you to write your answers," he told him. "I caution you not to try."

Yves grunted in response and Hans nodded, leaning forward to place the paper and pencil on the cot next to him.

"Very well. We shall begin." He sat back and crossed his legs once again. "I know you were in the practice of providing identification papers for members of the intelligence community. There is no use in denying it. However, we found no evidence of your activities as a forger at your house. I can only assume that you destroyed your equipment before we arrived. Or perhaps you have hidden it somewhere else. If that is the case, we will find it in time. It makes no difference. I am not particularly interested in your equipment. What I *am* interested in is who you provided identities for."

Hans paused and studied Yves for a moment.

"In May, three people came to see you. Two women and a man. Do you remember?"

Yves was still for a moment, then he very slowly nodded his head once.

"Good. I will tell you what I know, then you will fill in what I don't. Understood?"

Another slow and single nod.

"This trio came to see you and stayed for two nights. When they left you, they drove south, presumably to avoid the advancing troops. You provided documentation for one, or more, of these people. I know that at least one of the party was a member of the French intelligence. I'm interested in the women, the blonde in particular. Who was she?"

Yves was still for a moment, then he reached awkwardly for the pad and pencil. Hans watched as he struggled to write with a hand that was surprisingly steady for one so weak. After a moment, Yves had written one word: English.

Hans felt a twinge of surprise.

## When Wolves Gather

"English? You are sure?"

The man struggled to write again, and this time it was much longer before Hans had his answer.

French accent - clothes - but overheard things. Worked for English.

Hans sat back thoughtfully. Although outwardly calm, excitement was rolling through him. There could only be one blonde and English spy that moved so freely in France.

"What identity did you give her?"

The man wrote again.

Not her. Man.

"The man? You didn't provide papers for the woman?" Hans asked sharply, his eyes boring into Yves face.

Yves shook his head once and Hans frowned. That wasn't what he was expecting to hear at all. He had no idea who the man was, but he hadn't considered that anyone other than the woman would be in need of false identity papers.

"I want you to think very carefully, Monsieur Michaud," he said slowly. "Your freedom depends on your telling the truth. I want the names of all the people you provided documentation for, and we will get to those, but right now, I must know the truth about these three people. You only provided documents to the man? You are sure?"

Yves nodded once.

"What is the name you provided him?"

Hans watched as the old man wrote again. It was clear that it was a painful struggle for him to bend his head to see what he was writing, but Hans felt no remorse. The man had brought this on himself. If he had cooperated from the very beginning, he would not be in this condition.

Robert Lavigne.

Hans nodded, satisfied that the man had written the truth. There had been no hesitation.

"And the women? What were their names?"

It took the man longer to write this time, but Hans could detect no attempt to stall in his awkward attempts to write. Rather, the man was getting tired. When he finally finished, Hans looked at the names.

Geneviève Dufour - Josephine Rousseau.

"And which of these was the English agent?"

Yves pointed to the first name and Hans nodded briskly.

"Good. Very good." He picked up the pad and pencil and stood. "You are getting tired. I will arrange for a doctor to come this afternoon. For now, rest."

Hans turned towards the door, motioning for the soldier to leave before him. Once the guard was out of the room, he turned back to Yves.

"I believe that you've told the truth here," he said calmly. "That is good. If you continue to assist me, you will be back to tending your vines soon. I will ensure that you are kept comfortable here until I have everything I need. Get some rest now."

He left the cell and strode down the corridor, hearing the guard close and lock the door. If everything went well and according to plan, Yves would give him all the names of the intelligence agents he'd helped disappear. Then he would let him go, but keep him under surveillance. Sooner or later, more would come to see the old man. As they did, and as he passed their names onto Voss, what remained of the Allied intelligence network in France would be eliminated. And any fledgling resistance that might spring up would also be crushed. But more than all of that, Hans Voss now had a name to put to the English spy known to him as Rätsel.

Operation Nightshade was resumed.

⦿

Evelyn entered the bookshop located near Covent Garden and was immediately embraced by the warm and comforting smell of bound leather and old, worn pages that had survived the test of time. The bell above her rang cheerfully as she entered and bright sunlight sliced through the interior, picking out the dust particles dancing in the air. Just as quickly as it had entered, the light disappeared as the door closed behind her. Looking around, she took a deep breath, enjoying the hushed quiet of the shop. There were a few patrons browsing the shelves of used books mixed in with new published works, and as she entered, one man slid the book he was examining back onto the shelf and turned towards her.

He stood fairly tall and had black hair that was streaked with gray. Glasses perched on his nose and he was dressed neatly and unremarkably in a dark suit and overcoat, both of which were impeccably tailored to him. In fact, the superior tailoring was the only thing that made the man stand apart from any other in shop. In every other way, he was quite average and unassuming.

## When Wolves Gather

Evelyn smiled and moved towards him, holding out her hand.

"Why, my dear Mr. Marrow!" she exclaimed. "How nice to see you again!"

His lips curved and blue eyes twinkled behind his glasses as he grasped her hand. "Miss Ainsworth! Imagine running into you here. How are you?"

"I'm very well thank you." She released his hand and lowered her voice. "I'm glad you received my message. Thank you for coming so promptly."

"I was surprised to receive it, I must admit," he said, lowering his voice to match hers. "I'd heard that you were with the WAAFs and stationed in Scotland. What brings you all the way to London?"

"I'm afraid your information is rather outdated. I *am* in the WAAF, but I've been stationed in Northolt since January."

He let out a rather bitter laugh, shaking his head. "Have you? Well, I'm not surprised to hear that. Old information seems to be the norm in London these days, unfortunately."

Evelyn frowned. "You're exaggerating, surely?"

"Am I?" He sighed and forced a smile. "Perhaps I am. Never mind. What's on your mind? This obviously isn't a social call, given that we're meeting in a rather inferior bookshop rather than at Claridge's for lunch."

"I've been coming here ever since we returned from Hong Kong!" Evelyn protested with a laugh. "It may not look like much, but the gentleman who runs it really is a lovely man. He used to let me spend hours in an armchair in the back, poring over books that I probably had no business knowing about, much less reading. And he really does get in some rare gems and fantastic first editions."

"I had no idea you were such a bluestocking," Marrow said with a smile that belied his words. "Although, it shouldn't surprise me. Your father was always reading something or other."

"Yes. He loved his books." She smiled a little sadly, then shrugged. "He encouraged me to read widely, and I think I gave him a run for his money in that regard. But I didn't ask you here to discuss books."

"So I gathered."

"The thing is, I suddenly remembered that you used to work for the Security Service," she said, lowering her voice. "Do you still?"

He nodded. "Yes."

"Oh good!" She sighed in relief and moved around a display of books so that they were hidden from view from the few other patrons. "I wasn't sure, and I really didn't know where else to go, you see."

Marrow frowned and studied her for a moment. "What's wrong? Has something happened?"

"Yes, I'm afraid it has. Oh, not to me! Don't misunderstand. We're all right as rain in the Ainsworth household. Rather, I believe I overheard something the other evening and, well, I don't know what to do about it. I probably shouldn't have contacted you, but I honestly don't know anyone else who might be able to advise me."

"Advise you? What on earth did you overhear, Evelyn?" Marrow asked in concern.

"Well, I think I've uncovered a plot to commit treason!"

Marrow blinked and his frown grew. He drew her deeper into the store and further away from any listening ears.

"I think perhaps you should begin at the beginning," he said. "Where were you? And what, exactly, did you hear?"

"I was at a party at the Ramsay's. It was terribly crowded and I was getting rather annoyed at several conversations about the inconveniences of rationing, and the lax social standards that seem to be becoming the norm. Would you believe that some of my old acquaintances think it's appalling that women in uniform are being allowed into the Savoy and The Dorchester?" Evelyn demanded in a low voice. "As if we are lepers to be avoided!"

A faint smile crossed his face and Marrow nodded.

"Yes. I've heard the same arguments. You must realize that some people simply don't understand the need for auxiliary forces at all, let alone the role of women in the war effort," he said. "I wouldn't let it bother you too much. Those opinions are quickly becoming the minority as more and more women are proving their capabilities."

"Well, I quite agree, but it didn't lessen the shock at hearing old friends speak so plainly, especially in front of me. Why, they know I'm a WAAF!"

"I don't suppose they consider that you're really a woman in uniform. After all, you were one of them long before you donned the RAF blue. You're not wearing the uniform now, and I don't suppose you were the other night," he pointed out.

"No."

"Then it would be easy for them to forget that you are, indeed, a woman in uniform."

Evelyn shook her head.

"It still rankles, though. But that's all to explain why I went outside for some air halfway through the evening. I needed to get away for a few minutes, and I couldn't find Maryanne to leave altogether."

"Maryanne?"

## When Wolves Gather

"Gilhurst. Lord Anthony Gilhurst's sister, you know. We'd gone to the party together, you see. In fact, she's the reason I came to London."

"Ah, yes, of course." He tilted his head questioningly. "Why are you in London? Are you on leave?"

"Yes. I was at Ainsworth with my mother, but Maryanne wrote and said there was a party, and so I came to London. I've been thoroughly enjoying myself! I'd forgotten how much I miss everyone! Well, almost everyone," she amended with a flash of a grin. "Maryanne and I have been having a lovely time."

"Until the Ramsay's party?" Marrow prompted gently when she didn't continue.

Evelyn sighed and nodded.

"Yes. I was outside in the garden, sitting on a bench behind a hedge, when I heard two people talking on the other side. They didn't see me, and I didn't want to cause any awkwardness, so I remained where I was until they were gone. Unfortunately, I overheard quite a bit in that time."

Marrow watched her face for a moment, waiting for her to continue.

"Oh, now it all seems silly when I think it over," Evelyn finally said, shrugging and looking at him helplessly. "It's probably nothing."

"Why don't you tell me what you heard and I'll decide if it's nothing?" he suggested gently.

She looked at him for a moment, then took a deep breath and nodded.

"All right." She lowered her voice even more. "They were discussing a meeting, and the woman didn't want to go. She was afraid of being caught. She said quite clearly that if they were caught, they would be arrested and interned, or worse. The man didn't seem to think there was very much danger. He told her that the Nazis would be in London by September at the latest, and if they *were* arrested, they would be released when the Nazis came. He said they would then be hailed as heroes."

"You're sure of this? He said the Nazis would be here in September?" Marrow asked sharply.

Evelyn nodded.

"Yes. Quite sure. He went on to say that she would feel much better once she'd been to the meeting and seen everyone who was part of The Round Club."

"The Round Club? You're sure that's what he said?"

"Yes. He said she'd be surprised at the members, and then she would be much more at ease."

Marrow was quiet for a long moment, then he brought his sharp, blue eyes back to her face.

"Was there anything else?"

"There was quite a bit. He spoke of someone named Mata, who I think might be one of the leaders of this Round Club. He also told his companion that her father would be on the losing side when this was all over. I got the impression that he was discussing all of England losing to the Germans, and what would happen to the leaders in government who were opposing Hitler. He also spoke about the old ways, and the old England, being over." Evelyn stopped and pretended to think for a moment. "In fact, I got the distinct impression that, somehow, they are actively trying to help facilitate that."

They were both silent for a moment, Marrow lost in thought and Evelyn watching him through her lashes. She felt as though her performance was less than convincing, but he wasn't showing any signs of not believing her. And why should he? Everything she'd told him was true. The only thing that wasn't, and what she personally thought was lacking in her performance, was that she didn't know what to do with the information. Evelyn knew exactly what to do with the information, but playing the helpless young woman was the quickest way to get him to do what she wanted him to do.

After what seemed like ages, Marrow let out a long sigh and turned his attention back to her face.

"You were right to bring this to me," he said slowly. "It isn't nothing."

"Do you think there's something there, then? That it's really what it sounds like?" she asked.

"Oh yes. There's something there all right." Marrow moved deeper into the shadows of the bookshelves. "We've known about the Round Club for some time, but we haven't been able to discover who, exactly, is heading it up, or even who the primary leaders are. It's very difficult to find any information about them at all. We do have one or two leads in the lower members, but trying to determine who is part of the inner circle is something else entirely. We've been trying to infiltrate them for some time now, but haven't had much luck."

"You believe they're really that exclusive?" Evelyn asked.

"Oh yes." Marrow considered her for a moment. "I don't suppose you recognized the voices you overheard, did you?"

Evelyn feigned surprised. "What? Of course I did! Didn't I say?"

## When Wolves Gather

"No."

"Oh! I could have sworn I mentioned it. It was Miss Bethany Milner and Sir Ronald Clark."

Marrow sucked in his breath. "Miss Milner? Lord Giles' daughter?"

"Yes." Evelyn looked at him, noting that while he was obviously startled at Bethany's involvement, Sir Clark's didn't seem to be a surprise at all. "I suppose if she's involved, they *are* rather exclusive," she continued thoughtfully. "Do you really believe that members of society are actually supportive of the Nazis? It seems fantastic!"

"Unfortunately, that is exactly what I believe. There are many who don't want to think that it's possible, or want to ignore that it's happening, but we know that it is." Marrow shook his head and took off his glasses, rubbing his eyes. "This is just another nail in the coffin, so to speak. We know the Round Club is active, we know that it's comprised of members of all levels of society, and we know that it's based right here in London. What we don't know is who is in charge, who is funding it, what they're planning, or how, exactly, they're aiding the Germans."

He dropped his hand and settled his glasses back on his face.

"But none of that is your concern. Thank you for bringing this latest information to me. I know it couldn't have been easy for you to discover that…well, that there are those who oppose everything that you're doing for the war effort." He smiled at her sadly. "Your brother is flying against the Luftwaffe every day, and you are doing your bit as an officer as well. It must be difficult to learn that old friends are actively trying to welcome the enemy in while you're fighting so hard to keep them out."

Evelyn swallowed. He had no idea. While she had been in France, watching innocent men, women and children be slaughtered on the road by the Germans, Sir Clark had been in London organizing in support of the Nazi regime. Marrow had no clue of the fury simmering inside her, nor could he ever. He could never suspect that she was any more involved in the fight for freedom and information than an Assistant Section Officer in the WAAF would be.

"I'll admit I'm a little taken aback," she said finally. "It's not very pleasant. However, I suppose it's only to be expected. Throughout history, all civilizations have had their traitors. Why should we be any different?"

"Quite so."

"You know," she said after a moment, "I might be able to help you."

He looked at her quizzically. "What do you mean?"

She shrugged. "Well, I'm on holiday. There's no reason I can't stay in London and see what I can find out about this Round Club."

He frowned and shook his head. "No. It's far too dangerous."

"Dangerous?" She laughed. "Don't be absurd. There's nothing dangerous about it at all. I'm in a perfect position to learn anything I want to know without attracting the least amount of suspicion. I'm one of them. I've been part of their world since I was born. Why, only look at the other night! I knew nothing about any of it, and I wasn't even trying to learn anything. The information just fell into my lap! And even if they had seen me, neither of them would have considered me any kind of threat. I'm the perfect person to dig up information on this Round Club."

"This is no time to be reckless. This isn't some game to play, or a way to pass the time. You've done your duty by bringing what you heard to me. That's where your involvement ends."

"If I didn't know better, Mr. Marrow, I would think you were being patronizing," Evelyn said, her chin inching towards the ceiling. She looked down her nose at him. "I may not be part of the Security Service, or a man, but I can assure you, I'm more than capable of taking care of myself. And, as I've said before, I'm in a perfect position to gather information for you. All I have to do is go to parties and listen, something that I am already doing."

He stared at her for a moment and she could almost see him wavering.

"And you'll bring whatever you hear to me?"

"Of course." Evelyn smiled engagingly, her flash of aristocratic haughtiness gone. "I think it will be rather fun. There's a luncheon tomorrow that's been organized by the ladies' association of St. Paul's. Any lady who's anyone will be there. I'm sure I'll learn something. You have no idea how women talk at these things."

Marrow let out a short laugh. "So I've been told by my wife. Very well, but only if you promise to be discreet, and swear to me that no one will ever suspect anything. Your father would turn in his grave if he knew what was happening, and that you were about to jump right into the middle of it."

Evelyn thought of her father and his secrets and smiled faintly.

"Something makes me think that he wouldn't be very surprised," she murmured dryly, "but don't worry. No one will be the wiser, I promise you."

## When Wolves Gather

He sighed and nodded, resigned.

"We'll meet again on Wednesday. Shall we say ten o'clock in Hyde Park? At Speakers' Corner?"

Evelyn smiled. "Yes, all right."

"And you'll be very careful?"

"Mr. Marrow, you really must stop worrying about me," she said humorously. "I assure you, I will be the very soul of discretion."

## Chapter Seventeen

Evelyn looked at the clock hanging on the wall in the drawing room and closed her book. She really couldn't put it off any longer. She must telephone her mother and tell her that she was going to stay in London for a few more days. Her mother would be unhappy, and Evelyn hated when her mother was unhappy, but she really didn't have a choice. Not if she wanted to help apprehend members of the Round Club.

Her lips tightened and she set her book aside. Of all the things to encounter while she was on holiday, it had to be a ring of traitors right here in London. She wasn't even in France! They were right here, in England! Anger washed through her anew and Evelyn took a deep, steadying breath. Marrow had been quite right when he'd said that it couldn't be easy to learn that former friends and acquaintances were plotting against the Crown, freedom, and everything that she, Robbie, and Miles were fighting so fiercely to protect. Miss Milner and Sir Clark weren't close friends of hers, but their involvement raised the question of who else was part of the Round Club? Would she discover that someone close to her was part of this vile group? Was Maryanne?

A shudder went through her, and Evelyn got up restlessly. The thought of Maryanne being involved was laughable, but Evelyn knew full well that it wasn't outside the realm of possibility. The thought filled her with dismay, and she shook her head almost in denial. She hoped to God that no one she considered a friend would turn out to be plotting against King and Country, but of course it was a possibility. She knew there was only one way to find out, and she had to do it or she would go through the war wondering if everyone she knew and loved was a traitor. While she rather uncomfortably acknowledged that she herself was lying to everyone she cared about, at least she was doing it in support of her country. She couldn't imagine anything worse than discovering that any of those same people were in league with the enemy.

Crossing the room, Evelyn seated herself before the table with the telephone and picked up the handset. It was best to get this telephone call out of the way so that she could concentrate on putting all the skills that MI6 had taught her to work. The fact that she would

## When Wolves Gather

be doing it here in London was extremely disconcerting, but it was far better than sitting idly by while the Round Club went about its business in the shadows.

After a moment, she heard Thomas' voice over the handset and she smiled at the familiar, steady tone of the Ainsworth butler.

"Good evening, Thomas! This is Evelyn. Is Mother available?" she asked cheerfully.

"Good evening, Miss Evelyn," Thomas said, his voice softening slightly. "I believe she is in the drawing room. If you'll hold the line for a moment?"

"Yes, of course. Thank you."

Evelyn picked up a pencil and began drawing absently on a pad of paper. She imagined that her mother and aunts were in the drawing room with her uncle, having cocktails before dinner. With a pang, she thought of the warm companionship and briefly wished she was there instead of alone in London. While her family sat down to a nice dinner together, she would be having beans on toast and sausages alone in the kitchen.

"Evelyn dear! How are you? Is everything all right?"

Her mother's voice brought her out of her reverie and Evelyn smiled.

"Yes, indeed," she said, forcing a cheerfulness she didn't feel. "How are you? Am I interrupting drinks?"

"Yes, but that's quite all right. Agatha is making them tonight and you know how she always puts in too much sour," her mother said with a laugh. "How is everyone? Are you having a good time?"

"I'm having a wonderful time. That's why I'm calling. I'll be staying for a few more days."

"Oh no, you're not coming back?"

"Of course I'm coming back, silly!" Evelyn laughed. "Just not tomorrow as I'd planned. Maryanne and I have been having a grand old time, and tomorrow is the ladies' association luncheon. You remember how we always used to go? Well, I thought it would be fun to attend while I'm here. You don't mind, do you?"

"No, I suppose not," Mrs. Ainsworth said grudgingly. "Not if you're having fun. Did you go to the Ramsay's party?"

"Yes. It was just like they always are, except with less food. You wouldn't really know there was a war on if you don't look at all the bomb shelters and sandbags piled up everywhere. Did you know they've put a shelter in St. James Park? And there are anti-aircraft guns in the Flower Garden in Greenwich!"

"How perfectly horrid!"

"Yes, it takes some getting used to, I'll grant you. It's very strange, though. London looks quite different, but yet it's still the same. I saw Lord Pennington at Claridge's over the weekend. He sends you his regards and said to tell you that Lady Pennington would love to have you to visit in Bath."

"Isn't that nice! I must write her a letter. I haven't seen her in months."

"Have you heard anything from Robbie?" Evelyn asked.

"Not really. He telephoned last week, but we were at the church bazaar. They were raising money for the local defense fund." She cleared her throat. "We did have a letter from Gisele and Nicolas."

Evelyn stopped drawing and raised her head.

"You did? How did they manage that? I thought they couldn't get any letters out!"

"A couple that Adele knows managed to escape France in June. They carried it with them. They had to go through Spain, and just arrived in England last week."

Evelyn thought of her own hair-raising flight through France and swallowed.

"How terrifying it must have been! And they went through Spain?"

"Yes. Adele says that they aren't any the worse for wear. They're staying in Brighton at the moment with friends of theirs."

"What did Gisele say in the letter? Are they all right?"

"Yes. They are both well, or were at the time. They are at the chateau and, as it transpired, that part of France falls within Vichy, so they are at least in the unoccupied region. They write that they are unable to pass into the occupied territory without proper credentials issued by the Nazis. They were attempting to obtain what papers they need from the Germans so that they can travel to Paris and check on the house there. However, they've heard that the German officers are taking control of the better residences, so they think it may have been occupied."

"Oh, how terrible!" Evelyn exclaimed. "The thought of those people in Uncle Claude's house!"

"I know. It's perfectly horrid. Adele won't even discuss it."

"No, I don't imagine she wants to think about it at all."

"Other than that, Gisele said that everything was fine and not to worry about them."

"Well, that's a relief, at any rate!"

"How long will you remain in London? You know that I don't like you being there alone."

## When Wolves Gather

"I know. I'll come home at the end of the week. I just want to have a few more days," Evelyn said. "I only brought enough clothes for the weekend, and the ones I left here are rather dull, so I won't stay very much longer."

"Well, enjoy yourself, my dear."

"I will. I'll see you soon."

Evelyn hung up and stared across the room thoughtfully. She had realized, of course, when the details of the Armistice were released, that the chateau had fallen into the unoccupied territory. She'd been relieved when she saw that, knowing that Gisele and Nicolas were there. However, it was interesting that they were going to get the necessary papers so that they could travel between the occupied and unoccupied regions. From all accounts, it wasn't easy. One had to have very good reason to travel between the two and, even if the Germans allowed it, they still had to undergo thorough checks each time they crossed the demarcation line. But, if they did manage to obtain the passes, her cousins would be in perfect position to help in any resistance efforts. And she knew, without a doubt, that that was exactly what they had planned to do.

If she could find a way to contact Josephine, or even Leon in Bordeaux, they could perhaps arrange a way to make contact with Gisele and Nicolas. Evelyn would feel much better about the whole thing if she knew someone was keeping an eye on them. While her cousins were reckless on occasion, they weren't stupid. But they didn't know anything about this world Evelyn lived in, and she would be much happier if someone who did was there to help guide them.

Bill would have a fit if he found out that she was contemplating an introduction between her contacts and her cousins. He would tell her that she was risking exposing her own activities to her cousins. Perhaps he would be right to some extent, but Evelyn had absolutely no intention of Gisele and Nicolas ever discovering what she did, or whom she did it for. There was no reason for Leon or Josephine to even know that they were her relatives. She only wanted to watch from afar, through the eyes of others, to ensure that they didn't fall into trouble before they'd even had a chance to begin. Once they were involved with any resistance, it was up to them to stay alive.

Just as it was up to her to do the same.

Henry waited for a lorry to pass in the darkness before he went swiftly across the street. The telephone box was empty, thankfully, and he went inside quickly, closing the door behind him.

He was uncomfortable using this same call box for the standard message drop. Where before it had seemed the perfect solution, now it seemed more and more reckless. He'd passed a bobby just around the corner, and he couldn't help but wonder if the local policemen had noticed how frequently he came to this particular telephone booth to make calls. Or that it was always after dark. He supposed if they had noticed, they probably assumed he was having an affair, or something equally unimaginative. Yet the fact remained that the more he used this drop location, the higher the likelihood that someone would begin to take notice.

Another consideration, of course, was the fact that there were now several amateurs running about town. If they were also using the same drop locations, the chances of someone catching on were increased ten-fold.

Henry frowned as he quickly unscrewed the mouthpiece on the handset and tipped the rolled up piece of paper into his hand. He was just replacing the mouthpiece when an air raid warden came around the corner. Lifting the handset to his ear, Henry bent his head and pretended to be talking on the telephone. The warden glanced into the booth as he passed, but his stride never wavered as he disappeared into the darkness.

Exhaling, Henry hung up the receiver and tucked the paper into his pocket, stepping out of the booth. Now, in addition to the policemen on their beat, he had to worry about the wardens. A nuisance, that's what they were. They patrolled the streets as if they owned them, blowing their whistles if they saw even the faintest crack of light through curtains in the blackout. And they handed out their fines with even more gusto than the Roman tax collectors had. Damned busybodies, the lot of them.

Shaking his head, he made his way up the street to the local pub. Between the lot of amateurs running around playing at being a spy and the ever-watchful wardens and police, the risks of retrieving messages were beginning to outweigh the compensation. He would mention it to his handler when he had the opportunity. There had to be other options. He had a wireless radio. Why couldn't they make more use of that?

Stepping into the brightly lit pub, Henry blinked after the darkness outside. The few patrons inside glanced at him, then went

## When Wolves Gather

back to their pints without giving him another look. He went to the bar and ordered a beer, removing his gloves while the landlord poured it.

"Nice night," he said, setting the full glass before him.

"Yes, it is."

Henry paid him and carried his pint to a table in the corner. Sitting down, he laid his hat and gloves on the table and sipped his beer before pulling the piece of paper from his pocket. He opened it, scanning the message quickly, and his eyebrows rose in surprise. It claimed that a spy they referred to as Rätsel had just returned to England. They believed it was Jian.

Henry sipped his beer again thoughtfully. Now why did they think this Rätsel and Jian were the same person? The last he'd heard of the MI6 agent, she'd been sent to Belgium just before the German offensive into the Lowlands. He hadn't been able to discover anything else since. For all he knew, she was still in Belgium, or even France.

His lips pursed and he set down his glass. He supposed it was possible that they could be the same spy. The Germans had certainly been dogged in their attempts to locate Jian in the past. Perhaps that was because they knew her as this Rätsel.

Henry lowered his eyes to the message once more. It continued, claiming that she had gone by the alias Geneviève Dufour in France, and had returned by ship from Bordeaux. His instructions were to pick up her trail here in England.

Pulling a case from his pocket, Henry stared at the paper while he extracted a cigarette. They wanted him to find her here in England? And do what? What did they really think they could do here in England? This wasn't France. They couldn't simply send their Gestapo to her house and arrest her.

Henry lit his cigarette, then picked up the paper, holding it to the flame. As it caught, he laid it in the ash tray and glanced around. No one was paying the slightest attention to the table in the corner, and he lowered his eyes to watch the message burn. While he thought it was a wild goose chase, he would do as he was instructed. If it would keep Berlin happy, and keep their minds off the Ainsworth package, he would look for this Geneviève Dufour. If nothing else, it would keep him busy and away from the blasted Round Club for the time being. And that was worth any price.

## RAF Coltishall

Miles knocked on the door and reached for the handle when he heard the command to enter. He stepped into the office and closed the door behind him, standing to attention.

"You wanted to see me, sir?" he asked.

"Yes." Squadron Leader Ashmore looked up from the papers spread across his desk. "Have a seat, Lacey."

Miles nodded and went over to sit down in a chair before the desk as Ashmore sat back in his chair, rubbing his eyes tiredly.

"How are you holding up?" he asked after a moment, dropping his hand.

"Tickety-boo, sir."

"Good. It was a long day today. How's young Thomas coming along?"

"He seems to be picking up the ropes right enough. He's learned to keep moving and not fly in a straight line at last." Miles shrugged. "He keeps his eyes open and is a fast learner. That's all I can ask for from someone who'd never sat in a Spit before coming here."

"Yes. Bad luck, that." Ashmore shook his head. "Between you and me, that was a cockup from HQ. He was supposed to be sent to a Hurricane squadron down in 11 Group. Someone mucked up the orders. I was asked if I wanted him reassigned, but by then he'd already got the hang of it here."

"We need pilots, sir. I'd rather have Thomas than no one a'tall."

"Yes, that's what I thought." Ashmore pulled a silver case from his breast pocket and extracted a cigarette. "Smoke?" he offered.

"No, thank you."

Ashmore nodded and lit his cigarette.

"I've heard that the pool on you and Chris has almost tripled in the past week. Ainsworth is getting his share of bets as well."

"Well, there are enough Jerries to go around now," Miles said. "Thomas even got a piece of one today."

Ashmore grinned. "So I heard. Bertie said he couldn't contain himself."

"He was very excited," Miles agreed with a chuckle. "Well, and so he should be. It isn't every day that you get your first hit."

"No, indeed. And it shows he's keen. Lord knows we need all the enthusiasm we can get." Ashmore blew smoke out and studied Miles through the haze. "What's your impression? Is everyone holding up all right?"

## When Wolves Gather

Miles frowned.

"I think so. We're all getting tired, but overall everyone's in good spirits."

"No one's ready to revolt, then?"

"Because of the long hours in the air, you mean? No, not yet. The general feeling seems to be that it has to be done, so we'll go up and do it."

"Good. HQ has been on to me to keep an eye on morale. I gather 11 Group is getting hit rather badly. Air Chief Marshal Dowding is concerned about fatigue, among other things."

"He should be concerned about airplanes and pilots," Miles replied wryly. "Every day we go up, we lose more. And we don't have them to lose."

"I know, and I can assure you, so does he. He's been fighting to get more fighter production, but you know as well as I do that bombers are where the funding goes." Ashmore got up restlessly and went over to look out of the window. "Bloody ridiculous, really. The bombers won't keep the Luftwaffe out of England."

"What about that scramble the other day?" Miles asked after a moment of silence. "What was that about?"

"Lord knows. HQ swears there was a mass of enemy aircraft picked up by the radar, but you saw for yourself that nothing was there." He turned away from the window. "Air Vice Marshal Park has been adamant that 11 Group get their kites airborne within two minutes of a scramble. Perhaps that thought is spreading. It could be that Leigh-Mallory was gauging our speed, but I'd be very surprised."

"Two minutes?" Miles shook his head. "Even with the Spitfire's speed, I don't see how we can do it in two."

"We'll have to if we're to have any chance at all against the Jerries." Ashmore crossed back to his desk and stubbed out his cigarette. "11 Group will get the brunt of it when Göring does send his Luftwaffe in force, and make no mistake, he will. If they don't get up and intercept in two minutes…well, we all saw what happened in France."

Miles pressed his lips together grimly. "Understood, sir."

"I'm not saying it will be easy, but we have to find a way to do it." Ashmore seated himself again. "Park is quite right about that. The faster we get airborne, the faster we intercept the enemy."

"I thought the idea was to hit them in force with the Big Wing formation?" Miles asked. "Has something changed?"

Ashmore sighed.

"No. Nothing's changed. That is Air Vice Marshal Leigh-Mallory's orders for 12 Group."

"You don't sound as though you're convinced it will work," Miles said after a moment. "If you'll forgive me saying so, sir."

Ashmore waved a hand tiredly.

"No, I don't mind. I don't know if it will work or not. It takes a lot of time to gather several squadrons together to attack en-masse. If Göring comes over the North Sea, we won't have that time. So you see, I can readily understand where Park is coming from."

"HQ expects the main attack to come over the Channel," Miles said slowly. "If it does, and 11 Group does manage to get airborne in two minutes, then they will keep the Luftwaffe over the Channel. If they can't, and Jerry gets to London, then I think our Big Wing could be more effective."

"That's certainly the hope and plan." Ashmore sighed and shook his head. "This is all conjecture on our part, and a complete waste of time and energy. We'll follow orders and shoot down as many of the buggers as we can. In the meantime, I didn't call you in here to discuss the competing battle theories of two Air Vice Marshals who have never got along, and probably never will."

Miles grinned. "No, sir. My apologies."

"I've managed to get approval for you, Ainsworth, and Field to have twenty-four hours off this Friday. You have to be back first thing Saturday morning, but you're excused at the end of operations Thursday."

"Thank you, sir. And the rest of the squadron?"

"We're rotating through all of them, don't worry. The first two will go Wednesday. It means flying short-handed, but I think we'll manage all right. I had to fight to get permission for all three of you to go together."

"Thank you, sir."

"Now that you've managed to talk me into agreeing to let three of my best pilots go at the same time, what have you got planned?" Ashmore asked, tilting his head curiously.

"London, sir. I believe there was some talk of meeting Ainsworth's sister for dinner in London if she can swing it. She's in the WAAFs."

"Ah. And the Yank?"

Miles grinned. "Wants to meet her, I'm afraid."

"Well, I won't say that it will be an easy time here with all of you gone, but I will say you've earned it, the lot of you." Ashmore picked up his pen and prepared to go back to his paperwork. "Just be

## When Wolves Gather

sure to bring them back in one piece, and sober enough to fly, if you wouldn't mind."

Miles laughed and stood up, saluting.

"I'll do my best, sir."

## Chapter Eighteen

**London**
**July 30**

Evelyn hunched her shoulders against the cold drizzle that had engulfed the city and held her clutch purse over her head as she hurried along the pavement. The flimsy bag did little to protect her from the elements and she silently railed at herself for neglecting to bring the single-most important part of any Londoner's attire: an umbrella. It hadn't seemed as if she would need one when she left the house earlier, but the clear, if somewhat dull, day had taken a turn for the worse while she was trapped at that ladies' association luncheon.

What a waste of time *that* had turned out to be! She had been so confident that she would learn something, and indeed, there were several ladies of rank in attendance, Miss Bethany Milner included. Evelyn had even managed to get herself seated at the same table as Miss Milner, and had put up with her annoying whine for over an hour, but it had all been for nothing. She hadn't learned anything. She'd spent the entire luncheon engaging in mindless conversation with people she didn't really care for that much, and had come away completely empty-handed. Even Miss Milner had been perfectly respectable and vocal in her support of the bomb shelters and preparedness measures around London. In fact, if Evelyn hadn't overheard her herself, she would be tempted to doubt that Miss Milner was anything other than a patriotic heiress.

It was all very frustrating, and she had no idea what she would report to Marrow tomorrow. There was nothing to tell him, unless he was interested to know that St. Paul's had raised over two hundred pounds in their efforts to contribute to the local children's home.

"Ooof!"

Evelyn gasped as she rounded the corner and ran straight into someone. Strong hands steadied her as she stumbled backwards, and she looked up in startled dismay.

"Oh, I am sorry…" she began, then broke off as she recognized the man in front of her. "Lord Anthony!"

## When Wolves Gather

"Why, Evelyn! Maryanne mentioned you were in Town," he said with a smile, releasing her. "Are you all right?"

"Yes, I'm fine. I'm terribly sorry! I wasn't looking where I was going. This wretched rain!"

He glanced upwards and nodded, holding his umbrella out to shelter her as well.

"Yes, it's turned rather nasty. Haven't you an umbrella?"

"I didn't bring it out with me," she confessed with a laugh, straightening her hat. "I didn't think I would need one."

"That will teach you!" He looked around. "Come. Let's get out of this rain and somewhere dry. Would you care to join me for a cup of tea?"

"That would be lovely," she said, tucking her hand into his offered arm. "How are you? I haven't seen you in what seems like forever."

"That's what you get for running off into the WAAF," he replied, steering her across the street to a tea room. "I'm the same as ever. I've taken up my seat in the House and am endeavoring to help them see sense. And you? How is the air force treating you?"

"Surprisingly well, really. The accommodations leave much to be desired, as does the food, but the work is interesting. I'm enjoying it as much as I suppose one can during a war."

She ducked into the tea room as Anthony held the door for her, then watched as he shook out his umbrella and closed it before following her inside.

"Maryanne's gone into the ATS, but I'm sure she's told you." He looked around and led her to a table near a window. "She said she isn't cut out to sit at home and knit jumpers for the soldiers."

"Lord, no," Evelyn said in horror, sinking into the seat he held for her. "I can't imagine that at all."

"Nor could I." He sat across from her and grinned. "To be fair, no one was asking her to do that. Mother is working with the Women's Auxiliary, but she's at the house in Hampshire."

"Well, I think it's wonderful that she's in the ATS, although the uniforms are rather ghastly," Evelyn said with a smile. "It's certainly better than sitting by and watching as the men get to have all the fun and experience all the excitement."

He looked at her, his lips twisted.

"Excitement?" he repeated. "I'm not sure the boys back from Dunkirk would agree with that characterization."

Evelyn grimaced. "No. I suppose not."

"I do understand what you're saying, though. It's difficult to sit by while others seem to do much more important work than what you're able to do yourself." Something in his tone made Evelyn glance at him sharply, but his face was tranquil and, when he spoke again, his voice was even. "How is Rob? We saw him just recently, at The Dorchester, I believe it was."

Evelyn waited as a young girl came over to set down a tray with two pots of tea and cups and saucers.

"Would you like some sandwiches?" Anthony asked her.

She shook her head. "I've just come from a luncheon. I'm perfectly content with the tea."

Anthony nodded and thanked the server. Once she'd departed again, Evelyn looked across the table at him.

"Maryanne mentioned that you'd run into Robbie. He must have been in town to meet with the solicitor. He doesn't get very much time off these days."

"No, I don't imagine he does." Anthony poured tea into his cup. "It's appalling what we're asking these pilots to do, really," he said, lowering his voice. "They're short on machines, short on pilots, and yet we're asking them to fly against a superior force to defend England. I'm afraid Rob got the raw end of the deal."

"He doesn't think so," Evelyn said, sipping her tea. "He loves flying. Sometimes I wonder if he didn't get some of the recklessness from our French side."

"How are your French relations? They're not still there, are they?"

"My aunt and uncle are with Mother at Ainsworth Manor, but Gisele and Nicolas chose to remain in France. They are at the chateau in Monblanc. It's in the unoccupied territory, thank God."

"Your aunt and uncle must be worried sick."

"I'm sure they are."

"It's still shocking to me how quickly it all happened," he said after a moment. "No one thought France would fall so quickly. It really makes one wonder how on earth we'll hold out."

Evelyn looked up.

"We have the Channel to aid us," she pointed out. "Rommel's tanks can't roll through that very easily."

"Mm." He didn't sound convinced. "We can only hope."

Evelyn drank her tea and considered Anthony over the rim. She could see why Maryanne was concerned for her brother. He'd changed. The last time she'd seen him, he'd been full of confidence and life. Now, he seemed almost like a charcoal drawing of his former self.

## When Wolves Gather

The laughter was gone from his eyes, and his mouth had taken on a grimness that she had never seen. Either political life didn't suit him, or there was something else going on that he wasn't sharing with anyone. Whatever the problem, Lord Gilhurst was certainly not himself.

"How are you getting along in Parliament?" she asked after a moment. "Shall I be looking forward to watching your rise to prime minister?"

He laughed shortly. "Hardly. I have no such aspirations. Right now, I'm happy just to have a few of my father's cronies supporting me."

"Aren't you happy in political life?"

"I'm not unhappy. I suppose I'm where I should be. Sometimes I wish…"

"What?"

"Well, that I can do something more than what I'm doing." He smiled ruefully. "I feel rather useless, to be honest. Rob is flying his fighter planes, you're training women to support the RAF, and now even Maryanne will be driving for the war effort. Arguing policy on the floor doesn't seem very worthwhile in comparison."

"Then why don't you do something else?" Evelyn asked after a moment. "You could always join the RAF or Navy."

"And walk away from politics? My dear Evie, my father would have a coronary."

"It's not your father we're discussing."

"No, but he's very much a part of it." Anthony shook his head. "I've been considering it, but I really do think I'm better off staying where I am and working with the party."

Evelyn was quiet for a moment, then she smiled, changing the subject.

"What do you think of Churchill?"

"I like him," he said unexpectedly. "That's not a very popular opinion, I know, but I do. He speaks from his heart, and no one can doubt his commitment to England."

"If I'm to believe the newspapers, he seems to be under an extraordinary amount of pressure to discuss a peace with Hitler," she said softly. "Is that true?"

"There are some who are saying that he should consider the notion, yes, but I wouldn't put too much stock into what the rags are saying. They haven't got it right half the time."

"I don't see how we can possibly come to an agreement with Hitler," Evelyn said, setting her cup down. "It would mean having his Nazi thugs here in England. I can't think of anything worse!"

"If Hitler has his way, we'll end up with his thugs here anyway," he said with a shrug. "The facts do not favor our bid to stand against Germany, the Soviet Union, and Italy alone."

"I've known facts to be wrong before." Evelyn studied him. "You don't sound as though you think we can repel an invasion."

"I'm just being realistic, and preparing for the worst. We must be able to see things for how they are." Anthony shook his head and reached out to squeeze her hand. "But enough about the blasted war. We haven't seen each other in months, if not a year, and here we are discussing the most miserable thing imaginable. It won't do, you know. Let's talk about something else."

"All right. What shall we talk about?" Evelyn said agreeably.

"Let's talk about you."

"Me?" She laughed. "That won't take very long at all. There isn't very much to say. My life has become the WAAF, and that is very dull, I assure you."

"I've heard stories that you've become rather friendly with Miles Lacey," he told her, a twinkle in his eye.

"Oh for goodness' sake! It's fantastic how the gossip mills churn when I'm not even in London!" Evelyn exclaimed. "If this war was being run with such tenacious efficiency, Hitler would have been defeated in Norway!"

Anthony grinned. "It's true, then?"

"Miles is a friend. Rob introduced us last autumn. He's very nice."

"Mm-hmm." Anthony's grin was wicked.

"Oh, you're every bit as bad as your sister, do you know that?" she demanded with a laugh.

"I can't imagine why you're being so defensive. He's a good chap. I knew him up at Oxford, you know. He was a year or two behind me. Fantastic rugby player. In fact, I remember being rather surprised when I'd heard he'd taken up flying instead." Anthony poured himself some more tea. "He was with Rob when we ran into him the other week."

"Yes, Maryanne told me."

"We got to talking about politics, and he was surprisingly insightful," he said thoughtfully. "Once this war is over, he'll take over his father's seat, I suppose. We could do with a few more like him."

"That's high praise indeed," she said with a smile.

"I've always liked Miles. He started out a bit dodgy, but he's grown into a steady man. I suppose we can thank the RAF for that." He sipped his tea and grinned. "You could certainly do worse. He's got terrific prospects, and his fortune is secure, even in these unsettled times. His father has managed it well."

"Good Lord, you sound like a banker."

"All I'm saying is that he's a very good match for you, as I'm sure Rob would agree." Anthony set his cup down. "I'm rather amazed that you haven't snapped him up already."

"Perhaps he isn't willing to be snapped up."

Anthony let out a bark of laughter.

"Don't be absurd, Evie. He'd have to be blind, deaf, and dumb to let you get away."

"I really don't understand this fascination everyone has all of a sudden with my matrimonial prospects," she complained. "Why can't a Flight Lieutenant and an Assistant Section Officer simply enjoy each other's company and be friends? Why does it always have to turn into this?"

"Why, because you're Evelyn Ainsworth, my dear, and he is one of the Yorkshire Lacey's. It's just the way of it." He smiled at her. "And we've watched you go through season after season without falling prey to any of the hopeful idiots who tried so desperately to gain your affections. Did you know that Maryanne and I had a wager on Geoffrey Tate one year?"

"Geoffrey?!" Evelyn stared at him. "Good heavens! Who won?"

"She did. I was so sure you were serious about him."

"I'm terribly sorry. How much did it cost you?"

"Fifty quid. We haven't wagered since." He winked. "Miles might change all that. I really must remember to suggest it."

"Be sure to let me know how that one turns out as well."

"You won't give me a clue? An insider's tip?"

"My dear Lord Anthony, if you will insist on making wagers on something as silly as this, then you can take your chances without any assistance from me!"

◉

Evelyn unlocked the door and pushed it open, stepping out of the rain quickly. She let out a relieved sigh and bent to pick up a single letter that had been delivered through the post slot on the door. It was addressed to her in a feminine hand and bore the seal of the Billingsley's. Gillian was writing to apologize, no doubt, for being rather less than complimentary towards her. Carrying it over to the hall stand,

Evelyn dropped the letter onto the tray and set her purse next to it. She reached up to pull the pin from her hat, removing the wet accessory with a grimace. Not for the first time, she bemoaned the lack of her maid to assist her while she was in London. Fran really was a magician when it came to drying out wet accessories and making them look like new again.

Before she had the chance to finish the thought, the telephone rang shrilly, making her start. Evelyn set down the sopping hat and went over to the table with the heavy telephone, her lips twisting wryly. Oh yes. She missed her servants indeed!

"Hello? Ainsworth residence?"

"Now that's a voice I've been longing to hear," a deep voice said cheerfully, sending a rush of warmth through her.

"Miles!" she exclaimed in delighted surprise. "However did you know I was here?"

"Your mother told Rob, and Rob told me, so I thought I'd ring you up. You don't mind, do you?"

"No, of course not! You phoned at the perfect time. I just stepped through the door."

"How are you enjoying London?"

"It's rather wet right now. I've come home to change into something dry."

"It's been raining here as well. Makes for bloody miserable flying weather."

"Oh, it *is* nice to hear your voice," she told him, sitting in the chair next to the little table. "How are you?"

"Better now that I'm talking to you. Will you still be in town on Friday?" he asked. "We got our twenty-four hours of freedom and Rob, the Yank, and I will be coming to Town."

"Will you? All of you?"

"That's the plan. Chris wants to meet you."

"I have to return to Ainsworth. I was going to go up on Wednesday, but I can come back Friday," she said thoughtfully.

"Perfect! How early can you be back? I thought I'd come pick you up and we'd spend the day together."

"Oh, that would be lovely! But what about Rob and Chris?"

"Oh they've already made plans for the day. We thought we could all meet for dinner. How's The Dorchester? Would you like that?"

"You know I don't mind, but what about Chris? The Dorchester can be a bit stuffy. Will he be comfortable there?"

## When Wolves Gather

Miles laughed. "Oh, don't worry about the Yank. He'll fit in perfectly."

Evelyn smiled ruefully. "All right. I'm not implying anything. It's just that…" her voice trailed off.

"What?"

"Well, it's just that I've been hearing things while I've been here," she said, clearing her throat. "It seems that a lot of our peers don't approve of so many uniforms appearing in the more exclusive establishments. It simply occurred to me that it might also extend to your American pilot."

"What a load of bosh," Miles said disgustedly. "Who's been saying such rubbish? No, wait. Let me take a stab at it. Was it the Billingsley's?"

Evelyn was startled.

"How on earth did you know?"

"Lord Billingsley has been rather vocal about it recently, or so my father told me. There are a few others that I've run into, but by and large, most of our acquaintances are not of the same opinion."

"I seem to be running into it everywhere I go. Thank God I didn't bring my uniform to town with me. I'd be tempted to wear it simply everywhere."

Miles laughed. "And I wouldn't blame you."

There was a loud chorus of yelling in the background and the sound of something that sounded like a loud clang.

"Goodness, what was that?"

"Lord knows! I'm next to the repair hangar. It gets a bit loud. Are we settled for Friday, then?"

"Yes. What time shall I expect you?"

"Is ten too early?"

"Not a bit. I'll drive the Lagonda down and be here waiting."

"Wonderful! I'd better ring off now. We'll be going up again soon. I'll see you Friday."

"I'm looking forward to it."

Evelyn hung up with a smile and got up, her step suddenly lighter than it had been before. She went upstairs, humming a cheerful tune. Friday she would see Miles, and everything seemed brighter and more hopeful. And Rob too! She felt as if Friday were Christmas. She hadn't seen Rob since…goodness, how long *had* it been? Since before she left on that fateful trip to Belgium. She paused at the top of the stairs. It seemed like years ago, yet it was only three months since Hitler invaded the Lowlands. So much had happened! And she had been through so much! No wonder it seemed so long ago.

But that was all in the past. On Friday, she would see Miles again, and have dinner with him and her brother. And she'd finally meet the Yank!

Evelyn went down the hallway to her bedroom. But first, she had to dress for dinner with Bill, and then meet with Marrow in the morning. Friday would be a welcome respite, but until then, there was work to be done, even on holiday.

# When Wolves Gather

## Chapter Nineteen

Evelyn followed the maître d' through Claridge's to a table where Bill was already seated. As they approached, he stood and smiled.

"My dear Evelyn," he greeted her. "How are you?"

"Very well, thank you." She waited while the maître d' pulled out her chair and smiled as she sank into it. "I'm terribly sorry I'm late. It's been rather a hectic day. Is Lady Buckley joining us?"

"She'll be along later. She's dining with her Women's Club, but has promised to join us for dessert and coffee." Bill took his seat again. "She's looking forward to seeing you again. Would you like wine?"

"Yes, please."

Bill nodded to the maître d' and ordered a bottle of wine before turning his attention back to Evelyn.

"And why was your day hectic? You seem incapable of realizing that you're on holiday. Your days are not supposed to be hectic!"

Evelyn laughed.

"They're not, are they? I'm afraid I'm not very good at filling my days with frivolous nonsense anymore. It's amazing how quickly things change when there's a war on! I really can't imagine going back to the old normal now."

"Once this is all over, you'll be amazed how quickly it will return to normal," he said with a faint smile.

"I do hope so."

Evelyn fell silent as a waiter approached with a bottle of wine and waited while he opened it and poured a bit into Bill's glass. Bill sniffed, then tasted it before nodding his approval. The waiter turned to fill Evelyn's glass before filling Bill's. Leaving the bottle on the table, he nodded politely and turned to leave.

"I hope you don't mind, but I've already ordered for the two of us," Bill said.

"Not at all."

"Good. Now tell me what you did today."

"I went to a luncheon given by the ladies' association of St. Paul's," she said, reaching for her wine. "I thought I might learn something that could be useful to Marrow."

"And did you?"

"No, not even a snippet." She sipped her wine appreciatively. "It was a complete waste of time, and it was dreadfully dull. I don't know how I ever found those events tolerable."

"Marguerite says that some are more tolerable than others. I don't recall her mentioning St. Paul's."

"No, she wasn't there. And she didn't miss a thing, I assure you!" Evelyn set down her glass. "Although it seemed like half of London was in attendance. You would have thought that I would have overheard something, but it wasn't to be. After I finally got away, I ran into Lord Gilhurst in the street and we went for tea. That was much more informative."

"Was it?" Bill raised an eyebrow. "In what way?"

"Well, I'm not sure, really," she said slowly. "Maryanne is worried about him, you know, and after spending an hour with him this afternoon, I can see why. He's changed."

"So have you."

Her lips twisted humorlessly. "Very true."

"Tell me about Shustov," Bill said after a moment. "He sent a message?"

"Yes." She frowned. "It was rather disconcerting, as a matter of fact. It's quite obvious to me that the Soviets have several people in London, and the NKVD is in easy contact with all of them."

"Yes. MI5 has been trying to track them down, but for every one they uncover, two more are left at large." Bill shook his head, a heavy scowl on his face. "Why is it clear to you that there are several?"

"Well, because of the speed with which I was given the message! I learned that the code phrase was included in the radio broadcast one day, and had the physical message the next! It was put into a newspaper, which I retrieved at a corner shop in London. There was no delay, and the message was inserted into the classified section."

"It was an actual message? On a piece of paper?" Bill asked quickly, his eyes probing hers.

"Not on a separate paper, no, but it had been written in pencil in the newspaper itself."

He frowned.

"Yes. I see what you mean. Someone had to physically do it here in London that morning."

## When Wolves Gather

"Yes." Evelyn sipped her wine. "Rather alarming, really. Someone could have been watching when I went to get it, which makes for an extremely unpleasant feeling. I do know that I wasn't followed after buying the newspaper, though, so that was all right."

"And the message?"

She set her glass down with a frown.

"That's the other thing." She lowered her voice and leaned forward. "Shustov claims that a member of the Round Club is in contact with Hans Voss," she said grimly. "He said that they are looking for me here in England. The German SD has extended their reach and is determined to learn my identity."

Bill looked grim. "Anything else?"

"No." Evelyn sat back again, chewing her bottom lip. "I was taken aback that Shustov is obviously well acquainted with this Round Club when we've just learned of its existence ourselves. How on earth do the Soviets know more about it than we do?"

"We don't know that they do. He knows of its existence, just as we do. We don't know that he knows any more than that."

"Well, he knows one of them is in contact with Hans Voss," she pointed out. "That's more than we knew."

Bill grunted and reached for his wine. "Yes."

She watched him for a moment, her eyes narrowed.

"You don't seem the least put out by the fact that a Soviet agent seems to know quite a bit about what's happening here in London," she finally said in a low voice.

He sighed.

"It's not that I'm not concerned. Of course I am. But we've known that there are Soviet spies all over England since before the war. That Shustov is keeping an eye on what they send to Moscow is also no surprise. He's been doing it since your father and he met. He always seems to know things as soon as they happen."

"Well, it would have been nice if I'd been told of this before now," she muttered, reaching for her wine.

Bill looked faintly amused. "What difference would it have made?"

"I wouldn't have been so flustered with the speed with which he was able to get a message to me, for one. Do we have people in Moscow?"

"No."

She stared at him.

"No? Not even one?"

He shook his head. "Not that I'm aware of."

"Do you mean to say that the NKVD is running agents all over England, and we're deaf and blind in return?"

"Well, yes, I suppose so."

Evelyn sat back in her chair, stunned. "I assumed we had *someone* in the Soviet Union."

"We do. His name is Shustov, and you're in contact with him."

She waved her hand impatiently. "You know what I mean. Someone who is one of ours."

"Whether they are one of ours or one of theirs is immaterial if they give us reliable and accurate information," Bill said with a shrug. "It's true that they have shown themselves to be remarkably efficient at getting eyes and ears all over England, and yes, Jasper and I would prefer to have the same advantage in Moscow. But it's very difficult, and so we must make do with what we have. And what we have is you and Shustov."

"But…that's nothing!"

His lips twisted.

"You're doing yourself a great disservice there, my dear."

"Am I? Aside from the odd bit of intelligence that he passes on, he doesn't reveal anything to me about the NKVD, or anything that doesn't pertain directly to me." Evelyn shrugged. "I don't see that this is any kind of advantage to us."

"On the contrary, he tells you more than you realize." Bill leaned forward and lowered his voice. "And as he begins to trust you, he will share more. In time, you will be bringing us more information than you think. You must be patient. This relationship with Shustov was never meant to be anything but a long-term association. It's how it was with your father, and how it will be with you, for as long as we can keep it going."

Evelyn shook her head and reached for her glass again.

"It doesn't seem to be a very efficient way of doing things."

"You didn't feel this way before now," he pointed out, raising his eyebrows. "Why are you so disgruntled now?"

"Because now I realize just how well organized the Soviets are here in England," she retorted. "Goodness, we look like school children in comparison!"

"Perhaps," he admitted, "but it won't be for long. We're trying to win a war at the moment. The Soviets are not a priority right now."

"Perhaps they should be," she muttered under her breath. Then she sighed. "I'm sorry. I suppose I was simply surprised to realize…well, it doesn't matter. Shustov is clearly concerned for my well-being, and that makes me feel a bit better about the whole situation."

"Yes." Bill pursed his lips thoughtfully. "It *is* concerning that there is someone in direct contact with Voss, though. Having Henry in London is bad enough, but now there's another one? That's too many eyes looking for you, and here you are, right in the middle of London."

"Yes, well, I've been thinking about that. It's just possible that Henry and Voss's contact are the same person."

Bill looked at her for a moment.

"Oh? You think they're the same? Why?"

"I don't know. Perhaps because every time Henry reveals where I've been, the SD show up immediately. They seem inordinately interested in me, although I can't for the life of me imagine why."

"I rather think your pulling the wool over Voss's eyes in Strasbourg has something to do with it," he said with a flash of a grin. "The Germans don't take kindly to being made to look like fools."

"But it *must* be more than that!" she exclaimed. "They've been far too persistent, and now they're even looking for me here in England. To what end? So that they can get their hands on me when they invade? Why? Why am I so important to them?"

Bill was quiet for a moment, then he sighed.

"I see your point," he admitted. "Trying to find you on the continent when you're carrying documents is one thing. Actively pursuing you here in England does rather hint to something more ominous."

"I've been trying to think why I'm such a high value target for them, but I can't, for the life of me, come up with anything. In Oslo, I didn't have any critical intelligence on me. I did while I was in France, but how did Voss discover that I was the courier that had the plans from Stuttgart?"

"Don't forget Eisenjager," Bill added, tapping his finger on the table thoughtfully. "He was sent after you in Norway, long before you went to Belgium to get that package. And, from all accounts, he is with the Abwehr and not the SD. That's two agencies who want you."

"What do they know that we don't?" she asked, almost laughing. "I wish I knew why I was so valuable!"

"I don't know, but if we uncover Henry, we might be able to find out," Bill said slowly. "I think perhaps it's fortuitous that you've stumbled upon the Round Club. If you can discover who's a part of it, we can narrow the field of potential contacts with Voss. We can also determine if that contact and Henry are one and the same."

"Yes. I quite agree."

"When do you meet with Marrow again?"

"Tomorrow. I was to report any findings from the luncheon to him, but as it turns out, I'll be going empty-handed. He wasn't very happy about my getting involved to begin with. He's likely to scrap the whole thing now."

"Not if you convince him that it will be more beneficial to keep you in play."

"Yes, but how? I was supposed to come up with more information, proving that it was worthwhile for him to humor me, but I have absolutely nothing."

"Nothing you can share with him, at any rate." Bill was quiet for a moment, then he sighed and shook his head. "I know I'm going to regret this, but there is one way to convince Marrow that you're invaluable."

"Oh?"

"You suggested it yourself the other day."

Evelyn stared at him for a moment, then smiled slowly.

"Offer myself as a German-speaking asset to the Round Club?"

"Yes."

"I can certainly suggest it, but I thought you weren't very enthusiastic about the idea."

"I wasn't. I'm still not. I don't want any more people than are absolutely necessary to know about your affinity for languages, German in particular. That sort of information has a way of getting out, and with Henry lurking around, searching for you…"

"Yes. Yes, I believe I see what you mean." Evelyn was quiet for a moment, then shook her head. "I think we'll have to entrust that to Marrow at this point, don't you? I can't think of another way that will convince him to keep me on at the moment, can you?"

"No, and that's why I suggest it. You must be very careful. Having one of Voss's thugs here makes it damned difficult, not to mention dangerous, but we must find out who is in this club. Montclair and I have got nowhere looking for Henry ourselves. This might be the one chance we have to finally track him down."

"I understand. I'll be careful." Evelyn smiled coldly. "I do have one advantage over them, you know."

Bill raised an eyebrow.

"Oh? What's that?"

"I know they're looking for me here in London." She reached for her wine, a martial glint coming into her blue eyes. "The hunted has become the hunter, and no one ever expects that."

When Wolves Gather

# Chapter Twenty

**Speakers' Corner, Hyde Park**

Evelyn looked at the silver and pearl watch on her wrist and turned to look around. She was at the appointed meeting place in the northeast corner of the park, but there was no sign of Marrow. She sighed and walked a few feet before stopping. She would wait until quarter past, but if there were still no sign of him, she would leave. Standing around in the park indefinitely was not something that appealed to her, especially after her conversation with Bill last evening. The less attention she drew to herself, no matter where she was, the better at this point.

Evelyn turned and walked slowly to the other side of the area where people gathered to listen to politicians, artists, zealots, and everyone in between. Today it was empty and silent, but the path that ran past it was not. Despite there being a war, and it being the middle of the work week, several people were in the park. If Vladimir Lyakhov was correct, any one of them could be watching her, waiting to report back to Hans Voss. Or one of them could be a Soviet spy sent to keep an eye on her. Neither possibility was welcome to her, and a chill went down her spine. Of all the places that she should feel at ease and comfortable, London should be at the top of the list. Instead, she'd learned that it was no better than Paris, or Zurich, or Brussels. It seemed there was nowhere now that she could relax and be confident that she was among allies. The enemy, it seemed, had infiltrated them all.

A frown settled on her face and she pressed her lips together. And yet they were having no luck in reciprocating, either in the Soviet Union or in occupied France. Bill had told her last night that he was still trying to discover which agents were still at liberty in France. The only one that he knew for certain was still free and undetected by the Nazis was the one who had helped her escape Bordeaux two months before. Leon had contacted him a few days ago. He was safe.

For now.

When Bill told her, Evelyn had been surprised. While she hadn't said as much to him, she hadn't expected Leon to have escaped capture. Eisenjager had been in Bordeaux, and had tried to kill her as they were leaving. It had seemed inevitable that he would have reported Leon's involvement to the Gestapo. And yet, it appeared that he had not. Now why would that be?

She had puzzled over that for most of the night as she tossed and turned in her bed in Brook Street. The family house, which had become something of a haven for her in the past year, suddenly didn't seem as safe and secure as it had in the past. Every small noise had made her start in the night, giving her ample opportunity to think about why Leon was still free. Bill hadn't said whether or not he was still in Bordeaux. Perhaps he'd left the port city and was in hiding. Or perhaps he'd moved to another location within Bordeaux. But then what of his pâtisserie? Would he simply close? Or leave it to someone else to run? Or had Eisenjager truly not reported his existence to the Gestapo?

Shaking her head now, Evelyn dismissed the question from her mind. It really didn't have anything to do with her anymore. She'd escaped with Leon's help, and that was an end to it. It was simply another in a very long list of unanswered questions, and she knew as the war continued, that list would grow. It was inevitable.

"Miss Ainsworth!"

She turned and smiled brightly at Mr. Marrow as he walked quickly towards her. He wore a gray overcoat and carried an umbrella in one hand. As she turned, he lifted the umbrella in greeting.

"Mr. Marrow!" she exclaimed as he joined her. "I was beginning to think I'd got my times wrong."

"Not at all. I was delayed at the office. I apologize for keeping you waiting." He shook her hand and smiled down at her. "Shall we walk?"

She nodded and turned to fall into step beside him.

"I'm afraid I haven't anything very interesting to report," she confessed as they walked. "I went to the luncheon yesterday. Miss Milner was there, as well as quite a few others. I managed to get myself seated at her table."

"And?"

"And that's all. I didn't hear a thing out of the ordinary. Not a word!"

He sighed.

"I was afraid that would be the case, but of course it was worth a try. Well, that's that, then."

Evelyn looked at him. "What do you mean?"

"There isn't anything else to be done." He shrugged. "It was a good plan, but it didn't work. The best we can hope for now is that someone else will come forward if they overhear something, just as you did."

"Forgive me, but you're simply going to leave national security to the hope that someone else will come forward?" she asked in disbelief, stopping to stare at him.

He smiled faintly.

"Not entirely, of course not, but I'm afraid there isn't much more that you can do at this juncture. I do appreciate your willingness to try, of course, but there it is. If you *do* hear anything more in future, I hope you'll let me know, but for the moment, I think we're at a standstill, don't you?"

"I don't, actually." She resumed walking, catching his sidelong look of surprise. "I haven't been exactly forthright with you, Mr. Marrow."

"Oh? In what way?"

"There's something I haven't mentioned yet because, well, I was reluctant to do so. I know my father must have mentioned it to you at some point. He was very fond of telling everybody who would listen, but I doubt you would have remembered. I'm rather a talented linguist, you see. I speak several languages fluently and am very adept at dialects. One of those languages is German."

He paused and looked at her sharply.

"What?"

"With a Berlin accent."

"Now that you mention it, I do seem to recall your father saying that you had a tremendous ear for languages." Marrow continued walking, his umbrella tapping on the pavement. "Have you been to Berlin?"

"Once, many years ago. I was quite young, but it was there that I learned the accent."

"And you were reluctant to tell me this? Why?"

She smiled sheepishly.

"Well, I suppose because we're discussing English men and women who have thrown their lot in with the Nazis, many of whom have spent time in Berlin in the past. I suppose I must have been afraid that you would think I was one of them!"

"If you were, you'd hardly come to tell us of their plans," he said wryly. "Although, I do see your point."

They walked in silence for a few minutes, then he looked at her.

"How do you think you can use this skill to our advantage?"

"Well, the Round Club must be getting the information they're gathering out of England and to Germany somehow. What if something were to happen to that avenue of communication? They must be looking for multiple ways to move the information. I know I would if I were in their position."

"And you propose to offer yourself as a means to move it?" he asked her incredulously, stopping again. He stared at her. "Do you have any idea of just what you're suggesting?"

"Yes, of course I do," she said briskly. "I'm suggesting that I pose as a German spy and courier, in a position to ferry their information on to the German government. Or a handler. Or an agent. Whomever they would like."

"It's out of the question," he said, shaking his head. "It's far too dangerous. This isn't a game, Evelyn. This is war."

"Yes, and people will die in this war," she retorted tartly. "I'm an officer in the WAAF, Mr. Marrow. I'm well aware of what it means to be at war."

He stared at her for a moment, then smiled sheepishly.

"My apologies. Of course you are. I'm afraid I tend to forget that you're an officer in the air force now."

She inclined her head slightly, and he sighed, resuming their walk.

"However, that doesn't alter the fact that what you're proposing is extremely dangerous. And how on earth do you propose to pull it off when they know who you are? Your family is not exactly unknown, and you've been far from a wallflower over the years."

"Oh, that's quite simple. They will never know that it's me."

He frowned and glanced at her. "A disguise? It would have to be one hell of a charade, my dear."

"I've been known to fool one or two people before," she said dryly, unable to stop an ironic twist of her lips. "I was quite good at theatrics when I was younger, you know."

"I'm sure you were, but this isn't a play for the family's amusement. This is—"

"War," she finished. "Yes. I believe we've established that fact already."

He seemed nonplussed by her calmness for a moment, then he shook his head almost to himself.

"What would you hope to accomplish?" He tried a different tact. "As you say, you're an officer in the WAAF. You don't have unlimited time to commit to this enterprise."

## When Wolves Gather

"No, and that is why we must move quickly," she agreed. "As for what I can accomplish? At the very least, I'll be able to gather a few more names for you. I think, if we're very clever, I can be in a position where they will pass information to me to forward on to Germany. At that point, it will be up to you how to proceed, but we can at least prevent one packet of information from leaving the country. If we can discover how they move their information, you may be able to prevent more."

He was silent for a moment, then he sighed heavily. She'd won. Evelyn knew before he even looked at her, and a rush of satisfaction went through her. She'd convinced him.

"How long do you have?" he asked.

"Until the fifteenth," she said, making up the date on the spot. She knew Bill would work it out for her to have all the time she needed, but she couldn't very well tell Marrow that. Aware that she was placing an extreme time restriction on him, she shrugged. "I'm afraid that's when I'm due back at Northolt."

"That's quite a holiday."

"Yes, well, I've been supervising some rather intensive training for the past nine months. Someone obviously decided that I warranted a nice break. I'm not complaining!"

He chuckled.

"No, I don't suppose you are. Still, while it's a generous holiday for you, it doesn't leave me much time."

"No."

"I could certainly put together a believable cover for you, but it will take time, and that is something we don't have."

He fell into silence again as he thought, and Evelyn was content to walk beside him quietly. She wondered what he would come up with, or if it would be up to her to decide what part she would play. It was all strangely exciting, despite the grim knowledge that these were her fellow countrymen actively working against their government and neighbors. She had been looking forward to having a few weeks off after the course in Scotland, but only a few days had shown her that her old, idle life no longer held any interest for her. The bruise on her leg was a daily reminder that she was truly a part of the war effort now, and not simply as an officer behind a desk on an RAF station. How she could have thought she would welcome a few weeks of frivolous shopping was laughable, really.

Evelyn gazed across the park, a foreign feeling of not belonging taking root in her gut. She wasn't the innocent socialite anymore. Somewhere between Strasbourg and Bordeaux, she had changed and transformed into the woman who was now willing, and able, to kill a man silently with a knife if it became necessary. When had this happened? She suspected it had begun in a mountain ravine in Norway when she had left a man to die in order that she could continue. Or perhaps it was in Marle, when she had watched Asp die so horribly after struggling with Jens. Or was it when she had been confronted by a German major outside Reims and watched as Finn talked their way out of being searched?

No wonder shopping and luncheons no longer held the thrill and excitement they once did. How could they? How could London society possibly compete with cheating death?

"There is a girl, a typist with the telephone company," Marrow said suddenly, breaking the silence and pulling Evelyn back to the present. "She's one of ours. We've been working with her for months, and she's been primed to infiltrate the Round Club. I tell you this in the strictest confidence, you understand. You cannot breathe a word to anyone."

"I understand."

"She won't be at a high level in the Club, if she's able to make it in at all. However, she's managed to become friendly with someone who *is* rather high up. In fact, we believe that she has the ear of one of the inner circle." He cleared his throat. "That could very well be the way to bring you to their attention. I can rush a background and identity for you, and possibly have it finished as quickly as Monday. Once it's complete, our girl can recommend you to Molly. Because she's already gained her trust, it will move more quickly than it would if we approached this in the standard way. She can vouch for you to some extent. If we make your identity irresistible to them, they will reach out to you."

"And this Molly is the one you believe has the ear of one of the inner circle?"

"Yes. If she recommends you to them, then it will be up to you to sell the whole thing. If she doesn't, well, then the whole thing is a wash and you can return to Northolt."

"Do you know who Molly is?"

"No. She's a secretary of some sort, but we haven't been able to determine where, or who, she works for. Molly is a codename, and our girl hasn't been able to work out much about her." He stopped and looked down at her. "If we do this properly, I think it very likely that they will hunt you out. As you said, they need people to move the information out of England. That must be a priority for them. I'll

## When Wolves Gather

create a perfect opportunity, but it will be entirely up to you to make it work. Do you understand?"

Evelyn smiled. "Perfectly."

He tilted his head and studied her.

"You're very calm, and you're not asking very many questions."

"What is there to ask? You'll create a part for me to play, and I will play it. It's really very straightforward."

He blinked, then laughed shortly. "I suppose when you put it that way, it is."

"My only concern at the moment is that I have enough time to discover as much as I can once they've accepted me."

"You seem very confident that they will."

"Of course they will. They won't have a choice. As you said, I'm going to present them with a perfect opportunity." Evelyn smiled brightly. "They'd be fools not to take it."

"I think so as well, but you never can tell with these things. Sometimes everything is perfect and then someone throws a spanner in the works. We'll do our best, but if they don't take the bait, don't feel too badly. It happens more than you'd think." He looked at her. "Are you absolutely sure that you're up for this?"

"Definitely! I'm looking forward to it!" she assured him. "To be honest, I'm bored silly pushing papers and giving the same training over and over again. This will be a wonderful change of pace. I've always loved cloak and dagger stories. Now I can actually live one!"

"I think you'll find it's very different from what you read in stories," he said, shaking his head. "Very different indeed."

Evelyn's lips twisted, and she swallowed the urge to laugh.

"I'll send you a message with instructions at the weekend when I have a better idea of how things are progressing," he continued, seeming not to see the wry smile that had flitted across her face. "Are you staying in Brook Street?"

"Yes."

"Good. I'll send a message round on Saturday. By then, my people should have made some headway on your cover identity." He stopped and looked at her. "Thank you for doing this. If I had another way, I would never ask it of you."

She smiled up at him.

"You didn't ask," she pointed out cheerfully. "I offered, and there is nothing to thank. I'm simply doing what I can for my country. Nothing more."

"God willing you come to no harm doing so," he said. "Robert would turn in his grave if he knew what you were going to do."

"Oh, I wouldn't be so sure of that."

# When Wolves Gather

# Chapter Twenty-One

**Ainsworth Manor**
**August 1**

Evelyn took a deep breath and exhaled, looking up into the cloudless blue sky. Her mare tossed her head and huffed, and Evelyn laughed, leaning forward to pat her glossy chestnut neck.

"Yes, I know. You're ready for your brush down, aren't you?" she murmured. "Come on, then."

She straightened up and turned the horse's head for home. She'd arrived back last evening, having caught an earlier train than she'd originally planned. After her meeting with Marrow, all that had been left was to pack a bag and go home and, after a nice, leisurely lunch at a small cafe near Brook Street, that was exactly what she'd done. This morning, following an early breakfast, she'd gone for a ride, itching for some exercise and the feeling of the wind in her hair.

It was comforting to be home. Here she wasn't worried about being watched by invisible agents of the Soviet Union, Nazi Germany, or even both. She wasn't concerned with running into acquaintances who may or may not be traitors to the crown and their country. Here, she was away from all of that. It was a sanctuary, and Evelyn had never been more grateful for the expansive lands and familiar paths as she was now.

As she walked her horse along the bridle path that wound its way towards the stables, Evelyn sighed. She was happy to be home, but the restlessness that had driven her to London seemed just as pronounced this morning as it had been last week. For all the comfort and safety of her family seat, she couldn't ignore the feeling. It was as though she was physically unable to rest and relax. She was being driven by some unseen force to do more than she was able to do in Lancashire. Even her horse had sensed it, dancing impatiently as she'd saddled her earlier, and all but bolting once they were away from the trees around the house and Evelyn had loosened the reins to give her her head.

She frowned now as they walked back through the trees. Why was she so restless? She'd been completely exhausted when she returned from Scotland, both mentally and physically. It had been a grueling course that had drained every last bit of energy from her, and then taken some more for good measure. And yet, she hadn't been home for two days before she was ready to get moving again. What was wrong with her? Bill was right. She needed this holiday to recuperate and get her breath back, but she seemed unable to make use of it. Instead, she'd found something else to occupy her time.

Evelyn's lips twisted wryly. Of course it would have to have been her that overheard Sir Clark and Miss Milner in the garden that night. It was beginning to seem as though she was a magnet for this kind of thing. Even when she was minding her own business and on holiday, intrigue found her.

They broke through the trees a few minutes later and Evelyn went into the stable yard, smiling at the groom as he came out to meet her.

"Have a nice ride, then, miss?" he asked, reaching out to take reins as the horse and rider came to a stop.

"Yes, thank you, Barnes." Evelyn dismounted and stroked her hand down the horse's neck. "We had a lovely time, didn't we, Sass?"

Sass tossed her head and let out a huff, causing Evelyn to laugh.

"Well, at least I had a lovely time."

"Oh, I'm sure she did, too. She's just showing off for you, aren't you, my girl?" Barnes said, patting the horse's neck. "She's missed you, she has, miss. Every time someone comes into the stable, she looks for you."

"I've missed her as well." Evelyn gave her a final stroke, then turned away. "I met the new stable hand earlier. I didn't know Robbie had hired someone to help you, but I'm glad he did."

"It came as a bit of a surprise to me as well, but it wasn't Mr. Ainsworth who brought him on."

Evelyn raised an eyebrow and turned back.

"Oh?"

"No, miss. It was Mrs. Ainsworth. I believe someone suggested to her that we could use another pair of hands." Barnes grinned. "Can't say I'm sorry for it. It's mighty handy to have another man to help exercise the horses every day, and Wallace says he's right handy with the cars as well."

"My, it sounds like he's a godsend," Evelyn said with a smile.

"Yes, miss."

"Have you seen any of the others yet? Am I the only one up this early?"

## When Wolves Gather

"Mssr Bouchard was down a bit ago. He's taken a liking to Mr. Ainsworth's Shadow. He snuck him a lump of sugar. Thought I didn't notice," Barnes scoffed. "He'll be making that horse fat if we're not careful, and then what will I say to Mr. Ainsworth?"

"You'll tell him the truth, and Robbie will believe every word. We all know Uncle Claude is an old softie." Evelyn smiled. "Anyway, I'm sure it won't come to that."

"We'll see, miss. We'll see."

Evelyn grinned as she started out of the stable yard and back towards the house. Barnes had always hated it when any of them interfered with the diet of the horses under his care, and she and Robbie had been on the receiving end of stern lectures too many times to count. Yet all the horses were healthy and happy, and not one had ever got fat or ill from too many carrots or lumps of sugar.

"Evelyn!"

A voice called to her a few minutes later as she was crossing the south lawn to go to the terrace. She turned and smiled when Aunt Agatha came out from the trees carrying a basket filled with wildflowers and sprigs of fern.

"Auntie Agatha!" She waved. "You're up early!"

"Early? I've been up, tended the garden, had my breakfast, and gone for a long walk in the woods," the older woman said, joining her. "I don't know how you can lay in bed all morning!"

"I haven't. I've just come back from a ride." Evelyn tucked her arm through her aunt's as they walked towards the house. "You know I've always been an early riser. How are you? How are things here?"

"Oh, we're all managing. Adele, Madeleine, and I have been helping in the village with the Women's Institute. Claude has been helping the steward, with Rob's approval, of course. Did you know they're transforming the south pasture into farmland?"

"Yes. Mummy told me last week. I think it's a wonderful idea."

"Damien thinks that the government will requisition it if he doesn't do something. They've taken over a few pastures in the area and turned them into farms. They're being worked by the Land Army, or so they're called. I don't know what kind of army they are. They all seem to be women in trousers."

Evelyn grinned.

"Don't you approve? Of women in trousers, I mean."

"Don't be impertinent," Agatha said without heat, a twinkle in her eye. "You know very well what I mean. If a girl wants to traipse about in trousers, it's no concern of mine. And anyway, they can't very well wear anything else when they're out digging up fields, can they?

No. It's the government simply taking the land that I don't approve of."

"They do pay to use it, you know."

"Ha!" Agatha laughed. "A pittance. Hardly worth mentioning."

"Well, there *is* a war on, and food will only get more and more scarce as more of the supply ships are unable to get through. They have to do something."

"I know." She sighed. "I just hope for all of your sakes that this scheme of Damien's works. I hate to think of Robert's land being dug up and overrun with strangers."

"According to Robbie, the wool from our sheep is in very high demand, so I don't think it likely that he will lose very much of his land to the war effort," Evelyn said soothingly. "And even if he does, he will have it returned at the end of it."

"And then he will have to repair all the damage!"

Evelyn shook her head.

"You worry too much, Auntie. Let's get through the war before we start worrying about after it, shall we?"

"Evelyn! Agatha!" Madeleine waved from the terrace. "Where have you been?"

"I've been for a ride, and Auntie has been for a walk in the wood," Evelyn called back. "Is that tea?"

"Yes. Come and join us. I'll have Thomas bring more cups."

Evelyn released Agatha's arm and went through the opening in the low wall that surrounded the terrace.

"Good morning, Tante Adele," she greeted her other aunt, bending to kiss an offered cheek. "You look refreshed this morning. Did you sleep well?"

"I always do when I'm here," Adele replied with a smile. "The English countryside agrees with me."

"Where's Uncle Claude?" Evelyn sat down at the wrought iron table and stripped off her riding gloves.

"He's gone off to check on the progress at the south pasture," Mrs. Ainsworth said, lifting a bell and ringing it for the butler. "He's been helping Damien, you know."

"Yes, Aunt Agatha was just telling me. I'm glad. I know Robbie will be relieved to have Uncle's help with the estate. It worries him that he can't give it his full attention at the moment."

"How is Robert? Have you spoken to him?" Adele asked, sipping her tea. "He came here when we first arrived, but we haven't heard from him since."

## When Wolves Gather

"He's very busy. All the pilots are." Evelyn smiled as Thomas, the family butler, emerged onto the terrace from the drawing room with a tray in his hands. "Thomas, are you psychic?" she demanded with a laugh. "How on earth did you know we needed more cups and saucers?"

Thomas allowed a very faint smile to relax his features.

"I saw you and Miss Ainsworth crossing the lower lawn," he said, setting the extra cups and saucers onto the table, along with another pot of tea.

"Of course you did." Evelyn reached for a cup. "Well, I'm very glad of it. Thank you!"

He bowed slightly and turned back to the house.

"He really is invaluable," Agatha said, reaching for the other cup. "I don't know what you'd do without him, Madeleine. I really don't."

"Thankfully, that isn't something I have to contemplate for some time, yet," Mrs. Ainsworth replied. "We're very lucky that all but a few of the servants are too old to go war. I'm waiting for the maids and footman to go. I'm rather surprised none of them have signed up yet."

"Perhaps they're waiting to be called up," Agatha said, pouring tea into Evelyn's cup before her own. "I don't think I'd volunteer. I'd wait until I had no choice."

"Would you?" Adele seemed surprised. "I'd have thought you'd be the first in line when you were younger. Evelyn was, wasn't she?"

"Yes, and I told her at the time that she was being a fool, didn't I, Evie?"

"Yes you did, and my answer remains the same." Evelyn sipped her tea. "I'd rather be a fool than a selfish prig. If I'm able to do my bit, I should."

"Not everyone has your patriotism, my dear." Madeleine patted her hand fondly. "In our case, I'm rather glad of it. Once Fran, Megan, and Steven leave, I'll have to have a girl in from the village to help Millie with the housekeeping. And heaven knows who I'll be able to get to help Thomas."

"It will be all right, Mummy. Don't worry. It won't hurt us to take care of ourselves for a time."

"And so speaks the lips of youth and vitality," Adele said humorously. "What I wouldn't give for an ounce of your energy, Evelyn darling."

Evelyn laughed.

"I wish I could give it to you, Tante, but even if I could, you're hardly in need of it. The three of you are always busy!"

"We do try," Madeleine admitted with a smile. "And of course you're right. When the time comes, we will get along just fine. At least we'll still have Thomas and Millie, and Barnes and Wallace."

"And don't forget the nice Mr. Hanes that takes care of the gardens," Agatha added.

"The nice Mr. Hanes?" Evelyn repeated, her eyebrows soaring into her forehead. "Why Aunt Agatha! Never tell me that you've made friends with the gardener!"

Agatha flushed and Evelyn laughed, her eyes dancing.

"You have!" she exclaimed. "Do tell!"

"There's nothing to tell, Miss Nosy-body. He's a very nice man and we've had one or two discussions about the roses. That's all there is to it."

"I don't know where Lord Buckley found him, but I'm very glad he did," Madeleine said. "He's been helping wherever he's needed. He really is a jack of all trades. He even helped Wallace mend some electrical wiring in the garage!"

Evelyn smiled.

"I'm so glad. The more hands around here, the better." She looked across at Agatha's pink cheeks. "I'm sorry for teasing you, Aunt Agatha. It's just that I've never known you to like anybody before!"

Adele was surprised into a laugh at that, quickly muffled when Madeleine shot her a warning look. But Agatha didn't seem inclined to take offense. Instead, she smiled and shook her head.

"I don't, usually," she admitted. "I don't have any patience for platitudes and empty conversation. That is simply who I am."

"And we wouldn't change it for the world," Madeleine assured her.

"No. Not in the slightest," Adele agreed. "You're a very blunt woman, Agatha, but there is nothing wrong with that. One knows where one stands with you, and that is very much appreciated these days."

Evelyn looked at the three women and smiled. It filled her heart with joy to see her two aunts and mother finding a way to rub along together, especially after the rocky start they'd had. Perhaps this war was good for some things.

"Speaking of the staff," she said, setting her cup down. "Would it be all right if I borrowed Fran for a few days? I'm going back to London and it would be much easier with a maid."

## When Wolves Gather

"Yes, of course," Mrs. Ainsworth said, "but why are you so determined to go back to London? You've only just got back!"

"I know, and I'm sorry to go off again and leave you. It's just that I'm having so much fun!" Evelyn looked at her mother and smiled sheepishly. "I'd forgotten how fun it is to go to lunch and to go shopping, and not have to worry about whether or not the training went quite as well as I thought it did. I think a few days in Town is just what I need to refresh myself. It's lovely to be here too, of course, but not quite the same."

"Of course it isn't. The country is not London," Adele said with a nod. "And London is not Paris, but it still has much to recommend itself for all of that," she added with a grin.

"It did," Agatha said, "but now it's not the same at all."

"It *has* changed, but I'm enjoying it nevertheless," Evelyn agreed.

"Well, of course if you're enjoying yourself," her mother sighed. "How are the Gilhursts? You said Maryanne was worried about her brother."

"They're the same as always, I think. Everyone is under a tremendous amount of strain, and it shows. Maryanne has joined the ATS. She's going to be a driver."

"The army!" Madeleine gasped. "No!"

"Yes. Lord Gilhurst has already arranged everything. She said I inspired her." Evelyn laughed and pushed back her chair. "I can't imagine how, but there you have it. Well, I'm off to get changed. If it's all right with you, Mummy, I'll talk to Fran now. If she's willing to come with me, we'll leave in the morning."

"Yes, of course. I can see that it would be easier with a maid, and I'll feel a bit better knowing that you're not alone in that house. Will you take the train again?"

"I thought I'd take the Lagonda. Robbie left it here and it seems silly to take the train when it's just sitting gathering dust in the garage." Evelyn turned to go towards the open doors to the drawing room. "I'll speak to Wallace when I come down. That is, unless you'd rather I left it here?" She asked, looking over her shoulder.

Her mother shook her head and waved a hand airily.

"No. Take the car. Just be careful."

"I'm always careful, Mummy. You know that."

Evelyn stepped onto the gravel path that snaked through the rose garden. She'd come out in search of Rex Hanes, the gardener who'd captured Aunt Agatha's respect. Of course, he wasn't a gardener at all, but one of Bill's men. He'd been sent to keep an eye on things after a break-in that left both Bill and Evelyn uneasy. She'd been very grateful for his presence, but was rather surprised to find that he was still in residence. After she'd cracked the puzzle box, one of the primary reasons for his being there, Evelyn had assumed that Bill would re-assign him. Not only did that not appear to have been the case, but she was fairly certain that the new hand helping Barnes in the stables was also one of Bill's. Why was he *increasing* security? Not that it really mattered, she supposed. She knew she certainly would sleep easier knowing that there were people keeping an eye on things when she couldn't be here.

"Afternoon, miss," a voice said from the other side of a row of bushes. A head appeared, and then a torso, as Rex stood up, a trowel in his hand. "Having a nice wander through the gardens?"

"Yes, thank you," Evelyn said with a smile. "I was looking for you, as a matter of fact."

"Well, you've found me. What can I do for you?"

"What are you doing?" she asked, distracted by the trowel in one hand and what looked like a freshly dug up plant in the other.

"Digging out these weeds, the nasty blighters." Rex tossed the plant into a wheel barrow nearby. "They've all but taken over."

"Goodness, you mean that you're really gardening while you're here?"

Rex grinned and wiped perspiration from his forehead.

"I enjoy it, and it keeps me busy."

She made a face. "That's very kind of you to say, but you must be bored silly. Why are you still here? I would have thought that Bill would have recalled you."

"Sir William thought it would be best for me to stay on for a bit. He wants to be sure that we really have seen the last of our visitor."

"And the new man in the stables?"

"Ah, that'd be Walters, miss."

"And is Walters also here at Bill's behest?"

Rex had the grace to look sheepish.

"Yes, miss. After the last incident, Sir William thought it might be best if I had another set of eyes and ears to help. Truth be told, I don't think he'll rest easy until he's caught the spy running around London."

## When Wolves Gather

Evelyn looked at him over the bush, her brows coming together.

"You know about that as well, do you? What do you think? Do you think that's who broke into the house?"

"Hard to say, but I wouldn't be half surprised. Someone's looking for whatever your father left behind, and it stands to reason that it's 'im."

"Or her." Evelyn smiled wryly. "We don't know that the spy is a man. It could just as easily be a woman."

"I'd agree with you if it weren't for the fact that he's called Henry," Rex said, scratching his chin. "Never heard of the Germans calling a woman by a man's name before."

"That's true," she admitted, pursing her lips thoughtfully. "I suppose it's also true that he could come back. He doesn't know that what he's looking for is now gone."

"Exactly." Rex looked at her shrewdly. "Or that we know what it is he's looking for."

"Are you sure you're not bored babysitting here on the chance that he might return?"

"I'm perfectly happy here, don't you worry." He chuckled. "I've had my fair share of excitement in my years with Bill. I'm enjoying my time pottering around the gardens and helping where I can, and that's the truth. I keep a keen eye out, as does Walters. And Wallace and Barnes do their bit as well, even if they don't know anything about the intruder. If he's foolish enough to try a third time, he'll be in for a surprise."

"Well, that's a relief." Evelyn smiled and turned to leave. "I'll let you get back to your weeding, then."

"You be careful, miss," he said suddenly.

She turned back in surprise.

"Pardon?"

"If this Henry is what we all think he is, he'll be looking for you just as hard as he's looking for whatever it is that your father left behind," he told her soberly. "He may not realize it's *you*, if you get my meaning, but he knows there's a spy named Jian, and he knows she's in England. Until he's caught, you're at risk every time you go to London."

"Yes. I'm aware of that. I'm taking every care."

"Be sure that you do." He nodded and prepared to return to his weeds. "You'll be needed soon enough in France. It won't do to go and get yourself killed before you even leave England again."

"I'll do my very best," she said dryly, a grin pulling at her lips.

But as she left the rose garden and made her way back towards the house, Evelyn felt a chill of disquiet go through her. Rex was right, of course. She was aware of the risk each time she went into the city, and each time she entered the building on Broadway. Considering it now, she was forced to admit to herself that perhaps chasing the Round Club was a bit more reckless than it first appeared. And now she was going to go all in and pretend to be a German agent herself! Good heavens, what was she thinking? What was Bill thinking to allow it?

As soon as the thought came into her head, she brushed it aside with a slight shake and pressed her lips together. They didn't have any choice. She was in the perfect position to discover who the ring leaders were, and who they were in association with. Marrow had been very upfront about their lack of success. If the Security Service couldn't do it, then she had to try. The very fate of the King and Parliament might depend on it if the Germans made it across the Channel. It *was* tricky, though. If Henry was looking for her, she was about to throw up a veritable flare.

She just had to make sure that he didn't find her when he went to investigate.

And then there was the small matter of the stolen military secrets hidden in the back of her wardrobe in her bedroom. Evelyn raised her eyes to the second floor of the large manor house thoughtfully as she approached. They had to be dealt with as well. Until she could find a machine to read the microfilm, she had no idea how dangerous those papers really were. Her father certainly thought they were important enough to leave concealed in a safe deposit box that only she could access. But why? What were they? And why had he been so insistent in his last letter to her that she conceal their existence from the very agency that employed them both?

The answers lay in a locked box in her bedroom. She just had to find a way to read them. Perhaps she should take the microfilm with her back to London. At least there she had a chance of finding a machine to read them. A library, perhaps? Or even Marrow might be persuaded to lend a hand without being aware of it.

But even as she considered it, Evelyn felt an overwhelming sense of disquiet at the thought. If she were to be followed in London, or watched, and if the house in Brook Street were to be broken into, as the Manor had been, what then? Someone else would know about the secret her father had done so much to hide.

## When Wolves Gather

No. The films had to remain where they were for the time being. There would be time enough to find a way to read them after the Round Club had been dealt with.

And she would have to read them. For that would be the only way to discover exactly what she had carried back from Zurich, and what on earth her father had been so afraid to expose to MI6.

## Chapter Twenty-Two

**London**

Henry went quickly down the wide, shallow steps towards the marble-tiled lobby below. Various meetings had consumed his morning and now he had less than fifteen minutes to make it to a luncheon with the Spanish Ambassador. They were being joined by one of de Gaulle's puppets, an assistant, which Henry thought was absolutely ridiculous. Who was this person? One of the so-called Free French? What were his credentials for being invited to discuss the future of this made-up nationality comprised of traitors to Vichy? He was a nobody. Free French indeed.

Just yesterday, Vichy France had imposed the death penalty on any Frenchman who joined a foreign army. Yet de Gaulle was busy calling on his fellow countrymen to continue to fight alongside the British against the Nazi forces. He was encouraging them to go against their government, and condemning them to certain execution by the Vichy courts, yet even Churchill continued to support the French General's efforts to rally the Free French to himself. It was insanity. All that would be accomplished would be for a lot of Frenchmen to be hanged for treason when the Nazis took over London and sent them all back to France.

It was a hopeless cause, and he would have to listen to the bickering back and forth between the Spanish Ambassador and the Frenchman during lunch. He was expected to keep the peace between them, and obtain assurance from the Ambassador that Spain would not interfere with any moves the Free French made in the pursuit of their precious Liberté. Spain's wish to remain neutral should ensure as much, but these things were never cut and dry. It was damned silly, really. The entire luncheon would be nothing but a lot of empty words, and they would all come away convinced that they had made positive headway.

But it was something that had to be done if only so that he could determine just what Spain's position was towards the Free French. Once he knew that, he could forward the information on to Berlin.

## When Wolves Gather

He was crossing the massive lobby, heading towards the doors to the street, when a woman intercepted him, moving in the opposite direction. Her dark hair was pulled up neatly behind her head and a plain gray hat perched at an angle atop the glossy strands. She was dressed precisely in a conservative gray tweed suit, and she carried a stack of correspondence in her arms.

"Ah, Miss Pollack," he greeted her with a smile. "How is your day progressing? Better than mine, I hope?"

"Quite busy, as usual, sir," she replied with a nod. "Have you seen Lord Halifax this morning?"

"Only briefly, and from a distance. Why? Is there something the matter?"

"He'd like to have a word with you this afternoon. Would three o'clock be convenient?"

Henry sighed and nodded tiredly.

"Yes, all right. Tell him I'll be there."

"Thank you." Miss Pollack pulled an envelope from the stack in her hands. "This is for you."

Henry took the envelope with a brisk nod and Miss Pollack continued on her way, her low heels making a staccato sound across the tile. He watched her go, his eyes sliding down her trim figure to linger on long legs before he turned and continued on his way, tucking the envelope into his inner coat pocket.

So Lord Halifax wanted a word, did he? There was nothing very strange in that, but he found it interesting that he had been summoned on the very afternoon that he was lunching with the Spanish Ambassador. Very interesting indeed.

A few minutes later found him settled in the back of a cab on his way to the restaurant. Reaching into his pocket, he pulled out the letter Lord Halifax's secretary had handed him and tore it open. A single sheet of paper contained only two lines.

*Dukes in St. James. Nine o'clock. Room 323. ~ Molly*

A small smile crossed his lips and he tucked the letter back into his coat pocket. Well, that went a long way to making the day look more promising. At least, no matter what this intolerable luncheon held in store, he had this evening to look forward to. He must remember to tell his man not to wait up.

## CW Browning

**London**
**August 2**

Evelyn unscrewed the cap to her pen and pulled a piece of writing paper towards her. She and Fran had arrived in London an hour before and already the maid had the first floor swept clean of dust sheets. The room smelled of furniture polish and Evelyn sighed contentedly. She was so glad that she'd brought the young woman back with her.

"Would you like me to air the bedrooms, miss?" Fran asked, stepping into the parlor with a stack of clean towels in her arms.

"Oh, I don't think there's any need for that," Evelyn began, then paused. "Actually, perhaps you'd better. Rob is coming to Town with a few other pilots. We'd better prepare his room, and perhaps two others just in case."

"Yes, miss."

"Thank you, Fran. I'm so pleased you were willing to come along with me."

Fran looked surprised and smiled in pleasure. "Why, of course, miss."

She left the room and Evelyn heard her cross the hallway towards the stairs. Turning her eyes back to the paper before her, Evelyn felt a wry smile pulling at her lips. The look of surprise on her maid's face had brought home forcibly just how much she'd changed in the past few months. While Evelyn had always, she believed, treated their servants with respect and friendliness, something had changed over the past year. Since she'd been traveling and associating with men and women of quite different classes from herself, Evelyn's outlook had changed drastically. Fran was no longer simply her invaluable maid. She was a young woman who had her own life to live outside of her current employment, and Evelyn was very grateful that she chose to remain with them. It wouldn't last for much longer, but until Fran decided to do her bit to help in this war, Evelyn was extremely conscious of the debt that she owed to all the servants at Ainsworth. They helped maintain the standard of living that her family was accustomed to, and made her time home that much more comfortable.

Evelyn lifted her eyes to gaze thoughtfully out of the window. It couldn't continue, of course. None of it could. She wasn't quite sure *how* she knew that, but she felt it in her gut. The world was changing at

## When Wolves Gather

an alarming rate, and it was all thanks to the war. She and Robbie were working and fighting for their country, something that would never have even been considered just five years before. Their peers were joining up to do the same, working side by side with men and women from all walks of life. She'd seen it at Northolt, all classes working together on the station to fight a common enemy. Once that enemy was vanquished, the pre-war status quo would be changed forever. The working class would still be the working class, and the aristocracy would still be the aristocracy, but the attitudes would be changed. It was inevitable, really. Women like Fran would discover their worth outside of their presumed station in society, and the sharp distinctions between classes would have to become blurred. It was already happening out of necessity on military stations across England, and Evelyn wasn't so sure that was a bad thing. The stark divide between the classes had always bothered her, though she never could really put her finger on why. It had just seemed absurd that she wasn't supposed to go into a pub because of her station in life, and the pub landlord wasn't welcome in, say, The Dorchester for the same reason. What did it matter who one's parents were? A meal was a meal, and a drink was a drink.

The sound of the front doorbell made her start and she looked down at the blank sheet of paper before her. The letter she had meant to write had never even been started, and she picked up the cap to screw it back onto her pen. A moment later, she heard Miles' deep voice in the hall and her heart skipped in her chest. The door to the parlor opened and she turned in her chair, setting the pen down.

"Mr. Miles Lacey to see you, Miss Ainsworth," Fran announced.

"Thank you, Fran." Evelyn rose as Miles entered the room. "Miles!"

Fran closed the door discreetly as Miles came towards her, a smile on his face.

"Good morning!" he said, grasping her outstretched hands and pulling her towards him. "I'm a bit early, I'm afraid. I hope you don't mind?"

"Not at all!" Evelyn felt his arms go about her waist and leaned into him. "It's so wonderful to see you!"

His lips brushed hers and he held her close for a moment before pulling away and looking down at her.

"You look beautiful, and are very much a sight for sore eyes," he told her. "I couldn't sleep a wink last night."

"Couldn't you? I slept like a log," she teased, pulling away. "But never say you drove down this morning all the way from Norfolk?"

"We did. We were going to come down last night, but we didn't land until after ten. We decided to make an early start today instead."

Evelyn looked at his handsome face and noted the shadows under his eyes. He looked tired, and there was a somberness about his mouth that hadn't been there the last time she saw him. Miles was feeling strained, and it was beginning to show. In that moment, she knew why they had received this twenty-four break in the middle of what was undoubtedly the beginning of a fierce fight for England. Their CO was trying to prevent them from getting too tired too quickly. She thought of Fred, remembering how touchy he'd been when she asked if he was getting tired. She wouldn't make that mistake with Miles.

"You must be tired from driving," she said, forcing a bright smile. "Shall I have Fran bring tea?"

"Not a bit of it! I'm raring to go."

That brought a genuine laugh to her lips. "Very well, but where *are* we going?"

He winked. "Fetch your hat and you'll see."

◉

"You're having her do *what*?!"

Jasper stared at Bill in aghast disbelief. That gentleman stared back, unperturbed.

"It really is fortunate that she's in a position to be able to help," Bill replied. "After eight months, we're no closer to discovering Henry's identity. Here is an opportunity to tackle it from a different direction."

"Are you out of your mind? Have you been working too hard? Is that it?" Jasper demanded.

"Not at all." Bill crossed his legs and pulled a cigarette case from his pocket. "It was all her idea, you know."

"That I don't doubt." Jasper exhaled and sank into his seat behind his desk. "Why in blazes did you agree?"

"I've told you. She will be in a position to possibly discover who's involved with the Round Club, and quite possibly Henry's identity as well." Bill paused to light a cigarette. "And there's something else. We have another problem on our hands."

Jasper looked up sharply. "Oh?"

"Yes." Bill blew smoke upwards and frowned. "Shustov brought it to her attention."

"Shustov!" Jasper sat back and scowled. "When?"

"Just the other day. He contacted her and she picked up a message right here in London. It had been inserted in a newspaper."

"What did it say?"

"That someone here in London, in the Round Club, is in contact with Hans Voss." Bill met Jasper's gaze grimly. "They're expanding their search for Jian to England."

"What? How? But that's impossible!"

"Apparently not," Bill said dryly. "It isn't too fantastic, after all. They haven't had any luck in pinning her down on the continent, so they're coming here. They know she'll be off her guard on her own grounds. They're probably hoping to discover her identity and take care of her here."

"Good God! To what end?"

"To take her out of circulation."

"Right here in England?" Jasper stared at him. "Don't be absurd, Buckley. They wouldn't dare!"

"Wouldn't they?" Bill raised his eyebrows. "Who is there to stop them? We can hardly create a political incident out of it. We couldn't respond at all, and believe me, the Nazis know that."

"But...but...that's just not how it's done," Jasper blustered, his face red.

"Perhaps that's not how it was ever done before, but I think you'll agree that we're not dealing with a government that adheres to the ways of the past very much. Just look at what they did in France! Shooting refugees and bombing civilians are hardly the actions of international law-abiding soldiers."

Jasper exhaled and rubbed his face, never taking his eyes from Bill.

"You really believe they intend to hunt her down here in England?"

"I do."

"Then she should be decommissioned until the threat has passed. We've invested too much in her to lose her as an asset now."

"The threat will never pass if we don't discover who it is that is in contact with Hans Voss, or who Henry is."

"And you think she will be able to uncover either of those by masquerading as a German spy here in England?" Jasper looked skeptical. "This is unheard of, Bill. The whole thing borders on the fantastical, not to mention being highly unorthodox."

For the first time since entering Jasper's office, Bill looked amused.

"Everything we do is unorthodox," he pointed out. "Why should this be any different?"

"Well, for one thing, she'll be working for the Security Service!"

"Yes, well, there is that. I'll confess I'm not happy about that myself."

"And this Marrow chap? He seems perfectly sensible and respectable in the clubs, of course, but how do we know that he's competent at his job?"

"I've known Marrow for years, and he's as steady as they come. He'll not take any chances with Jian. He's a friend of the family, you know." Bill shrugged and a smile tugged at his lips. "I'm surprised she was able to convince him to allow her to do it, to be honest."

Jasper shook his head.

"I don't like it. You say the SD has someone looking for her in England, and now you're sending her right into the heart of the wolf's den."

"She can do what we haven't been able to yet," Bill retorted. "I have the utmost faith in her. If she says she'll learn the identities of the members of this so-called Round Club, then she will. And we must allow her to do it her way. Once she's in France, she will have to run her own operations, you know. We've trained her to do it. We can hardly protest at her using her skills here in England when we expect her to do it on the continent."

"But that's just the point!" Jasper exclaimed. "We trained her to do it *on the continent*, not here in England. That's what the Security Service is for."

"Yes, but the Security Service is in a shambles. They're clearly not equipped to tackle the Round Club without assistance."

"And you say Marrow agreed?"

"She met with him on Wednesday. He's working up an identity for her."

Jasper sighed heavily.

"It doesn't appear that I have any say in the matter. I *am* still the section head, am I not?"

## When Wolves Gather

"Of course you are." Bill got up to put out his cigarette in the ashtray. "That's why I'm here telling you what's been planned."

Jasper was betrayed into a reluctant laugh.

"So kind of you."

"I do try."

"What is the arrangement that she has with Shustov?" Jasper asked after a moment.

The smile faded from Bill's face and he retook his seat.

"I've absolutely no idea. She won't tell me."

"What? Why not?"

"She says it's for my own protection as well as hers. I suppose I can't really blame her. We have a mole here in our midst, and if her arrangement with Shustov is exposed, we'll lose him, and likely her as well."

Jasper grunted.

"I suppose so. I don't like it, though. I don't like that a Communist agent has such unfettered and direct contact with one of our own."

"Neither do I," Bill admitted. "We did insist that she go along with it, however. This is a beast of our own making."

"Well, it was the only way he would continue to feed us information, wasn't it? And I'm loathe to lose our only asset within the Soviet Union."

"Yes. I know." Bill exhaled. "And so we must accept this arrangement with good grace. Evelyn has a very good head on her shoulders. She will take care of herself."

"That isn't necessarily my concern." Jasper leaned forward. "How did he insert a message in the newspaper? Was it printed?"

"No. It was written."

"Written? Do you mean by hand?"

"Yes."

"How the hell did he manage that?"

"He's obviously got agents in London."

"In London? Don't be daft!" Jasper scoffed. "It's not possible."

"Not only is it possible, but I'd say it's fairly obvious. How else could a message be handwritten in the day's paper?"

"But the Security Service apprehended all the Reds in London!"

"They apprehended all the ones they know of, but for every one they catch, more go undetected. They admit that themselves. If you'll recall, Risto Niva did warn us in November. He claimed that there were several Soviet agents entrenched in England."

Jasper waved his hand dismissively.

"The words of a man who wanted to come to England. He would have said anything if it would give him a chance for freedom."

"In light of this message incident, I don't think we can dismiss it any longer. They are certainly here, and they are certainly active. The question is, how entrenched are they? And where?"

Jasper's brows pulled together in a scowl.

"This is all quite disconcerting," he muttered, "but of course I can see that you're right. However, as uncomfortable as it is, it's no concern of ours. We'll leave that to the Security Service. That is, after all, what they're in existence for."

"Yes." Bill pressed his lips together thoughtfully. "We must take care that our section is clean, though."

Jasper raised his brows. "Do you think they could be in government? In our own agency?"

"It's what we would do if we were fortunate enough to have people in Moscow."

Jasper glowered. "You really are a ray of sunshine this morning, aren't you?"

Bill chuckled and stood up.

"I'm simply stating facts. It would be the height of folly to pretend that the Soviet risk isn't as great, if not greater, than that of the Nazis."

He turned to leave the office and Jasper was silent until he reached the door.

"You will keep me apprised of developments, won't you?" he asked as Bill reached for the handle.

"Yes, of course."

**When Wolves Gather**

# Chapter Twenty-Three

Evelyn gazed out of the window as the hedgerows lining the winding road fell behind them and a small village loomed ahead. Miles had left London behind, heading west into the countryside, and she took a deep breath of the clean, country air that rushed into the open window beside her. She'd tied a scarf over her hair to keep it from blowing in the wind and, as she glanced over at Miles, she smiled at his disheveled waves being tossed about his forehead.

"Are we stopping in this village?" she asked. "Or continuing on?"

"I haven't decided yet," he said with a grin. "What do you think?"

She bit back a laugh. He had been stubbornly refusing to tell her where they were going since they left the house in Brook Street. Regardless of how she tried to trick it out of him, he'd remained mum on the subject.

"I think you don't have the faintest idea where we're going," she replied promptly.

"Then you'd be wrong, m'dear. I know precisely where we're going."

He winked at her and shifted gears, slowing down as they approached the small village.

"I don't see why you won't tell me, then. It's not as if I'm not going to find out."

"You really don't like to be surprised, do you?" he asked, looking at her.

"It's not that. I simply prefer to know what's going on."

"That's what comes of being an officer in the WAAF," he told her.

"Being an officer has nothing to do with it. We're never told anything, especially what's going on!" Evelyn turned her attention to the village shops that were passing by her window. "Much the same as you, I'd imagine."

"Oh, we're told what's happening once we're in the air," he said gaily. "They get us airborne before they tell us how outnumbered we are."

Evelyn shot him a look under her lashes, paused, then shook her head.

"We're not going to do it," she told him firmly. "We're not going to spend this lovely day talking about the war. I give you fair warning, Flight Lieutenant Lacey, that if you start, I'll walk back to Town."

He looked at her and grinned.

"Agreed. Not another word about scrambles or sorties will pass my lips."

He turned his eyes back to the narrow road as it curved to the left, then he slowed even more and pulled into a small car park in front of a squat building. A hanging sign above the door proudly proclaimed the name of the premises as The Fighting Cock, and a regal rooster stood atop a barrel beneath the name. Evelyn raised her eyebrows.

"We came all this way to go to a pub?"

"Not a bit of it." Miles stopped the car and left the engine running as he opened his door. "I'll just be a moment."

Evelyn watched as he ran around the front of the car and disappeared into the pub, her lips pursed thoughtfully. What on earth was he up to? She didn't have very long to wonder. Not even five minutes had passed before he was emerging again, a large wicker basket in his hand.

"What on earth is that?" she demanded through the open window.

"Part of the surprise."

He went to the boot and stowed the basket inside before sliding behind the wheel again.

"A picnic?" she asked.

He sighed and glanced at her before pulling out of the car park and back onto the narrow main street.

"Yes, Lady Nosy Body. I thought a picnic."

"Oh, how lovely!" Evelyn's lips curved in delight. "However did you manage it?"

"Well, I did have some help, I'm afraid," Miles admitted with a rueful grin. "The jolly fellow who is the landlord of The Fighting Cock happens to be a friend of my intelligence officer, Bertie. His son was at University with Bertie. Something of a brain, by all accounts. Bertie hasn't seen him since the war began. He joined the RAF, then disappeared. Bertie believes he's working on something very hush-hush

## When Wolves Gather

somewhere, but of course that's all speculation. Anyway, Bertie rang up the pub yesterday and spoke to Mr. Rutter, a very accommodating and sympathetic man who was happy to put together a luncheon for us. Amazing chap, old Bertie. Really indispensable."

"Intelligence officers usually are," Evelyn said with a smile. "You must remember to thank him for me. I can't think of anything I'd rather do. I was just thinking the other day that if there wasn't a war on, I'd be going on picnics and to garden parties just as we used to."

Miles looked at her, his eyes twinkling.

"Ah, but if there wasn't a war on, we'd likely never have met," he pointed out. "Which would you rather have? Me or garden parties?"

Evelyn pretended to think.

"Well, the parties *were* fun," she said slowly, drawing a laugh from him. "But I really can't imagine never having met you. Funny, isn't it? I feel as if I've known you forever."

"So do I."

They shared a smile, then Evelyn turned her gaze back out of the window. She watched as they turned down a narrow lane that ran through a hedgerow before winding its way through a lightly wooded area. A few minutes later, Miles pulled into a small clearing next to a river and stopped, shutting off the engine.

"Oh!" she exclaimed, looking at the sparkling water. "How lovely!"

"I thought you'd like it."

Miles got out and came around to open the door for her, helping her out of the Jaguar.

"I hope you don't mind sitting on the grass. I managed to pinch a blanket from the supply hut, but the ground still may be damp." He glanced up at the overcast sky and grimaced. "I hope it doesn't rain on us."

"I don't care a jot if it does," Evelyn told him. "I'm just happy to be here with you. We actually have an afternoon together, and I wouldn't mind if it poured buckets!"

Miles turned to the boot to get the basket.

"Hopefully it won't do that!"

⊙

Molly followed the footman across the hallway to the door of the drawing room. She tried not to feel in awe of the opulent surroundings, choosing instead to concentrate on the ramrod straight back in front of her. The Rothman residence in London was very intimidating indeed, having stood proudly as the family town house for over three hundred years. Lady Rothman liked to remind visitors every chance she got that the original structure had burned in the late 1500s, leading to the construction of the present house over the ruins of the old.

Molly had never understood Lady Rothman's pride over this fact. After all, most of central London had been rebuilt after the Great Fire, and yet that wasn't considered any great circumstance. Henry said it was because Lady Rothman felt insecure over her own family's limited heritage, and so she took inordinate pride in her husband's impeccable lineage. Perhaps that was the case. Whatever the reason, Molly always felt distinctly out of place and uncomfortable when she was called to Lady Rothman's drawing room. Her lips pressed together as the footman opened the door and announced her somberly. Henry said that was exactly how Lady Rothman wanted her to feel and that she shouldn't allow herself to be cowed. Of course, it was very easy for Henry to say that. His family was one of the most respected in England, while hers had a merchant background from East London.

"Ah, Miss Pollack!" Lady Rothman looked up from her writing desk and smiled congenially. "How lovely to see you again!"

She stood and nodded a dismissal to the footman. She was a very tall woman, saved from being ungainly by a willowy figure that had turned several heads in her youth. Age had been kind to her, and she had retained that slimness without succumbing to the middle-age thickness that beset so many of her peers. Her black hair had lost its luster, but her blue eyes were every bit as bright and lively as they had always been. As Molly held out her hand to her, she reflected that the woman before her was still handsome, but her choice of clothes left much to be desired. She was dressed in a rather plain cream colored suit with a skirt that did nothing to accentuate her slim figure. In fact, Molly had always considered Lady Rothman to look rather dowdy, though she would never dream of voicing that thought out loud. To criticize such a powerful woman would be social suicide, and Molly did admit to having some aspirations to better herself in that regard. With a smile, she clasped Lady Rothman's hand.

"Lady Rothman, I think you get younger each time I see you," she said cheerfully. "You really must tell me your secret. Is it rose water? I've heard that it does wonders for one's complexion."

"Heavens no! Never could abide the scent, my dear." The other woman motioned her to the settee and sank gracefully into a chair as Molly seated herself. "I've used a particularly good cream from

## When Wolves Gather

a little boutique on Oxford Street for years, but I confess that since the war began, it's getting more and more difficult to lay my hands on it. It's from Paris, you see. When I went last week, I had to settle for a far inferior cream made here in London. I was told that it's unlikely that I'll be able to find it again for quite a while."

"How frustrating!"

"Yes indeed." Lady Rothman crossed one foot behind the other and looked across at her. "Now tell me, my dear, how you have been? How is your work with Lord Halifax?"

"Very interesting. Thank you again for your assistance in obtaining the position."

"I've told you before, my dear, that it was my very good pleasure. I can think of no one I trust more to have in that position. And is everything going as planned?"

"Yes, it is. Just as you said, no one suspects a thing." Molly removed her gloves and set them with her purse beside her. "It's really quite remarkable."

"Of course they don't. Why ever would they? You're the very image of respectability and efficiency. It's why I chose you. And Henry? How is he getting along?"

"He's very well-thought of throughout both Houses, and I believe he is above suspicion. I certainly would never question him. He's getting rather impatient with the tasks that you're assigning to him, however. He thinks they're trivial and below him, and I must admit I tend to agree. A man in his position can be doing much more to help the cause. Why don't you trust him?"

"It's not that I don't trust him, Molly," Lady Rothman said slowly, "but rather that I'm cautious. It's my understanding that he has been working alone in London for quite some time now. He's not accustomed to being part of a larger group such as ours, and lone wolves can be dangerous. I just want to be sure that he is firmly with us before I commit him to more sensitive and crucial work."

Molly couldn't prevent the smug smile that curved her lips.

"Well, he's firmly with *me*, at any rate," she murmured with a laugh.

"I do wish you would be careful there, my dear," Lady Rothman said with a frown. "I don't believe that Henry is the right person for you. He's never been one to settle down, you know. All the mothers in London have quite given up hope for their daughters. It's very common knowledge that he's married to his work."

"I'm well aware of where his priorities lie," Molly said, keeping her voice light even as her spine stiffened.

"Very well, then. I'll say nothing more." She cleared her throat. "Tell me, have you heard much about Lord Gilhurst in Halifax's office?"

Molly's brows furrowed thoughtfully.

"Lord Gilhurst? Anthony Gilhurst? The son?"

"Yes."

"Not really. I believe he's a respected chair on the House, for all his youth, and I've heard that his father wants him to be more serious about his position in the party. Lord Halifax listens to him and thinks he has a bright future."

"Is it true that he's been vocal in his opposition to the war?"

"I haven't heard, but I can certainly look into it and find out for you. Why do you want to know?"

"Oh, his name keeps coming up in conversation," Lady Rothman said, waving a hand vaguely. "The duke is keen to get him onboard, and if the young lord really is becoming restless and disillusioned with the government's handling of the war, then he might very well be a good fit."

"I'll see what I can discover for you."

"Thank you. Now, do you have those documents that we discussed?"

Molly swallowed and nodded, reaching for her purse beside her. She opened it and pulled out a folded packet of documents.

"I have them right here," she said, closing her purse with a snap. "If I'm caught…"

"Don't worry, my dear," Lady Rothman said reassuringly, getting up and reaching out to take the packet from her. "It's not possible for anyone to ever suspect you. You're perfectly safe!"

Molly pressed her lips together briefly, then exhaled, pushing aside the uneasiness she felt at passing top secret documents to Lady Rothman.

"Yes, of course," she murmured, pulling her gloves on and standing. "I must get back now."

"Of course." Lady Rothman smiled warmly and shook her hand, watching as she went towards the door. "Miss Pollack?"

Molly paused and looked back.

"Yes?"

"Be sure to be discreet while asking after Lord Gilhurst."

"Yes, of course."

## When Wolves Gather

Evelyn watched as Miles packed away the last of their lunch into the large basket. The Fighting Cock had truly outdone themselves. They'd had a veritable feast of cold, roasted chicken, cheese, an onion tart that was absolutely delicious, and fruit for dessert. The landlord had even thoughtfully included a bottle of wine and two tumblers to drink from.

"That was delicious," she said, picking up her glass. "I'm so glad Bertie went to school with Mr. Rutter's son!"

"Yes, so am I." Miles closed the lid to the basket and leaned back on his elbow, reaching for his glass. "Although I must remember to ask Bertie how a pub landlord managed to send his son to Cambridge."

"Well, however it was, I'm very grateful to him." Evelyn raised her wine. "A toast to Mr. Rutter and The Fighting Cock!"

"Cheers!"

They sipped their wine and were quiet for a moment. Evelyn looked out over the rippling waves of the river that wound its way lazily through the countryside while Miles watched her.

"It hardly seems possible that there's a war on when this place is so heavenly, does it?" she asked suddenly.

"Are you enjoying it?"

She turned her head to meet his green gaze and smiled.

"I am. Very much."

"So am I." He sipped his wine. "This is just what we both needed. I think we've both earned a few hours of peace."

Evelyn looked at him, leaning on one elbow with his legs crossed at the ankles, completely at ease. He'd removed the silk neckerchief he wore in place of a tie, the top buttons of his shirt were open, and his jacket had been discarded. If it weren't for the RAF issued trousers, he would have passed for any idle man of leisure spending an afternoon by the river. She suddenly wondered what he was like before the war, before the uniform, and before his very survival depended on his skill as a pilot. Had he been carefree and reckless? She had a definite idea that he would have been an incorrigible flirt.

"What are you thinking?" he asked.

"I was just trying to imagine what you were like before the war," she said with a grin.

His lips curved in response and he gazed up at her, his eyes dancing.

"Oh? And what have you decided?"

"I think that you must have been a shocking playboy!"

He threw back his head and laughed, the murky sunlight catching his sparkling green eyes and picking out flecks of gold in their depths.

"Guilty as charged, but how did you know?"

"I believe there was mention of a serving maid by your friend Barnaby," she murmured wickedly.

"I should have known you wouldn't forget that little gem," he said, his grin rueful. "We *were* in school, my dear."

"Yes, of course."

"And shall I bring up Marc Fournier?"

Evelyn started and her eyes flared wide.

"Good heavens, has Robbie been telling tales again?" she demanded. "He does love to rub that in my face every chance he gets."

"Nevertheless, it appears that if I was something of a playboy, you were also something of a…" Her eyes narrowed dangerously and Miles grinned. "Belle of the ball," he finished smoothly.

Evelyn felt a laugh bubble up inside her and firmly repressed it. Tilting her head, she gave him an impish smile.

"What makes you think I'm not still?"

"What makes you think I'm not still a playboy?"

"Well, if you are, then you've certainly got more stamina than any other man of my acquaintance," she told him bluntly. "I don't know anyone who can spend three-quarters of his day in the air and still have energy left for much of anything at the end of it."

"Oh, you'd be surprised how much energy a good scrap will give you," he murmured with a wink.

Evelyn chuckled and leaned back on her elbows next to him.

"I think I'd be very put out if I discovered that you were doing this very thing with someone else," she said thoughtfully, staring up into the sky. "I might even be moved to do something altogether shocking."

"Really?" he drawled. "I can't imagine you doing anything shocking, Assistant Section Officer. You're the very picture of respectability."

An image flashed into her mind of an unconscious German SS officer sliding down the wall in an alley behind a hotel in Stockholm, and Evelyn swallowed.

## When Wolves Gather

"Oh, I think you'd be amazed at some of the things that I've done," she murmured, forcing her tone to remain light.

"Would I?" He leaned over until his lips were inches away from her ear. "Then I suppose it's a very good thing that I have absolutely no intention of ever doing this very thing with anyone else."

Evelyn turned her face to look at him and his lips captured hers, eliciting an involuntary sigh of contentment from her. The kiss was over almost as soon as it began, and she tried to ignore the flash of disappointment as he pulled away. It took her a second to realize that he was looking not at her, but into the sky, and then she heard what had caught his attention. Airplanes.

She turned her face to the sky as the low drone of engines grew louder. A moment later, a group of Hurricanes roared overhead. They flew in formation and Evelyn knew that they were going towards the Channel. She glanced at Miles and saw him watching them, his lips pressed together grimly. Sensing her eyes on him, he turned his head and the grim look disappeared.

"Hurricanes. It looks like they're going out." He reached for his discarded glass of wine and took a drink. "Speaking of Hurries, how is Fred Durton getting on?"

"About the same as you, I think," she replied. "He was shot down a couple of weeks ago. He ran out of ammunition and the Jerry followed him in."

"Good Lord! What did he do?"

"He says he was trying to outrun him." Evelyn turned to face him, studying him. "Is that possible? Do you outrun them?"

Miles hesitated, then sighed imperceptibly.

"*We* do, yes, but Spitfires are a darn sight faster than Hurricanes. We can."

"How? What's it like?"

He smiled faintly and reached out to brush a lock of hair out of her eyes.

"You ask the strangest things, Evie," he murmured. "Do you really want to know?"

"I wouldn't have asked if I didn't." She smiled and reached up to catch his hand in hers. "I want to know what you do up there."

"All right." He lowered their hands and his long fingers toyed with hers. "The 109s are fast. They were the fastest fighter in the game until the Spitfire came along. We can match them for speed."

"But if you only match them, how do you outrun them?"

Miles exhaled and glanced up from their joined hands.

"You're wandering into classified territory now," he said with a slight laugh.

Evelyn blinked and had to stop herself from letting out an unladylike snort. Good heavens, he was worried about telling her too much about the Spitfire while she herself was bound by the Official Secrets Act and had access to intelligence far and above anything he could ever know.

"I promise not to tell Herr Göring your secret," she said with a grin.

He chuckled and when he looked up again, his eyes were clear and sparkling with the passion that showed just how much he loved flying.

"We can't outrun them flat out, although I've come close a few times. We have to out-fly them, and that's what we do." He pulled his hand away from her so that he could demonstrate using both his hands. "You see, the Spit has a fantastic turning ratio, and we can maintain our speeds at very high altitude where the 109s cannot. So I lead them up like this, into a spiral so they can't get a clear shot, and take them up over thirty-thousand feet. Their engineering can't maintain that speed at that ceiling and, once I'm up there, I open up the throttle. They can't even begin to catch us then."

"When was the first time you did that?"

Miles looked at her. "Are you sure you want to know?"

"Absolutely."

"The Yank and I were in a scrap over France and were almost out of fuel. If we didn't get out of there, we weren't going to make it back."

Evelyn stared at him, then swallowed and nodded.

"That would do it."

"We weren't even sure it would work," he admitted. "It's one thing for the RAF to tell us what the kite can do, but it's quite another to actually have to test it. I'll tell you, both of us were damned glad the RAF was right."

Evelyn was quiet for a moment, inwardly shaken at the realization that much of what allowed Miles to survive and come back to her was sheer engineering on the part of his airplane.

"What? Now what are you thinking?"

"I was just thinking about how much the engineering of the airplane has to do with the success of the pilot," she said after a moment. "You have a fast airplane with a superior range and ceiling, and you've learned how to use that to your advantage."

## When Wolves Gather

"Yes. That's what flying is all about. Your Fred Durton has learned to fly the Hurricane to play to its strengths as well. It's what keeps us in the game."

"He's not *my* Fred Durton."

"I am, of course, very glad to hear that."

She met his gaze and smiled, her heart skipping a beat at the look in his eyes. Then the smile on her face faded.

"When Fred was shot down, his fuel tank exploded," she said in a low voice, dropping her gaze to her hands. She heard Miles' sharp intake of breath and glanced up. "He's all right," she said quickly. "It was one of the tanks in the wing. But as he so succinctly pointed out, if it had been the one in front of him, it would have been a much different story."

The grim look was back around Miles' mouth.

"Yes."

"He asked me if I would still go out to the pub with him if he was burned."

"And would you?"

"Of course I would." She met his gaze steadily. "Just as I would still go to the Savoy with you if you were burned."

"My darling Evelyn, if I'm careless enough to allow myself to be burned, you'd do better to stay well away from me," he told her not ungently. "I wouldn't be fit company for anyone, and would most certainly make the most miserable companion."

"Why? Because you'd be scarred?" Evelyn scowled. "I wouldn't care a jot about that."

"No, but I would."

Miles turned to reach for the bottle of wine. Taking her glass, he refilled it, and then his own. Evelyn watched him silently, noting that the grim look was still about his mouth. His hands were steady, but she knew the conversation had gone too close to home for him. With a shock, she realized that he was terribly afraid of being burned alive in the cockpit. Of course! What pilot wouldn't be? She'd seen the fear in Fred's eyes that day in her office, and she knew that if Miles looked at her, she'd see it again now.

He handed her glass back to her and she murmured her thanks, lifting it to her lips. She tried to cast about in her mind for something to say to change the subject, but nothing presented itself. They sat in silence for a long time, sipping their wine and looking out over the rippling waves of the river.

"Did he bail out?" Miles finally broke the silence.

"No. He landed outside Brighton and climbed out just before the fire reached the cockpit."

Miles smiled wryly and glanced at her.

"That sounds very familiar."

"Yes. I thought so as well."

"I'm very glad he made it back. He's a good chap."

"Yes, he is."

He glanced at her and the grimness was gone from his countenance. His eyes took on the devilish twinkle she was learning to recognize, and Evelyn felt her lips curving in response.

"I don't like that look in your eyes, Flight Lieutenant Lacey," she said warily. "I've seen that look before."

"I don't have any idea what you're talking about," he said, taking her glass from her hand and setting it aside with his own. "But I have just remembered that I was interrupted earlier by a squadron of Hurricanes."

Evelyn let out a gurgle of laughter as his arms went about her.

"How very rude of them," she murmured. "I hope you intend to do something about it."

His grin was wicked as his lowered his lips to hers.

"Oh, I do."

# When Wolves Gather

# Chapter Twenty-Four

**Moscow, USSR**

Vladimir Lyakhov turned the page and continued to read, the ticking from his watch the only sound in the office. Summer had brought with it warmer temperatures and he lifted a hand to wipe sweat from his brow. The window behind him had been open, but the noise from the street below had been grating on his nerves, leading him to close it and remove his jacket instead. Sitting in his shirt sleeves at his desk, he poured over the report from his man in Berlin. The heat in the small office was oppressive, though, and after another moment, he got up and walked over to the window again, throwing it open. Muggy but cooler air rushed in and he leaned his arms on the windowsill, gazing down into the busy road below.

Comrade Bogdan had been ensconced in Berlin for over five years now. He'd escaped the Nazi hunt for Communists by virtue of the fact that no one in Berlin realized he was Russian at all. He'd been born to a woman of impeccable German descent in a small hospital outside of Munich, the result of a brief but passionate affair with a Russian soldier. His mother had married a German factory worker before the boy was even a year old, and no one had ever thought to question Bogdan's heritage. As far as the Nazis were concerned, Otto Voigt was a pure-blooded German.

Vladimir had recruited him six years before in Munich, a year after Hitler had taken power. Otto, or Bogdan as he'd asked to be called, had proved invaluable over the years leading into the war. He'd reported regularly on the rearmament, and sent countless copies of munitions plans and schematics that he obtained from his contact within one of the main munitions factories. Bogdan himself was a clerk who had been inserted into the Abwehr through very careful planning on Lyakhov's part. When Vladimir asked him a few months ago to see what he could learn about a mysterious Abwehr assassin, he hadn't held out much hope that the man would succeed. After all, Eisenjager was a ghost even to his own people. However, Vladimir reflected now, he had seriously underestimated Comrade Bogdan's desire to make himself indispensable. The man wanted to help Mother Russia, and he would do anything in his power to do so, even if it meant discovering all that he could about a ghost who lived in the shadows.

Vladimir turned from the window and looked at the report on his desk pensively. Eisenjager was even more formidable than he'd known. If only half of what Bogdan had included in his report was true, the man was a greater threat than Hans Voss and all the SD agents put together.

Of course, he'd known he was dangerous. Everyone who'd heard of Eisenjager knew how skilled he was. His record spoke for itself. What Comrade Bogdan had uncovered, however, was much more chilling. Not only did the assassin have the training of the SS behind him, but he also had an unusual affinity for psychology which had, according to his superiors, been invaluable in several instances in allowing the assassin to become close to his target and build a rapport, gaining their trust.

This was something he must have learned after leaving the SS, Vladimir decided, his lips pressed together. The SS did not train their soldiers to build relationships that could then be exploited. That was a trademark of spies, not soldiers. Eisenjager would have been taught the psychology and manipulation once he'd joined the Intelligence Service.

And now he was one of their best agents, not least because he was also a cold-blooded killer.

Vladimir exhaled and rubbed his face, turning to stare blindly out of the window again. Eisenjager, not Voss, was the larger threat to the Ainsworth girl. How would an untrained and green agent defend herself against a ghost whose training was superior in every aspect? Was it even possible?

He'd sent a message to Lotus in London, warning her that someone in the Round Club was in touch with Hans Voss. He knew that she'd received it, and he could only hope that her people would take the threat as seriously as they should. If the SD was willing to go into England to get their agent, then there was little they wouldn't do to ensure that she was removed from the field of play. And if they were able to locate her and capture her?

Vladimir scowled. That must not be allowed to happen. Not only for her safety, but also for his own. If there was even the slightest hint of a rumor that he was working with a British agent, the Gulag would look like Heaven to him. Life wouldn't be worth living. His own people would make sure of that.

He'd narrowly escaped that fate last fall when he'd fallen under suspicion in the midst of an agency-wide hunt for a traitor. He'd survived by giving up Risto Niva as the traitor, and that had worked at

## When Wolves Gather

the time. However, he'd be unable to pull another such incident out of his hat if he came under suspicion again. MI6 had to find and eliminate the spy they had in their house before Voss found Lotus. It really was that simple. They had to infiltrate the Round Club and find who their mole was. It was the only way both he and Lotus had a chance to continue in this cursed war.

But what of Eisenjager? What was he to do about him? That he had set his sights on Lotus was fact. He'd lost her in Norway and, if everything he was reading about the man was true, that would have made her his own personal target. He would find her. It was only a matter of time. And what then?

Vladimir turned from the window, his brows settled in a deep and thoughtful frown. If only there was a way to get into Eisenjager's head! If there was a way for Vladimir to gain access to the assassin, he had all confidence that he could influence him for their interests. Vladimir was very good at that. The NKVD had ensured that all their ranking officers were. Psychological manipulation was child's play to them. If only he could find a way to get to Eisenjager!

His eyes fell on the report on the desk and he pressed his lips together as an idea came to him. Before he could give it any attention, however, a sharp rap sounded at the door. Starting, he crossed to the desk swiftly, flipping the folder closed.

"Come!" he called.

The door opened and a tall man stepped in, his dark eyes sweeping over him in surprise.

"Vladimir! Where's your jacket?"

"Right here. I was too warm sitting at my desk." Vladimir motioned to where it hung on the back of his chair. "How are you, Comrade Grigori? I thought you were in Stalingrad?"

"I returned last night." Comrade Grigori looked around and went over to a chair, seating himself. "It isn't very hot in here. Are you ill?"

"I've since opened the window." Vladimir sat down. "The noise from the street distracts me when I'm trying to concentrate, and I closed it."

"Ah. That I can understand." Grigori accepted the explanation with a nod. "Well, my old friend, put on your jacket. I've come to take you to lunch. We have much to discuss."

Vladimir raised an eyebrow as he looked across the desk at his colleague. "Have we?"

"Yes. I've just come from a meeting and I leave for Leningrad tonight. Come! I want to talk to you and the longer we stay here, the more likely we are to be interrupted and pulled into some kind of a meeting."

Vladimir grunted.

"No doubt you're right," he agreed, standing. "What do we have to discuss? I don't have anything to do with the operation that took you to Stalingrad."

"No, but that is not why I'm here." Grigori stood and watched as Vladimir pulled on his jacket and straightened his tie. When he glanced up at him, Grigori grinned. "Your work in Poland has not gone unnoticed, my friend. I've been authorized to discuss a new venture with you, and bring you onboard as soon as possible."

"A new venture?" Vladimir picked up the folder and locked it in his desk drawer, pocketing the key. "Do you mean a new operation?"

"Something like that. We'd be starting it together, and I've been given virtually unlimited resources. That's all I'm willing to say here, so get your hat and let's go. I thought we'd go to your favorite restaurant, if you think they'll have your table available?"

"Of course. They always have my table available."

Grigori laughed and clapped him on the shoulder as he came around the corner of his desk.

"Of course they do. You really must tell me how you manage it someday. Shall we?"

Vladimir nodded and walked with him to the door. He glanced at him as they passed out into the hallway.

"Unlimited resources?"

"As I said," Grigori said with a nod. "Believe me, Vlad. You want to be in on this. You, of all people, will truly appreciate the genius of it."

"You intrigue me, my friend. By all means, let us eat and you can tell me all about it."

"I thought that's what you'd say." Grigori glanced at him. "What were you working on just now? I'm not pulling you away from something pressing, am I?"

"No. It was just a report from one of my agents abroad. Nothing that won't wait."

**London**

## When Wolves Gather

"Do you want to hear something funny, Miss Ainsworth?" Chris asked, setting his glass down.

"Certainly!" Evelyn said brightly, smiling at him.

"You're nothing like what I imagined."

"Oh? And why is that?"

"Because, my dear, he was convinced that you had warts," Miles drawled beside her. "I'm sure I've mentioned it before."

Evelyn choked on her wine and gasped before snatching her napkin from her lap and covering her mouth as she erupted into a fit of coughing. They were seated at a table in The Dorchester, having arrived to meet Rob and Chris for dinner some time before. Rob, in true form, had brought along an old flame he'd run into earlier in the afternoon, who had also brought along her sister. The party of four had turned into a very merry party of six, and Evelyn didn't think they'd stopped laughing since they arrived.

"I think she's turning blue, old man," Chris said, reaching over to pound her on the back. "You didn't really tell her I thought she had warts, did you?"

"'Course I did." Miles winked as Evelyn's streaming eyes met his.

"But I never said that!"

"Didn't you? I could've sworn you did."

"Well, you're wrong." Chris sat back as Evelyn stopped coughing and caught her breath. "Drink some water, sweetheart. That always helps me."

"Good heavens, did you just call me sweetheart?" Evelyn demanded, lowering her napkin.

Chris grinned at her unrepentantly.

"It slipped out. I'm sorry. Won't happen again."

"At least it wasn't doll," Miles said. "He called a barmaid doll once. I thought that was only used in films."

"Well, I much prefer sweetheart over doll, at any rate!"

"Oh, then can I continue to call you sweetheart?" Chris asked, his eyes dancing.

"No, you may not!" Miles interjected.

"You *may* call me Evelyn," Evelyn said, shooting Miles a laughing look. "Miss Ainsworth sounds very stuffy among friends, and I hope you'll become a friend. I don't know any Americans."

"Well, now you do," Chris replied promptly. "We're not all that different from you guys, you know."

"I'd argue that you're very different," Miles said, putting out his cigarette.

"What part of America do you call home?" Evelyn asked, ignoring him.

"My family's from Boston."

"Boston? That's above New York, isn't it?"

"That's right. Hey Miles, your girl knows geography better than you."

"The United States isn't worthwhile geography, old boy. It's not old enough. Give it another hundred years and perhaps I'll be bothered to learn about it."

Evelyn laughed at that and reached for her wine.

"Is he always like this?" she asked Chris.

"Yes." Chris pushed back his chair and stood up, holding out his hand. "Care to dance, Evelyn?" He looked at Miles across the table. "You don't mind, do you?"

"Not if the lady doesn't mind."

"I'd love to dance," Evelyn said, taking Chris' hand and getting to her feet.

"Are you off to the dance floor, then?" Robbie asked, coming up with a buxom redhead on his arm. "It's a jolly good band this evening."

"Yes." Evelyn smiled at her brother. "Do keep Miles company, won't you?"

"Does he need keeping company? Are you feeling put out, old man?" Rob led his companion to her chair. "No need to worry. Yanks can't dance. Everyone knows that."

"Oh, for heaven's sake!" Evelyn exclaimed, tucking her arm through Chris'. "I don't know how you put up with them, Flying Officer Fields, I really don't."

"I'm used to it. I have younger brothers at home, you know. All kids are the same." He winked at her. "And please call me Chris."

Miles watched as the pair went off towards the dance floor and turned to Rob.

"I think the Yank just tried to insult us, Ainsworth," he said.

"It was a very clumsy attempt," Rob said, seating himself and feeling his pockets for his cigarette case. "I really thought we were teaching him better than that. Perhaps my sister has him rattled. She has that effect, you know."

"I don't think it's possible for the Yank to be rattled," Miles said thoughtfully, holding out his lighter when Rob finally extracted his cigarette case. "Very cool, that one."

"Is he really American?" the redhead asked from across the table. "I've never met an American before."

## When Wolves Gather

"It's sad, but there it is. He's really American." Rob lit his cigarette and handed the lighter back with a nod of thanks. "Jolly good pilot, though."

"Why is he flying in the RAF if he's American?" she asked.

"He went to Canada to join the RAF. Says it was to help us out." Rob shrugged. "Can't say that I'm not happy he's here, whatever the reason. He's saved my hide a few times."

"Mine as well," Miles agreed. "Miss Masterson, where's your sister?"

"Oh, Mary caught sight of an old friend and they're dancing," that lady said with a laugh. "She'll be along after this song, I'm sure."

"I thought perhaps we'd frightened her off. We can be a bit much sometimes, or so I'm told."

"Not a bit of it! I'm enjoying myself immensely. It's so lovely to see Evelyn and Robbie again. I'm ever so glad we came across each other this afternoon."

"A bit of luck, that," Rob agreed cheerfully.

"Robbie!"

Miles and Rob turned as Evelyn called his name, watching as she and Chris approached the table with a tall brunette. She was dressed immaculately in a shimmering evening gown and had an aristocratic dandy in tow.

"Look who found me on the dance floor!" Evelyn exclaimed.

"Miss Gilhurst!" Rob and Miles rose to their feet as the party approached. "Fancy meeting you here as well! How are you?"

"As well as ever, Robbie," Maryanne said with laugh, holding out her hands to him. "I couldn't believe it when Evie said that you were with her! It's been an absolute age since we've all been together!"

She turned to Miles and held her hand out with a wicked smile. "And Mr. Lacey! What a surprise!"

"Not such a surprise, I think," he murmured, taking her outstretched hand. "It's wonderful to see you again, Miss Gilhurst."

"Oh, you must call me Maryanne," she protested, looking around for her companion. "I'm sure you've met Giles. Giles, Rob Ainsworth and Miles Lacey."

"Yes, of course," Miles shook the young man's hand. "We belong to the same club, I believe."

"That's right." Giles wrung his hand and turned to do the same to Rob. "Jolly good to see you both. I see you're in uniform. Are you just down for the day?"

"Afraid so," Rob said. "We're due back in the morning."

"Rotten luck."

"But we have tonight," Maryanne said gaily.

"Indeed, and you must join us!" Rob told them. "We're just about to order dinner. Have you eaten?"

"Not yet. You don't mind?"

"Not at all!"

Rob made the introductions to Miss Masterson as Miles motioned to a waiter. He spoke to him in a low voice and in no time at all, two chairs were being added to the table and extra place settings were being laid out.

"I must say, this is turning out to be a lovely evening," Maryanne said a few minutes later as Chris held out the new chair next to him for her to seat herself. "Thank you, Officer Field."

"My pleasure, ma'am."

She looked up, startled.

"Oh! But you're American!" she was betrayed into blurting out.

"So I've been told," he said dryly.

Maryanne cast Evelyn a look as Chris took his seat between them.

"Why, Evie darling, you didn't mention he was an American when you introduced us!"

"I didn't think of it," Evelyn said with a shrug. "Don't worry. They're much like us. I'm fairly confident that he's been trained not to bite."

"Only under the right circumstances," Chris said without hesitation, drawing a laugh from both women.

"I'm so sorry, Officer Field. That was terribly rude of me. I just wasn't expecting your accent, you see," Maryanne told him. "And you're in an RAF uniform, so it did rather take me aback."

"Don't think any more about it," he told her with a smile. "I'm used to it."

Miles leaned towards Evelyn and lowered his voice.

"Chris doesn't stand a chance, does he?" he asked, his lips near her ear.

Evelyn gurgled with laughter. "Not one. She has that look in her eye."

"Poor Giles."

He straightened up again as the waiter returned to take their dinner order. Evelyn sipped her wine and looked around the table, her lips curving in amusement. Heavens, what a motley crew they were! A strange mix of aristocracy, RAF and, now, ATS all dining and laughing together as if it were the most natural thing in the world. But of course,

## When Wolves Gather

it was. They were all from the same background, even the Yank. The only unnatural part of it was that she was a spy.

"Miss Ainsworth, we danced together at the Rutherford's masquerade last summer, didn't we?" Giles asked after the waiter had departed.

"Very likely," she replied easily.

"Have you been to any of the balls yet this summer?"

"I'm afraid not. I haven't been in town."

"Oh, that's a shame. There have been a few, despite the war." Giles looked along the table at Maryanne. "Isn't that so, Maryanne?"

"Oh yes! But they aren't really the same, are they?"

"That's because so many people are joining up now," Miss Masterson said. "Why, even Lady Agatha's daughter has joined the WRENs. Tell me, Maryanne, are the rumors true? Have you really joined the ATS?"

"For once, darling, the gossip does not lie," Maryanne said with a nod.

"Miss Ainsworth, you really must talk her out of it," Giles said, turning his gaze back to Evelyn. "She'll listen to you. I've told her, but she won't have any of it. It's absolutely absurd for someone of her standing and breeding to join up. You know, I'm sure. Will you talk some sense into her?"

A short silence over the table and Evelyn felt six pairs of eyes staring at her. Not daring to look in Miles' direction, she turned to look at Maryanne instead, catching the look of amusement on Chris' face in the process.

"You don't think there's something in what Giles says, Maryanne?" she asked, only the faintest tremor in her voice.

"Certainly not," she replied promptly, her eyes dancing devilishly. "Do you?"

"While I'm sure a very compelling argument could be made, I can't say that I agree with him in this case, no," Evelyn said, pretending to give it some thought. "The country is in an awful pickle at the moment, and we need everyone who is able to lend a hand. I'm afraid, Giles, I can't talk her out of it because I think it's a wonderful idea! I told her so when she first mentioned it."

"But surely you don't agree with young ladies of your standing actually...working? Especially alongside God knows who!" Giles protested. "You can't possibly!"

"Oh, but I'm afraid that I do."

Miles pushed his chair back and stood as another awkward silence fell over the table and held his hand out to her.

223

"Before this turns into a battle of ideals and rhetoric, why don't we dance, Assistant Section Officer Ainsworth?" he asked calmly, his eyes dancing as they met hers.

"Oh, I hardly think it would be much of a battle, but I would like to dance, thank you!"

Evelyn placed her hand in his and tamped down the urge to laugh at the gaping look of shock on poor Giles' face. Miles' fingers closed over hers firmly and he led her away from the table, tucking her arm through his.

After they had gone, Giles looked around the table, his face pale.

"Good Lord, I didn't know she was a...what was it?"

"Assistant Section Officer, old boy," Rob answered cheerfully.

"I'm terribly sorry. I had no idea!"

"Oh, it's not me you need to apologize to, but never mind. I'm sure Evie won't think twice about it."

"For what it's worth, I think it's swell that you're joining the army," Chris drawled, smiling at Maryanne.

"Thank you," she said, reaching for her wine. "Where in America are you from?"

"I'm from Boston."

"And where is that, exactly?"

"North of New York."

"Oh! I've never been to New York, but I've always wanted to go." Maryanne smiled at him. "Is it really as grand as they say?"

Giles looked at Rob across the table.

"I feel like a right fool," he admitted in a low voice. "I always manage to put my foot in it somehow."

Rob laughed and held out his cigarette case, offering the other man a cigarette.

"I really wouldn't let it worry you. I can guarantee my sister won't let the incident bother her in the slightest. She's made of much sterner stuff, I assure you."

"She must be to be an officer in the air force," Miss Masterson said. "It's the WAAF, isn't it?"

"Just so."

"Don't you worry about her?" Giles asked after a moment.

Rob looked astounded.

"Worry? About Evie? Good Lord, no! Why ever would I do that?"

"Well, because she's working with people who...well...aren't like us. Don't you worry that she will, well, forget her upbringing?"

## When Wolves Gather

"My dear chap, believe me when I say that Evelyn knows precisely who, and what, she is, and woe betide anyone who might try to change that!"

## Chapter Twenty-Five

Evelyn looked up into Miles' face as they danced. The band was playing a ballad and, if he was holding her just a little too close, she certainly didn't mind. She loved to dance with him, and these were the moments that helped get her through the mountains of Norway, and the invasion of France. The memory of Miles and his warmth and humor could carry her through impossible times, and she was thankful for every second they had together. It was at times like this, with his arms around her, that Evelyn knew she was falling hopelessly in love. It was an impossible situation, but it was one that she was increasingly unwilling to walk away from. Especially after days like today.

"I can't imagine what got into Giles just now," he said suddenly, jolting her out of her reverie. "Does he actually believe all of that hogwash?"

"Some people do, you know," she said with a shrug. "You'll never convince them otherwise, and I've stopped trying. Actually," she tilted her head and her brows creased thoughtfully, "I don't know that I've ever really tried."

"That doesn't surprise me in the least. I can't imagine you letting anyone's opinion sway you." He smiled down at her, tightening his arms ever so slightly. "Do you know, Evelyn, the more I get to know you, the more I think there's so much about you that I'll never learn?"

"Whatever do you mean?"

"I don't know," he admitted ruefully. "I feel as if I've known you my whole life, and yet I feel like there's a whole other you that I'll never know."

Evelyn swallowed, her mouth suddenly dry.

"I can assure you, there is only one of me, Miles," she said, forcing a lightness she didn't feel. "And you seem to be getting quite familiar with me," she added with a flash of a teasing grin.

For once, he didn't return the banter, but looked down at her thoughtfully.

"Am I?" he asked softly.

# When Wolves Gather

She stared at him for a moment, her heart pounding. Oh, she'd always known that he saw more than he let on, her Spitfire pilot. She'd caught the speculative looks when she'd been foolish enough to slip and mention something she had no right to know or say. She'd always known there was a risk that he, out of everyone, would realize that she was living a lie, but she'd never imagined that it would actually happen. Yet now he seemed closer than ever.

The musky scent of his aftershave, which she loved, was wreaking havoc on her senses, and Evelyn put a little more distance between them as they danced, needing the space to think. His lips tightened a bit, but he didn't try to pull her back. Instead, he studied her face, his eyes pensive.

"What are you afraid of?"

His voice was low and soft, and Evelyn fought the impulse to pull him close and tell him everything. It was impossible. He could never know the truth. The Official Secrets Act forbade it, as did her own innate sense of self-preservation. Yet she knew instinctively that if she tried to lie or talk her way out of this, he would be even more persistent. He was like a hunting dog that had caught a scent. He wasn't about to give up.

"Losing you," she whispered, surprising herself. It was true, of course, but she'd never had any intention of telling him.

"I'm not going anywhere."

"But you are. You do. Every day you go up in your Spitfire, and you may not return." Evelyn bit her lip, then exhaled. "I'm afraid of this war, and what it's doing to all of us. It seems like the world is spinning out of control. Horrible things are happening to innocent people everywhere, and I feel so helpless. With every passing day, I'm changing, and I don't know if I'll ever be the woman I used to be. Nothing is the same, and I suppose I'm afraid that if I lose you, nothing will ever be the same again."

Miles released her hand and brushed his thumb along her jaw. If they weren't in the middle of the dance floor, she had no doubt that he would have kissed her. But they *were* on the dance floor, and suddenly Evelyn was very sorry for that.

"We're all changing, but we're changing together," he said softly. "I know that I won't be the same man I was before this all began, but I don't care about that. I'm facing each day as it comes, and waiting until I can face you each night. I can't say that I'll come back after every sortie. No one can. But I *can* tell you that as long as I have breath in my body, I'll fight to see you again."

Evelyn felt all the tension flow out of her and she couldn't tear her eyes away from his even if she wanted to. Everything Miles felt for her was there for her to see and, all at once, she knew that he was just as hopelessly in love with her as she was with him. He was right. He couldn't promise that he would always return, and she'd known that since the moment she met him. This was all they had: their stolen moments together. It was up to them to make them count and to enjoy them to the fullest so they could carry the memory with them; he to battle the Luftwaffe, and she to lie, and kill, for her country.

The thought made her shiver involuntarily and Miles frowned, feeling it.

"What is it?" he asked. "What are you thinking?"

"I was just thinking that tomorrow you go back to your squadron, and I'll have to return to my station soon, and we don't know where either of us will be this time next year."

He pulled her close again and tightened his arm around her.

"We will be dancing here, just like this." She looked up at him skeptically and he smiled. "Even if it's only in our minds," he relented.

Evelyn let out a short laugh and nodded, not trusting herself to speak. After a moment, she rested her head on his shoulder, moving with him in time to the music. He'd accepted her reply and had dropped the subject for now, but Evelyn knew it would arise again. Miles was far too astute to believe for much longer that she spent her days traveling around Great Britain training WAAFs. He would continue to hunt for answers, answers she was unable to give. But for right now, in this moment, they had each other.

And that would have to be enough to see them through what lay ahead.

◉

Evelyn crossed the road at the corner and turned to walk briskly along the pavement. When Fran had brought her breakfast this morning, there had been a small, sealed envelope on the tray, hand delivered early in the morning. The message was from Marrow, asking her to meet him at a little tea shop near Covent Garden. A surge of something akin to excitement had gone through her when she read it. Her cover must be ready. It was the only reason Marrow would want to meet, and that meant that it was finally time to put her money where her mouth was. It was time to embark on a charade that would, at its best, help them discover the names of some of the members of the

## When Wolves Gather

Round Club. At its worst, the operation would end in her being uncovered and killed by the traitors, or Henry.

The sense of anticipation and excitement had stayed with Evelyn as she dressed and went about her morning routine. She was beginning to recognize the feeling. It was the same nervous excitement she had each time she left England and went onto the continent. Once the operation was truly underway, the feeling would disappear. But until then, her heart beat a little faster, and her eyes were a little brighter with the expectation of adventure.

Turning down a street that would cut over to the market square, Evelyn exhaled and wondered if this insane plan would work at all. There was no reason that it shouldn't, but as she well knew, these things could quickly take on a life of their own and lead her down a path she never expected. At least she didn't have to worry about outrunning the German army this time.

At least, not yet.

She tightened her lips as she navigated through the sparse crowds in the square. Hitler would attempt an invasion. They all knew that. He would send his mighty Luftwaffe to take control of the skies and the air fields, and then the invasion would begin. It was up to men like Robbie, Miles, and Chris to prevent the German air force from gaining any kind of traction over England. If they could hold them off, England had a chance. If not…well, then instead of fleeing from the German army, Evelyn would be digging in to fight. There was nowhere left to run if England fell.

She just hoped and prayed that it wouldn't come to that.

Evelyn smiled as two children dashed in front of her, escaping their mother's watchful gaze momentarily to chase a couple of pigeons. They were carefree and laughing as the birds took flight in a panic, but the small gas masks hanging around their necks spoke of the ever-present war that loomed over them all.

"Sara! James! Get back here, you two!" a woman yelled from the entrance to the market proper. "And don't think I didn't see you run right in front of that nice lady. Apologize this instant!"

The children skidded to a stop, then turned to go back towards the woman. As they passed Evelyn, they stole a look up at her.

"Sorry, miss," the little boy said gruffly.

"I'm sorry too," the girl murmured.

"It's quite all right," she replied with a smile, nodding to the anxious mother a few feet away.

She was just continuing across the square when she saw Anthony Gilhurst walk into the market from the opposite direction.

Evelyn was just about to raise her hand to call and get his attention when he raised his walking stick in greeting to someone else. She shifted her gaze and watched as Sir Ronald Clark stepped out from behind a column further away. Sucking in her breath, Evelyn moved quickly to conceal herself behind the closest column to her, all thoughts of hailing Maryanne's brother forgotten.

From behind the stone pillar, Evelyn watched as Sir Clark strode forward to meet Anthony, his hand outstretched. The two men greeted each other warmly before turning to walk together towards the street on the other side of the square. Anthony looked around briefly before falling into step beside Sir Clark, and Evelyn frowned, her lips tightening. Sir Clark was completely at ease, striding out of the square, but that quick look around told her that Anthony, at least, was uncomfortable. Now, why would that be?

Evelyn glanced at her watch, then emerged from behind the column, following the two men. Why was Anthony meeting Sir Clark in the middle of the day in Covent Garden? As far as she knew, the two men moved in different circles entirely and had only a passing acquaintance. She knew she was probably reading into the meeting far too much, but Evelyn couldn't help herself. It was clear to both her and Maryanne that something had been weighing on Anthony's mind lately, and of course Evelyn knew that Sir Clark was a traitor through and through. Was Anthony following the same path? The thought would have seemed impossible to her a few weeks ago, but now she wasn't sure of anything.

The two men walked briskly through the street until they reached a small, respectable restaurant not far from the shopping district. Evelyn stopped and pretended to look at the wares displayed in a store front, watching from under her lashes as the men disappeared inside the restaurant. They were having lunch together, then.

Evelyn raised her eyes to the name of the restaurant above the door, then turned to retrace her steps thoughtfully. She was now late for her own engagement, but she would do it all over again without a thought. Why was Tony having lunch with Sir Clark in such a small and out-of-the-way place when the two men, on the surface of it, had absolutely nothing in common? And why did it bother her so much? There was no doubt a perfectly logical explanation, but the heavy feeling of disquiet emanating from her gut wouldn't allow her to consider it. Something was very wrong, and she was very much afraid that her dear friend may be getting involved in something that could land him in prison…or worse.

When Wolves Gather

# Chapter Twenty-Six

Henry stepped up to the curb and raised his umbrella, flagging down a taxi. As one pulled to a stop before him, he opened the door and got in quickly.

"Whitehall," he said shortly to the driver.

"Yes, sir."

The taxi pulled away from the curb and Henry stared out of the window pensively, his lips drawn together in a thin line. His day wasn't going well at all, and if he were honest with himself, none of his days had been going very well ever since he was given the order to hunt down Rätsel, the spy that Berlin was convinced was the MI6 agent known as Jian. Did they have any idea what an impossible task they'd given him? The sheer amount of refugees streaming into England from the continent was staggering, as he'd discovered when he began this ridiculous hunt. It was like searching for the proverbial needle in a haystack. Worse, even, as a majority of the refugees were women!

The name Geneviève Dufour had elicited no information whatsoever. She may have been known by that name in France, but no one possessing that name had come through the official ports and channels into England. Henry scowled. Of course she hadn't. If, as they claimed, it *was* Jian, there would be no record of her ever having returned in any of the usual outlets. In fact, he very much doubted that she would have entered the country in any official capacity at all. If she had been escaping France in the middle of the invasion, it was more likely that she would have arrived back in a fishing boat, or something equally untraceable.

In addition to the challenges of attempting to track down an MI6 agent, Henry was facing increasing pressure from Lady Rothman. She seemed to be of the opinion that he should be spending all of his spare time along the southern coast of England, looking for ways to sabotage the infrastructure. His scowl deepened. It went far beyond what he was willing to tolerate, but that was another thing that Berlin had been very clear about. They wanted him to give any and all assistance possible to Lady Rothman and the blasted Round Club. Did they realize just what she had him doing? For him to be running around England, wasting his time on silly boys' pranks, was a complete and utter waste of his talents and capabilities. He was a respected member of government, for God's sake! Yet Lady Rothman insisted on treating him like a schoolboy. It was damned insulting, that's what it was. He'd been at this much longer than any of the so-called Round Club. *They* were the amateurs, not him.

After a moment of stewing over the situation he now found himself in, Henry took a deep, silent breath and reminded himself that Lady Rothman and her amateur hour were not his concern. As long as they didn't get him caught, they could do as they pleased. He had more important things to worry about. Things such as the packet Robert Ainsworth had hidden so effectively before his death, and the mysterious visitor to the house in Blasenflue just last month.

His head snapped up and his eyes narrowed suddenly. He'd been unable to discover the identity of the woman who had gone to the old farmer's house. He'd thought he had a lead with the old man's daughter, but that had turned out to be a dead end, quite literally as it happened. He'd left France no further ahead than when he'd arrived. Now, Henry pursed his lips thoughtfully.

Could it have been Jian at the house in Blasenflue? Could MI6 have sent her there to look for the missing package? It seemed fantastic, really, because they knew just as well as he did that the house was empty and had been since the farmer's death. Yet, now that he considered it, it did seem rather strange that Jian had been on the continent at the same time that someone had gone to the house. Of course, according to Berlin, she was in France, not Switzerland.

He frowned. There was no reason to think that the agent would have gone to Switzerland in the middle of an invasion of France to visit an abandoned farm house. In fact, there was every reason to think the opposite. Travel between the two countries during the German Blitzkrieg would be fool-hardy in the extreme, and a complete waste of time. MI6 would have been more interested in getting their agent out of France than sending her on what they had to know was a wild goose chase.

But was it? As far as they were concerned, the house was empty. But what if it wasn't? What if something *had* been left behind, and whoever visited it last month was now in possession of something they had all overlooked? And what if that something was the package Ainsworth had hidden?

Henry shook his head and reached into his inner coat pocket for his wallet as the taxi came to a stop. It was absurd, of course. They had searched the house thoroughly. There was nothing there. Even if it *had* been Jian, there was nothing there for her to find. He really must

## When Wolves Gather

stop thinking that anything of note had happened in the mountains of Switzerland three months ago.

Passing the fare to the driver, he reached for the door handle. It was a vexing question, to be sure, but one that he needed to forget for the moment. Berlin wanted him to find Jian in London. An impossible task, but one that he had to do if he wanted to be rid of Lady Rothman and her ridiculous demands. Surely if he proved his worth to his handler, he would be exempt from playing with the Round Club. But how? How did he track down Jian when he didn't know who she was?

The house in Switzerland came back into his head as he climbed out of the taxi and began striding along the pavement. If, just for the sake of argument, it *had* been Jian to go to Blasenflue, she would have gone between France and Switzerland in the middle of an invasion. No small feat, that. How would Buckley have arranged it? A train would be out of the question. A car, perhaps? He shook his head. No. That would take too long, and Bill would have known that time was crucial to getting his agent in and out. That really only left an airplane.

Henry's lips curved as he walked. Yes. She would have flown into Switzerland, and then flown back to France. And Henry knew of only one pilot who was crazy enough to fly an agent about while the Luftwaffe was battling for control of the skies. If Jian had gone to Switzerland, Sam would have been the one to fly her in.

That was where he would begin.

Evelyn sipped her tea and considered Marrow over the rim of the cup. He appeared to be perfectly at ease, but she noted the slightly pinched look about his mouth, and the way his eyes darted around the small tea shop occasionally. He was uncomfortable with this meeting, though whether due to the location or herself, she couldn't tell.

"Everything you need to know about your cover identity is in this packet," he said in a low voice, pulling a leather portfolio from his case and setting it on the table. "We've included identification cards and papers, of course, as well as other personal items such as letters and receipts from a selection of shops. I suggest you include the receipts and some of the other pieces in your purse, and among your baggage, in case your things are searched. They will help to reinforce that you are who you say you are."

"Very well. And who am I?"

"Miss Sylvia Müller. You were born in Berlin and lived there with your parents until you were thirteen, at which time you were sent to a boarding school in England."

"Which one?"

"Harrowgate Ladies College."

"Good Lord, did my parents not like me?"

That garnered a faint smile, but he continued.

"At school you were an unremarkable pupil. You achieved average grades, were an average sportswoman, and got along well with your fellow students. All of that averageness made you remarkably forgettable. Aside from a few teachers and one or two girls, no one is able to recall a clear memory of Sylvia Müller."

Evelyn raised an eyebrow. "Was there really a Sylvia Müller, then?"

"Yes, of course."

"Won't that be a trifle sticky if she discovers that someone is impersonating her?"

"Oh, that's highly unlikely. She's been dead for four years. She was killed in a motor accident in Switzerland."

"Jolly good." Evelyn reached for a cucumber sandwich. "And what am I doing now?"

"You're a private secretary, working for Sir Oswald Blackney."

"Sir Blackney? But he's a prominent member of the House of Lords! And in the forefront of the public eye!"

"Precisely."

She stared at him.

"But…won't they already know his secretary? How do you propose that I take up a position in the household of someone who is a common name in England?"

"Sir Oswald has a number of private secretaries, and only one of them works and resides here in London. The others he keeps at his various estates." Marrow smiled at her. "You really must trust us, my dear. We're very good at what we do. No one will raise any question at your employment."

"And Sir Blackney?"

"Is more than happy to oblige us in this matter. This isn't the first time he's been useful to us, and I daresay it won't be the last."

Evelyn was silent for a moment, digesting that. It seemed that everyone in her social class had something to hide these days.

## When Wolves Gather

"When did I decide that a secretarial life was the life for me?" she finally asked, setting aside the disturbing question of her peers for the moment.

"When your father passed away from a heart attack in 1933. Your mother was left without an income in Germany, and turned to the Nazi party when Hitler promised food and work."

"As did I?"

"Just so. You returned to England to make a living, sending a portion of your paycheck back to your mother every quarter."

"Siblings?"

"One brother."

"And is he a faithful Nazi as well?"

"He was, before his death in the siege of Calais."

Evelyn glanced up sharply.

"Is that what happened to the real Sylvia's brother?"

"Yes."

"Am I to suppose that this was my motivating moment to want to pass information back to my countrymen in this time of war?"

Marrow grinned.

"You may, indeed."

"Well, that all seems quite neat and tidy."

"Yes, but it will be up to you to sell it."

"I may need to muddy it up a bit," she said thoughtfully. "It seems a bit too neat for my liking. Perhaps I was ambivalent in this war until the death of my brother. Perhaps I even sympathized with my adopted country. What was his name?"

"Hans."

"Perhaps Hans and I were estranged," she continued, her brows together. "Perhaps he didn't like the idea of my living and working in England. Perhaps he thought my place was at home with Mother."

"If it will help you convince them that you're Sylvia Müller, make up any situation that you like. I will caution you, however, not to make it very complicated. The more complex the lie, the easier it is to slip and give yourself away."

"Quite right." Evelyn finished her cup of tea and reached out to pour some more from the pot on the table. "I'll be sure to keep it simple."

"You'll need to memorize everything in that packet, Evelyn. There can be no mistakes. These people will be looking for any indication that you are an impostor." Marrow shook his head and rubbed his face tiredly. "By all rights, you should have weeks to prepare for this kind of operation. It's sheer folly for me to be sending you out cold like this."

"Yes, but we don't have weeks," she said calmly. "I'm not worried, and neither should you be. I'm perfectly capable of memorizing my part and seeing this through successfully."

"But should anything happen or go wrong…"

She waved a hand impatiently.

"What could possibly happen? Don't be ridiculous. In the very worst case, they will decide that they don't trust me and won't use me, and that will be an end of it."

*Always providing that Henry doesn't uncover me first,* she added silently as she lifted her cup to her lips.

"This is all providing that they take the bait at all," Marrow said. "Our girl will pass your name on to Molly tonight. She has all the information she needs to make a convincing recommendation. She'll meet with Molly tonight, and beyond that, we wait to see if the Round Club responds."

"I think they will. You've made me almost irresistible. Not only will I be a perfect conduit to move their messages to their agents abroad, but I also have access to information through Sir Blackney that they may have use for."

"Quite so. Well, here's hoping that they see it the same way." Marrow drank some of his tea and then cleared his throat. "In the meantime, you need to get yourself down to Dorchester."

"Dorchester?"

"Yes. Sir Blackney has holdings throughout southern England, but he's agreed to allow us the use of his Dorchester estate. This will be an additional enticement for the Round Club."

"Oh? Why?"

"Sir Oswald keeps a yacht in Dorset, within easy distance of his Dorchester estate. With the use of the yacht, you can very easily take physical packets and information to the Channel Islands, or so we hope they will think."

"And the Germans have control of the Channel Islands," Evelyn finished. "Very neatly arranged. And Sir Oswald is aware of all of this?"

"Very much so. It was his suggestion to employ the lure of his yacht." Marrow smiled. "As I said, he's been of assistance to us in the past. He well knows how to play this game. He's agreed to indicate that his secretary has access to his yacht in order to attend to his business interests. If the Round Club believes that you can use the yacht, they will realize that you could meet an agent of their choosing in the

Channel, or even go as far as the Channel Islands themselves to deliver their packages."

"That's very thin," Evelyn said after a moment. "It seems to me that there are a lot of "ifs" and suppositions there. What on earth would his secretary have to use the yacht for? And I would think he would want to know each time the yacht was used, in which case, he would know it wasn't on his behalf."

"I didn't say that it was perfect," Marrow said with a shrug. "We only had a few days to come up with the whole thing! This was the best we could do in such a short time."

Evelyn laughed sheepishly.

"Yes, of course. I'm sorry. I'll make it work, don't worry. I'll think of something if they question that particular aspect too closely. What of the staff at the estate?"

"They have no idea that you aren't Sylvia Müller. As far as they're concerned, you've been working at one of Sir Oswald's other estates and are visiting Dorchester for the sea air."

"The sea air?"

"Yes."

Evelyn looked at him doubtfully.

"For heaven's sake, don't tell me that I have a weak constitution. I don't think I could abide having to wander around swathed in blankets, taking powders and drinking tonics."

"Not at all. Sir Oswald thought you could use the change of scenery. You've been melancholy since the death of your brother."

"Oh! Well that sounds reasonable enough. How will I know if they've taken the bait?"

"We assume that they will contact you. Until they do, you'll have to sit tight in Dorchester. If you don't hear something in the week, we'll have to accept that they did not."

"And I return to London?"

"Just so."

Evelyn pressed her lips together grimly.

"Then let's hope they contact me quickly."

## Chapter Twenty-Seven

Evelyn paid the driver and climbed out of the taxi, going up the shallow steps to the front door laden with bags and boxes. Lifting an arm with difficulty, she managed to press the bell with her little finger. She'd been to the shops after her meeting with Marrow, but they were hardly the shops that she was used to frequenting. If they had been, she would not be carrying her parcels home with her. She would have arranged for them to be delivered. As the fingers in her left hand began to go numb from holding packages at an awkward angle, she reflected that there was much to be said for the convenience of being waited upon as one of the premier socialites in London. Still, it couldn't be helped. These were purchases that could not be made at any of her regular establishments.

The door swung open and Fran hurried to relieve her of some of the packages.

"No, no, it's quite all right, Fran," Evelyn said cheerfully, sweeping into the hallway. "They aren't heavy at all. I'm afraid I got rather carried away this afternoon. I'll carry them up myself."

"But miss!"

"It's quite all right!" Evelyn was already halfway up the stairs before Fran even had the front door closed. "I'll take care of them myself. Is tea ready?"

"Yes, miss."

"Thank heavens! I'm famished."

"I'll set it out in the parlor, miss."

"Thank you, Fran. I'll be down directly."

Evelyn reached the top of the stairs and whisked herself around the corner and out of sight before Fran decided to come and assist her after all. The last thing she needed was to have her maid see these ridiculous items that she'd purchased. Her lips curved suddenly into a wry smile as she went towards her bedroom. Her maid would think she'd lost her mind, and there would be no explaining half of it.

A moment later she'd closed the door behind her and, crossing to the bed, dumped the entire collection of bags and boxes onto the coverlet. Rubbing the hand that had begun to lose feeling, Evelyn surveyed the mess before her and exhaled. She had no idea where she'd

## When Wolves Gather

hide it all from Fran. It would have to be in one of the spare bedrooms, but heaven forbid if the maid went in to clean the wardrobes in the next day or so. Luckily, there were a few items among the pile that were legitimately hers, purchased to try to avoid Fran's suspicion. She just had to hope that Fran wasn't very curious, or wouldn't notice that the few new items would not account for the sheer number of bags.

And there were a fair number of bags. Sylvia Müller was a respectable private secretary, and her transformation into the woman would be considerably more involved than she had imagined at the outset. It was all because of the identification papers, of course. Marrow had had to work within the strict confines of basing his descriptions on a real woman. While the Security Service had made them as general as they could, there were certain aspects that could not be changed; such as the lamentable fact that Sylvia Müller had black hair.

After giving it considerable thought, Evelyn had reluctantly decided that dying her hair was out of the question at this point in time. Reaching for a box, she pulled off the lid and lifted out a black wig of medium length. The shopkeeper had shown her how to manipulate it into several different styles, but the one she was most concerned with was a neat chignon behind her head. Once she'd practiced a few times, Evelyn was confident that she would be able to master the look without anyone being able to see the edge of the wig. But she didn't have very much time to practice at all, and she would have to do it when Fran was unlikely to interrupt.

Examining the raven locks in her hands, she pursed her lips. The hair was silky and smooth, and didn't seem as though it would handle very many different hairstyles, but the young woman who sold it had assured her that it would hold up to many performances.

*Well, it only has to hold up to one at the moment,* she thought, setting it back into the box. *If it can do that, I'll try not to think about the exorbitant price I had to pay.*

Moving the box to the side, Evelyn unpacked the assortment of clothing, shoes, stockings, and makeup that would create a believable Sylvia Müller. She had an appointment on Monday morning to go to an address and have her photograph taken for the false identification papers. Marrow would be there to approve the transformation, and then she would be on her way to Dorchester by the first train Tuesday morning. It was all very straight-forward, and the only aspect of the entire operation that bothered her was how on earth she would explain to Fran why she was dressed so ridiculously. Or where she was going for an indefinite amount of time.

Evelyn pursed her lips thoughtfully as she sorted through everything on the bed, separating the items that would remain in her bedroom from those moving into one of the spare rooms. The simplest solution would be to send the maid back to Ainsworth Manor, but she could hardly do that so soon after bringing her back with her. She would need a very good reason, and she would need it quickly. She had much to do in the next twenty-four hours, and when she was finished, Evelyn Ainsworth would be nowhere in sight.

### August 4

Molly followed the ram-rod straight back of the butler into the sitting room where Lady Rothman was seated on a settee. She waited for the august personage to depart before crossing to Lady Rothman quickly, her face flushed.

"My dear Mata, I'm so sorry for intruding on you like this on a Sunday morning," she said breathlessly. "I wouldn't have come, but I have new and urgent information that I didn't think should wait until tomorrow."

"How intriguing," Lady Rothman murmured, waving her into a seat. "I confess I was very surprised to receive your note. We are fortunate that my husband is away this morning, and so we need have no fear of being interrupted. Shall you take tea?"

"No, thank you." Molly shook her head. "I won't keep you long. Do you recall that receptionist that I've been cultivating?"

"The typist with the telephone company?"

"Yes, that's the one." Molly leaned forward slightly. "She came to see me last night, and you'll never guess what she told me!"

"My dear Molly, you may dispense with the theatrics. I have no intention of guessing when you are quite clearly here to tell me."

Molly flushed, but her excitement never wavered.

"She came to me with something she'd heard from her sister at dinner a few weeks ago. You'll perhaps remember that her sister is a housemaid at Sir Blackney's town residence. Well, she told Agnes over dinner that she believes that his private secretary is a German spy!"

Lady Rothman stared at her.

"Mr. Chivers? Don't be absurd. The man is as fervent a Tory as I ever did see."

## When Wolves Gather

Molly frowned.

"It wasn't a man she spoke of. It was a woman."

Lady Rothman tilted her head, thinking for a moment.

"Does he have more than one secretary?"

"Agnes claims that he has several, but this one is usually at one of his estates." Molly furrowed her brows. "She didn't say which estate, but no doubt it's of no real importance. What I found interesting, and what I'm sure you will as well, is that the sister is absolutely convinced that the secretary is a Nazi sympathizer at the very least, and most likely a spy."

"Why on earth would she think such a thing?"

"It seems the woman, a Miss Müller, was born in Berlin but moved to England six or seven years ago when she obtained a position as a private secretary." Molly smiled faintly. "That was the entire basis for Agnes's sister to believe that she was a German spy. Agnes told her that she was being paranoid and to stop reading her dime novels late at night. She sent her away and went about her business."

"Very sensible."

"Yes. But then she says she got to thinking about it and decided that it wouldn't hurt to do a little investigating. I won't bore you with all the ins and outs of the people involved, but you'll remember that Agnes's connections are one of the reasons that I'm grooming her to join the Round Club."

"Yes, of course." Lady Rothman waved a hand impatiently. "What did she discover about the secretary?"

"Well, Miss Müller is currently in Sir Blackney's house in Dorchester. She went at his suggestion for a change of scenery. It turns out that her brother was killed at Calais, just before Dunkirk."

"Brother?" Lady Rothman raised her brows. "A German soldier?"

"Better. SS." Molly smiled. "By all accounts, Miss Müller took his death rather hard and Sir Blackney was concerned that she would become quite poorly. He packed her off to Dorchester for a change of pace and sea air."

"While this is all very fascinating, I'm not sure why this would indicate that this woman is a German spy, or even sympathetic to our cause."

"Agnes believes that she is passing information to an agent on one of the Channel Islands."

Lady Rothman scoffed and stared at her in astonishment.

"How can that be possible? You know how difficult it is to move physical information out of the country. Why, we've been unable to do so ourselves and look at all the resources we have available to us!"

"I know. I thought the same thing, but then Agnes told me that the secretary has full access to Sir Blackney's yacht. He keeps it moored in Dorset, and she's been seen taking it out at all hours."

Lady Rothman was silent for a long moment, then she stood and began to pace slowly about the room.

"It seems fantastic," she murmured. "Why would Sir Oswald allow his secretary to make use of his personal yacht?"

"Agnes believes that all his secretaries are given access in order to facilitate his personal correspondence with his interests on the Continent. Of course, once the war moved into France, it became more difficult."

"But apparently not impossible, not if he allows his secretaries to take on the risk of going across the Channel." She paused in her pacing to shoot Molly a sharp look. "How reliable is this Agnes? How do we know that we can believe her?"

"She's never given me bad information before," Molly answered promptly. "And she certainly did her homework on this one. She even went down to Dorchester on the train one day to talk to one of the hands on the yacht."

"Oh? And what did she find out?"

"That they'd gone out to Guernsey not two nights before to drop off food and supplies for one of Sir Blackney's old footmen."

"Just food and supplies?"

"Well, she'd hardly tell the crew of the yacht that she was giving information to the Germans there, would she?"

Lady Rothman chuckled unexpectedly.

"No. I suppose not." She returned to her seat on the settee. "You're right, my dear. This is very interesting indeed."

"That's not everything, ma'am." Molly cleared her throat. "Agnes says that Miss Müller has found out about the existence of the Round Club, and she wants to offer her services as a courier to us."

"How on earth did Agnes discover that?!"

Molly grinned.

"I told you that she would be a perfect fit with us. Once she was convinced that the woman was genuinely sympathetic to our cause, and actively moving what intelligence she could gather from her employer, Agnes arranged for a meeting."

"That was very rash," Lady Rothman said disapprovingly. "She had no right to do such a thing without permission."

## When Wolves Gather

"Yes, and I've addressed that with her. However, the fact remains that Miss Müller is very keen to help us in any way that she can."

"Why?"

"Agnes believes that it's because of her brother. She thinks that when he was killed, it was the push that Miss Müller needed to join the fight."

"Hmm. That's very possible," Lady Rothman admitted. "Grief is a very powerful motivator."

"If she is willing to assist us in any way possible," Molly said, leaning forward earnestly, "Miss Müller may very well be just the answer we've been looking for."

## Chapter Twenty-Eight

Evelyn looked up in surprise when the front door bell rang. She glanced at the ornate clock on the writing desk and set down her pen, startled to find that it was already past three. She'd been writing letters for the better part of two hours now, and she stretched, letting out a jaw-cracking yawn. Who on earth was coming to visit on a Sunday afternoon? There were only a handful of people who knew she was even in residence after all. A moment later, a soft knock fell on the door of the parlor and Fran opened it.

"Miss Gilhurst, Miss Ainsworth," she announced, standing aside for Maryanne to sweep into the parlor.

"Maryanne!" Evelyn exclaimed, getting up. "What a surprise!"

"I hope you don't mind my dropping in like this," Maryanne said cheerfully. "I was visiting Lady Shriver and thought that I'd stop by as I was in the vicinity."

"No, of course not! Can I offer you tea or coffee?"

"No, no. I had something at her house and, to be perfectly honest, if I have to drink anything more I'll burst."

Evelyn laughed and nodded a dismissal to Fran. As the door closed behind the maid, she went over to sit in a chair, motioning Maryanne to the sofa.

"Good heavens! Well, we can't have that," she said. "How is Lady Shriver?"

"As well as can be expected. You've heard that Lord Shriver passed away?"

"Yes. My mother told me while I was at Ainsworth. I gather it wasn't unexpected?"

"Lord, no. He'd been having trouble with his heart for years. He stopped going about in the spring and they say that he declined rapidly after that." Maryanne stripped off her gloves and laid them on the small table beside the couch. "Lady Shriver seems in good spirits, all things considered. She was on an absolute tear about redoing the drawing room."

"Well, I suppose she wants a change. It must be difficult losing your husband after a long illness."

Maryanne tilted her head and looked at her.

## When Wolves Gather

"As opposed to suddenly? Did your mother want to redecorate after your father died?"

"Not that she mentioned."

"Well, I daresay the Shriver drawing room could use some updating. It's a very dark and heavy room, filled with perfectly horrid gothic pieces." Maryanne looked around. "This room is very nice and bright. What a relief! I almost feel as if I've come from a cave!"

"Oh Maryanne, it's not that bad! Lady Shriver's drawing room *is* rather gloomy, I'll grant you, but it's hardly a cave!"

"Well, by the time she's finished with it, it will be all yellow and cream, with poppies."

Evelyn looked startled.

"Poppies?"

Maryanne nodded, a wicked laugh in her eyes.

"Yes, darling. Poppies. I don't know how I didn't choke on my tea when she told me. Poppies everywhere, and not the wishy-washy colors. She wants the cheery bright red ones! Those are her words, not mine."

"Goodness!" Evelyn couldn't stop the grin that pulled at her lips. "It almost makes me wish I didn't have to go back to Northolt."

"I really must remember to make Tony send me a detailed description once it's finished," Maryanne agreed. "Lord knows where I'll be by then."

"How long will your training be?"

"Six weeks, and then I'll be posted, oh, somewhere squalid, I'm sure. But do you know, I'm quite looking forward to the whole thing? I think it will be a grand adventure."

"It will certainly be different from what you're used to," Evelyn said with a smile. "You must promise to write faithfully and let me know how you get on."

"Oh, I will. Can I write to you at Northolt? I haven't because I didn't know if they frowned on that sort of thing."

Evelyn burst out laughing.

"Yes, of course you can! It's the WAAF, not a detention camp!"

"Very well, then. I promise to write very long and boring letters." She picked up her purse and fished inside for her cigarette case. "I so enjoyed myself the other night. It was perfectly wonderful to run into you. I haven't had that much fun in months!"

"It was a very nice evening," Evelyn agreed, getting up to cross over to the side table and a box of cigarettes. "It was almost like old times again."

"I'm sorry that Giles was such a bore. He really does stick his foot in it sometimes. He has very old-fashioned ideas, and his views are appallingly limited to whatever his silly mother spouts into his ear. I tell him so all the time. I'm used to him, but I hope you weren't offended."

"Not at all. It was all rather amusing to be honest." Evelyn lit a cigarette with a match and waved the flame out. "I think Miles was more bothered by it than I was, actually. He seemed to be very annoyed when he took me to dance, which is interesting because he's well aware of the opinions of some people on women joining up and all that. He knows some of our acquaintances feel that way. I suppose he didn't think it extended to me, which is silly really. Of course I would be lumped into the same category."

"I think it rather caught us all off guard," Maryanne said. "I know that I certainly didn't expect Giles to say anything like that. But, of course, I assumed that he knew you were a WAAF. I thought everyone knew."

Evelyn grinned suddenly.

"His face really was priceless when Miles addressed me by my rank. He looked as if he'd swallowed a lemon."

Maryanne laughed and tapped ash off her cigarette into the ash tray on the table.

"The American was very cool about the whole thing, wasn't he?" she asked after a moment. "He seemed to be enjoying it immensely."

"Well, they don't have quite the same conservative views in America, do they?" Evelyn moved to sit again, carrying an ashtray from the side table with her. "I believe they're rather more open-minded than we are, although they certainly seem to have their own peculiar class system."

"I was taken by surprise when he opened his mouth," Maryanne said with a laugh. "I simply wasn't expecting an American accent with the uniform. I didn't even know we had American pilots flying in the RAF until last night!"

"It's not common. Miles says that there are only a handful, and they're scattered through the squadrons." Evelyn lifted her cigarette to her lips and inhaled, blowing the smoke out thoughtfully a second later. "Do you know something? I think we're going to get quite a lot of foreigners flying for us. We already have the Poles, and now I suppose we must have some French and Belgians."

"The Poles? Do we really?" Maryanne sounded shocked. "How did they get here?"

## When Wolves Gather

"They escaped when Poland fell and made their way here, or so Miles says." Evelyn laughed suddenly. "The RAF tried to make them all learn Polish phrases to help with the communication, but that didn't go over very well."

"No, I don't imagine it would. I don't think I would want to learn Polish to communicate in my own country." Maryanne shrugged. "Not that I have anything against them, mind, but I much prefer English. Do you know Polish?"

"No, I'm afraid not. I haven't got that far yet."

Maryanne grinned.

"Too busy learning Russian?" she teased. "When Rob slipped last year and said that you were multi-lingual, I nearly swooned. I never would have taken you for a bluestocking!"

"Is that what I am? I simply find languages fascinating, and I have an ear for them, so why not?"

"I struggled to learn French, and when my governess tried to force Italian down me, I thought I should die," Maryanne announced with a laugh. "I'll leave the languages to you, my dear. At least the Americans speak English, although Pilot Officer Field does use some strange phrases that I've never heard before. I suppose that's how they all talk over there. I wonder who his people are?"

"What on earth do you mean?"

"Well, it's obvious that he comes from some kind of upper echelon. He's well-spoken, for an American, and clearly well-educated. His manners are impeccable, which surprised me. He must have been raised in similar circles to our own, don't you think?"

"Well, I suppose so. I hadn't given it very much thought, to be honest," Evelyn said in amusement. "I did ask Miles if he would feel comfortable at The Dorchester and he laughed and said he would fit right in. So I suppose he must come from an influential family. But why all this interest, Maryanne? Are you falling for an American?"

Maryanne looked faintly horrified as she put her cigarette out.

"Heavens no! Can you imagine what Tony would say? Let alone my mother!" She shuddered theatrically. "I'm curious, that's all. He was telling me a little bit about Boston, and I do think I'd like to visit it some day."

"And visit him as well?" Evelyn asked wickedly.

Maryanne laughed.

"Go ahead. I suppose I deserve it for teasing you about Miles, although it's not the same thing at all."

"Isn't it? Why not?"

"Well, because he's American, darling."

"Yes, so I noticed."

"Well, an American is simply out of the question." Maryanne paused, then grinned. "Although, he *is* dreadfully good-looking."

"Yes, he is," Evelyn agreed. "And I don't see why his being American should have anything to do with anything. After all, as you pointed out, he obviously comes from similar social circles to us. If you'd like, I can find out just who his people are," she added devilishly.

"There's absolutely no need, my dear. I'll probably never see him again." Maryanne looked at her watch and reached for her purse. "I really must be going. I have one other stop to make before going home and changing for dinner. Tony and I are dining at Claridge's this evening."

They stood and Maryanne looked at Evelyn.

"Do you have plans for dinner? Why don't you join us?"

"I don't have any plans, actually," Evelyn said slowly. "Do you think Tony will mind?"

Maryanne waved a hand dismissively as Evelyn pressed the bell to summon Fran.

"Of course not! He'll be delighted to see you. And to be honest, I think it will do him a world of good to be reminded of happier times. He's been an absolute bear to be around lately."

"He's still not himself?"

"No, and if I thought it would do any good, I would suggest that we go down to Devon and spend some time at the manor with Mother." Maryanne pulled her gloves on as the drawing room opened and Fran appeared to escort her to the front door. "But I know he'll simply say that he can't take the time away."

She held out her hand to Evelyn with a smile, and Evelyn grasped it, meeting her gaze.

"I'll see you tonight, then," she agreed. "What time?"

"Shall we say seven? Come round to the house and we'll have a drink first."

"Very well."

"Splendid!" Maryanne released her hand and went towards the door. "We'll make it my going away dinner and have a wonderful time."

Evelyn kept her smile until the door had closed behind her friend, then the smile disappeared. She crossed to the window and watched as, a moment later, Maryanne emerged onto the pavement out front and turned to walk up the sidewalk. Seeing her standing at the window, she waved gaily and Evelyn lifted her hand in response before turning away from the glass.

## When Wolves Gather

As she had parted from Marrow yesterday, she had asked him if he knew anything of the small restaurant near Covent Garden where Lord Gilhurst and Sir Clark had gone to lunch. He had looked at her and asked rather sharply why she was asking. She'd shrugged off the question, saying that she was just curious, but it hadn't fooled him. She wasn't surprised. She hadn't asked very tactfully, blurting it out like an over-eager schoolgirl. However, after staring at her hard for a second, he'd told her what she'd already guessed. The restaurant was a suspected meeting place for The Round Club.

Things weren't looking very good for Lord Anthony Gilhurst, and Evelyn had absolutely no idea what to do about it.

◉

Fran looked up from her ironing in surprise, setting the iron on the stove as Evelyn walked into the bright, sunny kitchen at the back of the house.

"Is there something the matter, miss?"

"Not at all, Fran. I wanted to speak to you and I didn't see any reason to call you into the drawing room when I can just as easily come in here." Evelyn pulled a chair out at the table and sat down. "I'm really very grateful that you came to London with me."

Fran flushed with pleasure and picked up the iron, returning to the sheets.

"It's quite all right, miss. I don't mind at all."

"I know, but I still appreciate your willingness to come." Evelyn cleared her throat. "I've just accepted an invitation to go to Devon with Miss Gilhurst for a few days. It seems silly for you stay when I won't be here, so I thought perhaps you'd rather go back to Ainsworth."

Fran didn't show any surprise in the sudden change of events, a testament to the fact that she was well-used to Evelyn and her restless travels. In fact, Evelyn reflected, she almost looked as if she'd been expecting something like this.

"If you think it'd be best, miss," she said with a nod, the iron never hesitating in its steady and even swipes across the linen. "How long will you be gone?"

"Only a few days, but I know Maryanne well. The few days are just as likely to become a week, and then I'll be on my way back to Northolt."

"I understand, miss. I'll return to Ainsworth Manor, then. When will you leave?"

"We're motoring down tomorrow. I'll book you on the morning train back to Ainsworth." Evelyn smiled at her. "Would that be all right?"

Fran looked surprised.

"Yes, of course, miss. You don't need to ask."

"Well, I feel that you should have some say," Evelyn said humorously. "You may want to do some shopping first, for instance. Do you?"

"Shopping?" Fran smiled and shook her head. "No, I'm all right, miss. I'll toddle off on the morning train and be back in time to help Millie with the lunch."

"Oh, well, if that's what you'd like then no doubt Millie will be grateful for the assistance." Evelyn stood. "I'll go write a letter for you to carry back to Mother explaining everything."

"Very good, miss."

Evelyn left the kitchen and went back down the hallway to the drawing room. She would explain to her mother that she was going to stay with Maryanne at their house in Devon for a few days. She wouldn't question her daughter going off like this. Like Fran, she was used to Evelyn taking off at a moment's notice. It had been a common enough occurrence before the war.

Seating herself at the writing desk a moment later, she reached for a pen. It didn't sit well with her, all this lying to her family, but Evelyn was becoming more and more adept at it as the months went by. This really was the best way, she decided, unscrewing the pen cap. Maryanne was leaving for the ATS and would be gone from London, making it very unlikely that anyone at Ainsworth would learn that she hadn't gone to Devon after all. It was a tidy little lie, and one that would arouse no suspicion anywhere.

If Evelyn felt a pang of discomfort at the ease with which she was betraying her loved ones, she pushed it aside. It was war, after all, and they could never know what she did in her service of said war. This was simply who she was becoming, and there wasn't anything she could do about that at the moment. Her loyalty was to her country and MI6, and that meant living a lie. She'd known it when she agreed to work for Bill, and now she reminded herself that she'd made that choice with her eyes wide open. There was no turning back now.

# When Wolves Gather

# Chapter Twenty-Nine

Lady Rothman watched as her host pulled a piece of dried jerky from the pocket of his jacket and fed it to one of his many King Charles spaniels. Lord Chartwell had at least four that she knew of, though only one was in the garden with them today. His love for the beasts was well-known throughout society and every hostess who invited him for a stay in the country had to be prepared to have at least two of his beloved spaniels accompany him.

"And you're sure of this?"

The question caught her by surprise, spoken without him looking up from his dog.

"Yes. It seems there cannot be any doubt. I made inquiries myself after Molly made me aware of the situation yesterday. This secretary appears to be everything that she claims to be."

Lady Rothman watched as the Duke of Stafford straightened up. The spaniel shook itself after finishing its treat before turning to trot along the gravel path ahead of them.

"Sir Blackney has at least three personal secretaries," he said, clasping his hands behind his back and resuming their walk. "Why a mere squire thinks he needs that many secretaries is beyond me, but there you have it. And this one is in Dorchester, you say?"

"Yes."

"He's hardly ever in Dorchester. I've only known him to be in residence there but once a year, and only for a few weeks then." Lord Chartwell shook his head. "Still, it's none of my business how the man runs his affairs. Have you told anyone else about this Miss Müller?"

"No. I thought it best to discuss it with you before committing to any plan of action."

"Quite right."

"If she is everything that we think she is, she could be invaluable in getting physical information out the country and to our contact on Guernsey," Lady Rothman said slowly. "She could be the very answer to our difficulties."

"Yes," he said thoughtfully, watching his dog. "The challenge has become even greater since the authorities have begun eyeing everyone with suspicion these days. It's a sad state of affairs indeed when a respected peer of the realm can't go about his business without constantly looking over his shoulder. Would you believe that a sniveling office clerk had the appalling temerity to serve me with a summons last week?"

"What? What was the reason given?" she asked, looking at him in shock.

He waved a hand vaguely.

"Consorting with radical individuals. It's a damned nuisance. I've contacted my solicitors, of course, and nothing will come of it."

"Nevertheless, it's certainly a problem," she replied, shaken. "Why, if they dare to serve *you* with a summons…"

Her voice trailed off and Lord Chartwell looked at her. He clucked his tongue and reached out to squeeze her hand reassuringly.

"Don't you let it worry you. My solicitors will nip it all in the bud, mark my words. Now, back to this secretary. She will have to be vetted, you understand. We must be very sure."

"Yes, of course. Do you have someone particular in mind?"

Lord Chartwell was quiet for a moment, then he nodded slowly.

"Yes. Send Sir Ronald Clark down to talk with her. He speaks German well. He spent time in Berlin in '38, you know. Knows Hitler and Goebbels personally. If the woman isn't a true sympathizer, Clark will make short work of sniffing it out."

"That's a fantastic idea. I'd thought perhaps Henry could go, but I do think Sir Clark is the better choice."

"Ah yes. Henry. How is our young friend coming along?"

Lady Rothman frowned.

"He's very stubborn. Do you know, I think he believes himself above the rest of us?"

Lord Chartwell looked at her, amused.

"My dear Lady Rothman, Henry thinks himself above most of England, and so do we. You can't hold that against a man. He's been working with Berlin for over two years."

"Yes, I'm aware of that."

"Well, then, you must give him some space. What have you been assigning to him?"

"Surveying the southern coast."

Lord Chartwell stopped walking and looked at her in astonishment.

"Surveying the coast?" he repeated. "No wonder he's being difficult! You can't ask a seasoned spy to run around taking photographs of telephone wires and country bridges!"

252

## When Wolves Gather

"You said to start him out slowly!"

"Yes, but I didn't mean that slowly! I meant not to have him raise any suspicion in his offices or in Whitehall! Do you have any idea what kinds of information a man in his position is privy to?"

"Well, yes, but—"

"I'll be amazed if he stays with us at all if you've been sending him all over England on a fools errand," he continued ruthlessly. Then he exhaled and shook his head. "My apologies. It's been a trying week, and that took me by surprise. I'd advise you to allow him to begin gathering intelligence on what countermeasures, if any, are being put into place to repel an invasion. I mean on a military level. Which airfields are the most crucial to our fighter response? Which naval yards? Which factories? These are things he can discover easily, and things which the Abwehr can use."

"Yes, of course."

"Is he still having relations with Molly?"

Lady Rothman flushed pink.

"I hardly think that's any of our business," she murmured. "Really, my lord, you're as bad as she is for bringing it up."

He was amused, his short flash of anger a thing of the past.

"Of course it's our business, my dear. As long as they are in a close relationship, we can keep our association with Henry a secret. I don't need to tell you how important discretion is at this juncture. If he is still meeting with Molly in private, she can pass on any information to us, eliminating any need for contact between us."

"Well, when you put it in that light, then I suppose you're right," she agreed reluctantly. "However, I do think it's disgraceful how the youth today act without any decency whatsoever. It's appalling what they get up to."

"Yes, well, Molly is of a different class. We can't expect too much, can we?" He whistled sharply as his spaniel darted off the path. The dog returned promptly, looking very disgruntled at having been called back from what was undoubtedly the beginning of a chase after a rabbit. "She's very useful, of course, and her position makes her invaluable, but girls like her *will* be that way. At least in this instance, it is all to our advantage."

"I would have expected more from Henry," Lady Rothman said.

"My dear Mata, you really must learn to ignore these things. These types of affairs have been happening for centuries, and will continue." He chuckled. "I daresay I sowed my fair share of oats in my day. It's all to the better. Builds character."

Lady Rothman snorted.

"From what I've seen, Henry is not lacking in character."

"Arrange to meet with Sir Clark as soon as possible. I want to have this Miss Müller investigated immediately," Lord Chartwell said. "Herr Schmidt is waiting for the list of our members, along with the names of those who are opposed to us. We must find a way to get those, and all the other information we've gathered, to him without any more delay."

"Of course. And if Sir Ronald agrees that she is legitimate?"

"Then by all means, proceed with all haste. The sooner we start moving intelligence, the better for everyone."

⊙

"When are you due back to your posting, Evelyn? It must be soon."

Evelyn sipped her wine and smiled across the table at Anthony.

"Not for another week, actually."

"Another week?" he raised his eyebrows in surprise. "That's a long time, isn't it?"

"Yes, it is. However, I haven't had any leave since Christmas, so I suppose the WAAF decided I was due a nice holiday." Evelyn set down her glass and looked at Maryanne. "That's what you have to look forward to, Maryanne. Months of work with little time off."

"Yes, but at least I know going into it that that's how it will be," Maryanne replied with a short laugh. "I'm prepared. Besides, here you are with a lovely, long holiday, so perhaps there's hope for me."

"Are you nervous?" Evelyn asked.

"No, not nervous. Apprehensive, perhaps. I have no idea what to expect. I won't have the faintest clue what to do or where to go. How on earth did you get on when you first joined?"

Evelyn shrugged.

"I followed everyone else and tried not to make a mess of things, I suppose. It will be easier than you imagine. You'll learn a lot in your training, and the rest you'll learn as you go."

"I hope so. I want to make a difference, you know. I know it won't be much, but I want to do my part. I'm tired of feeling as if I'm not doing anything."

"I don't think you'll have to worry about not doing anything," Evelyn said with a smile. "They'll keep you busy, I'm sure."

## When Wolves Gather

"I'm very proud of you, you know," Anthony said, looking at his sister. "I know how important this is to you, and also how much it took to decide to do it. It's ridiculous how some of our peers are making such a fuss over women doing their bit."

"Did you hear what happened the other night?" Evelyn asked, her eyes twinkling.

"I told him," Maryanne said.

"Giles can be an idiot most times," Anthony said, reaching for his glass. "I'm not sure why you go about with him as much as you do. I find him rather dull."

"He makes me laugh and is usually good for the occasional gem like the other night. It makes life interesting, darling. Evelyn wasn't bothered by it, so no harm was done."

"Nevertheless, it was dreadfully impolite, as much to you as it was to Evie."

"Perhaps. Well, it's all water under the bridge now. I leave for the army in a few days, Evelyn will go back to her station, and the war will go on despite the narrow-mindedness of some of our acquaintances."

Anthony was quiet for a moment, then he sighed heavily.

"I hope it's not all in vain, what the two of you are sacrificing to help in the war effort, but I'm very afraid that it will be. Some are saying that an invasion is inevitable and, if they're right, it will all have been for naught."

"I don't believe an invasion is inevitable at all," Evelyn said a little more sharply than she intended. "The people who are saying that are not taking into account the pilots who will fight to keep the Luftwaffe out of England."

"They are very brave, without a doubt, but there are so few of them compared to Hitler's air force," he pointed out. "I don't know how we can even hope to keep pace."

A short silence fell over the table as Maryanne looked at Evelyn, her eyes filled with compassion.

"Really, Tony," she finally muttered. "I'm sure Evelyn is well aware of the odds. Do you need to underline them for her?"

Anthony looked at Evelyn sheepishly, his lips tightening briefly before he gave her a small smile.

"I'm so sorry, my dear," he said. "I'm clearly as bad as Giles. That was thoughtless of me. Will you forgive me?"

"There is nothing to forgive. You only speak the truth." Evelyn took a steady breath and reached for her wine. "I know that things look grim, but I refuse to accept that a squalid little painter will topple Great Britain that easily. I must have hope, you see, otherwise there is no point to anything I do."

*And I will be one of the first executed as a spy,* she added silently.
"Yes, of course."

"And what of you, Tony?" she asked after a moment. "Have you decided whether or not to do something to aid in the war effort? Or shall you concentrate on your political career and do your part through Parliament?"

"What? Were you thinking of doing something yourself?" Maryanne asked, surprised.

"It was simply a thought," Anthony replied, looking uncomfortable. "You know that I've been restless these past months."

"Yes, but I didn't know you were considering doing something different!"

"It really doesn't signify," he said brusquely, waving a hand impatiently. "It's nothing. I'll continue to do whatever I have to in order to keep my loved ones safe."

Evelyn studied him from under her lashes. He looked almost angry at the questions, almost as if he were being attacked. Her lips pressed together and her eyes narrowed. He did feel attacked. She could see it in his body language, and in the way his hand tightened on his glass. Lord Gilhurst was feeling decidedly guilty about something, and with that last comment, she knew he'd decided to throw his lot in with the Round Club.

"Of course you will," Maryanne said soothingly, her brow furrowed. "No one is suggesting otherwise. You've always done what was best for the country, and for us."

"I've certainly tried." Anthony seemed appeased and he swallowed a mouthful of wine before forcing a smile. "I seem to be making a habit putting my foot in it this evening. Forgive me."

Maryanne nodded and looked relieved when their food appeared at that moment. They were quiet while their dinner was laid before them, and once the waiter had departed, she looked at Evelyn.

"What are your plans for the remainder of your leave?" she asked.

"I'm going down to Weymouth for a few days," Evelyn lied, picking up her utensils. "I'm meeting Tante Adele and Uncle Claude. They want a little break from Auntie Agatha, I'm afraid."

"Oh dear. Is it that bad?"

"It would appear so. I'm sure after a few days away, they will all be the best of friends again."

## When Wolves Gather

"Your Aunt Agatha is rather impressive," Anthony said, his lips pulling into a grin. "I still remember the time she upbraided me in the middle of Hyde Park for all the world as if I was a boy in short trousers again."

"You deserved it," Evelyn said, laughing at the memory. "I seem to remember you teasing me unmercifully that day."

"Me? Tease you? You must have me mistaken with someone else, Evie. I would never dream of doing such a thing."

The mock angelic look on his face made both women laugh and, as Evelyn reached for her wine, she felt a pang at the easy camaraderie between them. She'd been close to the Gilhursts for what seemed like forever, and she quite counted Tony as a second brother. Yet he was on a path that would pit him right up against herself, and everything she believed in.

"When do you leave?" Maryanne asked, drawing her attention from her grim thoughts.

"Tomorrow morning."

"Oh, what a shame! You won't be back before I leave for my training!"

Evelyn smiled at her friend.

"Don't worry, darling. You'll do splendidly. I have every confidence in you. And we'll see each other again soon."

"That's true." Maryanne brightened. "And when you see me again, I'll be in a uniform just as ugly as yours! Won't that be a laugh?"

"You'll be surprised how quickly you become accustomed to that ugly uniform. When every woman you see is wearing it, it doesn't seem that terrible!"

"You will write to me, won't you?" Maryanne asked suddenly. "I don't know how I'll manage without someone I know to talk to."

"Of course I will," Evelyn said reassuringly. "And I'm sure we can arrange to meet in London on an evening off."

"You really must stop fretting, Maryanne," Anthony said. "I've never seen you so excited as the day you signed up. You will be back here before you know it, and as Evie says, you can meet as often as you like. After all, it's not as if either of you are leaving the country."

Evelyn winced inwardly at that. Certainly Maryanne wouldn't leave England, but she would. And when she left, there was never a guarantee that she would come back.

## Chapter Thirty

*5th August, 1940*
*My Dear Evelyn,*
*I really enjoyed our day together. I wish it could have been longer, but it's best that we returned when we did. While we were lounging on the bank of the river sipping wine and feasting on cold chicken, my squadron lost a pilot over the Channel. His name was Barnes, and I didn't know him well. He was in Green section. He'd only been here a few weeks. Rob said that it's getting so he doesn't even want meet the new pilots anymore. I can see his point. We're just getting to know them when they're killed.*

*Did you see the news out of Vichy? A French military court tried Charles de Gaulle in absentia for treason, and found him guilty. He's been sentenced to death. His crime? Leaving France and coming to England, and then trying to rally the remaining French troops to himself. It's a damn farce. The charges, the trial, the verdict - it's all so that Vichy can ingratiate themselves to Herr Hitler. Their government is simply a puppet for the Nazi party, doing everything they ask and taking no notice of their own people in the process. Frankly, it's frightening to watch.*

*Chris had a letter from home today. He says the Americans are more and more divided. Charles Lindberg is advocating for isolationism, and says that the United States should mind its own business and stay out of it. But other prominent members of the government argue that they should send aid to help Great Britain. Both sides are being very vocal, and Chris says it's only a matter of time before things come to a head over there.*

*He's disgusted by Lindberg and his crew. He thinks that if they were here, and saw what was really happening with their own eyes, that it would be different. He says that the average American thinks that we're simply sitting around, sipping tea and eating biscuits, waiting for them to come save us. He says if they saw how desperately we were fighting, they would*

## When Wolves Gather

*want to help because that's the American way - to help anyone willing to help themselves. I'm not so sure that he's right. It seems to me that the Americans are a rather selfish lot. They've watched as most of Europe has fallen to the German Blitzkrieg. If that doesn't make them sit up and take notice, I don't think a few pilots being blown apart over the Channel will make any difference. I said as much to the Yank, but he laughed at me and told me to wait and see.*

*It's a long day tomorrow, so I must turn off the light and go to sleep. I do hope you're enjoying the rest of your holiday. I miss you already and can't wait until we see each other again.*

*Always yours,*
*Flight Lieutenant Miles Lacey*

### Dorchester
### August 6

Evelyn looked around the bedroom as the door closed behind the housekeeper. It was a very modest, smaller bedroom, but furnished with taste. The four poster bed had no curtains, but the rich wood gleamed from regular polishing and the bedspread was immaculate. A writing desk was positioned before a large window that would let in the morning sun, and a wardrobe stood open and empty against the far wall. A worn armchair was placed near the fireplace and Evelyn imagined that in the winter the room would be very cozy indeed with a fire roaring in the hearth. It was a comfortable room, and one that perfectly befitted a personal secretary.

She had been greeted on her arrival by a thin woman with graying hair who introduced herself as Mrs. Besslington, the housekeeper. Her husband, the butler, was currently in London with his Lordship, but they had Frank, the first footman, in his absence. She'd informed Evelyn that she'd been expected, and hadn't seemed in the least surprised that a secretary was coming without Sir Blackney. Obviously she was accustomed to his staff coming and going, and that made Evelyn's job that much easier. She'd been concerned about explaining her presence, but it seemed Sir Blackney had already addressed that particular problem for her.

# CW Browning

Setting her case on the bed and bending over to open it, she reflected that while Mrs. Besslington had seemed friendly enough, she didn't appear to be interested in the secretary that had showed up at her door. Once she'd shown Evelyn to her room, she'd departed promptly. There were no attempts to question her or learn anything about her, and for that, Evelyn was grateful. She already felt like a fool, made up as she was.

Her lips curved and she went over to the small mirror fixed on the wall near the bed. The black wig that she'd purchased had easily been arranged into a very prim and neat bun at the back of her head, and her face had been artificially lined with the skillful application of makeup before she left the house this morning. She would have to be careful with that, she thought critically, tilting her head as she studied her reflection. If she had to reapply it, she would have to get the lines just right. However, it had been easy to make herself look ten years older than she was, and the addition of a rather grotesque wart on her cheekbone near her hairline completed the image. She'd even managed to fix a very small piece of the wig hair into the putty that formed the base for the wart, making it appear that hair was growing from it. She'd been very pleased with the result, laughing almost uncontrollably when she saw it fixed to her skin. It was positively horrid, and she loved it.

Evelyn turned away from the mirror and pushed the wire-rimmed glasses up on her nose, going back to her suitcase to unpack. Her normally trim figure had been transformed into a rather frumpy, stocky frame with the addition of layers of padding wrapped around her waist beneath her clothes, and if her ankles looked a little slender for the rest of her, the thick stockings she wore took care of that. It would make for a very warm time in the summer heat, but it couldn't be helped. Hopefully, she wouldn't be in this disguise for very long.

She had no idea how long she could expect to wait for the Round Club to make contact with her. The arrangement with Marrow was that she would remain in place for a week. If she hadn't been contacted by then, she would leave and they would consider the operation a dud. But Evelyn would be very surprised if that were to happen. Marrow had made it enticing enough for them, offering a direct route to German agents on the Channel Islands. She really didn't see how they could afford *not* to explore the possibility of using the secretary. If, for whatever reason, they decided not to take the bait and didn't contact her within the week, her orders were to return to London. She had one week.

Bending to scratch her calf under the uncomfortable stocking, Evelyn thought wryly that one week might just end up being too long

## When Wolves Gather

in the August sun. God-willing the powers that ruled over the blasted Round Club would come calling long before that.

⊙

The day was cloudy and a brisk wind pulled at Lady Rothman's hat as she walked along the path that snaked through Regents Park. She glanced up at the overcast sky with a wary eye. She hadn't brought along her umbrella because she hadn't considered that it would be necessary, but now she was rethinking that decision. While the weather forecast said nothing about rain today, this was England, and she'd been caught in an unexpected shower enough times in her life to regret her rather foolish optimism.

"Ah, Lady Rothman!"

A voice called to her and she turned inquiringly, smiling when she saw a rather portly gentleman making his way unhurriedly towards her. Sir Ronald Clark was a man of average height who was completely unremarkable, with the possible exception of his extraordinary mustache. He eschewed the current trend of very thin mustaches, preferring to maintain his full, but neatly trimmed, facial hair with pride.

"Good morning, Sir Ronald," she greeted him as he joined her. "How are you this fine morning?"

"Never better, my dear Lady Rothman. Never better!" He turned to fall into step beside her, adjusting the pace to his own leisurely stroll. "How is Lord Rothman? Still terrorizing the House?"

"As much as he is able, I'm sure. I haven't seen very much of him of late."

"It's this blasted war. It's keeping everyone busy, or so I'm told." He nodded to an acquaintance that passed, then lowered his voice. "What was so urgent that you wanted to meet here? I thought we were trying to be discreet."

"There can hardly be anything unusual in meeting by chance while out for a stroll in the park."

He grunted.

"If one ignores the fact that I *never* go for a stroll in the park."

Lady Rothman laughed. "I know. I thought the fresh air would do you good."

He looked at her askance.

"Good Lord, not you as well! My man's been on to me for the past year or more. He's convinced I'll have a heart attack."

"We're only concerned because we care, dear Sir Ronald. We can't lose you, you know. You're far too useful!"

He was betrayed into a laugh.

"Useful, eh? And what needs doing now? Go on. You might as well tell me and we'll get it over with."

"There's someone in Dorchester that we want you to meet. She's one of Sir Blackney's personal secretaries. Her name is Sylvia Müller and she claims to be from Berlin."

He looked down at her thoughtfully.

"Is that so?"

"Yes. I understand that she's rather keen to join our cause and do something to aid the Fatherland." Lady Rothman cleared her throat and lowered her voice. "My sources say that she is willing, and in a position to move physical packets of information to the German agents on Guernsey. If that is truly the case, she would be invaluable to the organization."

He was quiet for a moment, then he shook his head.

"I don't know," he said skeptically, pausing to look at her. "All the German agents in England have been apprehended. If she's an agent who is able to move information, why wasn't she caught with the others?"

"I've been looking into that and I think I've discovered why we're just hearing of her now. Her brother was killed at Calais."

He raised his eyebrows.

"You think that she's suddenly decided to become active because her brother was killed?"

"Can you think of any better motivation?"

He pursed his lips for a moment, then turned to continue walking.

"No, I suppose not. How long has she been in England?"

"She attended boarding school here, and returned to take a secretarial position when her father died in '33. She supports her mother, sending her money each quarter."

"And her family?"

"Devoted Nazi party members from all accounts."

"Well, I suppose I should go to Dorchester and meet her, then. I'm surprised she's allowed to remain so close to the coast. Isn't Sir Blackney's estate within the five-mile radius imposed on German nationals?"

"Actually, I don't believe that it is," Lady Rothman said, after a moment's thought. "However, it makes no difference, really. She isn't

## When Wolves Gather

normally in Dorchester. Sir Blackney sent her down for a bit of a break. She took the death of her brother rather hard, I understand."

"Lord, I hope I won't have a weeping woman on my hands," he said without compassion. "Nothing worse than the waterworks you lot employ. Still, I'll see what I can suss out. If she's not who she says she is, I'll know soon enough. No one can fool me. I'm far too well-versed in the German culture. Spent a year there, you know, in '38. I know how they think."

"Yes, that's why we'd like you to go meet her," Lady Rothman said hastily when it appeared that Sir Clark was on the verge of launching into a story. He did love to go on about his time in Berlin, but she didn't have the time to indulge him this morning. "The duke was of the opinion that you were the best person for the job."

"Quite right. Quite right. I'll catch the train in the morning. I'll know if this Miss Sylvia Müller is really a Berliner, mark my words."

◉

Evelyn pulled a leaf from a tree and turned it over in her fingers as she inhaled deeply, enjoying the scent of boxwood mixed with the fresh, evening air. The day had been overcast for the most part, and now the fading light was casting deep shadows across the estate. The only sounds to be heard were the distant call of sea birds, and the occasional rustle of a squirrel in upper branches of the old trees.

Exhaling in contentment, Evelyn paused to look around. Sir Blackney's estate was expertly landscaped and maintained, including the walking path that wound through the woods on the south side of the property. After dinner, it was here that she had come to explore, wanting the peace and tranquility of the untamed woods. Her day had been tedious and lonely, spent in the confines of the small downstairs office, ostensibly to work on correspondence for Sir Blackney. She'd dined alone in the large dining room with a book to keep her company. Despite her protests, Mrs. Besslington had appeared shocked at her suggestion that she eat in the kitchen with her. As far as the housekeeper was concerned, a personal secretary was someone who was a member of the house, not the servants, and no amount of arguing would convince her otherwise. Still, she supposed it was for the best. The less interaction she had with anyone, the better all around.

A distant drone filled the air, the sound unmistakable to anyone who had spent any amount of time on an airfield. Stopping,

Evelyn tilted her head back and scanned the sky, looking for the airplanes. After a moment, they appeared on the horizon above the trees. It looked to be a group of at least ten small fighters. A whole squadron, more than likely. She watched them, squinting to make out the silhouettes. Hurricanes, it looked like, and they were heading out over the Channel. Moving fast, they streaked across the evening sky in perfect, steady formation, black contrasts to the clouds streaked with pale pink and purple from the sinking sun. Evelyn's breath caught in her throat and she felt her chest tighten as emotion welled up inside her, taking her by surprise.

She'd seen enough squadrons of Hurricanes flying overhead at Northolt, but this was different. The quiet peace of the evening was at such glaring odds with the war planes flying overhead that she felt almost as if she were in a dream. Yet she wasn't dreaming, and those pilots were going to meet an enemy that was just as lethal and fierce as they themselves. Pilots like Fred, and Robbie, and Miles were above her, ready to battle the fearsome Me 109s in order to reach the bombers attacking the convoys in the Channel. She knew the battles were becoming more and more fierce from things Miles had told her. Fred had been shot down, and so had Robbie. They were losing pilots already, and Hitler hadn't even begun to turn his attention on England. When he did, Göring's Luftwaffe would come over in force. This was only the prelude.

Evelyn watched the squadron of fighters until they disappeared from sight, wondering how many would return from the sortie. Were there new pilots in that squadron who were unseasoned and inexperienced? Miles and Robbie both said those were the ones they lost more often than not.

Turning, Evelyn started back towards the house, her peaceful stroll at an end. She sent up a silent prayer for the safety of those pilots, and for all of her own pilots that she loved and cared for. It seemed surreal that they were in the middle of war when the breezes blew so gently and the boxwood smelled so strongly, but they were. And she had to do her part to try to shorten it as much as possible. It was why she was here, dressed in this ridiculous get-up.

As she passed out of the trees and started across the wide expanse of lawn, Evelyn felt a shiver go down her neck. Turning her head, she was just in time to see a shadow duck behind a tree not ten feet away. Taking a deep breath, she turned her head back and continued. Her stride never faltered, but her heart had skipped and pounded in her chest. They were watching. They knew she was here.

Now all she had to do was wait.

**When Wolves Gather**

# Chapter Thirty-One

Evelyn got off the bicycle that Mrs. Besslington had loaned her and leaned it against the outside of the Post Office. She'd received a message, delivered before breakfast, asking if she would be so kind as to go into the village today, as interested persons wanted to speak with her. The entire message had been composed for all the world like something out of a spy film, making her almost laugh aloud when she read it. Whoever had written it had even capitalized the words they wanted emphasized, leading her to believe that she was dealing with an amateur. Why, she almost expected to be followed by someone in a trench coat and hat with false spectacles. Alas, such an amusement was not to be, and she had pedaled into the village in complete solitude.

Where she was to meet these "Interested Persons" was a mystery. The note hadn't given any particulars aside from the time. She was to be in the village High Street at one o'clock. Evelyn lifted the sleeve of her jacket to look at her delicate gold watch just as a clock tower chimed the hour. *Well, here I am,* she thought, lowering her hand and turning towards the entrance to the post office. *Now where are you? Who are you?*

The entire arrangement seemed absurd to her, but then she wasn't an amateur. If the situation weren't so serious, it would be laughable. This was the organization plotting to aid the Nazis in taking over Britain? But as soon as the thought flitted across her brain, Evelyn's lips tightened. The local agent who sent her the message was hardly one of the upper ranks of the Round Club, and it would be complete folly to discount the entire organization because of the silliness of one.

She was just stepping into the small building when something caught her attention out of the corner of her eye. Turning her head, she scanned the High Street quickly, her pulse quickening when she caught sight of Sir Ronald Clark standing halfway up the street. He was talking to a man dressed in work clothes, and his silhouette faced her, but there was no mistaking him. Pausing in the door to the shop, she watched as both men finished their conversation and turned, as one, to look in her direction.

Sir Clark stared at her for a moment, then said something to the other man before beginning to walk down the street towards her. The man turned and went in the opposite direction after one final look at Evelyn. She watched Sir Clark move with his leisurely stride down the pavement, her heart pounding. The man was well known to her, and she to him. If even one part of her disguise was off, he would surely recognize Evelyn Ainsworth, the daughter of Robert Ainsworth, and one of the richest heiresses in England. And then what?

*I'll be up the creek without a paddle, that's what.*

Changing direction, Evelyn stepped out of the doorway and back onto the pavement, turning to collect her bicycle. Pushing it beside her, she walked towards the portly gentleman coming towards her. There was only one way to find out if her disguise would hold up. She knew the accent would. If she could pass muster with the likes of Herr Obersturmbannführer Hans Voss, she could certainly get past Sir Ronald Clark. No. If she failed, it would be because he recognized her.

"Excuse me!" Sir Clark called when she was a few feet away. He raised his hat off his head. "Miss Sylvia Müller?"

Evelyn paused and looked at him inquiringly, her lips curved in a polite smile.

"Yes?"

She spoke in English, but gone was her upper crust accent. In its place, she spoke with the soft, generic tones of someone who had learned to speak English as a second language. She would allow a very faint hint of her German to affect certain words, giving the impression that she had worked hard to learn to conceal her Berlin roots.

"My name is Sir Clark. Sir Blackney said I might find you here." Sir Ronald was all smiles. "I hope I'm not intruding?"

"Not at all, Sir Clark. I am simply doing some shopping."

"May I walk with you?"

Evelyn hesitated for the briefest of seconds, then inclined her head stiffly.

"Of course."

He turned to fall into step beside her and she stole a glance up at his face. So far, so good. She began to relax.

*Now, let the grilling commence.*

◉

Sir Clark watched the scenery whizz by as the train rocked rhythmically, lulling him into a state of languor. It was past tea time, and he was looking forward to his dinner. After leaving early this

## When Wolves Gather

morning to traipse down to Dorchester, he hadn't had time for anything to eat. He'd only just arrived in the village when Miss Müller presented herself. The disruption to his normal schedule had been worth it, however. The woman was everything they needed, and more.

He felt like rubbing his hands together in glee, but of course he wouldn't. Instead, he stared out of the window and reflected that surely God must be on their side. It was the only possible explanation for such a perfect agent dropping right into their hands. And she really was perfect.

Miss Sylvia Müller was quiet and unassuming, unlike so many women these days, and he'd been gratified to find that when she spoke English, it was only with the faintest trace of her German accent. Quite remarkable, really. So many Germans had such a difficult time with the English language, and their accent really was appalling for the most part. He much preferred to speak German when conversing with a German for the simple reason that he found their butchering of the English words quite repulsive. But Miss Müller had learned to conceal her accent quite well. She'd confided to him that she'd worked hard to mimic the English as much as possible once the war started. She'd realized that her accent would make her hated by the locals, and so she had worked to lose it. When he asked her if it had worked, she had smiled faintly and shrugged. It hadn't, really, but she imagined the animosity would be much worse if her accent were thicker. She said she didn't think many people knew *what* the faint accent was that they were hearing, and so she was treated as any other foreigner: with polite suspicion.

Whatever the reason and outcome, Sir Clark was glad that she spoke English well. It made everything much easier. Nevertheless, he'd conducted much of the interview in German, and there could be no doubt that the woman had been born and raised in Berlin, or thereabouts. She claimed that her mother had moved out of the city when her father died, and he saw no reason for that not to be the case. Her accent was exactly what he was used to hearing from his many friends in Berlin, right down to the little nuances of dialect that made that area of the Fatherland unique.

She was a bit older than he had been expecting, but he supposed that didn't account for very much. If anything, she would be possessed of a bit more patience and wisdom than a younger woman, and would be less inclined to take reckless risks. She appeared to have a very good head on her shoulders, along with a steady temperament that he found pleasing. In fact, the only flash of emotion that he'd detected from her was when she'd been discussing her brother. Sylvia Müller had loved her brother very much, despite them not having seen each other in over two years. The bond they had shared was evident in the way she spoke, and Sir Clark believed with every fiber of his being that she would do anything to avenge his death.

And that was all to their benefit.

He'd go to see Mata as soon as he returned to London and advise her that the secretary would be the perfect addition to the Round Club. He knew that she and the duke were concerned about moving the intelligence they'd gathered over the past months quickly. He would suggest that Molly transfer the first packet to Sylvia Müller at the weekend.

The time had come to stop playing games, and to start doing what needed to be done.

# When Wolves Gather

# Chapter Thirty-Two

**Somewhere over the North Sea**
**August 8**

"Cowslip, this is Blue Leader. Approaching angels 4 now."

Miles spoke into his radio calmly as he led his section to the coordinates HQ had given him when they scrambled them ten minutes before. He glanced to his right. Chris was there on his wing, scanning the skies above them. On his left, young Thomas was flying nice and close. His dip in the drink had taught him well, Miles reflected with a flash of amusement. Thomas was also scanning the sky above and below, looking for enemy fighters.

"Roger, Blue Leader. Continue angels 4 and steer vector 2-1-0. Bandits twenty plus."

Miles stifled a groan and felt his body tense as his hands involuntarily tightened on his control stick.

"You heard him, gentlemen. Twenty plus. Keep your eyes peeled."

"They've got to be kidding with these numbers," Chris muttered. "Three against twenty? It's damn suicide."

"It's only suicide if you're foolish enough to get yourself killed," Miles replied.

"Tally ho! I see them!" Thomas cried a second later. "Seven o'clock below!"

"Yes, I see them."

Miles stared down at the writhing mass of fighters and bombers. They were attacking a convoy of merchant ships and he could see one ship in flames far below. It was a speck, really, with funnels of black smoke twisting into the air. There was no hope for that one, but the other four were still afloat.

There were many more than twenty enemy aircraft. It looked to be closer to fifty plus. The good news was that he picked out a few Hurricanes in the melee. The bad news was that there were only a few. They were outnumbered by more fighters than Miles cared to count, and he clamped his jaw shut grimly. As Chris said, it seemed like suicide to get into the middle of that.

"Right. Mind our chaps, lads," he said, nudging his stick to send the Spitfire into a dive. "Here we go."

A second later, Miles pressed his gun button, sending a line of bullets towards an Me 109. The fighter banked to the left as he fired and his shot missed, streaking past harmlessly.

"Damn!" he swore to himself. "They know we're here! Watch your tail!"

As he spoke, two 109s shot into his peripheral view and he turned quickly to avoid having them latch on behind him. After some vicious maneuvering, Miles came up behind one of the Me 110 fighter-bombers that were so deadly in attacking the convoys. They were fast, and able to dive and fight with precision. However, they couldn't turn worth a damn and he had every intention of exploiting that fact. Approaching from the bottom right, well out of range of its single rear-facing machine gun, Miles unleashed a burst of ammunition straight into the belly of the airplane.

"Miles, behind you!" Thomas cried breathlessly.

Miles broke away as smoke began pouring from the stricken aircraft. A 109 fired at him from behind just as he twisted out of the way and, instead of hitting him, the fighter hit the 110 in the tail, adding to the damage Miles had already wrought.

"He shot his own man!" Thomas crowed. "Bloody marvelous!"

Miles had no time to enjoy the moment as two more 109s dove towards him. Twisting up and to the left, he looked behind him to find three more on his tail. Six of the devils! How in blazes was he going to get out of this mess?

Relying on the superior speed and maneuverability of his Spit, Miles twisted and dove, avoiding fire and trying to get into position to take at least one of the bastards out. Pushing his kite to what had to be the edge of her limits, Miles turned into a tight, inverted spiral, trying to get away from two fighters and into position to shoot another. Just as he thought he had a shot, the small shadow shot out of range, twisting and turning to come towards him, head-on.

Miles looked behind him at the three still trying to get a shot at him, and then back at the fighter streaking towards him. It was a flight leader, he realized with a start. The yellow stripe on his nose was visible now, and Miles grit his teeth. As much as he wanted to take that bastard on, he had to live to be able to do so.

## When Wolves Gather

Pulling up, he arched into a loop, taking the three 109s with him. As he came around to fire at the one closest to him, Miles felt his machine shudder violently as bullets ripped into his tail. Swearing, he broke away and checked his gauges furiously, memories of losing altitude and crashing on a beach in Belgium coming to the forefront of his mind.

"You're hit, Blue Leader!" Chris cried.

"I'd noticed, Yank."

Chris shot into his peripheral and fired at the fighter behind him. It was with great satisfaction that Miles saw smoke appear and the little bastard who'd clipped him dropped out of the fight, turning back towards France.

"All my gauges are functioning," he said. "Can you see anything?"

"Nah. No smoke. Nothing." Chris passed behind him. "Just some holes in the tail."

That was all Miles needed to hear. With a grunt, he turned and dove back into the fray, Chris on his wing. Thomas was engaged with two 109s as he tried to get to another 110 and Miles joined him. They were there for the bombers, after all. If they could take out a couple of the 110s, he'd consider that a job well done.

Before he could begin to maneuver for a shot, the yellow-nosed fighter shot towards him, guns blazing. Miles swore again and broke away, narrowly avoiding being hit a second time.

"You bloody bastard!"

"I've got Uncle Tom," Chris said breathlessly. "Go get the asshole!"

"With pleasure," Miles muttered, pulling up and twisting away from the group around the 110.

Yellow Nose followed and Miles realized that he must have seen his own airplane markings. If the stakes weren't his life, he supposed he would have found amusement in the situation: two flight leaders, both with several kills painted on their planes, trying to get the best of the other. There was something to be said for besting a pilot who had earned the right to lead others. Not only did it deal a blow with the loss of experience for the other side, but there was something very satisfying in getting the better of a ranking pilot. It made for a fierce battle, and one that would end only in defeat for one of them. Miles clamped his jaw and focused all of his attention on his adversary. He had no intention of being the one who went down today.

Squinting against the glare of the sun, Miles turned, twisted, dove, and arched in a tight dance with the other pilot. While the Spitfire was much more maneuverable, the enemy had skill. He didn't try to make his machine do what he knew it couldn't, and stayed with Miles twist for turn, avoiding all attempts to land a shot.

"Damn, you're good."

Miles felt a twinge of uncertainty as he arched up and around, trying to get a jump on the fast opponent. He was better than Miles, and Miles freely admitted it. He flew with precision, and without mistakes. No matter what trick Miles pulled out, he was there to avoid and counter. It was as if he was inside Miles' head, seeing every move before he made it.

Miles squeezed his eyes shut against the glare of the sun, and suddenly pulled up, turning to face his opponent head-on, just as the Jerry had done earlier. Caught, the 109 sped towards him, and Miles sucked in his breath. He was flying straight towards a smaller fighter, and neither one of them was backing down. He had to be mad!

The distance between them closed rapidly, and in another second they would collide. The German was obviously as mad as he was, and Miles swallowed. Sweat poured down his forehead and his breath was coming fast and heavy when he pressed the button on his control stick, the 109s nose within spitting range. His airplane shuddered, sending bullets tearing through the side of the fighter as he streaked to the right at the last possible second. At the same time that his bullets were ripping into the 109, Miles felt his own machine lurch and tremble and knew, without a doubt, that he'd been hit again.

Afterwards, Miles would have no idea how he missed flying into the German's wing as he passed, but miss it he did. After a desperate look at his gauges, he twisted around to get onto his opponent's tail. Before the Jerry could react, Miles pressed the button again and shot another burst into the fighter. Smoke, thick and black, began pouring from the 109 and it dropped out, heading back towards France, losing altitude rapidly.

Miles exhaled and reached up to wipe the sweat out of his eyes, relief rushing through him. The feeling was short-lived, however.

"On your six, Blue Two!"

Miles looked around quickly until he located Chris with three 109s on his tail. Diving to take aim at the one closest to him, his machine shuddered slightly and he scanned his gauges again. Everything was reading normally and he shook his head, his lips pressed together grimly. Something wasn't right, but he couldn't worry about it. As long as he could still fly, his job was to continue.

## When Wolves Gather

Centering one of the 109s in his crosshairs, he sent a line of ammunition towards it, hitting it in the tail. It spun out to the right, dropping briefly, then coming back.

"They're like green flies at the beach," Chris gasped. "God, they're—"

He broke off suddenly and Miles watched as the Spitfire lurched to the left suddenly.

"I'll be damned!" Chris sounded almost cheerful. "The bastard got me!"

Miles spared him a quick glance before turning his attention to the 109 that had landed the shot on Chris.

"It's your tail. He shredded it," he said, focusing on the fighter before him. "Get out of here and go home while you'll still make it."

"And you?"

"We'll be along shortly. Save me some tea."

⊙

Evelyn looked up from her book as another squadron of fighter planes flew overhead. She'd come outside after lunch just as a group of them had flown over, and this was the third group in an hour. She watched them for a moment, wondering if she knew any of the pilots. They were Hurricanes, but unless they were from Northolt, it was very unlikely.

"Here's the afternoon post, Miss Müller," a voice said behind her. "Mrs. Besslington asked me to bring it to you."

Evelyn turned to see an under-footman approaching with a stack of envelopes in his hand.

"Thank you," she said. "Would you mind placing them on my desk, please? I'll be in shortly to attend to them."

The young man nodded and turned to go inside, but Evelyn stopped him before he reached the door.

"Tell me, do the airplanes always fly over so often?" she asked.

The footman turned and looked into the sky at the fighters in the distance.

"They have in recent days, aye. More and more of them are coming and going. The Germans are attacking the convoys, or so they say."

She looked at him.

"Don't you believe it, then?"

He shrugged.

"I suppose I have to, seeing as all those fighter planes are going out every day. Wouldn't put it past the Jerries, not after what they done in France."

He nodded to her and turned to go back into the house while Evelyn turned her attention back to the now-specks in the distance. She counted them quickly before they disappeared from sight. She would count them again when they came back. It was a silly thing to do, really, because she wouldn't know if the airplanes coming back were that squadron or another. Yet it made her feel as if she were part of it, somehow.

How many *would* come back? The fighting was getting fiercer and fiercer up there. The grimness about Miles' mouth that day by the river had spoken more plainly to that than anything else. The Luftwaffe was ramping up their forays into the Channel, and the bombing of port cities was becoming more and more frequent. Hitler was turning his eyes to his next conquest, and those fighter planes were the only things standing in his way.

She lowered her eyes to her book and tried to concentrate on the words, but she was finding it impossible. Restlessness was rolling through her, and she finally closed the book impatiently. How could she sit here and read while men like Miles and Rob were flying to meet the enemy? While she sat in the summer afternoon warmth, they were defending ships being attacked by bombers and fighters alike.

Evelyn let out a huff of frustration and stood up, laying the book on the arm of the chair and walking towards the lawn. Perhaps a short walk around the grounds would help to clear her head and make her feel less melancholy. It wasn't as if she wasn't doing anything, after all. She was doing her part by trying to catch a group of traitors who would happily hand all those pilots over to the Nazis and not think twice about it. Who knew what damage they could do if she didn't discover their names! Right now, they were an invisible threat, but once she gave them a name and a face, their power would be limited.

And then all those boys getting shot down won't have given their lives for nothing.

As she stepped onto the grass, Evelyn's lips tightened. She would find out who these people were, and she would hand the names over to Marrow. A shadow passed over her face. It seemed likely that Tony would be one of them, and that brought a wave of sorrow over her. It didn't seem possible that she could very well have to give up such a dear friend. It would destroy Maryanne. Yet she had no choice. If Tony had been foolish enough to cast his lot with traitors, then it was out of her hands to protect him. And she wasn't even sure that she

## When Wolves Gather

wanted to. They went against everything she believed in, everything she and Robbie and Miles were fighting for. Why, even Chris had come from America to fight for them! She would do absolutely everything she could to make sure they were all brought to account.

And she had no doubt that she would get her opportunity. The interview with Sir Clark yesterday had gone very well. He'd even conducted an hour of the interview in German, which had amused her to no end. She kept thinking of that day in Strasbourg, so long ago now, when she'd sat across from Hans Voss. Sitting across from Sir Clark in the garden of the local pub had been nothing compared to Strasbourg. She'd fooled Voss easily enough, and Sir Clark was no SS agent.

Yes. She was confident that he'd gone away convinced that she was exactly what she wanted them to believe she was. And he'd never once suspected that he was, in fact, sitting across from Miss Evelyn Ainsworth, the socialite who had joined the WAAF at the start of the war.

Her lips curved faintly and Evelyn looked up into the overcast sky. She had no doubt that she'd passed muster. Now all she had to do was wait.

◉

Molly finished fastening her skirt and reached for her blouse, which was tossed over the back of a chair. She glanced at the man in the bed, reclining against a mound of pillows, watching her with a cigarette in his hand.

"Don't look at me like that," she said, pulling on the shirt.

"Like what?"

"Like I'm doing something dreadfully terrible." She began doing up the buttons. "I *have* to leave. I'm meeting Mata in the garden at eleven."

"Then return when you've finished."

"I can't! I have to be at work early in the morning, and so do you, for that matter."

Molly turned and sat down at the vanity, picking up a hairbrush.

"So I do. You're quite right." He smoked his cigarette and watched her for a moment. "Shall I see you on Saturday?"

"I'm afraid not." She met his gaze in the mirror. "I'm going down to the seaside to meet with a woman who is…well, she's a German agent."

The man stilled, his eyes piercing.

"What?" he asked softly.

"You heard me." She set the hairbrush down and turned to face him. "She's a secretary, one of Sir Blackney's, and she's from Berlin. Sir Clark met with her today. We thought she was simply a German who wanted to help her Fatherland, and Mata sent Clark down to make sure she was legitimate."

"And?"

"She told him that she already has a contact on Guernsey. She's been taking intelligence that she's gathered from Sir Blackney's correspondence to him on the squire's yacht."

He frowned.

"If that's so, how is it possible that I've never heard of her?"

"Don't feel bad, Henry. Neither Mata nor the duke had either!" Molly got up and went over to sit on the side of the bed. She took the cigarette from his hand and lifted it to her own lips. "I'm the one who told them about her!"

Henry raised his eyebrows.

"You? How did you meet her?"

"I didn't. You remember I told you about Agnes, the girl I've been working with who wants to join the Club?"

"Typist, or some such thing?"

"That's it. Well, she found out about her from one of Sir Blackney's housemaids. She told me." Molly handed the cigarette back to him and smiled, unable to contain her excitement. "I made some inquiries and, sure enough, it turns out that she is just the sort of person we've been looking for! Her brother was killed in Calais and that's why she's suddenly so keen to join the cause."

"It sounds like she has no need to join the Round Club if she already has a contact in the Channel Islands," Henry pointed out, leaning over to put the cigarette out in the ashtray by the bed. "Why would she bother?"

Molly frowned.

"Why shouldn't she? Honestly, Henry, you always insist on making things difficult. Why are you being so contrary?"

"Am I?" He looked surprised. "I thought I was being helpful."

"Well you're not. It doesn't matter why she wants to be of assistance to the Round Club. She does, and we need her to move

## When Wolves Gather

information for us. In fact, that's what I'm doing on Saturday. I'm taking her a packet for her to move on to Guernsey."

Henry was quiet for a long moment, staring at the bedspread thoughtfully. Molly watched him for a moment, chewing her bottom lip. He didn't look happy.

"What's the matter, my love?" she asked. "Is it because I'm doing something this weekend?"

He glanced up and made an impatient motion with his hand.

"Not at all. I simply question why Mata has you running down there so quickly. I'd have thought she would wait and do some more research."

"How much more research should she do? She sent Sir Clark, and you know what an authority on Berliners he is. He swears that she's exactly what she says she is."

"Hm."

Molly made a face and leaned forward to press a kiss on his lips.

"Don't be cross because I have the chance to have a bit of fun," she murmured.

He smiled against her lips and pulled her closer. A few moments later, she pushed herself away breathlessly.

"Now look what you've done. I have to do my hair again." She scrambled off the bed and went back to the vanity. "You know, if you were less surly, Mata would give *you* more to do. Then perhaps you'd be the one taking the packet down to Dorchester."

Henry looked up at that.

"Dorchester?"

"Yes. Didn't I say? She's at Sir Blackney's estate in Dorchester."

Henry watched her, then stretched.

"And does this paragon of a spy have a name?"

"Sylvia." Molly finished brushing her hair and twisted it back into its prim bun with deft fingers. "Sylvia Müller."

## Chapter Thirty-Three

**Leningrad, USSR**

Vladimir looked up at the knock on his door and glanced at the clock. It was after eleven at night, hardly the time to pay a social call. With a sigh, he closed his book and pushed himself out of the armchair, walking across the hotel room to the door.

"Yes?" he called through the door.

"It is Maschov," a familiar voice answered.

Vladimir grunted and opened the door, removing his hand from the pistol in his pocket.

"It is late," he said, turning to go back to his chair. "I hope this is important."

"You asked to be alerted immediately if I heard anything more about Eisenjager," Maschov said, closing the door and advancing into the room.

Vladimir eyed the man with interest.

"It's been two months. I'd given up hope. What have you learned?"

"I believe he is in Liechtenstein." The man leaned against the back of the other arm chair. "Do you remember Igor?"

"From Stalingrad?"

"Yes. He has been following the movements of an Austrian who is suspected of, among other things, collaborating with the Romanians to help Jews escape through Switzerland."

"I've heard of such a man," Vladimir said slowly. "It is said that, along with the Jews, he also aids men and women trying to leave the Soviet Union."

"Precisely."

"What has this to do with Eisenjager?"

"Nothing. It merely explains how Igor came to be in Liechtenstein. While there, he has learned that the German assassin keeps an apartment in Vaduz. That apartment has been occupied now for three weeks." Maschov cleared his throat. "Igor believes Eisenjager has gone to roost."

"How did he discover this apartment?"

## When Wolves Gather

"I do not know," Maschov admitted. "I've never known his information to be wrong, however."

Vladimir was thoughtful.

"No. Neither have I." He looked up. "How does he know the apartment is occupied?"

"Milk is being delivered. The standing order was resumed three weeks ago." Maschov pulled a notebook from his pocket and thumbed through it until he found what he was looking for. "Two bottles of milk are delivered twice a week. Lights are seen behind the curtains at night, but no one is ever seen entering or leaving." He looked up. "Igor asked me to make it clear that the surveillance was only for the space of five days. He had to pull his man and reassign him to a high priority detail."

"And in that time, no one was seen at all?"

"No."

Vladimir pressed his lips together and was silent for a long moment before shaking his head.

"And why would Eisenjager go to Vaduz and stay in an apartment without leaving?" he wondered, tapping one long finger on the arm of his chair.

"If I may offer a theory?"

Vladimir waved his hand impatiently.

"By all means. Speak."

"I have heard whispers that a target escaped in France, and the SD and the Abwehr were both involved in the failure. If that rumor is, in fact, true, then perhaps Eisenjager was one of those involved, and is being punished."

Vladimir considered him for a moment, then nodded.

"Perhaps. And perhaps someone else is in the apartment in Vaduz." He exhaled. "If you hear anything else, report to me directly."

Maschov nodded, straightening and turning for the door.

"And Maschov?"

"Yes?"

"Keep this between us."

"Of course, comrade."

The man left and Vladimir got up to lock the door. So the SD and the Abwehr had lost a target in France, had they? His lips twisted and he went to pour himself a drink from the bottle on the side table. It could, of course, have been anyone. Lotus was certainly not the only agent on the continent during the race through the Lowlands and France. And yet, Vladimir thought it likely that she was the only agent that would interest both the SD and the Abwehr.

279

Carrying his drink back to his armchair, Vladimir settled himself down again and reached for his book once more. He knew Lotus had escaped Belgium. A code in the radio broadcast had informed him that she'd made it to Switzerland to successfully set up contact arrangements between them. She had then fled through France, very clearly making it safely back to England, as she had received his message last week. It would appear that she accomplished all of that while, once again, evading enemy agents.

Vladimir stared across the room pensively, his book laying closed on his lap. There was no disputing the girl's luck anymore. She was inordinately blessed with it. In Norway, he had intervened and saved her life, though she would never know that. That had not been luck. But making it out of France when the deadly assassin was once again on her trail? That was pure luck. She hadn't the skills yet to take on the likes of Eisenjager and hope to come out alive. It was a very sad, but very real fact. The English hadn't trained her properly before sending her into his world. But how long would her luck continue?

Lyakhov's lips tightened into a grim line. If he could but have the training of the young agent for only a month, he could turn her into the formidable threat that Britain needed in this war, but that was not possible. All he could do was watch from afar, and hope to God that they came to their senses and properly trained the weapon they had in their possession.

For Vladimir needed Evelyn Ainsworth to survive, and he needed her to succeed where others would not. If she didn't, three years of careful planning and maneuvering on his part would be wasted.

**London**
**August 9**

Henry sat back and read over the message he'd composed, ready to send to Berlin. It wasn't that he mistrusted Molly and her information, exactly. It was more that the entire situation didn't make sense to him. Why would a German agent, already established with her routes of contact, suddenly wish to join forces and assist an organization like The Round Club? And how did she even learn of it to begin with?

He paused in his reading to gaze across the library thoughtfully. He supposed this secretary could have learned of the

## When Wolves Gather

club's existence from her contact on Guernsey. But why would she think it would be advantageous to offer her services as courier to them? Any agent worth any respect knew that the odds of being betrayed increased in proportion to the number of people who knew of their existence. Why would she risk it?

He lowered his eyes to the message and read it through, then reached for the paddle of his wireless radio. She wouldn't, not if she had any sense. Something wasn't right there. He could feel it in his gut. If it turned out to be as he feared, he had to alert Molly as soon as possible. It was entirely possible that she could be walking into some kind of trap.

The simplest way to set his mind at ease was to contact Berlin and ask, and that was precisely what he was doing. His message asked if they had an agent embedded in Dorchester under the cover of a personal secretary. He informed them that a secretary was claiming to have contact with a man on Guernsey, and could they confirm that this was their agent?

If they responded that the woman was, indeed, known to them, then all would be well. Molly would have her evening of "fun", as she put it, and his handler would commend him for being careful and proactive in assuring the safety of the Round Club. However, if they had no knowledge of this woman, then he would not only be saving Molly from what could only be a trap, but he was showing his handler what fools Mata, Clark, and the duke were. No matter the outcome, Henry came out ahead.

He finished transmitting the message and shut the wireless down, closing the case and locking it. They wouldn't answer immediately, and he had to leave for a meeting with Lord Halifax. He would check in with them later.

Standing, he carried the case over to an open cubby concealed behind a bookcase. The house had been standing since Cromwell's time, and the cubby was leftover from his ancestors and their need to hide documents and artifacts from the Roundheads. He set the case inside and pushed the bookcase back into place. Handy things, those cubbies. They were all over the house, but he only used a few of them. If he ever did fall under suspicion, the Security Service would have a hard time proving anything. Any and all evidence of his treasonous activities was securely hidden away. If Cromwell's men couldn't find the hiding spots, the present day authorities certainly wouldn't.

Henry turned to leave the library, collecting his briefcase as he went. When he contacted his handler this evening, he would also give him the latest development in his search for Jian. While it had been an impossible task, Henry had managed to uncover a few breadcrumbs, and he was confident that those crumbs would, eventually, lead him to the agent Berlin so desperately wanted.

Henry was downright cheerful when he took his hat, gloves, and cane from his butler and went out the front door. He'd succeeded in tracking down the only pilot crazy enough to fly an agent in and out of Switzerland during the Nazi Blitzkrieg. He'd located Sam in Barcelona a few days ago and had a very interesting telegram back from him. He had, indeed, flown a woman into Switzerland, and then back to Paris a few days later. He couldn't tell him any more than that, and Henry was sure he didn't know any more than that. Buckley worked strictly on a need to know basis, and Sam wouldn't have needed to know anything aside from where to pick up and drop off. But what he did know, and shared quite readily with Henry, was a description of his passenger.

MI6 had locked down everything even remotely pertaining to Jian months ago. Henry was certain that they knew they had a spy in London, but he was also certain that they had absolutely no idea who it was. Because of that, their internal investigation was kept secret from everyone. Sam had no reason to question Henry's story about needing to complete a report for the archives, and had given the information readily. Henry's lips twisted as he nodded to his driver and got into the back of his car. MI6's commitment to secrets and clandestine operations was the very thing that enabled him to get exactly what he needed to track down their prized agent. How very typical!

His amusement was short-lived and the smile faded as the car pulled away from the curb and began to make its way to Whitehall. Buckley was hunting for the spy in London in earnest and, while Henry wasn't afraid that he'd be caught, it would be foolish of him to ignore the risks of digging around too openly in MI6 affairs. He didn't have any fear that they suspected him, he'd been much too careful for that, but he *was* concerned that he wouldn't be able to discover Jian's real identity and apprehend her before the Nazis invaded England. Once they began, she would disappear, and so would any hope of handing her over triumphantly to the Gestapo.

He had to find her before the invasion, and now that he had a description, he was off to a very good start.

## When Wolves Gather

Evelyn stepped out of the small village post office, pulling on her gloves and turning towards her borrowed bicycle. She'd just sent a telegram to Marrow apprising him of where they were in the operation, and she was confident that she'd impressed upon him that their plan was poised to be a resounding success. It had been with some measure of personal satisfaction that she'd composed the message. She knew he'd never expected this operation to go anywhere.

As she turned her bicycle around and climbed on, the all-too-familiar sound of Merlin engines filled the air. She looked up and searched for the Hurricanes. After a moment, they appeared above her, heading to the Channel. There were six of them today. Yesterday, out of the ten that flew over her in the garden, only eight returned. That squadron had lost two airplanes. How many of these six would return?

She pedaled out of the village, wondering if Miles and Robbie were up there, then she shook her head. Yes, of course they were. All the pilots were up every day now, battling Göring's fighters and bombers, trying to save ships, and the men who sailed on them. It was a very sobering thing to consider those airplanes that hadn't returned yesterday, and to know that that was the reality that Miles and her brother faced every day. Some would not return. Planes would be lost, pilots would be killed, and it was all to keep the people of Great Britain from falling under the subjugation of the Nazis. They were fighting for their very survival against a seemingly unbeatable foe.

Evelyn swallowed and took a deep breath as she rode along the quiet, winding road that would take her back to Sir Blackney's house. Seeing Miles and Rob the other night had been lovely. Meeting the Yank, as they called him, had been wonderful as well. But now she almost wished she hadn't met them for dinner. While it had been a truly fun evening, it only served to remind her of how much she missed her brother and Miles, and had introduced her to a new pilot to worry over. What if any of them were killed? What if they all were? How could she possibly bear it? She had really liked Chris. She found him to be funny and intelligent, and it was quite clear to her that he fit in perfectly with her brother and his friend. Their camaraderie was evident to anyone who clapped eyes on them. And yet, if she were to look at the results of her counting experiment yesterday, one of them wouldn't survive the month.

It was one thing to know the numbers and odds on paper, and quite another to witness it in action, as she had yesterday.

And that wasn't even the worst of it, she reflected. The skies were deadly, yes, but there was just as much danger here on the ground. She'd seen what the German bombers had done to cities, towns, roads, and civilians alike in Norway, Belgium, and France. In Holland, Rotterdam had been flattened by the Luftwaffe. Just because they were on the ground, it didn't mean that they were safe. In fact, they were facing an even greater threat on ground as they had to contend with the enemy within their own people.

Anger washed through her anew and Evelyn pressed her lips together. That, at least, was something that she could do something about, and it would be her very great pleasure to do so.

---

Henry sipped his whiskey and soda and set the glass down on the polished desk surface. He looked at his watch and went to the bookcase, pulling out a worn copy of Plato's Republic. Reaching into the empty slot on the shelf, he depressed a hidden catch, releasing the book case. It was time to check in with Berlin and see if they'd been able to find any answers for him.

A few moments later, he had the case open and the radio ready to transmit. Taking another sip of his drink, he sat down to write out a message, briefly explaining that he had a lead on Jian and believed that she gone to the abandoned house in Switzerland in May. He promised to have news soon. There. That would go a long way to getting him out of running Lady Rothman's errands like a lap dog.

He sat back after transmission with his drink in his hand and stared across the library pensively. This whole war wasn't going quite as planned, as evidenced by the fact that they were still fighting at all, and he was getting rather fed up. When the war had commenced, he'd never been one of those who said it would be over by Christmas. He knew that it would be a long and drawn-out affair. What he hadn't expected was that Winston Churchill, of all people, would take over as prime minister and keep them fighting a losing battle. Really, who could have possibly predicted that? And now he was stuck playing at amateur hour with the Round Club, putting his own cover at risk daily. It really was absurd. This wasn't how it was supposed to go at all.

He lifted his glass to his lips and shook his head. The only light in the mess was that he had a very good lead on Jian and, in turn, on whatever she had removed from that house in Blasenflue. If Ainsworth had managed to conceal anything there, and she had retrieved it, then he would have the missing package in short order. His promise to his handlers would be kept, and his reward would be great. He had no doubt of that.

## When Wolves Gather

The radio came alive and Henry sat forward, grabbing the headset again. He picked up a pencil and listened, then began writing on his pad of paper. The message was short, and for that he was grateful. He wasn't in the mood to engage in a lengthy discussion at this time of the evening. When he was sure the message had finished, he removed the headset and set about decoding the response.

NO AGENT OF THAT NAME OR DESCRIPTION KNOWN. PROCEED WITH CAUTION. KEEP INFORMED OF OTHER MATTER.

Henry stared down at the decoded words and his eyes narrowed. So it was as he feared. The secretary was a hoax, no doubt sent by the Security Service. They obviously knew of the Round Club, then, and possibly even knew who the members were. Certainly they were now aware that Sir Clark was one. How many others did they know? And was his name associated with them?

His fist clenched, crushing the paper, as fury went through him. He'd known it was dangerous to get involved with them, but Berlin had insisted. Now they were *all* at risk!

He packed up the radio again and got up to put it back in its hiding place. He had to go see Mata immediately. There was no help for it. If Lady Rothman was suspected, they would undoubtedly have her under surveillance, and that would expose him as a potential accomplice, but what choice did he have? This was not something he could risk writing down to be delivered. He would have to hope that his own precautions would protect him for suspicion.

As he closed the bookcase and turned to go to the door, he reflected that, luckily, there was no reason in the world why he shouldn't visit Lady Rothman. They were part of the same circles, after all. It would take much more to implicate him with the damn club, and he'd been very careful from the very beginning. No. He would be safe, for now. Moving forward, he would ensure that any other communication between himself and Mata went through Molly.

But first, he had to alert her to the fact that Miss Sylvia Müller was a British agent.

## Chapter Thirty-Four

**Dorchester**
**August 10**

Evelyn sat at the desk in her bedroom, her eyes on the pistol before her. The Browning P-35 was in pieces on a soft cloth while she meticulously cleaned the components. It was a high-powered pistol that was, in the hands of an experienced shot, capable of hitting a target over 50 meters away. Evelyn was very pleased to have it, as it was far superior to the standard firearm MI6 had issued to her. As with any firearm that she handled, she cleaned it regularly, and there was little to do with it now. Yet she went through the motions, ensuring that nothing would impede its performance tonight. She had to be able to count on the gun in the event that things were not as they should be.

Not that she had any specific qualms about her meeting tonight. Everything was progressing just as she and Marrow had planned. Sir Clark had sent her a message last night, delivered by the same man she had seen with him in the High Street. Evelyn had read the instructions twice before burning the telegram in the fireplace in her room. She was to meet a woman named Molly tonight on the road to Weymouth. The message had been very clear about the exact location, as well as the time. She would meet this Molly to accept a packet which she would then take to the Channel Island of Guernsey, passing it onto to an agent there. Once she was in possession of the packet, further instructions would follow.

It was simple enough. She'd meet Molly tonight, get the package, and then wait to be contacted again. While she was waiting, she would contact Marrow and alert him to her success. He would direct her from there. All she had to do was get the packet tonight.

When dawn had broken, it had found her on the road to Weymouth to investigate the proposed meeting place. Evelyn's lips tightened as she gently swiped a brush through the barrel in her hand. As she'd approached the appointed spot, she'd felt her first twinge of discomfort. It was a very remote place, in the middle of the countryside, and the nearest village was quite some distance. The lane

## When Wolves Gather

was lined on one side by a thick hedgerow that formed a boundary for a large field. On the other, a rise in the ground was topped with trees, forming an almost textbook kill box. It was the perfect setting for an ambush.

Her lips twisted now as she remembered the first time she had ever heard the term 'kill box.' It had been on a mountainside in Norway, and the meaning behind the name had been made very clear to her in the events that followed. The ravine had, indeed, turned into a kill box, and she had barely escaped with her life.

But this wasn't Norway, and she wasn't being hunted by an SS battalion. She was meeting another woman in a perfectly civilized fashion on a country lane in England. There was absolutely no reason for her to feel as wary as she did.

Evelyn slid the barrel back into the frame of her pistol, locking it into place. Reaching for the spring, she took a deep, soothing breath. It didn't mean a thing that the meeting place was perfectly suited for an ambush. It was a country lane near the coast in the South of England. Areas like that were everywhere. In fact, they would be hard-pressed to find a spot anywhere between here and the coast that was completely open and unable to lend itself to such concealment.

She was being overly cautious in taking her gun and going prepared for the unexpected, but if the past few months had taught her anything, it was that the unexpected was to be expected. Evelyn slid the spring back into place gently and picked up the metal ring to hold it in place. Everything would be fine. She would get the packet and take it to Marrow, and her role would be finished. There was absolutely nothing to worry about.

Evelyn finished assembling the gun and pulled the slide back, peering down the empty barrel before releasing it. She reached for the magazine and slid it into the handle. Everything was ready. All she had to do was wait until after dinner, and then leave.

Tomorrow morning it would be over, and hopefully she would be in possession of at least a few names of the traitors. And then she would return to Ainsworth Manor and her holiday.

### RAF Coltishall

Miles jumped off the wing of his airplane and nodded to Jones.

"Rearm and refuel, Jones," he said unnecessarily, "and the engine was doing a bit of sputtering on my way back."

"Were you hit, sir?"

"Not this time."

"Perhaps it was just the low fuel, then. We'll take a look."

Miles nodded and turned to watch as Chris rolled towards them on the landing strip.

"Any more kills, sir?" Jones asked hopefully.

Miles shot him a look, then shook his head, a reluctant smile curving his lips.

"You boys still have that blasted pool going?" he asked. "Sorry to disappoint. We didn't hit a thing. Rotten weather up there. I'm still sitting on eight confirmed and two probable."

"Ah well, at least you're still in the lead," Jones said cheerfully. "The Yank is stiff competition, though. He's got eight confirmed as well, but only one probable. He's one hell of a pilot, that one."

"Yes, and thank the good Lord for that," Miles replied as Chris pulled his Spit next to his and shut the engine down. "The more bastards we shoot down, the fewer come back."

"Very true, sir! Very true."

Jones nodded respectfully and turned to attend to Miles' airplane as Chris climbed out of his cockpit.

"I didn't think I was going to make it in," he called before jumping off his wing. "I came in on fumes!"

"So did I." Miles went to join him just as Rob came around the side of his airplane.

"I think we all did," Rob said cheerfully. "Awful weather up there. Did you see the squall coming back?"

"See it? I nearly flew into it!" Chris exclaimed. "Jerry's nuts if he thinks he can hit anything in this."

"Which is probably why we didn't see hide nor hair of them," Miles said.

The trio began walking across the grass to the buildings in the distance and Rob looked at Chris as he pulled his cigarette case from his pocket.

"Nice of you to return with us, Yank," he said conversationally. "Didn't feel up to a tour of Great Yarmouth today?"

"Hey, it's not my fault some damn Kraut took a chunk out of my tail the other day. That detour was courtesy of one of Göring's finest. I'm just glad they were able to fix my kite. I've grown fond of the old girl."

## When Wolves Gather

"I'd be wary of flying around in a patched up Spit myself, but to each his own."

"Rather that than no Spit at all."

"Very true, Yank," Miles agreed. "And none of us can say we're flying pristine machines."

Rob grunted at that, acknowledging the truth with a rueful shrug.

"True enough. I suppose with as much as we're flying, it's bound to happen," he said. "We're up more than we're down these days. How many raids can Jerry send after our convoys in one day?"

"I don't think you want to know," Miles muttered. "I have a sneaking suspicion that the answer is a lot more than he is."

"What happened to the old argument that Hitler didn't have the airplanes to mount something like this?"

"I think he's very clearly illustrated that that was a whole load of bollocks."

"Yes, and now we're facing them. I think you're right, Miles. I think it's going to get a lot worse before it gets any better."

"Worse? How much worse can it get?" Chris demanded. "We're already flying patrols and sorties four times a day!"

"The poor sods in the south are doing that, and going up every night as well," Miles pointed out. "Be glad you're in 12 Group, my dear boy. 11 Group has it much worse."

"I heard Gravesend lost three airplanes yesterday," Rob said. "Pilots bailed out."

"How the hell did they manage to lose three?" Chris wondered. "We haven't lost any since Uncle Tom landed in the drink."

"As I said, they have it much worse."

"Makes you wonder how they're still sending planes up," Rob said. "At that rate of loss, how on earth do they still have a squadron? Still, I suppose it's not like that every day. Stands to reason it can't be. Can it?"

"I wouldn't wager on it. Northolt lost four yesterday, or so Bertie said earlier."

Rob frowned and was silent, mulling that over.

"Well, if things are that dire, then we're really in for it, aren't we?" he finally said. "They must be running low on airplanes."

"Yes, and if I had to venture a guess, I'd say that it must be bloody hell for the ground crew to keep up with the repairs," Miles said. "Stands to reason that they're getting shot up more than we are, but they don't have more mechanics."

The three were silent for a moment, digesting that, then Chris exhaled.

"Well, isn't that just a cheerful thought," he muttered. "What happens when the Krauts actually try to invade England? If this is just them going after the convoys, what the hell will it be like when they come after us?"

Miles and Rob were silent for a long time, Rob sucking on his cigarette and Miles tramping through the coarse grass with his hands in his pockets and his head down. When he finally lifted his head, his mouth was set in a grim line.

"I don't know, Yank, but I have a feeling we're going to find out, and sooner rather than later."

# When Wolves Gather

# Chapter Thirty-Five

Evelyn coasted to a stop once she was out of sight of the front gate and got off the bicycle, leaning it against a tree. With a quick look around the deserted lane, she turned to cut through the hedge that ran along the road. She'd told Mrs. Besslington that she was going into town to the pictures. While the housekeeper had seemed surprised, she hadn't said anything beyond that Evelyn should take a Macintosh, as it had been raining off and on all day. Accordingly, Evelyn wore a spare raincoat borrowed from one of the maids. As much as she'd protested that it wasn't necessary, she was glad of it now. The overcast sky which had been the author of two sudden downpours already had looked ominous as she pedaled down the long driveway and out of the gates.

Because the staff of the estate were aware of her plans, she'd had to hide the bag she was taking along to her meeting with Molly on the edge of the estate. There was no easy excuse for why she wanted to carry such a large satchel with her to the pictures, and she couldn't leave it behind. Not only did she have no idea how large the packet would be that she was expected to take to the Channel Islands, but she also had a map of the county and her heavy makeup inside. If, God forbid, she was caught in a downpour as Mrs. Besslington feared, she'd have to repair her disguise before meeting with Molly. Even though the woman had never seen her, she'd undoubtedly been given a description by Sir Clark. Evelyn had to maintain the disguise at all costs.

Making her way to the shrubs where she'd hidden the bag, Evelyn glanced up at the darkening clouds. Perhaps she would be lucky and the rain would pass over them. It had this morning. The raincoat *did* have a rather generously sized hood, but Evelyn knew she couldn't rely on that to protect her if the heavens were to open up.

She retrieved her bag and hung it across her body, going back to where she'd left her bicycle. The ride to the meeting point would take around forty minutes, and she wasn't due to meet Molly for two hours. Her hope was that she would arrive well ahead of the other woman to ensure that no surprises were lurking in the trees above the road. Once she knew it was safe, then she would retreat and arrive again at the appointed time. It never hurt to be too careful, after all.

## CW Browning

Evelyn climbed onto her bicycle and started off again. An excited knot settled in her stomach, and her senses were alert as she rode away from Sir Blackney's estate and into the quiet countryside. After all the uncertainty on Marrow's part, she was only a couple of hours away from hopefully learning the identities of at least a few of the traitors who made up the Round Club. What else might be in the packet? Plans for how they would proceed to overthrow the King and Parliament? Her heart beat a little faster at the thought. For they must have such plans. Why else would Sir Clark have been so confident in the garden that night with Miss Milner? He'd been very sure that they would escape all repercussions for their actions, something that could only happen if the current regime was replaced. How on earth did they hope to accomplish it?

Before she could consider the question any more, headlights lit up the lane behind her and Evelyn glanced back. A car was coming along the road quite fast, and she moved to the very edge of the pavement to allow it plenty of room to pass. As it pulled up alongside her, however, the vehicle seemed to slow down. She glanced over and, in the fading light, saw a man behind the wheel of a sleek, dark sports car. That was all she had time to notice before he pulled suddenly to the left directly in front of her, coming to an abrupt stop and blocking her progress.

Evelyn let out a gasp and braked, stopping just before she crashed into the side of the car. Her heart pounding, she watched as the driver's door opened and the man got out, coming around the back of the car quickly.

"Miss Müller?" he demanded harshly.

Through her shock at almost having run into a car, Evelyn felt another wave of alarm roll over her. She knew that voice! Gasping again, she stared at Anthony Gilhurst as he advanced towards her, his lips pressed together unpleasantly.

"You *are* Miss Müller?"

Evelyn got off the bicycle and stood with it between them, her hands suddenly trembling. Pulling the wool over Sir Clark's eyes with her disguise was one thing, but was it good enough to deceive a man who was like a second brother to her? She supposed she was about to find out.

"Yes?"

"You must come with me. We can put your bicycle in the boot of the car."

Evelyn stared at him, her brows furrowing.

"What? Why? Who are you?"

## When Wolves Gather

Despite the blood pounding in her ears and her heart pounding in her chest, Evelyn was very pleased to hear the faint accent tinting her English. Even under pressure, she was able to keep up the facade.

"I'll explain in the car," he said in a clipped voice. "Come. We haven't much time."

He reached out to grab the handle closest to him, beginning to pull the bicycle towards the boot of the car. What on earth was he doing? Why was he here? All at once, her shocked stupor shattered. He was one of them. He was one of the traitors, and he had come to intercept her! Why? What was happening?

"Wait! You can't do that!"

She reached out to grab the bicycle, her mind spinning. She didn't know what he was up to, but Evelyn knew beyond a shadow of a doubt that she couldn't get in the car with him. Even though it was Tony, she couldn't trust him as far as she could throw him. But she had to be very careful and pull herself together. Think! What would Miss Müller say?

"I won't go with you. I don't know you!"

His grip tightened on the other handle of the bicycle and his mouth twisted into a grim scowl.

"We don't have time for this," he growled. "You must get into the car!"

"Absolutely not!"

The look her words brought to his face made Evelyn's breath catch in her throat and she inwardly shivered. Tony's temper was legendary, and Maryanne had told her more than once that sometimes her brother could be terrifying. She'd always thought Maryanne exaggerated, but now she was catching a glimpse of that temper, and it truly was unnerving. Perhaps if she hadn't faced much worse over the past year, she would even be terrified as well. Instead, after a second of stunned shock, fury went through her.

How dare he? How *dare* he be angry because she wouldn't jump to do his bidding?

Anger gave her strength and Evelyn ripped the bicycle away from him, but before she could do anything further, Anthony wrenched it away and threw it aside. She sucked in her breath as he grabbed her arm.

"You're coming with me, Miss Müller," he snarled. "I've had enough of this!"

Evelyn grit her teeth as his fingers dug into her arm painfully through the raincoat. She couldn't respond with her skills as a fighter.

Through her anger and budding panic, she knew that well enough. Miss Müller would have no such skills. She would be forced to fight as any other woman would fight.

Twisting in his grip, Evelyn pulled back one foot and kicked him hard in his shin while she clawed at his face with her free hand. Though she'd always thought such methods were ineffective and silly, Anthony let out a startled cry of pain as her nails dug into his lean cheek. Taking advantage of his momentary surprise, she wrenched out of his grasp and turned to run. She didn't have any clear idea of where she was going to go, but she knew that she had to get away from Lord Gilhurst quickly before something happened that she would very much regret.

She ran to her left, intending to dart into the field adjacent to the lane. She never saw the dip in the ground amid the roadside rushes and brambles. When the ground suddenly sloped downward, Evelyn lost her balance and pitched forward. Instinctively throwing her hands out to brace herself, she let out an involuntary cry as her hands went into water instead of hitting the ground. The brambles and plants along the road had concealed a low ditch, filled with water and reeds from the day's frequent downpours! Her arms went into water up to the elbows before her palms sank into soggy earth and mud. Unable to brace herself in the muck, Evelyn fell, face first, into the water.

Her first thought was that she couldn't breathe, but her second was even more horrifying. Her disguise! The makeup would be washed away by the water! Almost as soon as the realization hit her, Evelyn felt strong hands grab her arms, hauling her out of the ditch. Panic rolled through her, fierce and numbing. Anthony! He would know her in an instant!

"Come here, you—"

Anthony broke off abruptly as he spun her around, staring in absolute shock. He released her and stumbled back a pace, his eyes wide and his face paling in the twilight.

Evelyn didn't think; she reacted. Lunging forward, she drove her fist into his abdomen. As he grunted and fell forward, her other hand was already slicing through the air to make contact with his temple. Moving quickly, she caught him as he fell forward, unconscious. Dragging him away from the ditch, she laid him down in the grass before hurrying back to her bicycle. He wouldn't be out for long, and she had to be gone before he woke up. She had to find somewhere to repair her makeup, and then she had to get to her meeting with Molly. The meeting was the priority.

She'd deal with Tony later.

# When Wolves Gather

Evelyn shook her head and peered at herself in the small hand mirror. She'd found a dilapidated and disused farm building about twenty minutes after fleeing the roadside. Gaps in the roof let in what was left of the evening light, but it was nearly impossible to see clearly. From what she could see in the murky gloom, the water from the ditch had wiped out most of her face makeup, but thankfully the wart was still in place. When she fell, that side of her face had been turned upwards, and some of the makeup there had survived. The rest, however, had streaked and run off.

When she'd first pulled the mirror out of her satchel and examined her face, she'd simply stared in dismay. It was much worse than she'd feared, and Evelyn didn't think it was possible to repair it without removing all that was left and starting over. But that wasn't an option, and Molly was waiting, so she took out her paints and tried to do her best. The end result was very far from perfect, but it would have to do. The darkness would be on her side, helping to conceal much of her face, and Molly had never met her. She had to hope that it would be enough.

She closed the mirror and began to gather her makeup to put it back in the bag, her hands shaking. Evelyn scowled. Adrenaline was still coursing through her, but so was her anger, and something else. It was an emotion she couldn't name, causing her to tremble and her breath to come fast, and it was all tied up with Anthony.

It was one thing to suspect that a dear friend had fallen into company with traitors, but it was quite another to have it confirmed. Somewhere deep inside, she supposed she was hoping there was some other explanation for his meeting Sir Clark, and for his comments that were so suggestive of a shifting view on this war. Perhaps she didn't really believe that Lord Gilhurst was capable of turning his back on the country that afforded him his rank and standing in this world. Or perhaps she simply didn't want to face the fact that someone she cared for was not who she'd always thought he was. Whatever the reasons, seeing him in the road tonight had shaken her to her very core.

And now he knew that *she* wasn't who she said she was either.

Evelyn finished packing everything back into her bag and closed it, looking at her watch in the gloom. Perhaps it was better this way. If Anthony was arrested and locked away, he could hardly expose her as…as what? He had no idea who she really worked for. He would assume that she was working with the Secret Service, which of course she was at the moment, but he had no idea of her *real* work. Between them, she was sure she and Bill could come up with something that would keep him far away from the truth. And that task would be made much easier if he were incarcerated as a traitor.

Turning towards the door, she felt a sinking sensation in the pit of her stomach. If Tony were arrested, Maryanne would be devastated. If she ever found out that Evelyn had been part of it, she would be furious. And really, how could she not find out? Anthony had *seen* her! He was bound to tell his sister, and then Evelyn would lose both of her friends. She stopped and sucked in her breath as something else occurred to her. Even worse than that, Rob would discover that Evelyn had been involved!

Walking out of the dilapidated old structure, Evelyn felt as if she was watching from afar as her world imploded, and there was absolutely nothing she could do prevent it. Except there had to be a way to prevent it! She and Bill would think of something. They had to, or her wartime career would be over.

She grabbed her bicycle and began wheeling it across the grass towards an old cart track not far away. But that was tomorrow's headache. Tonight, she had to meet Molly, and she was now running late.

◉

Bill looked up at the knock on his office door, glancing at the clock on the wall. It was past eight o'clock and Wesley had departed over two hours ago. He wouldn't still be here himself but for the fact that Marguerite was out of town and he had a pile of late reports that had come in from France just before five.

"Yes?" he called, sliding a folder over the report he was studying and rubbing his eyes.

The door opened and Jasper peered around the door, unsurprised to see him at his desk.

"Good, you're still here," he said, his body following his head into the office. "I thought you might be. I saw that a slew of messages came in from the continent."

"Yes, from France. A few of my people made it into the unoccupied zone before the Germans set up the border. They're relaying messages as they can." Bill stretched and waved Jasper into a chair. "Why are you still here?"

## When Wolves Gather

"I'm not. I've just returned from dinner to pick up my cigarette case. I left it behind." Jasper sat down and crossed his legs comfortably. "I'm glad you're still in. I want to congratulate you on Jian's outstanding performance at the training course. The instructors were universally impressed by her performance. One of them said he would never have dreamt it possible for a woman to make it through the whole thing. He said he's watched some rough and tumble men completely crumble, unable to do half of what she managed. Did you know she fell twelve feet off an obstacle?"

"No."

"Well, according to that chap, she did, and it wasn't pretty. There was some concern that she had broken something, but she refused to stop. Said that if she was in enemy territory, she wouldn't be able to stop if she took a tumble. Limped for the better part of two days, I'm told."

"That sounds very much like something she would have said," Bill said with a wry smile. "And I'm not surprised in the least. She's tough, which is why I wanted her."

"Well, she's earned the respect of some very formidable Commandos right enough. I couldn't be happier. You must be sure to pass on my regards when you see her next."

"I will." Bill got up and went to unlock the cabinet against the wall. "Drink?"

"I'll take a brandy if you have any."

Bill nodded and opened the cabinet doors, reaching for a decanter.

"What's Winston's final decision regarding the training course? Has he made one yet?"

"Oh yes. He considers it a resounding success and is going forward with both the new branch and the training course. It's already in process. He's calling it the Special Operations Executive, and his instructions are to 'set Europe ablaze.'"

Bill chuckled and carried a glass of brandy over to Jasper.

"He has such a flair for the English language. How does he intend to do that?"

"By training men and women to go into France, work with any resistance there, and sabotage the Germans by any means necessary."

Bill's eyebrows rose and he turned to pour himself a whiskey.

"Sabotage?"

"Among other things, yes. Guerrilla warfare, disrupting supply lines, blowing up train tracks, that sort of thing." Jasper sipped his brandy. "The training is key, and the first official class could go through as soon as October. The first candidate I put forward for the official start is the agent that Jian brought back with her, Oscar."

Bill nodded and went back to his seat.

"That's a good choice. I think he'll welcome the chance to go back. However, I'm not sure that I'm happy about you moving him from MI6. His knowledge and experience are invaluable."

"Yes, I know, but that same experience will enable him to blend in with the locals and help coordinate with resistance groups." Jasper shrugged. "Winston asked me for one candidate that I thought would be a good fit. It was Oscar or Jian. I thought you'd prefer him."

"Good Lord, yes!"

Jasper chuckled.

"It might prove useful to you to have him there in a completely different capacity. There's nothing to stop him from sending back any information that he happens to gather along the way. I'm sure we can come to some sort of arrangement with the people heading up the SOE."

"Very true." Bill sipped his drink. "Has any more progress been made on our spy here in London?"

"No," Jasper said with a shake of his head.

Bill uttered an exclamation and got up impatiently, taking a quick turn about the office.

"We have to do better than this!" he exclaimed. "If we can't find a rat in our own hold, we might as well pack it in now and save ourselves a lot of trouble."

"I agree, but we're doing everything we can. It's devilish tricky. We know it's someone of some standing, and it's someone who had access to our operations. That narrows the field considerably, but there are still a lot of people who can be responsible. I've got a team quietly investigating all of them, as you're aware, but they have to be extremely discreet. The tip about the Round Club was helpful. If our man is the same one in contact with Voss, we can eliminate about half the names on our list. They don't fit the profile for someone who would be involved in the club at that level. But it still takes time."

"We don't have time."

"I'm aware of that, and I assure you, I'm trying to find him. It would be better, of course, if you had kept Jian tucked away and out of sight," Jasper added.

Bill grunted and went back to his seat.

"No doubt it would, but she wasn't having any of it, not after she discovered the existence of the Round Club. Well, after all, it's what we trained her to do."

## When Wolves Gather

"Yes, but not here in England."

"Here, there, does it matter? She's doing her job. She's gathering intelligence that will help us defeat enemies of the Crown. It just so happens that those enemies are right here in London, unfortunately." Bill rubbed his eyes tiredly. "I won't deny that I'm worried about Henry finding her while she's digging around, but what other choice did I have? She was the perfect person to try to determine just who's involved."

"Yes, well, of course if the blasted Security Service was in order and on their game, she wouldn't have had to get involved at all, would she?" Jasper shook his head disgustedly. "It's a right shambles over there."

"Yes, I know. That's probably the only reason Marrow agreed to it at all. He knows the family, you know. Was a friend of Robert's."

"That's not surprising. Robert had friends everywhere. It's what made him so wonderfully efficient. He knew secrets no one else did."

"And he took many of them to the grave with him." Bill sighed. "Jian is a lot like him, but without the secretiveness, thank God. We don't have to worry about her not sharing crucial intelligence and hiding it from the world."

"Are we any closer to finding that package?" Jasper asked after a moment.

"Unfortunately, no. She hasn't given up, though. If it can be found, she'll be the one to do it."

Jasper nodded and finished his drink.

"Well, at least we know the Jerries don't have it either. Have you had any contact with her?"

"No, and I don't expect to until she's finished this operation with Marrow."

"Well, I certainly hope she's taking every precaution. The last thing we need is to lose her right here at home."

## Chapter Thirty-Six

It was dark when Evelyn finally arrived at the meeting spot. The clouds obscured any light from the moon, and the complete blackness was the kind only possible in the country. Despit that, she hadn't switched on the torch fixed to the front of her bicycle, approaching as quietly as possible. Her run-in with Anthony had shaken her, and she didn't feel comfortable at all. Perhaps because of that encounter, all her instincts were screaming and a knot of dread had taken up residence deep in her belly. Something was wrong, but she had no idea what. Until she met with this Molly, she wouldn't know what had brought Anthony out to Dorchester.

Why had he tried to get her into his car? The thought popped into her head, repeating itself as it had since she left the old shack. Had they changed the meeting place and he was supposed to deliver her somewhere else? Or was his appearance something much more sinister?

She shook her head with a frown, making her way through the darkness. She had to put it out of her mind for now. She had much more important things to worry about. Coasting to a stop on the deserted road, she listened intently to the silence. While she may be experiencing grave misgivings, she was here now, and there really was no turning back. She'd committed to a course of action, and she must see it through, regardless of the impulse to turn around and run. The weight of her pistol was comforting in her coat pocket, and Evelyn was suddenly very glad she'd brought it along.

An owl hooted in the distance, breaking the absolute silence, while a breeze rustled against the hedgerow. A shiver went through her as Evelyn shot a look behind her, bracing one foot on the pavement. Nothing but darkness yawned behind her, and she turned to face forward again. Remaining on her bicycle, she strained to see in the darkness. Then, after a moment, she got off and began walking it forward. Inky blackness prevented her from seeing much more than a few feet in front of her, and she was just deciding whether to turn on the torch after all or not when she saw it.

Apprehension slid through her as she made out the shape of a car pulled to the side of the road, just below the hill that led to a

## When Wolves Gather

spinney at the top. It was a few feet in front of her and, as she stared at it, the headlights suddenly came on, blinding her.

Evelyn lifted her hand to shield her eyes from the sudden brightness, her heart leaping into her throat. Peering around her hand, she watched a shadow emerge from the driver's door.

"Hello?" she called in her faintly accented tone. "Are the lights really necessary?"

"I thought they would make it easier to see," a woman replied. "Miss Müller?"

"Yes." Evelyn frowned and moved out of the direct glare of the headlights. "And you?"

"My name is Molly."

The woman followed her until they were standing out of the beams of light and next to the car. Evelyn lowered her hand, examining the other woman. She was slightly taller than herself, with dark hair pulled back and secured behind her head. The filtered light cast her features in shadow, but Evelyn had the impression of high cheekbones and full cheeks.

"You are late," Molly said.

"I was delayed on the road. A motor car almost ran me over."

"How alarming for you! I trust you're not hurt?"

"No." Evelyn saw the woman studying her in the darkness and was grateful for the shadows that she knew obscured her face as much as they concealed Molly's. "I was instructed that I was to receive a package from you," she said briskly. "Do you have it?"

"Not much of one for conversation, are you?"

"I don't see any benefit to wasting time."

Something like a twisted smile crossed the other woman's face.

"How right you are." She withdrew something from her pocket and Evelyn's breath caught in her throat as light slanted across a black pistol. "I couldn't agree more."

Evelyn stared at the gun, her mouth going dry as her heart pounded a rapid tattoo in her chest.

"What is the meaning of this?" she demanded, allowing her accent to thicken. "Why do you point a gun at me?"

"Because, Miss Müller, I know that you are not who you claim to be," Molly told her calmly. "You are *not* in contact with anyone on the Channel Islands, or in Berlin."

"I don't know what you mean," Evelyn said, buying time while her mind spun. How had they found out? Tony couldn't possibly have alerted them already. Could he?

"Yes you do, and it begs the question who, then, are you?"

"I am Sylvia Müller, Sir Blackney's personal secretary."

"Yes, so we're reliably informed." Molly frowned. "That part appears to be true, but the rest?" She shrugged. "Lies. The people in Berlin have never heard of you, and neither have the agents on Guernsey. I don't know who you really are, or who you work for, but it really doesn't matter. The game you're playing ends now."

"I don't play games," Evelyn said, her voice chilling.

"Neither do we, and due to your tardiness, I'm now really very pressed for time." Molly motioned towards the incline beside them with the gun. "As much as I would love to continue this conversation, I have another appointment that I must keep this evening. Go on with you. We're going into the spinney up there, where we won't be disturbed. You may leave your bicycle. You won't be needing that."

Evelyn hesitated for the briefest of seconds, then laid the bicycle on the ground before glancing up the incline. She could disarm the other woman easily here and now, but it would be a useless waste of energy if there were others in the trees who would shoot her before she could get the package. She would have to go up there with her, if only to ensure that she was truly alone. At least she knew that Anthony hadn't come before her. If he had, Molly would know exactly who she was, and Evelyn had no doubt that she wouldn't have been able to resist telling her. Molly was very pleased with herself, and gloating over the unmasking of Miss Evelyn Ainsworth? She wouldn't have been able to resist. No, she hadn't heard anything from Anthony yet. But if not him, then how the devil had they found out?

"It's not my bicycle, you know," Evelyn said, abandoning the accent. "I borrowed it from the housekeeper."

"I'm sure someone will happen across it in the morning," Molly said dismissively. She pulled out a torch and switched it on, illuminating the hill before them. "The bicycle is the least of your worries. Walk!"

Evelyn made a face in the shadows as she moved up the slope towards the trees, keeping a wary eye on Molly and the gun in her hand. She hadn't answered Evelyn's question about the package. Did she even have it with her? Or had she come empty-handed, knowing that it was a trap. Lord, she hoped not! To go through all of this only to go away empty-handed would be the worst possible failure.

"Do you actually intend to use that toy?" Evelyn asked as they neared the top of the incline.

"You'll be the first to find out," Molly replied with a short laugh.

## When Wolves Gather

"How overwhelmingly banal." Evelyn reached the top of the incline and looked down her nose at the other woman. "And a bit dramatic, don't you think? Have you thought this through? Have you ever actually shot anyone?"

"If I were you, I'd be more concerned with my own skin at the moment. Go into the trees."

Evelyn shrugged and walked into the spinney, picking her way past a bramble bush.

"I'm simply trying to help you. It really doesn't seem as if you've given this much thought. How are you going to dispose of me, for instance? You can't very well just leave dead bodies lying about. It's not done."

Reaching a relatively clear area void of undergrowth, she cast a quick look around. The light from Molly's torch didn't reveal any hidden accomplices, and Evelyn's shoulders relaxed.

"Don't concern yourself with that. It's all been taken care of," Molly said, walking up behind her. "I can't say that you will be given a proper burial, but then I don't suppose you'll notice."

Evelyn waited until she was close, then swung around, going straight for the hand with the gun. The speed with which she moved took Molly by surprise, and before she could react, Evelyn's fingers had closed around her wrist, wrenching it sideways at an impossible angle with her arm. She felt the crack as the bone snapped just as Molly let out a cry of pain, cut short abruptly when Evelyn slammed the side of her hand into her throat. Robbed of the ability to make any sound, Molly reached out frantically with her good arm, trying to grab Evelyn's neck. Avoiding her grasping hand easily, Evelyn leveled a blow to her temple with her elbow, catching her as her eyes closed and she fell.

She eased the woman to the ground and checked for a pulse. She should be unconscious, but Evelyn had hit her a little harder than she intended. Sifu had warned her often enough that the difference between a corpse and an unconscious opponent was the force behind the blow, and it was with anxious fingers that she pressed against the side of Molly's neck. She had no desire to stand trial for killing a woman on the road to Weymouth.

Relief went through her when she felt a pulse, and Evelyn exhaled silently. Looking around, she saw the gun illuminated by the discarded torch. It had fallen harmlessly to the ground when she broke Molly's wrist, and Evelyn reached for it now. If arrangements had been made to dispose of her body, then there must be others with her. They would be waiting nearby, and they would be expecting to hear a gunshot.

Picking up the gun, she aimed it high into the trees and squeezed the trigger. A deafening report echoed around the spinney and a there was a rush of wings and squawking as sleeping birds were startled from their slumber. Turning, Evelyn tossed the gun away and reached for the belt on Molly's coat. She pulled it out before rolling the woman onto her stomach and tying her hands securely behind her back. Her breath was coming quickly now. She didn't have much time. The others wouldn't be far, and as soon as they heard the shot, they'd come to take care of the body.

Reaching to her own neck, she undid the scarf tied there and used it to gag the unconscious woman. She would be found, but Evelyn hoped to be gone by then. She didn't want to risk Molly raising an alarm before she'd gone two steps.

Once the woman was bound and gagged, Evelyn grabbed the bag that Molly wore across her body. She picked up the torch and held it with one hand while she opened the flap. She sincerely hoped that the package was inside! She didn't have time to search the car below. In fact, she didn't think she really had time to search the bag, but she could hardly leave it. Not when she'd come this far.

Shining the light into the bag, Evelyn experienced a mix of relief and excitement at the sight of a brown paper-wrapped package tied securely with twine. Grabbing it, she pulled it from the bag just as the sound of underbrush crunching made its way into the spinney. They were coming!

Evelyn jumped up and turned to run towards the trees, her heart pounding once again. She wasn't going to make it. The realization hit her just as two men burst into the spinney behind her. A gunshot rang out and Evelyn stumbled as the wood splintered on the tree beside her. Without hesitation, she reached into her pocket and pulled out her Browning, turning as she raised her arm. The forgotten torch cast enough light over the area for her to clearly see the two men running towards her. She fired. The man on the right stumbled, a stunned look on his face, and stopped. He swayed for a second, then fell backwards as blood spread across his chest.

Evelyn shifted her aim to the other one to find his weapon pointed right at her. She sucked in her breath, but before she could fire again, another shot rang out from behind her. The man fell back a pace, a bullet hole in his forehead.

Evelyn stared, stunned, as he fell to join his companion on the ground. Spinning around, she gasped to find Anthony lowering a pistol.

"Tony!"

He moved forward, his eyes on her pistol.

## When Wolves Gather

"I don't suppose you'll consider lowering that, will you?"

"That depends on what on earth you're doing here!" Evelyn found her voice, the gun never wavering.

"Saving your life, from the looks of things," he said dryly. "We're on the same side, you and I, although I'm damned if I know how or why."

A shout echoed through the trees, some distance away, and Anthony cursed under his breath.

"You must go," he said urgently. "For God's sake, put that gun away and listen to me! You must get away from here!"

Evelyn hesitated, then lowered her pistol, struggling to make sense of what had just happened.

"I...I don't understand."

"I don't have time to explain, Evie. Those weren't the only ones with Molly. There are four others, and by the sound of it, they're on their way now. The shots will have alerted them that something went wrong. You can't be caught here!"

He dug in his pocket and pulled out his keys, pressing them into her hand. His eyes met hers in the darkness and Evelyn saw only concern in his face.

"Take my car. It's parked about a quarter mile along the road behind a hedge."

"But...what about you?" Evelyn came out of her stupor, her fingers closing around the keys.

"I'll take care of Molly and the others. Just go!"

Evelyn swallowed, hearing voices on the other side of the spinney. With one final look at Anthony, she turned and darted through the trees. She emerged into a field and, in the darkness, she couldn't see what was before her. Remembering the ditch filled with water, Evelyn turned to her left and began to sprint away from the spinney, glancing up at the moonless sky. For the first time that evening, she was grateful for the clouds that immersed the countryside in almost impenetrable darkness. They would prevent anyone from seeing her running into the night, leaving the spinney, and Anthony, behind.

## Chapter Thirty-Seven

Evelyn finished making herself a cup of tea and turned, sipping it. She'd arrived back in Brook Street in the pre-dawn hours, going straight to bed and falling into an exhausted slumber. This morning she'd arisen feeling very much refreshed, and more than a little confused as to how she'd made it through the night before with little more than a scratch.

The entire drive to London had been spent trying to make sense of what on earth had happened. She felt as though her world had been tossed upside down in the space of two hours, and Anthony was right in the middle of everything. What the hell was he doing? And why had he let her go? He'd given her his car to get away, for God's sake. What did any of it mean? What did he mean when he said they were both on the same side? How was that possible?

Shaking her head, Evelyn rubbed her eyes. She was no closer to answers in the bright light of day than she had been in the darkness last night. But with the new day had come at least one welcome thought: Anthony couldn't possibly be one of the traitors, not after what he'd done last night. And that was a very welcome thought indeed.

She looked at the sealed package laying on the table. Despite everything, she'd accomplished what she'd set out to do. It hadn't been done in quite the manner she'd planned, it was neither pretty nor easy, but it had been done.

Taking another sip of hot tea, Evelyn wondered how Anthony had fared after she left. He would have had to spin some tale to explain his presence there, and it would have to be one that would convince the Round Club that he'd had nothing to do with the two dead men, or an unconscious Molly. She pursed her lips thoughtfully. Molly hadn't seen him. No one had, save the man he'd killed, and Evelyn had no doubt the man was dead. One simply didn't survive a bullet shot to the head. If no one had seen him, he could spin just about any story he liked. Who was there to disprove it?

Evelyn sighed and carried her cup over to the table, seating herself and picking up the package. She was dwelling on things she couldn't possibly know the answers to until Anthony himself shared

## When Wolves Gather

them with her. Since he had to come to retrieve his car eventually, she had no doubt those answers would come. For now, she had the package to examine.

She untied the string and pulled the brown paper away from a leather pouch. It was the type of pouch that carried diplomatic papers, and she turned it over to find it tied closed with a strip of leather.

"Well, let's see what was almost worth my life," she murmured out loud, undoing the knot and opening the flap.

If Marrow had any idea that she was going through the contents, he would no doubt have her arrested. They were, after all, what would become classified documents when she handed them over to him tomorrow. He'd be furious if he ever discovered that she'd looked at them, but she had absolutely no intention of passing them on without doing so. Bill had trained her too well for that.

She carefully slid out a stack of papers, held together by a clip at the top. On top was a letter, written in German, instructing the reader that everything contained in this pouch was genuine and had been obtained and compiled in the strictest secrecy. Evelyn snorted, the grandiose language making her feel as if she were reading a poorly written novel. They really were prone to the dramatic, this Round Club.

Lifting the letter, Evelyn found herself staring at a list of names beneath it. Her pulse leapt as she read the neat description at the top of the paper. It was an account of the senior members of the Round Club: the inner circle. Even though she'd hoped to find something like this among the papers, Evelyn hadn't really expected it to be there. It seemed very foolish to write out a list of all of their leadership. What if it fell into the wrong hands, such as hers? Yet here it was, the single document she'd been hoping to find.

She let out a gasp and shock went through her at the first name on the list. Lord Chartwell, Duke of Stafford? Impossible! Yet there was the name, neatly printed in ink, and at the very top. Next to it, a note had been added: Founder. Good Lord! He was the head of the whole thing! The second name was equally shocking: Lady Rothman.

Evelyn sat back in the chair heavily, staring at the names silently, her mind spinning. She couldn't believe it! Lady Rothman? She had been to countless lunches hosted by the woman, and her mother considered her a close acquaintance. Why, both Lady Rothman and Lord Chartwell had been at her father's funeral! And they were actively plotting to help Hitler gain control of Great Britain? It seemed beyond belief, but it clearly was not.

Her lips tightened as she scanned some twenty-odd names, all very well known to her. None were as shocking as those first two, although they all left a bad taste in her mouth. How on earth could she ever be civil to any of them again? How could she converse with them at parties, or exchange pleasantries at the theatre or in a restaurant? How could she even look at any of them again without spitting in their faces? They were traitors, one and all, and their united goal was to bring an end to the country that she and her brother were fighting with their lives to defend.

    Rubbing her eyes, Evelyn took a deep breath and forced herself to remain calm and think rationally. Emotion had no place in any of this. This was business. This was work. It was just plain bad luck that it was happening right here in London.

    Her eye fell to the last name on the list, and she frowned. There was Tony, just as she'd suspected for the last week or more. It didn't make any sense! Why would he have done what he did last night if he was one of them? None of it made any sense!

    Shaking her head, she lowered her eyes to the papers before her once more. Pushing the question of Anthony out of her mind, she stared at the list, absorbing the sheer scope of the Round Club's reach. It was much larger and more prestigious than she'd ever imagined. Marrow couldn't possibly arrest all of them without causing an uproar, not to mention the severe upheaval in the government and social structure of England. It was like a nightmare.

    Shaking her head, Evelyn removed the clip from the sheaf of papers and went through them systematically. Aside from the List, she was amazed at the veritable treasure trove of information that was there. Alongside diagrams and photographs of the defenses and infrastructure of the entire south coast of England, and of London, she also read detailed plans they'd made to execute a coup, overthrowing Parliament and the King when the German invasion began. The absolute nerve of them!

    Her eyes narrowed and her lips tightened again when she read that the Führer had instructed for the invasion to commence in August, or September at the latest. So it was coming, and very soon. The onslaught would begin, and it would be up to Miles, Rob, Chris, and countless other young men to repel the Luftwaffe and make an invasion impossible.

    Evelyn reached for her tea, willing herself to calm down and breathe once again. Getting hysterical over what hadn't happened yet, even if it *was* coming, would serve no purpose other than to make her a nervous wreck. Then she would be of no use to anyone.

    After a fortifying sip, she set the cup down and continued to go through the papers. There were all kinds of rough maps and names

## When Wolves Gather

of bridges and rail lines, as well as a copy of the train timetables so the Germans would know exactly when the trains were running. She shook her head, anger rolling through her. That alone would cost hundreds of Englishmen and women their lives, as the Luftwaffe would know precisely when to bomb the tracks to cause maximum devastation. After seeing how they attacked the roads in France, Evelyn had absolutely no doubt that they would do the same here with the rail lines. And Lady Rothman and Lord Chartwell were handing them the means to do it on a platter!

Tamping down her fury, Evelyn forced herself to scan through the rest of the papers. She had to remain detached and unemotional so that she could properly evaluate the wealth of information before her. Even after reminding herself of that, when she came across the name Henry a few moments later, she felt her stomach clench and her heart drop.

There were several references to 'Henry' and his movements and assistance. It almost seemed to be an accounting of what the London spy was doing, but it was very vague. Her lips twisted and Evelyn couldn't help but feel somewhat vindicated. It seemed even the Round Club wasn't very sure of anything when it came to Henry, and he was part of their organization. At least MI6 weren't the only ones stymied by the man.

She frowned a second later at a reference to Walter, "the man in Lyon." There was a spy in Lyon? What did the Round Club have to do with the city in France? And what did it matter to them if there was a German spy in Nazi-occupied France? She went back through the papers but could find no other reference to Walter aside from this one. Frowning, she re-read the sentence, her brows furrowed. It appeared that this Walter was known to one of the inner circle, but that was all it said. Clearly they thought Walter was already well-known to the Germans. But who was he? And why was he even mentioned at all?

After puzzling over it for a while, Evelyn finally gave up and exhaled, getting up from the table. The answer wasn't in the packet. All she could do was make sure Bill was aware of him so that he could forward the information to his agents in France.

She returned to the table a few moments later with the small camera that she'd been issued to carry with her abroad. It was a tiny little thing, able to be concealed in the lining of her purse or coat. Bending over the table, she began snapping photographs of every page of the packet. There was a lot here, and Bill would want to see all of it.

When she was finished, Evelyn carefully replaced all the sheets just as she'd found them and clipped them together again. She slid the packet back into the pouch, tying it closed. She would re-wrap the whole thing just as it had been when she received it, and then she would deliver it to Marrow. He would never know that photographs had been taken and passed on to MI6.

Picking up her cup, Evelyn finished her tea and looked at the clock. She must get dressed to go out. She had to send a telegram to Marrow, letting him know she had the package. Once it was delivered, her part in this operation-turned-mess would be over.

And then what would she do to keep herself busy?

Evelyn started when the front door bell sounded. She looked at the clock and screwed the cap on her pen, pushing her chair back. It was early afternoon and she was writing out her report of the entire fiasco the evening before in case Marrow wanted a proper debriefing. She had no intention of going to the headquarters, wherever that might be, and spending a day answering questions. She hated doing it with Bill, and she wasn't about to do it with Marrow. Crossing the room to the door, Evelyn acknowledged that she might not have a choice, but she hoped the written account would be enough to forestall any formal debriefing.

In the hallway, she hesitated only a second before resolutely reaching for the handle. The very fact that she was uneasy in her own home was enough to make her irritated. If the Round Club had discovered her identity, she had much larger problems on her hands than a possible assassin at her front door.

"Anthony!" she exclaimed, opening it wide. "Come in. I've been expecting you."

"Hello, Evelyn!" Anthony smiled and stepped into the house. "I imagined you might. I'm very happy to see that you're safe and sound."

"Yes, of course I am," she said, closing the door. "Come into the drawing room. I sent my maid back to Ainsworth, so I'm unable to offer you anything beyond a cup of tea, I'm afraid."

"That's quite all right. I've just come from lunch." He set his hat and gloves on the hall table and followed her into the drawing room. "I really am glad to see that you're safe. Did you have any problems with the car?"

## When Wolves Gather

"None at all. It was right where you said it would be, and no one followed me." Evelyn waved him into a seat as she sat down on the settee. "And you? What happened after I left?"

"I told them you were already gone when I got there." Anthony said, seating himself. "It wasn't difficult to convince them that I'd arrived only seconds before them."

Evelyn nodded and studied him for a moment, then cleared her throat.

"Tony, what in blazes were you doing there?"

"I could very well ask you the same thing, Evie."

"Yes, but I asked first."

He stared at her for a moment, his face unreadable, then he sighed.

"I shouldn't be here, and I certainly shouldn't be explaining anything to you," he muttered, "but I know you won't leave me in peace until I have. Your disguise was outstanding, by the way. I had absolutely no inkling it was you until that ditch water washed half of it away."

"Thank you."

"Why were you pretending to be a German spy?"

Evelyn clucked her tongue and shook her head.

"Oh no. You first."

"Very well." He crossed his legs comfortably. "I went looking for Sylvia Müller, but not to threaten her, as you so obviously thought. I went because I had to warn her - you - that the people you were meeting knew that you weren't a German agent. I knew what they meant to do, and I couldn't very well allow an innocent woman to be killed. When I saw that it was you, well, I couldn't believe my eyes."

"I don't understand. I thought you were part of it! I *saw* you with Sir Ronald in Covent Garden."

He looked up at that.

"Did you? When?"

"The other day. I followed you and watched as you both went into the restaurant."

"And you thought...yes, I can see why you would, I suppose." Anthony exhaled. "There's no help for it, then, but to tell you everything. You asked me once why I didn't do something else when I said I felt like I wasn't contributing to the war effort. Well, the fact was, I am. Six months ago, I was approached by the Security Service to assist them in hunting out members of an organization that they believed were going to attempt to overthrow our current government. I didn't believe that such a thing was possible, but I began listening at the

311

clubs and dinner parties, and I started to hear things. I learned that not only was it possible, but that my own peers were part of it. I agreed to help the Security Service, and have been working with Marrow ever since to discover everyone who is involved. I've been trying to infiltrate the Round Club at the highest level, and have finally gained the trust of Sir Ronald Clark who, as I believe you're aware, is part of the inner circle. That meeting that you witnessed was, I believe, the final vetting process."

Evelyn studied him for a long moment. He was telling the truth, she decided. His voice was quiet and steady, and his eyes never flickered or wavered on her. He hadn't been conflicted about the course of this war as she'd presumed. He was trying to do his part to save his country in the most practical way available to him.

"Then you're not one of them?"

"Not in the way you obviously believed," he said with a twisted smile. "I'm trying to do the same thing that you are. I'm trying to find out who they are so that we can stop them. At the moment, that means pretending to be a Nazi-sympathizer."

"But how did you come to be there last night?"

"Yesterday afternoon I was summoned to Lady Rothman's drawing room, where I found Sir Ronald and Lord Chartwell. There, I was told that he was the founder of the Round Club, and that Lady Rothman was his number two."

"They told you this? Why?" Evelyn demanded.

"Because they'd accepted me into their confidence. I've finally made it into their circle." Anthony felt in his jacket for his cigarettes and pulled out his case, offering her one. "You don't appear shocked at all by Chartwell and Rothman's involvement," he remarked, his eyes on her face.

"No." Evelyn took a cigarette. "I'm afraid I'd already deduced as much. I was very shocked when I realized. Why, they were both at Daddy's funeral! It's unfathomable that they would be involved in such a thing."

"Unfortunately, it's very much the truth." He lit her cigarette and then his own. "While I was there yesterday, someone came to see Lady Rothman. I didn't see him, as she spoke with him in the adjoining room and he was out of sight, but I recognized his voice. I still can't place it, but I'm sure it's someone I know well. He told Lady Rothman that he'd contacted Berlin, and that it was confirmed that they didn't have any knowledge of an agent matching the name or description of Miss Sylvia Müller."

Evelyn's lips pressed together.

## When Wolves Gather

"That's how they found out," she breathed. "They contacted Berlin directly."

"Yes. Lady Rothman was furious. Then she calmed down and told him that they would continue with the operation as planned. When he began to argue, she said that Miss Müller must be killed and that was the simplest way to accomplish it."

"That was rather extreme. Why not simply break off all communication?"

"Because, my dear, you had already met with Sir Ronald. You knew that he, at least, was a traitor." Anthony tapped ash into the ashtray next to his chair. "After leaving Lady Rothman's, I went to see Marrow. I got the whole story from him, and he sent me to get you out of it. I was to take you back to London without delay, and Miss Sylvia Müller would simply disappear."

Evelyn looked at him ruefully.

"Except I wouldn't cooperate. I'm terribly sorry about that."

"Yes, well, had I known it was you, I could have explained. As it was, when I woke up, you were long gone. I did try to follow you, but I could find no trace of you, the bicycle, or even tracks to follow. All I could do was go along the road to where I knew they would be, and wait for you to show up." He shook his head and rubbed his eyes. "I had no idea what I was going to do, but I certainly couldn't allow you to be killed. Good Lord, what would I tell Rob? I saw you arrive and watched from the trees, staying hidden as you and Molly went into the spinney. You know the rest."

Evelyn was silent for a long time, digesting it all. So Anthony had been working with Marrow all the while! She was conscious of a profound sense of relief, and she shook her head, a smile curving her lips.

"Well, I must say that I'm very relieved to hear that you're not a traitor after all. You have no idea what I've been going through!"

"I can't say that I'm not a little disappointed that you ever believed that I was. Good Lord, Evie, you've known me for years! How could you think that I would betray my king, my country, my family?"

"Well, how could we think that the Duke of Stafford would, yet he is," she pointed out. "I was seeing traitors everywhere I looked! Of course I didn't want to believe it, but I thought I was seeing irrefutable proof."

"That will teach you to jump to conclusions," he said with a flash of white teeth. "Well, that's my part in it. Now it's your turn. How in blazes did you end up masquerading as a German secretary?"

313

"I overheard Sir Ronald and Miss Milner talking in the garden at the Ramsey's party," she said, getting up and putting out her cigarette. "I knew Marrow was working with the Secret Service, so I went to tell him. He's an old friend of the family, you know. I was rather taken aback by the discovery of the Round Club, as I'm sure you were, and I offered to help."

"Why in God's name would you do that?!"

"How could I not?" She gazed at him, amused by his discomfiture. "I could hardly sit by and do nothing, and I really was the perfect person to attempt it. You know that I speak German, and I was at a loose end until I have to return to my station. Do you really imagine that I would miss out on a chance for a bit of adventure before I returned to Northolt?"

"But Evie, the danger! Look at what happened last night! You were almost killed!"

She waved a hand dismissively.

"Yes, yes, Marrow kept harping on the danger as well. It's quite absurd, you know. We're at war, and I am an officer in the WAAF. There's very little that I do that does not involve some degree of danger."

He frowned and looked skeptical, but he couldn't very well argue the point. They *were* at war, and she *was* an officer in the Women's Auxiliary Air Force. At least, as far as he was concerned, she qualified to herself. She couldn't stop her lips from curving wryly. As for the danger, oh, if he only knew! Last night had been unexpected, and certainly hair-raising, but it was hardly the most dangerous spot she'd been in.

"But what about Molly?" she asked, going back to her seat. "What's happening with her?"

"Marrow wants to simply observe for now. The Round Club is in a complete uproar. The men we shot are both dead." He looked at her, his gaze suddenly piercing. "You killed a man last night, Evie."

She swallowed. She knew he expected her to be shocked and upset at the very least, but the most she could summon was a grimace of distaste.

"I thought I might have," she said in a low voice. "You know what a good shot I am, and I was aiming for his heart."

"Well, lucky for you that you are. If you'd missed, it could have ended very differently." Anthony put out his cigarette and blew his cheeks out, shaking his head. "What a bloody mess. Molly is furious that you got away, and so is Lady Rothman. It's a very good thing that

## When Wolves Gather

Sylvia Müller doesn't exist, and that no one has any idea that you're involved. They will be searching for the secretary for months."

"What about you?" Evelyn asked, her brows coming together in concern. "Don't they suspect something? How did you explain your part last night?"

"I told Lady Rothman that I'd overheard the whole thing yesterday and went down to Dorchester to see if I could lend a hand."

She stared at him in disbelief.

"That's it? That was your story?"

He laughed at the look on her face.

"Yes. You know, Evelyn, sometimes it's easier to keep things simple. You'd be surprised what people are willing to believe when they're too busy looking for much more complicated lies."

Evelyn stored that away for future pondering and shook her head.

"I'd say you're extremely lucky that Lady Rothman appears to have a very limited imagination," she murmured. "What will you do now?"

"Continue as I was before. I really must beg you to say nothing of this to anyone. My position is precarious enough as it is."

"Good heavens, Tony, as if I would breathe a word!" She was quiet for a moment, then she looked at him ruefully. "And anyway, it seems I must ask the same of you. If anyone so much as suspects that Sylvia Müller and I are the same person, I'll be in a pickle."

"Your secret is safe with me, rest assured." He stood up and smiled down at her. "We had quite the adventure last night. I expect you'll be more than happy to return to your station after that."

Evelyn stood up and laughed lightly.

"I must admit that I never dreamt anything exciting would happen. I thought it would all be terribly straight-forward."

"Yes, well, I wish it had been. I was almost sick with dread last night, thinking you'd be killed and there was nothing I could do to stop it." Anthony turned towards the door. "I never want to feel that again. I'll be very happy when you're back in Northolt and out of harm's way."

He stopped suddenly and turned to her as a thought occurred to him.

"Good Lord, you *are* really a WAAF, aren't you?" he demanded, his eyes widening. "You're not secretly working for Marrow as well, are you?"

Evelyn laughed.

"No, I'm not working for Marrow," she assured him. "This was a one time offer. You may rest easy on that score."

He exhaled, relieved.

"Thank God for that!" He turned back to the door, missing the flash of amusement in her blue eyes. "You know, Rob would have an absolute coronary if he knew what you got up to in your spare time."

"Then it's a good thing he will never know, isn't it?"

Anthony turned at the door and held out his hand to her.

"Take very good care of yourself, Evelyn. Please don't get involved in anything like this again. I don't think I could handle the strain."

"Don't worry. I'll be back to work soon," she said cheerfully, her voice a little unsteady. "There's no need to worry about me."

Her fingers tightened on his when he would have pulled his hand away.

"Please be careful, Tony. If Lady Rothman and the duke were willing to kill a secretary who knew nothing about anything, think what they will do if they discover they've been betrayed by a member of their inner circle."

He nodded, his face grave.

"Oh, I'm well aware. I'll be careful."

**When Wolves Gather**

# Chapter Thirty-Eight

**Portsmouth**
**August 12**

Evelyn entered the tea shop and looked around. It was very quiet at this time of the morning, and she caught sight of Marrow seated at a table towards the back. Only one other table was occupied, graced by two women with shopping bags at their feet. She nodded pleasantly to them as she passed, making her way to where Marrow waited.

"Good morning," she greeted him. "I'm sorry I'm late. I'm afraid I had to take a detour on my way in. Did you know the city was bombed?"

"Yes. I take it you came in that way?" Marrow waited until she was seated before retaking his chair.

"Yes. I had no idea. I haven't looked at a newspaper in a few days." Evelyn pulled the strap of her bag over her shoulder, setting it on the floor beside her chair. "It's terrible! An entire street is blocked with rubble!"

"Yes, I know. The Jerries came over yesterday. The docks got the worst of it, I'm told. I wouldn't have arranged to meet you here if I'd realized the damage was so widespread." Marrow motioned for another cup and saucer. "The woman who runs this shop told me there's something happening over Dover this morning. She heard it on the wireless."

Evelyn frowned.

"Dover? Are you sure?"

"I'm not, but she is. She's worried they'll come back with another bombardment today."

"I suppose I would be as well." Evelyn smiled as a matronly woman came over with a clean cup and saucer and another pot of tea. "Thank you very much."

"You're welcome, miss," she said with a nod. "You just let me know if you need anything more."

She left and Evelyn reached for the little milk jug on the table.

"Why *are* we meeting in Portsmouth?" she asked. "I could have met you in London."

"I have business here and came down very early. I thought it would be an easier distance for you from Dorchester than going all the way to London."

Evelyn poured milk into her cup as he spoke, then reached for the teapot. Anthony obviously hadn't told him that she'd returned to London yesterday, and she saw no need to enlighten him.

"Thank you," she murmured.

"I understand you had quite an experience the other night," he said, clearing his throat. "Are you all right?"

"Perfectly, thank you." Evelyn sipped her tea and smiled at him. "I'll admit that things got rather hairy, but it all worked out in the end."

"Evelyn, for heaven's sake, you don't have to pretend that nothing happened," Marrow said in exasperation, lowering his voice. "You must have been terrified!"

Evelyn set her cup down.

"I think I was more angry than frightened," she replied calmly. "It wasn't until later that I acknowledged that the whole thing could have turned out very differently."

"I'm exceedingly glad that it didn't," he said fervently. "What on earth would I have told your mother?"

"Presumably not the truth." Evelyn laughed at the look on his face. "Oh, Mr. Marrow, don't look so appalled! Nothing happened and I'm none the worse for wear, I promise you. The entire operation was a resounding success because I got the package."

He stared at her, clearly surprised.

"What?"

"Yes. Weren't you told?"

"No!"

"How strange. Perhaps he didn't realize I'd taken it."

She reached down for her bag and cast a quick glance around the shop. The two other customers were deep in conversation on the other side of the room, not paying them the slightest heed, and the owner was nowhere in sight. Pulling the paper-wrapped package out of her bag, she handed it to him with a smile.

"There you are. So, you see, I even came away with the goods, as they say in the films."

Marrow took the package, shaking his head in amazement.

"I assumed she hadn't brought it along. Why *did* she? If they knew you were a fraud, why risk carrying it with her?"

## When Wolves Gather

"She said she had another appointment. I believe she was going to give it to someone else, perhaps for safe-keeping rather than risk carrying it all the way back to London."

He pursed his lips thoughtfully.

"You may be on to something there. They didn't know who you were, only that you weren't who you claimed to be. If they thought it was a trap, and there was any possibility of her being followed, she would hardly have carried it back to London with her."

"What will happen to her?" Evelyn asked after a moment. "After all, she was going to shoot me!"

"I'm keeping a very close eye on her. After the events of the other night, I can't move to detain her just yet. It would cause difficulties for our mutual friend."

Evelyn tightened her lips, but she could understand his position. If Molly were taken into custody, Anthony would fall under suspicion. Even if they couldn't prove anything, he would be excluded from information and watched constantly. It was best to make the Round Club believe that they'd got away with everything. They would hunt for Miss Müller and the missing package for months before they realized they'd both disappeared, and Anthony's cover would remain intact.

"Well, I can't pretend that I'm not disappointed that she will get away with it, but I can readily understand why you're choosing this course of action," she said after a moment. "I suppose in the long run, it's for the best."

"Just so." Marrow drank some tea, then met her gaze. "Evelyn, you performed outstandingly well out there," he said slowly, setting his cup down. "Much better than I could ever have dared hope. I know that you're well-established in your position with the WAAF, but I'd like you to consider coming over to the Security Service. I can arrange it easily as a transfer of sorts. You would fulfill your military obligation in service with us. You would be invaluable."

Evelyn resisted the urge to laugh and, instead, smiled prettily at her father's old friend.

"Thank you, but no. My place is with my girls," she said. "While I did thoroughly enjoy myself, and I *did* you know, despite everything, I've made a commitment to the WAAF. I really must return to Northolt."

He nodded, a rueful smile on his face.

"I expected that you'd say that," he admitted. "It would have been foolish not to try, however. If you ever change your mind, I'll very happily welcome you into my section. Just say the word. I need more people like you."

"I will be sure to remember that if I ever tire of my current occupation."

Marrow looked at his watch and finished his tea in one gulp.

"I'm sorry to cut this short, but I must leave for an appointment." He picked up the package and slid it into his briefcase. "I can't thank you enough for what you did, and this information will, hopefully, go far towards to enabling us to break up this Round Club once and for all. I don't think it's too dramatic to say that England owes you a great debt."

"Nonsense," she said briskly. "Just promise me that you'll stop them."

"I'll certainly do my best." Marrow stood and held out his hand to her. "Safe travels back to Northolt, Evelyn. And thank you again for everything. I do wish it hadn't ended the way it did."

"Believe me, so do I," she said with a smile, standing and grasping his hand. "But do you know, for all that, I wouldn't go back and do anything differently? Isn't that strange?"

He smiled.

"Perhaps, but I won't tell anyone."

Evelyn laughed and watched him leave before sitting down to finish her tea. Her smile faded as she thought of the papers she'd photographed the day before. She'd met Bill for dinner last night and delivered the film. The twinge of guilt that she felt in knowing that she had betrayed Marrow's trust was tempered with the knowledge that there was information in that packet that directly affected her, and MI6. Bill may be able to glean a clue as to Henry's identity, and any help in that department was worth any price.

Her lips twisted as she reached for the teapot to refill her cup. After hearing about her harrowing experience on the road to Weymouth, Bill had been furious. He was convinced, as she was, that it was none other than Henry who had contacted Berlin and blown her cover. He had wanted her to retreat to Scotland, there to stay hidden until they had tracked him down. It was absurd. She wasn't about to go into hiding in her own country just because an imaginary secretary had been targeted by the spy. She'd said as much to Bill, telling him not to be an old fool.

Evelyn chuckled to herself now as she remembered the look on his face. He'd seemed unable to decide whether to be deeply insulted, or to laugh. Thankfully, he'd seen her point a moment later when she reminded him that Henry had no idea that Miss Müller and

## When Wolves Gather

Jian were one and the same. As far as Henry was concerned, nothing had changed as regards to Jian. He still had no idea who the agent was, where she was, or how to begin to find her. And, because of that, nothing had changed with her, either. She wasn't going to stop going to London on the very minuscule chance that Henry might find her out.

Bill had eventually relented, but he *had* managed to extract her promise to spend the rest of her leave at Ainsworth Manor. As Evelyn opened her purse to take out money to pay for her tea, she sighed. Because of her excursion into Dorchester, he had insisted on tacking another five days onto her holiday. He was absolutely determined that she rest, but what he didn't understand was that rest was the very last thing she wanted.

She laid some coins on the table and stood up, collecting her bag. How could she take a lovely long holiday while Miles and Rob were fighting constantly overhead? Coastal cities like Portsmouth were being bombed more and more frequently, and now something was happening over Dover. Every time a German formation crossed over the Channel, the pilots of the RAF had to scramble to meet them head-on. They weren't getting any nice long holidays. They were exhausted, but still had to get up there and fight. How could she feel easy about resting when men like Fred and Chris were fighting what had to seem like a losing battle every day?

As Evelyn walked out of the tea shop, she looked up into the clear, blue sky. The sun was shining brightly and a brisk, salty breeze blew in from the ocean. It was a lovely summer day and, despite her bleak thoughts, her spirits lifted. She didn't know what tomorrow would bring, but today she could relish the fact that she'd done what she could for her country, and done it well. In a roadside spinney, on the way to Weymouth, they had defeated the Nazi agenda. It had been a small victory, but a victory nonetheless. And even the small victories had a way of adding up into something big.

Great Britain was fighting, on many different fronts and in many different ways. It wasn't only the pilots, sailors, and soldiers in the thick of it now. War had come to the people, and the people were taking sides.

As she walked down the narrow street to where she'd left her car, Evelyn smiled. If Hitler thought he could Blitzkrieg his way into England as he had everywhere else, he was in for a shock.

England was fighting for her life, and she would not fall easily.

# Epilogue

Evelyn drove along the winding road, her hair blowing in the wind that whipped through the open windows. She'd left Portsmouth behind and was cutting across West Sussex before turning north towards London. The beautiful weather was a lovely change from the past week of heavy clouds and showers that had plagued the island. She inhaled the fresh, crisp air, smiling at the joy and freedom she felt. It must be the sun, she decided. She was inordinately happy, despite having almost been shot the a few nights before.

A formation of fighters caught her attention and the smile faded somewhat. She had seen countless groups of fighters flying overhead on her drive, and it seemed to her to be more than usual. She knew that 11 Group was taking the brunt of the scrambles to intercept German bombers, and she was driving along the southern coast, but it was still disconcerting.

What had happened at Dover this morning? Was that the reason for the increased fighter activity? Or were the Jerries coming after Portsmouth again? She was passing Tangmere, and Evelyn knew from Fred that that station was one of the most hard-pressed in 11 Group. Was that why she was seeing so many fighters? Because she was passing a very active air station?

Evelyn hadn't gone another quarter mile when her attention was drawn to another mass of airplanes, and an icy chill streaked down her spine. These airplanes were coming from the Channel, and they weren't Hurricanes or Spitfires.

Evelyn slammed on the brakes, staring at the outlines of the machines in the distance. Stukas!

Her heart pounded in her chest as Evelyn hit the accelerator and pulled off of the road, stopping the Lagonda in a shallow ditch that ran alongside. She opened the door and jumped out, grabbing her bag from the passenger's seat and running towards a hedge a few feet away.

The peaceful, sunny day was shattered a moment later as an awful screeching filled the air. Evelyn dove behind the hedge and covered her ears, watching in horror as the bombers went into a steep

## When Wolves Gather

dive, tearing down from the sky. Following their projected path, her gut clenched as she caught sight of towers in the distance. They were attacking the radar towers at Poling!

Poling was part of a chain of radar towers that stretched along the entire southern coast of England. It was those towers that allowed the RAF to scramble their fighters and intercept the enemy before they'd crossed the coast. Without those towers, Fighter Command would be blind.

Squeezing her eyes shut, Evelyn huddled behind the hedgerow and tried to block out memories of that awful noise in another time, and another place. Then the road had been filled with families fleeing an invading army. As the Stukas screamed towards the towers, she buried her head in her knees, seeing overturned carts and bodies strewn across the ground, covered in blood.

When the first bomb hit the towers, the ground shook from the impact, jarring Evelyn out of her panic-induced memory. Her eyes flew open and she lifted her head, watching as more bombers began their descent.

Suddenly she knew why there were so many fighters up in the air today. They were being scrambled to repel what could only be the beginning of the Luftwaffe's assault on England. It was beginning in earnest at last. Hitler was moving to take England, and he was starting by taking away their radar towers.

The Battle for Britain had begun.

# Author's Notes

**1. Special Operations Executive (S.O.E). (aka Ministry of Ungentlemanly Warfare, aka Churchill's Secret Army.)** The Special Operations Executive was a secret organization formed by Winston Churchill in July, 1940, with the expressed purpose to "Set Europe Ablaze." It was tasked with the mission of performing acts of sabotage, espionage, and reconnaissance in Nazi occupied Europe. Agents were trained in what was referred to as "ungentlemanly warfare" before being parachuted into occupied territories where they then worked with local resistance groups. The organization was kept under strictest secrecy during the war, and only a handful of people even knew of its existence. Those people were sometimes called the "Baker's Street Irregulars" after the location of the headquarters, which was on Baker Street.

   - The training for the S.O.E was rigorous and difficult. The recruits were subjected to intensive mental and physical screening before they could advance to the actual training. Once the agent advanced to the Paramilitary School, they underwent hard physical training in addition to learning: silent killing, weapons handling, demolition, map reading and compass use, elementary Morse Code, raid tactics, foreign weapons, and parachute training. After the intensive 5-week course, those who passed were then sent on to "Finishing Schools" were they were finally told who they were working for (S.O.E). The final training was extensive and very concentrated. They learned advanced Morse code, were trained in advanced explosives, and learned how to survive behind enemy lines. The S.O.E. was, essentially, looking for a "PhD who could win a bar fight." (World War 2 Spy School: The Complete 1943 S.O.E. Counter Espionage Manual, Ian Hall, pp 7-13)

   - Those recruits who were skilled enough to complete all three levels of training were sent into occupied territory. They had an average life expectancy of 6 weeks.

   - In June, 1940, Churchill created the Commandos for the purpose of executing specialized raids on the enemy. (the actual

## When Wolves Gather

Commando Units weren't operational until 1941) The training Evelyn undergoes in this book is purely fictional, and my imaginative blending of two of Churchill's most aggressive secret organizations in the beginning of the war. The real training for S.O.E. didn't actually commence until the winter of 1940-1941.

2. **Anti-Italian Riots in England**. On June 10, 1940, Mussolini declared war on England. That night, anti-Italian riots occurred across England and Scotland. Mobs formed and went through the cities and towns, attacking Italian-owned businesses. They ransacked and looted the businesses, many of which were also where the owners lived. Sadly, the Italians were, for the most part, British citizens and had lived and worked in England for decades. Such was the anger at the actions of Mussolini that English neighbors turned against their Italian friends. Cities in England that were hardest hit by the riots were: Liverpool, Cardiff, Swansea, and Newport, while in Scotland Glasgow and Edinburgh took the award for most violence.

- On June 11, Churchill announced that all Italian males between the ages of seventeen and seventy who had lived in Britain for less than twenty years would be subject to internment. In addition, any male or female on the MI5 suspect list would also be subject to internment. A large number of these men were actually deported to Australia or Canada, and were not reunited with their families until after the war.
(https://ww2db.com/Anti-Italian Riots)
(https://trove.nla.gov.au/newspaper/article/25807870)

3. **British Traitors**. At the outset of the war in 1939, British authorities interned hundreds of men and women whom they deemed to be "Fifth Columnists." These people were accused as fascists who supported Hitler and the Nazi Party, actively working to ensure a German victory. In the decades following the war, scholars and government officials alike have denied the existence of any Fifth Column, instead claiming that it was all a witch hunt to excuse the internment by the government of British subjects. However, classified documents held by MI5, the Home Office, and the Treasury Solicitor's department show that between 1939 and 1945, more that seventy British men and women were convicted of working to help Nazi Germany win the war. Not only was the "myth" of the Fifth Columnists real, but many of them were convicted of treason. These documents, released to the National Archives between 2000 and 2017, reveal that Hitler did, indeed, have

British traitors active throughout the war. Here are a few of those exposed:

- Hastings William Sackville Russel, 12th Duke of Bedford. He was a diehard fascist and great admirer of Hitler. In 1940, he tried to negotiate peace terms with Germany. He also funded pro-Nazi groups with his considerable fortune. Despite these and other actions, his privileged status protected him from prosecution or internment.
- Admiral Sir Barry Domville, former Director of Naval Intelligence. He was a close friend of Heinrich Himmler, and praised the work done by Hitler. He led an organization called "The Link," which disseminated Nazi propaganda. He was interned under Defence Regulation 18B.
- Lord Semphill. He admitted to selling military secrets to Japanese Intelligence for more than 15 years. Despite this, he was never prosecuted or interned, and retained his seat in the House of Lords.
- Captain Archibald Ramsay. He was a Conservative MP, and a fascist and anti-Semite who founded "The Right Club." Along with his wife Ismay, he plotted one of three violent coups d'état uncovered by MI5 in 1940. He was interned under Defence Regulation 18B but allowed to keep his seat in the House of Commons.
- John Beckett, former Independent Labour MP. He became a fascist in the 30s, and formed a series of pro-Nazi groups, all backed with the Duke of Bedford's money and influence. In 1940, MI5 undercover agents uncovered his plans for a revolutionary coup d'état. He was interned under Defence Regulation 18B.

(Hitler's British Traitors: The Secret History of Spies, Saboteurs and Fifth Columnists, Tim Tate, Icon Books Ltd, 2018)

- Not all the traitors had such distinguished pedigrees. Many were common people: a Scottish hairdresser, a conman, a freelance journalist, and a drunkard are just a few more examples. In this book, I have fictionalized real situations, and I hope illustrated the very real threat that was present in England in the summer of 1940.

4. **Spitfire and the Glycol Tank**. While the Spitfire was undoubtedly the darling of the RAF during the war, it did have its quirks. One of those was the glycol tank. The glycol header tank was positioned in the nose of the airplane, in front of the engine, and was how the Merlin engine was cooled. However, if the pilot allowed the engine to idle for too long before takeoff, the glycol in the tank would boil, having the opposite effect and causing the engine to overheat and seize. If the glycol tank reached 110 degrees, the aircraft would be enveloped in a

## When Wolves Gather

cloud of white smoke, the engine would seize, and the plane would crash. Pilots had to taxi out quickly, turn into the wind, and take off without delay before the glycol reached high temperatures. An example of this in action is the experience of then Flying Officer Geoffrey Page in May, 1940. On his first flight in a Spitfire, Geoffrey Page started the engine and motioned to the airman on the ground to pull the chocks. In the time it took the airman to run under the wings and pull them, the glycol coolant temperature went from 0 to 70 degrees. That was before he could even release the brakes! By the time he actually began his takeoff, the temperature was already at 109 degrees.

- To make it even more interesting, glycol is extremely flammable. The glycol tank's position at the front of the aircraft caused it to be exposed to enemy fire. If hit, the glycol tank could explode, sending flames into the engine and upper and lower fuel tanks. The bad news for the pilots was that the fuel tanks were located in front of the cockpit wall. While the lower fuel tank was self-contained, the upper tank was not. This could, and did, send flames into the cockpit when the tanks were hit by enemy fire.

- After the Battle of Britain, armored plating was added around the glycol tank to reduce the risk of fires when hit. Eventually, the upper fuel tank was also made self-contained, further reducing the number of pilots burned in battle.
(Fighter Aces of the RAF in the Battle of Britain, Philip Kaplan, pp 56-57) (Battle of Britain, Len Deighton, pp 40-43)

5. **Hurricane and the Fuel Tanks**. The Hawker Hurricane had a different glycol and fuel tank configuration from the Spitfire. The glycol tank was located behind the engine and directly in front of the fireproof bulkhead that separated the engine from the reserve fuel tank. However, the reserve fuel tank was located directly in front of the cockpit. The main fuel tanks were located in the wings. While this configuration did make it more difficult for the glycol tank to take a direct hit from enemy fire, it had its drawbacks as well. The main fuel tanks in the wings were self-contained, making them much safer for the pilots flying the aircraft. However, the reserve tank in front of the cockpit was not self-contained, nor was the tank armored. As a result, if the reserve fuel tank was hit, or if flames made it to the tank, the resulting fire went straight into the cockpit. One such victim of this was Geoffrey Page, the same pilot who flew the Spitfire above.

- On August 12, 1940, Geoffrey Page was serving in 56 Squadron, flying the Hurricane. He took return fire from a Dornier 215 and was hit in the front reserve tank. According to his account, within

seconds the cockpit had become an inferno. He managed to bail out, but was on fire as he descended into the Channel. Page suffered severe third degree burns over his face, hands, and torso. It was two years before he was able to return to active duty, and flying. Despite his injuries, he went back to flying fighters and survived the war. He retired as a Wing Commander and passed away in 2000.
(Fighter Aces of the RAF in the Battle of Britain, Philip Kaplan, pp 65-83) (Battle of Britain, Len Deighton, pp 44-47)

6. **Chain Home**. Chain home was the codename for the twenty radar towers built by the RAF prior to, and in the beginning of the war. The original twenty towers ranged from Ventnor in the south to Orkney in Scotland. It was an early warning radar system, developed to detect and track aircraft. One of the first practical radar systems, and the main component of the world's first integrated air defense system, Chain Home played an integral and crucial role in the Battle of Britain, and throughout the war. The towers detected incoming aircraft and the information was then forwarded to a central location in Fighter Command. There the signals were interpreted and collated, and then relayed to the pilots for them to intercept. The system was invaluable for allowing the fighter pilots to intercept the Luftwaffe.

- Chain Home was limited to high altitudes, however. Any airplane flying in at low altitudes was not detected by Chain Home towers. Those were detected by low-level radar stations, but fed into the same Dowding system – sending the information to a central location in HQ.

- In addition to the radar, the RAF also relied on ground spotters to report visual confirmation of incoming aircraft. These spotters sat with binoculars in nests along the coast, telephoning in reports of formations, including the number and type of aircraft. In many cases, these served to confirm the radar reports.

German reconnaissance, along with the reports from spies within England, alerted the Germans to the presence of the radar towers and, on Aug. 12, 1940, they commenced an assault on the radar towers. However, the attacks on the sites were not very successful. The towers themselves proved to be almost impervious to bombing due to their open, steel frames. In addition, the receiver huts were placed a little distance from the towers, providing some safety. While some of the locations were knocked out, most notably the Ventnor tower, all the towers were repaired and the system fully functional within hours of being hit. It's worth noting that after this initial onslaught, the German commanders decided that the towers were too difficult to

## When Wolves Gather

destroy and left them alone for the rest of the war. If they hadn't made that decision, the outcome of the Battle, and the war, may have been quite different.
(https://military-history.fandom.com/wiki/Chain_Home)
(https://en.wikipedia.org/wiki/Chain_Home) (The Battle of Britain, Richard Hough and Denis Richards, W.W.Norton & Company, 1989)

7. **Battle of Britain – Part One**. The Battle of Britain, the greatest air battle in World War 2, raged from July 10 – Oct 31, 1940. For many of us today, when we think of the Battle, we think of those fierce, dark days of August and September when so many planes and men were lost. That was, indeed, the heart of the Battle, but the fighting began long before that. To truly understand the awesome scope of what those young men—many no older than 20 years of age—accomplished, we have to understand that these pilots didn't simply wake up on August 13th to a sudden onslaught of enemy bombers and fighters. Rather, they had been fighting them for months over France and the Channel. Those who survived were already battle-weary before the real hell began.

- In early July, with France secured, Hitler turned his sights on his last remaining foe—Great Britain. The Kriegsmarine sent its U-boats and E-boats into the Channel and the North Sea, attacking all shipping convoys that it could detect. The Luftwaffe supported their efforts from the sky with deadly Stukas and light bombers, accompanied by the Me 109 and 110 fighters. RAF fighter squadrons were scrambled daily to try to protect the merchantmen and sailors on the ships.

- In addition to the convoys, the Germans were also within easy range of the port cities along the southern coast of England. They began to bomb cities such as Portsmouth, Bristol, Cardiff, Plymouth, and Brighton, accounting for 192 civilian casualties in July.

- Aircraft production in England had been ramping up since May 14th, when Lord Beaverbrook became Minister of Aircraft Production. Suddenly, everyone recognized that aircraft had to be made a priority if they were to have any chance at all against the Luftwaffe. When Beaverbrook took over in May, planned aircraft production for fighters that month was 261 machines. The actual output for that month was 325. For June, planned production was 292. The actual output ended up being 446. The improvements continued through the rest of the summer, ending with 972 aircraft produced in August alone.* If not for these rapid improvements in fighter production, the Battle of Britain would have ended very differently.

# CW Browning

- Even with the increased fighter aircraft production, the RAF was still at an appalling disadvantage going into the Battle. In July, official estimates were that around 700 fighters (Hurricanes and Spitfires combined) would be the complete force defending England against 1,576 long-range bombers and Ju 87s, and 1,089 fighters (Me 109 and 110s combined). To make matters even more grim, while the fighter production was ramping up substantially, the RAF was faced with the problem of not having the trained pilots to fly the new aircraft. The production was outpacing the pilot pool, and as a result, pilot training was being cut down to very bare bones to get the pilots into the aircraft as quickly as possible.

- By mid-August, when the Luftwaffe unleashed its full force upon England, new pilots were climbing into the cockpits of Spitfires and Hurricanes with less than 8 hours total flying time in ANY aircraft. It was then up to them to survive against the German pilots.

- Between July 10 – July 31, the RAF lost 69 fighters and shot down some 155 German aircraft. In that same time, the Germans sank 18 small coastal vessels, one or two larger vessels, and 4 navy destroyers. Although they were holding their own, and performing above the expectations of the Luftwaffe generals, the RAF pilots were already getting tired, and the main attack had yet to come.

*(The Battle of Britain, Richard Hough and Denis Richards, pp 102-153) (Fighter Aces of the RAF in the Battle of Britain, Philip Kaplan, Pen & Sword Aviation, 2007) (Battle of Britain: A day-to-day chronicle, 10 July-31 October 1940, Patrick Bishop, Quercus Publishing, 2013) (Spitfire Pilot: A Personal Account of the Battle of Britain, Flight Lieutenant David Crook DFC, Lume Books, 2015)

Other Titles in the Shadows of War Series by CW Browning:

The Courier

The Oslo Affair

Night Falls on Norway

The Iron Storm

Into the Iron Shadows

Other Titles by CW Browning:

Next Exit, Three Miles (Exit Series #1)

Next Exit, Pay Toll (Exit Series #2)

Next Exit, Dead Ahead (Exit Series #3)

Next Exit, Quarter Mile (Exit Series #4)

Next Exit, Use Caution (Exit Series #5)

Next Exit, One Way (Exit Series #6)

Next Exit, No Outlet (Exit Series #7)

The Cuban (After the Exit #1)

The Trouble with Enzo (After the Exit #2)

Games of Deceit (Kai Corbyn Series #1)

Close Target (Kai Corbyn Series #2)

# About the Author

CW Browning was writing before she could spell. Making up stories with her childhood best friend in the backyard in Olathe, Kansas, imagination ran wild from the very beginning. At the age of eight, she printed out her first full-length novel on a dot-matrix printer. All eighteen chapters of it. Through the years, the writing took a backseat to the mechanics of life as she pursued other avenues of interest. Those mechanics, however, have a great way of underlining what truly lifts a spirt and makes the soul sing. After attending Rutgers University and studying History, her love for writing was rekindled. It became apparent where her heart lay. Picking up an old manuscript, she dusted it off and went back to what made her whole. CW still makes up stories in her backyard, but now she crafts them for her readers to enjoy. She makes her home in Southern New Jersey, where she loves to grill steak and sip red wine on the patio.

Visit her at www.cwbrowning.com
Also find her on Facebook, Instagram and Twitter!

Printed in Great Britain
by Amazon